IRRESISTIBLY WILD

J. SAMAN

Copyright © 2023 by Julie Finkle

All rights reserved.

No part of this book may be reproduced in any form or by any electronic or mechanical means, including information storage and retrieval systems, without written permission from the author, except for the use of brief quotations in a book review.

❀ Created with Vellum

1

C allan

"It's like something out of a horror film out there," the hostess says to me as I step inside the restaurant, shaking excess rainwater from my hair and shirt. Another flash of lightning streaks across the sky immediately followed by a loud crack of thunder. She jumps, stifling her loud gasp with her hand. "Sorry," she apologizes, her face flushing in embarrassment. "I hate thunderstorms."

The lights flicker and she tenses. So do half the people sitting at their tables and in the bar.

Today has been an epically shitful day and this thunderstorm is the coup de grâce.

"Any chance at a table for one?" I ask.

"Your usual table is taken, Dr. Barrows. Are you okay with one more in the center of the room?"

She gives me a contrite smile and all I can do is sigh and nod. A table in the open isn't my favorite thing and if I had the buffer of my friends with me, I wouldn't care so much—they garner far more attention than I ever do—but right now, all I want is my favorite sushi, a couple of glasses of something alcoholic, and a quiet moment to sort through my thoughts.

With any hope, I won't be recognized, but that's not how this day seems to be going for me so far.

"Thank you," I say as I take my menu that I don't particularly require and sit down, dropping my napkin onto my lap. The hostess walks off and immediately my water glass is filled by a busboy just as the lights flicker again. Thunder rumbles loud and aggressively enough to be heard over the din of Friday night diners who were brave enough to say fuck you to the storm.

That's not what I am.

I'm a man on the edge of his sanity.

I wasn't in any state to be around my friends who offered to come and join me or have me over for dinner, or even to go home alone and drown myself in a bottle of bourbon. Today is not just an insane summer storm. Today is also the summer solstice and with it, I desperately tried to save a group of doomsday cultists who took a crap load of cyanide before feeding it to their children.

Out of all fifteen who came through my emergency room doors, I was able to save two children who are now up in the ICU fighting for their lives.

As if that wasn't tragic or disturbing enough, I received a call that my Harvard Medical School mentor dropped dead today. It was a standing joke that Dr. Lawrence would die in his classroom and that's exactly what he did. He's the reason I got into Harvard, as he was my neighbor growing up. One of the reasons I wanted to become a doctor in the first place.

Even when I was off touring the world with my best friends as the drummer for our band, Central Square, my dream was to become a doctor, not a rockstar.

But his death came with a huge request from the medical school administration. One I can't say no to because I feel as though I owe Dr. Lawrence. The last thing I ever wanted to do was teach medical school, but now it looks as though that's happening. Starting on Monday.

So yeah, crappy fucking day.

My eyes scroll along the menu just as movement captures my attention along with the scent of something sweet. Cherries and almonds. My gaze climbs up my menu, latching onto a pair of vibrant blue eyes that appear a little manic.

"Hi. Are you sitting here alone?"

"Pardon?" I blink at her.

She puffs out an exasperated breath, her long golden-blonde bangs flying up along with it. "Sorry. Dumb question, as clearly, you're alone at the present time. What I'm asking is are you alone, alone? As in dining solo? As in not expecting a friend or lover or significant other or date to arrive in the next few minutes?"

"Why?" I hedge because she wouldn't be the first pretty woman to approach me after recognizing me.

She shifts her weight to her right foot as her head flies over her shoulder, catches on something that makes her grimace, and then she turns back to me. "No time to explain. Just play along and I'll pay for your dinner as a thank-you."

"What?" My eyebrows scrunch together. The pretty thing isn't making a whole lot of sense, and I'm in no mood to decipher whatever the hell she's trying to say.

"You're all about the one-word answers and I like that in a man since I talk enough for everyone, but if you could just smile and pretend you adore me, that would be—"

"There you are," a guy says, half-out of breath as if he's just sprinted here. "Why did you leave? Our food just arrived."

The blonde gives him a withering glare. "I never ordered any food with you."

"Yes, you did. I sat down and we started talking. I ordered you another drink and a round of appetizers."

"Um. No. That's not what happened at all."

"Sure, it is," the guy protests, moving in closer to her.

The woman's hands fly out protectively, stopping him. "Uh, not so much there, Sweaty Joe. I was having a drink and you started talking to me. I told you I was here to meet someone using the universally polite way to blow someone off, but you decided to order me a drink even though I declined it and then a round of appetizers."

He shakes his head, growing agitated. "No. You told me the person you were meeting wasn't here yet. I took that to mean he stood you up and his loss was going to be my gain."

She pans her hand in my direction. "Well, here he is so you can go back to the bar now."

"Uh-uh. I bought you a drink and food. That entitles me to something."

"*Entitles you to something?*" The woman is incredulous and frankly, so am I.

"Yes. I don't buy drinks and food for every woman. It's called quid pro quo, honey, and I expect something in return for my generosity." He looks her up and down lasciviously. "Besides, you wanted me. I could tell. You were flirting back."

The woman's face flushes with rage as if she's about to eviscerate him right here in the middle of the restaurant. "You're crazy! I was definitely not—"

I stand, having seen enough. "She was not flirting with you because she's here to meet me." I walk over to her and wrap my arm around her waist, pulling her into my side. Maybe that's a bold move and maybe it isn't, but my protective instincts are firing on all cylinders, and I don't want this guy near her. She comes easily enough, so I don't overthink it.

The guy's dark eyes swirl, almost looping in opposite directions. He's short. Stalky. Sweaty. And his pupils are blown out. He's on something and my guess is cocaine judging by the white powder crusted beneath his nostril.

He ignores me completely in favor of her. "Forget this asshole. Come back to the bar with me and have the drink I bought you."

"She told you no, and now I'm telling you to fuck. Off."

"Listen, man. I don't know what—"

I remove my hand from her waist and get right up in his face, no longer caring if we're making a scene and people are watching us. I grip him by his shirt and haul him up until he's forced to stand on his tiptoes. "When a woman says no, or that she's not interested, or asks you to back off, you listen. It's not a negotiation. Get out of here before I change my mind about rearranging your face." I give him a small shove, making him stumble into an empty chair, then I tug the woman back into my side. "She's mine."

He glances around the restaurant, noting all the curious eyes on him, and then he straightens himself. "Whatever. Trashy bitch wasn't worth it anyway."

He stalks off, back toward the bar, only to be intercepted by the manager before he can get there. Frank meets my eyes, and I give him a nod. They'll kick him out and he'll never be allowed back in here again.

I release her immediately and retake my seat, running my hand through my slightly too-long-on-top hair.

"Wow. That was not what I was expecting at all." She takes the seat opposite me and reaches for my water, downing half of it. I watch, slightly amused by that.

She's a firecracker.

She blows out a heavy breath as she sets my glass down and wipes at her lips. "Can you believe him?" She pans her hand in the direction he went. "The guy was so pushy at the bar and normally I would have tossed the drink he bought me in his face and told him where he could stick the food he ordered, but it hasn't been my best day, and I was a bit flustered." She softens, her eyes meeting mine. "Thank you for coming to my rescue like that. I'm obviously not meeting anyone here tonight. I figured once he saw you that would be that, but I guess one should never underestimate the power of cocaine and the madness it breeds."

She sits up straight, folding her forearms on the table, settling in like she has no plans to go anywhere else, and for the first time, I get a good look at her. I know how incredible her body feels against mine and I know how delicious she smells, but seeing her up close like this is a sucker punch I'm not prepared for.

Huge doe-like blue eyes, lighter and more luminescent than mine. Oval face framed by long, flowy blonde hair, the color of honeycomb. A petite nose that turns up slightly on the end and boasts a tiny diamond stud on the right side and full, pillowy pink lips.

She looks like a young Scarlett Johansen.

Fucking hot—and definitely sexy—even though she's not wearing anything all that sexy. Just a plain black crop T-shirt that hits her waist and ripped baggy jeans.

"Anyway." She clears her throat a little self-consciously and I realize it's because I haven't said anything yet. I've been too mesmerized by her face. "Thanks again. Your dinner is most definitely on me."

She moves to stand, and I reach out, circling her wrist with my hand to stop her. I didn't even do it consciously, but that small point of contact warms my hand and makes my skin buzz.

"Or you could stay and join me," I offer, not even sure that's what I want. I wanted to be alone, but I also can't deny that I want to talk to her more if for no other reason than it affords me the opportunity to look at her. "I haven't had my best day either, so I'm not sure what sort of company I'll be, but after that guy, I'd rather not send you back to the bar by yourself or even out in the storm alone."

She licks her lips, the hint of a barbell in her tongue peeking out as she does, and then after a moment of deliberation, she sits back down. I remove my hand from her skin.

"Today sucked," she starts without any preamble. "All I wanted was to eat some sushi, have a big, fat drink, and unwind my mind, and then that asshole came in and killed all my chill."

A smirk hits my lips, and I can safely say it's the first smile I've had all day. "Well, I was in the same boat until some beautiful, crazy woman came over and asked me to be her fake date."

"Actually, I prefer crazy beautiful. It's all in the phrasing, don't you find?" She rests her chin on her hands. "And I don't know what you're complaining about. Asking to be someone's fake date sounds like the start of a great night to me."

I lean forward, angling my head. "You think so?" I challenge, my smirk growing into a devilish grin because I can't drag myself away from the way her blue eyes heat and sparkle. We went from strained and a bit tense and awkward to fun and flirty in a nanosecond, and I'm digging the hell out of it.

Maybe this is what I needed to drag me out of today. Her.

"I think we'll find out after we order." She bobs her head to the left, indicating our waiter who now stands over us. "But I'll tell you this, choose our sushi wisely or this thing is over before it even begins."

"Who says I want it to begin?"

A coy smile curls up the corner of her lips as she rims the empty wine glass of her place setting with the tip of her finger. "Oh, I think we both know you do." She sits back and waves a hand toward me. "Order away. I'm into everything."

Hell.

I order us a massive boat of several different kinds of sushi, some edamame, and then I pause. "Gyoza?" I pose to her.

"Pork and pan-fried?" she counters.

I give her a look. "Is there any other kind?"

"Not for me there isn't."

I look back up at the waiter. "We'll have an order of that and two doubles of Don Julio 1942. One large ice cube in each, and keep those coming, please."

The waiter leaves and my pretty companion wiggles in her seat and then drops her elbows onto the table. "Tequila?"

"You've never had it with sushi?"

She shakes her head.

"I hate sake."

"Same. But I usually go with white wine instead."

"Then tonight, it seems, you're living a bit on the wild side."

The lights flicker once again as a massive rumble of thunder shakes the restaurant, making our empty place settings and water glasses rattle. It doesn't appear to bother her in the slightest.

She runs a delicate manicured finger along her chin, her nails black and shiny. "You should be warned, that's not just tonight. I always live my life a bit on the wild side if I can help it, and I promise that's not an exaggeration. I'm a lot. Just ask the last guy who fell in love with me after I warned him not to."

Something darkens her features at that, but I don't bother exploring it.

"Hmmm." I tap my lip, my gaze dancing about her face. "I can tell you're younger than me. He was a boy, right?" I shrug indifferently. "I'm not worried about it."

But even as I say the words, something odd hits me. A twinge. A warning. Like I'm calling myself a liar, which is ridiculous.

She studies me, liking this game we're playing just as much as I am. Not only is she beautiful, she's exciting. Different. Intelligent. Quick-witted. Just sitting here, I have to fight through the pheromones she's putting off.

I'm helplessly fucking magnetized.

"No," she says as if she's come to some conclusion. "I imagine you have the reverse problem. Gorgeous. A bit mysterious. Not afraid to dine alone, threaten a man, and call a woman you've never met before yours." She's delighting in this now, giving me a long once over, sticking on my chest and arms, before dragging her gaze back up to my face. "Oh yes. I can see it all now. You have women falling at your feet. Am I right?"

"You don't expect me to answer that do you?"

She laughs, the sound light and sweet like spun sugar. "Definitely not. It was one hundred percent rhetorical since I already know the answer is yes." She laces her fingers together and rests her chin on them once more. "So tell me, stranger, are you a one-night-only sort of guy?"

"Depends. Are you a one-night-only sort of girl?"

"I am now," she declares with a scrunch of her nose that makes the tiny stud glint against the light. "Who has time for love and relationships?"

Unfortunately, not me. At least that's how it's been since I started med school, and before that, it was random groupies after random shows we played. I was eighteen when Central Square started touring and twenty-two when we fell apart. But now that two of my best friends have found love and are happy and I'm in my thirties, I can't help but start to want that for myself.

But that's for another night, and certainly not with this woman.

"What's your name?" Because I swear, she's familiar even if I can't place her. Could be from the emergency department with the number of people I see coming in and out of there.

"Are we doing names?"

I laugh. "I didn't realize we weren't."

"We weren't, but now I'm curious. I'm Layla. No last name."

"I'm Callan. Also no last name."

She squints at me, and I regret pressing the whole names thing. People in Boston know me as Callan Barrows from the band Central Square. We were one of the biggest pop/rock bands of our time until our manager, Suzie, dropped dead of a stroke in the shower at the age of twenty-two. We were five guys—plus Suzie—who all grew up in Central Square, Cambridge, and Suzie was the girlfriend of Zax, our bassist, and the twin sister of Lenox, our pianist.

After that, we couldn't find it in us to go on, but in truth, I was done before that. I did college entirely online, premed college at that, which wasn't easy. I had to find lab time in between tours.

I wanted Harvard Medical School, and I had an in for it with Dr. Lawrence and the money I was willing to pay. I had mentioned to Greyson—our frontman and Zax's younger brother—that I was thinking of leaving the band. Suzie died two weeks later, and I felt more guilty for wanting to leave the band than I ever had before. That all happened eight years ago, but this is Boston and we're still among their favorite celebrities.

She continues to scrutinize me, but our tequila is delivered, and she doesn't press it further, and I'm grateful.

Whether she recognizes me or not now, I don't think she initially did, and I like that about her. I'm not Dr. Barrows or Callan Barrows, drummer for Central Square to her. I'm just a guy who saved her from a dickhead and is now having dinner with her.

I raise my glass and she does the same.

"What are we toasting to?" she asks, swirling the clear liquid around the block of ice.

"To an unexpected turn of events?" I suggest.

"I'll say." She holds her glass out to mine and we tap them together before she tosses back every drop of tequila.

I choke out a laugh. "That's sipping tequila."

She runs a hand through her hair, flipping the long strands over to the other side of her neck. "Is that what that was?" Her lips smack. "Who knew? I'll sip the next one, I promise. You have no idea how badly I needed that."

"Actually, I do." I toss down mine the same way she did and signal our waiter for our next round. "I had a bad day too, remember?"

"I know we shared names, but I don't feel like sharing my woes."

I wipe away the excess tequila from my lips. "Good thing, because I had no intention of sharing mine."

She beams at me. "Awesome. You're that kind of guy. Hot and broody."

A gust of breath hits the air as she takes me completely off-guard. "I've never been called broody." If anything, I've always been the easy-going guy. The dependable one.

"No? Only hot?"

"Is that what you're calling me? Because I can safely say, I've never wanted a woman to think I'm hot more in my life than right now with you."

"Gorgeous? Hot? You're everything in between for sure. That dimple in your cheek is doing crazy things to my insides, but you didn't hear that from me." She gives me a wink before turning a little serious. "But for real, are you not normally this broody?"

"No," I admit. "I'm normally considered the nice guy."

"The nice guy," she parrots as if testing the words on her tongue. "I can work with that. I don't necessarily need broody to get off."

I guffaw just as the gyoza and edamame are set before us.

I raise my eyes to hers, unabashed lust in my gaze as I stare directly at her. "Then what do you need to get off?"

2

L ayla

I'LL BE honest with you. I spotted Callan walking into the restaurant before the asshole at the bar even started with me. Callan walked in and it was as if the entire place froze and then simultaneously moaned. The woman on my left certainly did. He was captivating and confident, but there was something in his eyes that said he was unapproachable.

That piqued my interest, and I did a slow drag, taking in his tall form and muscular physique, and then turned back to my drink. I wasn't here for that tonight and didn't have it in me to try.

Even if he was, *is*, hot as all fuck.

But then that guy got seriously pushy. He got right up in my face, touching me in ways he had no business touching me, taking liberties with my food and drinks I did not give him, and I needed an out. Usually, you tell a guy you're there to meet a date and they back off. Not this one, and Callan was the only guy sitting alone.

And when he got all alpha male possessive? Yeah, that was also hot as all fuck.

So now I'm sitting here, eating edamame, flirting shamelessly, and drinking heavily as I desperately try to wipe away what is easily one of the worst days I've ever had. And coming from a woman who lost both her parents in a car accident when I was six, that's saying some serious shit.

"What do I need to get off?" I parrot, actually thinking about that. Normally I'd say something witty and possibly a bit crass. That's the road I was headed down, but his question made me pause and with that, I'm once again thrown off my game. "Honestly?"

"Sure," he says flippantly, taking a sip of his freshly delivered tequila before setting the glass down. "I like honesty and feel like that's the plane we're on. Not to mention, it's an answer I'd like to hear."

"All right." I snap apart my chopsticks, buying a few extra seconds before I force my gaze back up to his. His eyes are blue, but not just any blue. They're cobalt. Deep and lustrous like the metal. Almost familiar to me. He's familiar to me. "I don't know what would get me off tonight. My mind is a hot mess of a minefield, and it doesn't seem to want to stop exploding. I'm flirting with you, and it's fun and diverting and I don't want to stop. Maybe that's all I need right now. Someone to take my mind off everything else."

My absolute favorite professor ever dropped dead earlier today. Right in front of me. And there was nothing I could do about it, though I tried. The man was dead before he hit the floor, but I'm a freaking med student. Saving people is what I want to do, but I couldn't save him. I did CPR for over ten minutes while waiting for the EMS crew to arrive and pronounce him dead.

To pile onto that—not that there is anything more tragic or upsetting than that—about thirty seconds after they zipped the body bag and loaded him onto the ambulance, I received a call from my landlord informing me that my apartment flooded due to a massive leak in the roof.

All of my stuff is destroyed.

I moved into that apartment two months ago after moving out of my ex's place and it was finally starting to feel like home. Now this.

I don't care so much about my furniture—that can all be replaced —but I had things in there. Things from my childhood. Things that I've collected and held on to. Things that *cannot* be replaced. Then there's the other thing. The thing I should no longer care or think about. The reason why I will only do one-nighters and refuse to make time for love or relationships for the foreseeable future.

I squish a piece of gyoza between my chopsticks, dip it in the sauce, and then pop it into my mouth. I chew as he marinates on what I just put out in the air between us. He watches me as I swallow, and then I chase down the dumpling with more tequila.

Sitting forward, he polishes off his second drink and then stands. My eyes track him and my body shifts back in my chair automatically.

"Come with me," he says, extending his hand out to me.

"What?"

"You said you were wild. Prove it. Come with me," he repeats.

"Wild and stupid aren't synonymous. Where are we going?"

"Someplace where I can take your mind off everything. Something tells me it'll do the same for me, and then we'll come back and eat our sushi, and if I'm lucky, maybe I'll get to take you home with me to finish things off."

Heat swarms through me like a pack of bees, dancing with the butterflies already fluttering in my belly.

"Have you ever done this before?" I don't know why I ask. Maybe to know what level of player he is. Maybe to ascertain if my instincts are leading me astray.

He grins, his expression guileless as he answers, "Never. Not like this anyway."

Throwing caution to the wind, I wipe my mouth with my napkin and stand, placing my hand in his. It's warm and strong, and his palms are calloused, and immediately I'm hit with that same dizzying sensation I felt when his hand captured my wrist.

I don't know him. Yet it feels as though I do.

I trust him. I can't explain that either. It's instinctive. Something inside me that tells me I'll be safe with him. It also tells me I'm going to love every second of whatever he has in mind for me.

He intertwines our fingers just as more thunder booms from beyond the glass windows. It pops a smile to my face and makes my heart jump. Excitement ripples through me as he leads us through the restaurant to the back. For a moment, I expect him to take me into the bathroom, but he doesn't. He continues on, clearly knowing his way around, and then he's opening a door that simply says office on it.

"What are we doing? Whose office is this?"

He doesn't answer me. He just drags me inside the empty and dark room. The lights stay off as he shuts and locks the door. On my next breath, he has me pressed up against it.

"I've wanted to do this from the first second I saw you," he murmurs before his lips crash down onto mine in such a forceful, dominating way I instantly moan. My fingers thread into his hair, thick and soft and long enough to grip. He tastes like tequila and desire, and I'm intoxicated by it.

I haven't been kissed in two months and it was just a random guy in a random bar a few nights after I moved out of my ex's. A guy I forgot about the second after the condom came off. He was my get under someone new to get over someone old, and he didn't quite do the trick well enough.

He sure as hell didn't kiss me the way Callan is. All tongue and lips with occasional teeth.

Hot.

His kisses are hot.

His breath pants against my mouth while his hands roam the curves of my hips, all the way up along my ribs, so his fingers can tickle the sides of my breasts. He growls at the soft feel of them through my shirt since I'm not wearing a bra and then he dives back into my mouth, consuming me until I have to push him back to catch my breath.

Dark and hooded eyes, barely visible in the almost blackness of the office, hold mine.

"Let's see how wild I can make you."

He drops to his knees in front of me and I gasp. His hands slide up under my shirt, squeezing my bare breasts. I tremble and sigh as he runs the rough pads of his thumbs over my hard nipples. I don't have the biggest breasts in the world, but the way he's touching me, it's as if his hands can't get enough of them.

His mouth licks and nips at my belly, pulling at the button of my jeans with his teeth. I laugh lightly when he slips off without undoing it only to be punished by a hard squeeze to my tits. He gets the button undone, followed by the zipper, and then his hands are on my hips, dragging my jeans down. One flipflop hits the floor and he's helping me to pull one leg free.

Deft fingers slide into the sides of my panties and then my free leg is out of that too, the satin hanging limply around my other ankle along with my jeans.

My nails scratch his scalp, anxious for his mouth on me. I'm dripping at the thought of it. At that skilled tongue doing wicked things to me. At how I didn't have to ask or shove his head down. This is the reason he brought me in here.

He wants to do this.

A stranger on his knees in an office of a restaurant is about to eat me out and I'm about to let him.

"I hope you're good at this," I tease, needing to defuse the sharp tension. He hasn't touched me since he undressed me from the waist down. He's been silent, stroking my belly and breasts, and, well, staring at my pussy, I guess.

I swallow air in giant gulps.

His head tilts up and I can just make out the lines of his face and the sparkle of his eyes. "Baby girl, I'm a fucking master at this. I'm about to eat you so good, my tongue in your pretty cunt is all you'll be able to think about for the rest of the night until I give you my cock later."

Ho-ly-shit! What on earth have I gotten myself into?

"I don't know about all that nice guy stuff when you say things like that."

"Me either." Without wasting another second, he grasps the back of my knee and places it on his shoulder, exposing me to him. He leans in and inhales me, the scent of my arousal tearing a groan from him that I feel in my bones. My fingers rip at his hair and my thoughts scramble. It's insanely fucking intimate and a lot and it turns me on like nothing ever has before.

His hand wraps around me, clutching my ass and pressing me deeper into him, holding me exactly where he wants me. The flat of his tongue licks from my opening up to my clit where it then swirls around and around. I cry out only to stifle the sound by biting into my lip. It turns into a loud whimper only to become a full-fledged moan when he slides two fingers inside me.

"Fuck," he growls. "You're fucking soaked, beautiful. And goddamn delicious."

I can't speak. I can't do anything other than hold onto him while I mindlessly grind into a stranger's face and take in everything he's doing to me. The way his fingers are pumping in and out of me, angled to hit that perfect spot on my inner wall. The way his tongue flicks and his lips suck on my clit. Everything he's doing is pure magic. Spinning me up higher and higher into euphoric bliss.

I writhe against him, holding his head in place as I fuck his mouth and face and fingers. It's wet and noisy and there is a restaurant full of people just beyond the door. That only seems to turn me on more. His tongue and lips focus on my clit, and I rub against him, needing more, so damn close I can feel the heat of it licking at my skin and coiling low in my belly.

A spring ready to snap and be set free.

"I need it," I gasp as he pumps me harder. Faster. Deeper.

"Then take it." His lips latch onto my pulsing clit, and he sucks it straight into his mouth, teasing it with his tongue, and I explode. Flickers of prismed light glitter behind my eyes. I clench around his fingers, rolling my hips into him, and quivering uncontrollably. My knee threatens to give out on me, buckling and forcing the hand he had on my ass to grasp my hip to hold me up.

He continues to lap at me, licking me until the last of the waves subside. Lowering my foot to the ground, he helps me back into my underwear, jeans, and flip-flops. I'm useless, just standing here watching him like some voyeur and having an out-of-body experience that I only want more of.

He stands, licking his lips and wiping at his chin with the back of his fingers, only to lick those clean as well. My eyes have adjusted to the darkness by this point, and I stare at him, dazed and a bit confused, and totally giddy and high.

"We should get back to our table," he says and a laugh bursts from my chest.

"Right. Dinner."

He smirks, coming in and pressing his lips to mine, spreading me open and making me taste myself. "Unless you'd rather go somewhere else. Take the sushi to go. I live two blocks from here."

Two blocks. His place. Sushi to go. Frankly, I don't care so much about the food. Swallowing down the small burst of nerves that tickle my heart, I stare into his eyes and say, "Lead the way."

A smile lights up his face, making that dimple in his cheek pop. Such a boyish feature on a man who is anything but. He doesn't hesitate. Retaking my hand the way he did earlier, we exit the office unobserved and then just as we reach our table, loaded with all the sushi we ordered along with a fresh round of tequila, lightning flashes so bright it reflects off the wet streets outside the window. Thunder cracks two seconds later, and then the power flickers and goes out.

Some women scream and a child starts crying.

"Shit," he hisses, gripping my hand tighter. "You okay?"

"Um. Yes?" I think so. Adrenaline races through me and I take a calming breath. "It feels like something out of a horror movie."

"Interesting. That's exactly what the hostess said to me as I walked in."

"Well, she was right."

All around us people are talking in harried voices, anxious and unsettled. "Don't move. A generator should kick on in—"

The lights snap back on. Some people are on their feet, others are gripping their tables as they stare around, unsure of what's going on and what to do.

"How did you know about the generator?" I ask only to think better of it and add, "Come to think of it, how did you know about the office?"

His gaze skirts along mine briefly as he releases my hand so he can fish out his wallet and drop what appears to be four one-hundred dollar bills on the table. "I'm a silent owner. Let's go unless you want the sushi."

"It's a lot of food to waste."

"Give me a second then."

He walks off, speaks to a random waiter, and then a second later he's back and the waiter is boxing up our food and handing him a huge to-go bag.

I shake my head. This man is full of surprises. If his cock is anywhere nearly as talented as his mouth and fingers are, who needs food? I bet he could sustain me on orgasms alone. I can't wait to tell Meils, my older sister—and guardian after our parents died—about this. She'll naturally freak out, but that's also part of the fun in telling her.

I'm almost tempted to take a covert selfie of me with Mr. Hottie McSterious, but that feels creepy, and I'd slaughter a guy if he ever did that to me.

Ugh. I just realized I'm going to have to move back in with my sister and her husband again. Though I will get my nieces out of that deal.

"Why do you have to move back in with your sister and her husband?"

"Huh?"

Callan smirks at me as I give him a brilliant impression of a deer in headlights.

"Did you not realize you were musing aloud?" He fights his amusement as he leads us to the exit.

A blush slams into my chest so fast and furious it's like I just dipped my body in tomato sauce. "Um. No. I hadn't. How much did I say?"

We're both peering out the windows at the hellacious storm we're about to venture into. "Well, let's just say I'm relieved you don't plan on taking a covert selfie of me, because yes, that's creepy. Mr. Hottie McSterious is my new favorite nickname, and I'd be happy to spend the night sustaining you on orgasms, because yes, my cock is just as talented as my fingers and mouth are."

Yeesh. I spilled it all. I make a mental note to ask my friends and sister if that's something I do on the reg or if that orgasm truly did scramble my brain.

"I should be embarrassed, and I am, but all I caught from that is you confirming how talented your dick is."

He laughs, loud and hard. "If we weren't in public, I'd kiss you, but since we are, it'll have to wait until we get to my place. Are you ready to make a run for it? I'm hoping your flip-flops will hold up."

I glare balefully down at my feet. These are the only shoes I have right now. Same with my clothes. Dear Lord, that's going to be a nightmare to deal with tomorrow.

"Me too, actually, but there's only one way to find out and I'm not drunk enough to walk the streets of Boston barefoot."

"I won't ask. On three?"

"One. Two. Fuck it!" I push open the door and drag him along after me, shooting us out into the pelting rain, wind, and unrelenting thunder and lightning.

"Jesus! I've never seen it like this here before. Run!"

He gives my hand a firm yank and then we're flying up the street. We're both instantly soaked, and my flip-flops are barely able to stay on my feet. Oddly enough, I'm having the best time with him despite how things went for me today.

And I can't wait to see where this night takes me next.

3

C allan

RAIN PELLETS us with the force of bullets. We're soaked, saturated to the bone, as we race up the street. One of her flip-flops goes flying and she has to stop and grab it, hopping as she puts it back on. Finally, we reach the front door of my brownstone in Beacon Hill. I don't bring a lot of women home. I don't like women knowing where I live, especially the ones who recognize me.

But this girl... she has no clue who I am.

Maybe that's what I like about her. She doesn't know and she doesn't care, yet she's still here with me. She turned a royally shitty day into something a hell of a lot more fun. Because she's fun. And fucking beautiful. And her pussy? Holy hell, I can't wait to be inside her pussy. Or taste it again. Or feel it come on my fingers.

She's quirky and definitely a bit on the wild side as she said.

But her trust in me right now? That sort of floors me.

We just met an hour ago, but it feels as if we already know each other, which I know makes no sense, but there you go. Some people you can know for years, and they still feel like a stranger to you. Then there are people you meet, and they immediately feel as if you've known them your whole life.

She feels like the latter.

Unlocking the door, I flip on the lights and then bring her in. She glances around but doesn't linger on anything for too long. The first floor is the kitchen and dining areas along with a smaller family room, an office, and my exercise room. But brownstones are built up, so the rest of the living spaces are on the second and third floors.

I go into the kitchen and set the bags of sushi on the counter and grab us a couple of clean towels to wipe down with, but it's not nearly enough. We're dripping everywhere.

"You have power."

"I have a generator," I explain. "It doesn't power everything, just most things."

"Does it power your dryer?" she whispers, turning to face me and taking the towel from my hand.

"It does."

She peeks down at herself and then back up at me. "Do you mind throwing my stuff in your dryer then?"

Oh. Good call. "Not at all. Come with me."

"You say that a lot," she quips, smiling coyly at me. Her blonde hair is hanging around her face like a waterfall and her clothes are sticking to her body, showing off her braless tits and hard nipples.

I smirk, stepping into her. "I'm hoping that's how this night goes. You *coming* with me. Before me and after me as well. But for now, I can throw your stuff in the dryer, and give you something to wear and we can eat the sushi and have another drink and relax if that's what you want."

I want her to know she has options. While I did bring her here with the hope of a night full of dirty sex, that's not all this has to be.

Her gaze latches on the bags of sushi. "You should put that in the fridge. I'd hate for all that fish to spoil before you have a chance to eat it."

Before *I* have a chance to eat. Message received.

I pick up the bag and give her my back as I walk it over to the fridge, intentionally hiding the frown I'm annoyed I'm sporting. Once that's done, I spin back around to find her walking toward my stairs and just as she reaches the bottom step, she pivots to face me and her eyes lock on mine.

"It doesn't look like you're coming yet." Her hands grasp the hem of her shirt and then she's pulling it up and over her head, revealing her slightly smaller-than-handful-sized tits and pink nipples. My mouth waters and my hands twitch for another feel of them. Her skin glows, pale and pretty, but with a hint of a flush. Not in embarrassment because there's no trace of that anywhere on her, but in obvious arousal. My cock hardens in my pants, a state it's been in nearly all night since she sat down.

My gaze drops to her pants.

"What about those?"

"What about them?" she tosses back at me.

"I can't put them in the dryer if they're still on you."

"True."

She undoes the button and zipper and then goes about the process of peeling wet denim from her skin. As if in a trance, my body floats toward hers, standing behind her, and somehow my hands are on her bare hips, holding her steady though she doesn't need me to since one of her hands is holding onto the stair railing.

My thumbs drag up and down her cool, damp skin and then slide up along her ribs. She frees herself from her jeans and panties, standing beautifully naked in front of me.

Her breath hitches when my hands start massaging the globes of her ass. One finger slides down the center of her cheeks, going lower, all the way down until I reach her opening.

"Let's see if you're wet enough for my cock." I slip a finger inside her and pump it in and out. She emits a breathy hum from the back of her throat. "Close. But I want you wetter. I want this pussy to be dripping before I slide inside of it."

She gasps when I push a second finger in only to immediately pull them back out. I slip them into my mouth and suck her off them as I bring my mouth to her ear.

"Go up the stairs. I want to watch from this angle."

She moans, but wordlessly does what I ask, making a fucking meal out of it as she sways her hips with every step. I have the best view of her pussy from this angle—pink, wet lips, and a tight hole.

God, she's pretty.

I slip out of my clothes, leaving on my boxer briefs, and then pick up her discarded items. I pull the condom out and then toss my wallet on the table near the stairs. Then, like an anxious schoolboy, I jog up the steps to her, losing my cool with every second I see her like this.

"Which way?" she asks, and I point to my right.

I have an idea. Something I've never done before but suspect she'll be up for since she seems to be up for anything and everything.

She turns and immediately heads in that direction, her tits bouncing slightly as she goes. I open the door to my laundry room for her, guiding her over to the machines. Opening the empty dryer, I throw our stuff in and turn it on, the gentle hum filling the room.

"You're very neat and organized."

I chuckle lightly as I take her hips and pick her up, dropping her on top of the washing machine. "My father was an Army doctor for thirty years. Neat and organized was ingrained in me from birth."

I part her legs and step in between them. The height is perfect. "What are you—"

I turn on the washing machine to a spin cycle even though it's empty.

"Oh!" Her eyes widen and a stunning smile spreads her lips. "I've never done this."

"Me either. How does it feel?"

She giggles as the drum inside the machine starts spinning around. "It tickles."

I spread her legs wider, opening her up for me, and my thumb starts to trace her swollen clit. "And now?"

Her eyes close and she licks her lips. "Now it feels really good. It's vibrating through me and with you doing that?" A gasp escapes from her lips as the washer picks up speed. "Fuck, that feels so good."

Bending down I flick her clit with my tongue and her hand shoots out, grasping my hair and holding me there. She's dripping now. I can see it on top of my washing machine and it's so fucking hot my cock jerks in my briefs.

I give it an impatient rub, needing contact, needing her.

"Ah! Callan! Yes! God, yes. Please don't stop." She rocks into me, wiggling and pressing herself deeper against the washing machine, wanting more of the vibrations. I eat her, play with her, touch her, working her up higher and higher.

"I want to watch you come like this. All over my washing machine. And then I'm going to slide my cock in you and fuck you on top of it."

That does it. My dirty words and my tongue and the machine set her off and she comes on a loud cry, her head back and her pussy grinding against my mouth. I've been with plenty of women over the years. Many put on shows for me, thinking that's what I wanted, or were so nervous or unsure of themselves that they just took whatever I gave them.

Layla knows who she is.

She knows what she likes. And she's unafraid to ask for it and take it. It's part of what makes her easily the sexiest woman I've ever been with, and I haven't even been inside of her yet.

"On here or somewhere else?" I ask as her body begins to sag.

"If you want it somewhere else, you're going to have to carry me. My legs are mush."

Hmmm. Tempting. All so tempting. But I'm not sure I can wait any longer.

I slide down my boxer briefs, roll on the condom, and then scoot her to the edge of the machine. I glance up while rubbing the head of my cock against her opening.

"Right here." I point to my eyes and then slide inside her, watching what it feels like through her eyes as she does the same with me. Once I'm seated all the way to the hilt, I give us both a second to acclimate because if I move, even a tiny amount before I get myself under control, I'm going to blow my load.

Because *fuuuuck* she feels good.

It feels like a goddamn wet fist is gripping my cock, and the washing machine is still going, and I can feel that too. I inhale a deep breath through my nose, exhale, and then repeat. And once I think I'm ready, I slide out of her and then thrust back in and hold once more.

"Like that? Slow and steady or do you want to get pounded before the machine stops?"

Hazy blue eyes hold mine and she licks her lips. Her hands are back, palms planted firmly on top of the machine for support and to improve our angle. Long legs wrap themselves around me.

"Pound me. Don't stop until I beg you to."

Motherfuck. She's perfect.

I do as she asks. I start to pound into her. Punishing thrusts that have her tits bouncing and the machine inching back into the wall. Deep, hard fucks that have me bruisingly gripping her hips to hold her against me. I ram into her over and over again, forcing loud cries and sharp moans from her mouth along with deep, low, guttural growls from me.

I'm sweating, my ass cheeks are clenching, and I can't stop watching her.

Her eyes are closed now, her head tilted back exposing her long, graceful neck. I haven't kissed her once since we got back here, and it pisses me off enough that I grab her by the back of her head and force her mouth to mine. Our kisses are wet and sloppy, a conglomerate of panting breaths.

We continue to fuck, unbridled and unhinged, both chasing our pleasure in the other. She goes over the edge first, her nails raking down my back and her "Oh fuck, oh fuck, oh fuck, yes," in my ear. My cock thickens, my balls draw up tight, and then I unleash myself inside her with a roar. I still, clinging to her, holding her close, trying to catch my breath.

Buzzzzzz.

The washing machine signals the end of its cycle and then stops, the sound making us laugh with breathy smiles.

"That was fun."

She's fun.

"Wanna take a shower and go another round?" I ask, pulling back far enough to meet her eyes.

"Definitely. Are you a twofer or a threefer sort of guy?"

I bark out a laugh as I pull myself out of her and remove the condom. "I'm an 'as many times as you can take it before you pass out' sort of guy."

The goddess smiles at me, all bright sunshine eclipsing the gloom outside, and something foreign inside my chest twinges. I ignore it as I help her down and we go for round two in the shower followed by round three in my bed.

This is not how I thought this night was going to end when I walked into the restaurant.

She's not something I ever saw her coming.

Which is why I'm not shocked when I wake up at four a.m. alone. It's also why I don't bother second-guessing myself when I grab the pillow she was using and bury my face in it as I force myself to go back to sleep while breathing in the faint scent of her.

I don't know her last name, and she made it clear last night was all she was looking for from me. I'm sure I'll never see her again.

And I can't help but be a little disappointed by that.

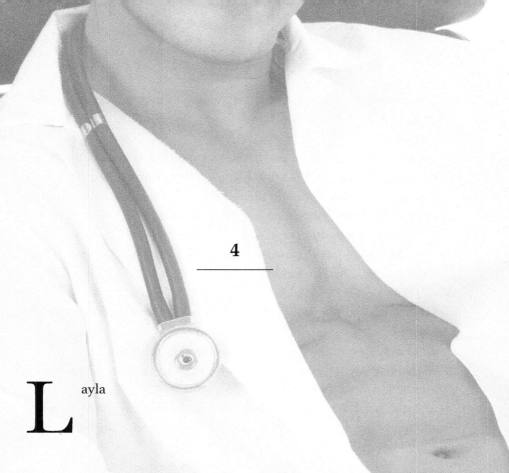

4

L ayla

A STRONG HAND grips mine as we carefully step on the waterlogged hardwood floor. Surrounding me is nothing but devastation. The visual remains of my apartment so closely mirror my insides that I'm ready to throw up right here.

"That was—"

"My sofa," I answer Stella, my voice already shaking. She took this morning off from her restaurant to come here and be with me for this. Stella has been my best friend since I was fourteen. She's also my stepcousin since she's the daughter of Landon who is Oliver's older brother and Oliver is married to my sister Amelia. That was a mouthful.

After I snuck out of Callan's somewhere around three this morning, I snuck undetected into Amelia's and Oliver's place and passed out until my landlord called me to tell me that the fire marshal officially cleared the place for me to come in and gather any salvageable belongings.

Salvageable.

That was the word he used, and as I stand here, the roof over my head gone and replaced with a soaked blue tarp, I see he wasn't kidding. The storm last night along with the roof that caved in makes this place look like something out of *The Wizard of Oz*.

"Maybe we should just—"

I shake my head. "I can't go, Stella, and I can't have someone else do this for me. I have to be the one."

"Okay. I get it. And I'm here with you."

I give her hand a squeeze because I fucking love this woman with my entire heart.

"I haven't even told Amelia and Oliver about this yet."

She gives me a funny look I catch out of the corner of my eye. "I thought you slept there last night."

"I did, but I didn't get there until after three. They didn't wake up and they were already out the door taking the girls to ballet class before I got up."

"Oh. Well then. And where were you before that?"

At her suggestive tone, I throw her a side-eye. "Is this the place where we're going to talk about my one-night stand?"

"If talking about your one-night is worth talking about then yes."

"Definitely worth talking about. But later. After I'm done here and you're plying me with alcohol."

"Deal."

"Bedroom—"

"First?" she finishes my sentence since that's what we do with each other. "That's what I was thinking too."

We both nod and then move toward the bedroom like any second the floor will give out beneath us. My apartment wasn't big. The third floor of a three-family house, it boasted a small galley kitchen, a small living slash dining area, and my bedroom.

"Oh fuck. I can't."

Those words leave my lips the second I step over the threshold and take in the bedlam. My bed is covered in black stuff, the frame half-broken. Same with my dresser, the mirror above it shattered. But neither of those is what I'm even remotely focused on. My bookshelf, my precious, precious bookshelf filled with all my precious, precious books is absolutely decimated. The books are spread out across the floor in heaps and bunches, the pages scattered, many torn from the books. All wet and ruined beyond repair.

"Stella." That's as far as I get before I start to cry. And crying isn't particularly my jam. When your life isn't all roses and sunshine, you learn to go with the flow and make the best of every situation and not waste time on such trivialities as crying.

But I'm crying now, and I can't stop.

Stella lowers herself to her hands and knees.

"Careful!" I cry out. "The glass."

She throws up a hand as if she's already aware of it and starts to crawl over, picking up one of my mother's paperbacks. It falls apart in her hands and it gets worse from there. The box that held the small keepsakes from my parents is upside down on the floor, the lid gone. Stella turns it right side up, and I sob, my hand clapping over my mouth.

My ticket stub to the first Red Sox game I went to with my parents. My mom's old charcoals. The note from the tooth fairy when I lost my first tooth that was in my dad's handwriting. All gone.

"That was—"

"I know, babes. I know what it was." She sets the remains down, sitting back on her haunches and looking up at me, matching my heartache. "I'm so very sorry, Layla."

I nod. And cry. And sob. A lot.

"You should move in with me and Delphine."

I shake my head, sucking in a deep breath to calm myself down enough so I can talk. "You only have a one-bedroom."

Stella met the half-Black, half-Creole beauty from the South Bronx while she was finishing up culinary school in New York. Stella convinced Delphine to move back to Boston with her and they opened Stella's here. It's a farm-to-table restaurant that sources all local ingredients, oftentimes straight from Stella's garden and green-house she has on top of the building the restaurant is housed in. It's a massive success and they're in the process of opening another restaurant in the South End closer to their place.

"We could move. I've been thinking about it anyway."

I roll my eyes. "Shut up, bitch, and stop being so perfect and thoughtful. You're not moving and certainly not for me."

"What? Are you saying you don't want to live with me?"

I laugh at the feigned hurt in her voice and it feels good, some of the tightness in my chest lifting with it. "I'm saying I don't want to live with you and Delphine. The last thing I want to hear is you having sex every night. Oliver and Amelia's place is fine until I can find something else."

"You know Oliver is going to offer to buy you a place again. A thousand says Grandma will too."

"I know, but I need to find my own way a bit."

"I get it. I do. Growing up Fritz isn't always as easy and glamorous as we make it seem."

I smile at her teasing tone. I won't lie, being part of the Fritz family is the best. I don't care about the fame that comes with their name, and I don't care about their billions either. About nine years ago, my sister Amelia reunited with Oliver Fritz at their ten-year high school reunion. They started with a fake engagement—long story there—and subsequently fell in love.

Oliver became the big brother I never had. He also adopted me when he married Amelia, so he's not only my stepbrother, but he's also a stepfather in a way since both he and Meils are fifteen years older than me. I even took his last name, becoming Layla Atkins Fritz. And once you become part of the Fritz family, that's it. You're theirs and they love big, and they love hard, and I can't get enough of any of them.

She's right—for Stella's father and his siblings, it wasn't always so easy and glamorous for them.

"Okay. Let's grab whatever we can and then I'm taking you to the restaurant to get you drunk so you'll tell me all about your hot one-nighter."

An hour later I'm day drinking at the bar. Stella called in reinforcements in the form of my sister. I cried on Amelia's shoulder, and she told me I can stay with them as long as I need to, and now she and Stella are grilling me on my one-nighter with Callan.

"He did what with you?" That's Amelia and I start cracking up because I'm on my second cocktail now. Stella drops a plate of jambalaya—one of my favorite dishes ever—in front of me and I moan at how good and spicy that smells.

"I bet that's how she sounded when he did it too."

I shovel a hot bite into my mouth and nod my head as I chew. "It totally is. I mean, it was ridiculous and if I hadn't had the day I had just had, I maybe, possibly, probably wouldn't have allowed a stranger to go down on me in an office of a restaurant, but my fucks to give weren't to be found."

Amelia is staring at me, her gray eyes pensive. "I want to be upset in some older sister, former guardian kind of way, but it's just not happening. First, because it's freaking hot. Second, because you had a hell of a day and a round of dirty sex always helps that. I just don't love the risks you took, but, yeah." She shrugs.

"I can't explain it. I just felt safe with him," I defend. "I would never—*could never*—imagine doing that again." I pause, thinking about that. "Maybe that's a lie. I don't know." I wave her away. "Anyway, it was fun, and the sex?" I take another sip of my drink. "It was just as delicious and spicy as this jambalaya."

It's like three in the afternoon and the restaurant is closed between lunch and dinner so it's just us right now. Otherwise, I wouldn't be as vocal about this as I'm being.

Stella drops her elbows onto the bar top. "So then why did you bang and bounce?"

I give her an unimpressed look. "Because repeat dick isn't in my playbook at the moment. I was with Patrick for two and a half years and spent a solid year of that swearing I wouldn't fall in love with him because I had a goal, and my goal wasn't to be fucked with. Then my goal and his goal lined up and it was like, yes, awesome, he's my guy. Then after six months of living together, he feeds me some bullshit about how he loves me, but he needs to focus on school and maybe we just need a break and not a breakup and we fight about it and then he goes out and fucks Molly Lin the same goddamn night we call a break but not a breakup!"

Amelia pats my shoulder and I sag.

"I didn't want to love him."

"I know," she says, giving me a sideways hug. "I had a shitty college guy too, remember?"

I wince. Her shitty college guy broke up with her because our parents had just died, and she had to move back to Boston to take care of me. Talk about devastating on multiple fronts.

"He was epically shitty," I remark. *And I love you for being the best sister on the planet.*

"But look how well it all turned out. She got rid of the loser and met a hot guy while pretending to be his fake lady and the rest is history."

I point my fork at Stella. "Don't think for a second that's going to happen with me and Callan. It was a one-off. That's it."

She shrugs. "I'm just saying... never underestimate the unexpected."

"WHAT IS it that has you standing over here in the corner smiling?" Octavia Abbot-Fritz, a.k.a my stepgrandmother, asks, and the smile I didn't realize I was sporting springs into full action. I take a sip of my martini—clearly, it's a drinking sort of weekend—to cover it a bit, but it's too late. Octavia's caught a scent and that's all the bloodhound needed.

"Nothing," I lie, not ready to tell her about Friday night with Callan. I had a lot of fun with him and felt a pang of guilt and remorse when I snuck out in the wee hours. Part of me wanted to stay.

Part of me wanted to see what could happen next and that's why I had to go.

After what my ex put me through, I decided to focus all my time and energy on becoming a doctor and that's what I'm doing. I don't have the mental or emotional capacity for anything else, and Callan is the sort of guy a girl could easily fall for.

No thanks.

"I'm just having a good time watching all the kids play in the pool." That part isn't a lie. I am having a good time doing that.

Today is my nieces Keegan and Kenna's sixth birthday and Octavia, ever the grandma supreme, went all out for it as she does with every birthday. We're talking full pool party for all the cousins—there are at least fourteen Fritz children running around—along with a magician, a bouncy house, a princess photo booth, and a cake that puts Amelia's and Oliver's wedding cake to shame.

The storm that tore through Boston as well as my apartment Friday night is gone, leaving hot sunshine in its wake. It is a Fritz party after all, and nothing else would do. I wouldn't be shocked if Octavia called God herself and demanded perfect weather for today. Naturally, God would listen.

"That's not why you're smiling like you have a secret you're reluctant to share," Octavia comments dryly, taking a sip of her own drink and staring out at the massive grounds of the back of the Fritz compound. "Besides, I happen to know you don't have a lot to smile about right now."

It's unfortunately true.

After dealing with it all morning yesterday, then day drinking it all away after, Amelia took me home and we talked with Oliver, who got all father-figure on me and demanded I allow him to drop way too much money on a new place for me. I love him, but I told him I'd simply stay with them until I figured my stuff out.

He wasn't happy about that.

Oliver has a giant heart and is a fixer.

Amelia finally, sorta, talked him down. After doing three loads of laundry, I have enough clothes and a few pairs of shoes to be okay.

That's it though. That's all I have left. My renter's insurance and my landlord's insurance will financially cover my losses, but there are some things money can't replace.

That's why Rina made me this cocktail, and I have to say it's doing wonders for my mood.

"At least my computer wasn't there. I have all my school stuff on it, so that was a break."

Octavia touches my arm, calling my attention away from the screaming, laughing children over to her. "Our offer still stands, Layla."

Just like that, I'm choked up once more. I swallow and clear my throat and nod. And when I'm able to form words that won't squeak, I utter, "I know. Thank you. But I can't accept."

She called me this morning to tell me she wanted to get me a new place. I died a bit. I never thought I'd be so lucky to have a family like this.

Fuck their money. Their love is priceless.

"What does Oliver have to say about that?" Her green eyes sparkle against the sunshine, her blonde bob kicking up a little in the wind. "I know he offered the same and I know it's not the first time he has."

"No, it's not, and yes, he offered again. But I can't let anyone buy me an apartment. Especially not the type of apartment you'd all want to buy me. You're already too generous with paying for medical school, and Oliver bought me a car *and* paid for college. I can't accept anything else. I just can't. It already sits heavy on my chest that I've accepted so much. I'm twenty-three and I'll get some money back from insurance. I'll be fine."

She squeezes my arm. "You're family, Layla. Ours. You're a Fritz and this is what we do for each other. What good is having all this money if I can't spoil my grandchildren with it?"

I laugh and I'm not the only one. Stella joins us, rubbing her elbow against mine. "I'm sorry, Grandma, but are you suggesting that's not what you're doing now?" Stella pans her hand around the backyard.

"I make no apologies. Look at all those smiles."

"Oh, we're looking," I deadpan. "Those are some very happy faces. But a birthday party isn't quite the same as an apartment."

"Oh, boy." Stella gives me a grim look. "Is she trying to talk you into letting her buy you a condo again?"

"Yup," I reply, humor light in my voice. Not that Stella is one to talk. She's every bit the billionaire the rest of the Fritzes are and that's just with her trust fund.

"Hush it, you two." Octavia winks at us, taking another sip of her drink, and I do the same with mine, needing it more than I care to think about.

"In all seriousness, what will you do?" Stella's girlfriend, Delphine asks. "Stella told me about the state of your apartment." Her dark eyes meet mine, her lips dipping down into a frown. "I'm so sorry. I feel like we just moved you in there and now this."

"That's because you *did* just move me in there. It's only been two months."

"Damn." She shakes her head, her tight black curls springing around her face. "You know you're always welcome to stay with us."

"I offered that... what?" Stella looks mockingly at me, her head tilted making her impossibly long blonde hair tickle around her butt. "Ten times yesterday? It got to the point of begging."

I roll my eyes at my friend and give her hair a tug. "You did beg, and it was very sweet if not a little desperate." She gives me an elbow jab and I kiss her cheek. "Seriously though, I appreciate all of your offers, I truly do, but I can't camp out on your couch, and I can't let you buy me an apartment. I'll move back in with Meils and Oliver and the girls until I can find something new closer to school. I still have my old room there. It'll be fine."

Octavia shakes her head ever so slightly, pursing her lips to the side. She's upset that I won't let her drop a couple of million on an apartment for me, but thankfully she isn't pressing it any further.

"Are you doing okay about your professor?" Octavia questions, changing the subject.

"Grandma!" Keegan yells from the top of the waterslide. "Watch me!"

"I'm watching, baby," Octavia calls out, waving at her. Keegan goes flying down, curving around in a loop before splashing into the pool feet-first, her wet, red hair flying around her as she goes. The twins are all Amelia, though they did get Oliver's green eyes.

"I'm doing okay," I tell her after Keegan comes sputtering up in delight, jumping straight into Oliver's arms. "It was rough, and I'm still shaken up by the whole thing. Not to mention we have no idea who will take over teaching the course. The only good thing is that we're on a summer schedule and the classes are shorter, and a lot of the work is done outside the classroom."

"Well, I'm sure whomever they decide on you'll love just as much."

I give my grandmother a wan smile. Somehow, I doubt that.

5

L ayla

"Oh my fluffing Christmas, did you hear?" my friend Murphy shrieks as she races toward me, grabbing my arm to stop herself as she skids on the floors.

"Hear what?" I demand as I help her upright so she doesn't assplant.

"Thanks. Sorry. Did you hear who they named as the interim professor for this class?"

Reluctantly I continue to head toward our classroom. The last time I was in here I was doing CPR on our dead professor. I shudder.

Her brown orbs go wide when I shake my head. "Are you for real? Didn't you read the group chat texts yesterday?"

"No. I was at my nieces' birthday party and after I texted Friday about Dr. Lawrence and my apartment, I was sort of done. I needed the weekend to get my shit back together and besides, keeping up with the group chat is a full-time job."

She cackles. "Truth. Okay." She shakes my arm in excitement, forcing me to halt before we enter the class. "Listen to this. You're going to pee yourself. I nearly did. The new guy is young."

"Anyone compared to Dr. Lawrence is young."

"Fine. That's true. But this guy is not only young, he's also like so freaking hot. And famous! Rock star famous. There's already a bet going on in the class to see who will nail him first. I'm giving myself two weeks to seduce him. I've been obsessed with him forever."

"What? You know him?"

She gives me a look. "Dude, everyone knows him. Because he's famous." She playfully smacks my shoulder. "Are you not listening?"

"I'm listening. It just doesn't sound good is all. Is this person even qualified?" Half the time any hotshot, superstar doctor comes in here they're all ego and little knowledge. It's as if they think we'll absorb their brilliance through osmosis, and they don't have to teach. "Dr. Lawrence was the best professor I've ever had. Anyone they bring in won't be able to replace him half as well."

"Yes, but this new guy is an emergency room attending. He was also the favorite protégé of Dr. Lawrence. He's legit. And hot. And famous. A rock star, Layla. I'm not even joking."

"Great." I don't mean it. I don't want anyone to replace Dr. Lawrence. Hot. Rock star doc or not.

We pull open the heavy door and enter the tiered auditorium-style classroom and my breath stalls in my chest when I see who is standing in the front of the classroom by the SMART board. My chest heats to lava decibels and my insides squirm like worms in the dirt.

Small pieces of what Murphy just said along with everything else from Friday night start shooting through my head like bullets, hitting a mass of targets.

Oh. My. Hell.

"Murphy." I grab my friend's arm, squeezing it.

"Ow. What?" She shakes me off, but I can't drag my gaze away.

"The new professor?" I point a shaky finger. "Is that him?" *Please say no, please say no, please say no.*

"Yep. That's him."

Of course, it is. How awesome for me.

"You said rock star?"

"Rock star," she parrots, oblivious to my inner turmoil "As in an actual rock star. Callan Barrows was the drummer for Central Square. That kick-ass band from all those years ago that broke up when their manager died. He became a doctor and word has it, he was the protégé of Dr. Lawrence. This could not be any better. Eye candy— because hello, he's ridiculously hot—and famous. Hot doc for the win!"

"Right. What emergency room does he work in?"

Please don't say it, please don't say it, please don't say it.

"MGH."

Yup. Because that's how my life is going right now.

My hot one-night stand is my new professor. And my new boss.

I knew he was somewhat familiar. I knew there was something beyond my physical attraction to him. I knew he had money, and I vaguely considered he was a doctor because I saw a medical journal sitting on his coffee table and his father was one. I just hadn't given it much thought because hello, I was not there to learn about him or discuss his profession.

He was also upset on Friday. He mentioned how he too was having a bad day, and if he was close with Dr. Lawrence, that could easily explain it.

This is a nightmare.

"A nightmare? Why?"

Argh! Clearly I do that speaking my inner thoughts aloud thing with more than just with my hot-one-night-stand.

But what the actual fuck am I going to do?

I clear my throat, hoping my voice comes out even. "No reason. I just miss Dr. Lawrence is all."

"Oh. Sure." Her voice fills with sympathy. "I totally get that. I can't believe you were there for that."

Meanwhile, I'm staring down our professor like some sort of visual stalker. I don't want him to look at me, but I also want to know the second he does so I can catch his face and see if he freaks out the way I am.

I drop into a seat in the back and at the end of the row trying not to collapse into a fit of panic-induced hysteria.

How is this a possibility?

I mean, there have to be odds to this, and they can't be very high, right?

Callan Barrows. I snicker. Dr. Hottie McSterious works so much better for him.

I slink down in my chair, open my laptop and position it in front of my face, hoping to be invisible and make a quick escape after class when his eyes finally meet mine. Dark blue. Instantly shocked. He stares and stares as if he's trying to make sense of my being here.

And when he has all the pieces put together, boy is he unhappy to see me.

Can't say I blame him.

We had hot, hot sex all night. I moaned his name, scratched my nails down his back, lost count of the number of orgasms he gave me, and then fled like a thief in the night the second he fell asleep.

"Wow. Why is he staring at you like he wants to kill you?"

"No clue," I lie to my friend only to think better of it. "Actually, he sort of works with Oliver. I don't think he knew I was a student here."

"What do you mean?"

"Remember I told you Oliver got me a position in the—"

"Emergency room at MGH!" she finishes for me. "Holy fried cheeseballs. You're going to be working with him?"

"So it seems," I answer, still locked in a visual battle with my guy. I'm almost starting to find this amusing except it isn't. I know it, and so does he. It's trouble. For both of us if anyone ever finds out.

"Damn. I'm so jealous. Think of all the storage rooms he could pin you against the wall in. I'm totally putting my money on you banging him first then."

I cough out a guffaw that startles half the class. I clear my throat and ignore the curious stares. "That won't be me, babe. I refuse to be the med student who ends up forced into podiatry or men's health treating erectile dysfunction and baldness because I screwed my teacher and boss."

Screwing your professor or student is never a good thing. It's a frowned upon, forbidden thing. I don't know all the rules related to that, I just know that at the very least, it's unethical because he grades me. It's also the sort of thing that follows you around like a 'kick me' sign on your back, giving everyone the right to take a shot at you.

Not that I plan to screw him again. No man is worth that fate. I don't care how hot the sex was.

"Wow, you really thought that through."

"Doesn't make it less true."

Callan's jaw is tighter than a drum as he finally looks away.

I have two and a half more months with him as my professor. Plus, there's that other not-so-small thing. The thing neither of us knew about when he took me to his bed and he's still in the dark about.

That only makes this worse.

This is going to get complicated and messy in a nanosecond if I don't clean this all up.

But how the fuck do I tell Oliver, who got me a summer position helping in the emergency room, that I can't work there because of a certain doctor without outing what happened between us?

It's impossible.

Our situation is a storm we have to weather and will instantly grow to resent the destruction it leaves us in.

There is no escaping him. Here in the class or there in the hospital. He'll be all I know and all I see and all I feel because, for the past three days, he's *all* I've thought about. Best sex of my life and it had to come from the man who is now my professor.

He rounds the desk at the front of the room and taps his laptop keyboard with so much vitriol and force I'm shocked the thing didn't break apart. He reads something on the screen and when he finds whatever it is he's looking for, he looks like he's ready to explode.

Frustrated hands run through his thick, brown hair, and then it's all over. With the flip of a switch, he's calm, composed, and now ignoring me completely.

Phew! That's a relief.

"Good morning, everyone." He calls attention to the class as if he didn't have their undivided attention already. Everyone in here is locked on him.

The women especially.

"As you all know by now, we lost a great man on Friday," he continues. "I knew Dr. Lawrence my entire life. His loss will echo the halls and be felt for decades to come."

He moves back to the front of his desk and then sits on the edge of it, staring out as he commands the room. The way he did in the restaurant Friday night when he walked into it.

"The medical school has asked me to finish up the remainder of your Essentials Homeostasis II course and out of respect to Dr. Lawrence, I agreed until they find a permanent replacement. I'm going to assume you're all up-to-date on the course curriculum and have been meeting your lab and simulator requirements. I'll break you up into your groups in a few minutes to review the neural pathways you should have all been studying, but if anyone has any questions for me prior to that, now is the time to ask."

Daria's hand shoots straight up in the air as she starts to speak. "Are you really Callan Barrows from the band Central Square? I grew up listening to your music. I love it."

He sighs. "Yes. Any other questions? Perhaps about my medical background since medicine is why we're here."

"So, you're like friends with Zaxton Monroe, Greyson Monroe, Asher Reyes, and Lenox Moore?" she persists, ignoring his direct remark about focusing on his medica background instead of personal.

Callan leans back on the edge of the desk, his hands behind him. "Yes."

I snicker at how deadpan he can make a one-word answer. It's the same as it was when I first ran over to his table on Friday.

"Oh, my God. They're like so swoony. I'm obsessed with Asher

Reyes. Oh, and Greyson Monroe too. His voice is like... ugh." Daria fans her face and Callan stares at her in exasperation.

"Are we done with the Central Square—"

"Will they come to class?" Alfred cuts him off.

"No. Anything else? Last call?"

"Are you single?" Daria giggles and so do the two girls sitting beside her.

He stands and glares down at them, his voice allowing no room for argument when he replies. "That's not a question I ever answer and certainly not one you need the answer to. Now that we got those out of the way, from here on out, it's medicine and medicine only."

"Wow," Murphy whispers, leaning toward my ear so only I can hear her. "This is going to be an interesting summer."

No joke.

6

L ayla

CLASS ENDS and for a few moments, I linger. Only he's surrounded and that doesn't seem as if it will be changing anytime soon. I need to speak with him, and judging by the way his gaze catches mine—the first time since I first sat down over three hours ago—he's thinking the same thing.

I give him a smirk and toss my hands up in the air in a *what can do you do* way and then climb the steps to leave. I don't make it far. A very unexpected and unwanted person is waiting for me in the hall leaning casually against the window opposite the door I'm exiting.

My ex's face is buried in his phone, and I wonder if I can keep going without him seeing me. Except, because this is the way my life is going right now, his head pops up the second I go to make a break for it.

"Hey! There you are," he exclaims with a big, bright, beaming smile. The ones he used to give me when he'd see me after class or when he'd come to pick me up for a date or later when he'd come home from class, and I'd have dinner already going for us.

"What are you doing here?" Yeah, I'm not nearly as happy to see him as he is to see me.

He frowns at my less-than-warm greeting. "I wanted to talk to you."

He pushes away from the window and closes the space between us until he's close. Too close. After the last few days I've had, I'm in no mood.

"No thanks." I start walking. Unfortunately, he keeps pace until he grows flustered by my obvious attempt to brush him off and grabs my arm, pulling me to a stop.

"Come on. Don't be like that." He catches my chin and forces my gaze up to his brown eyes. I shake off his touch and he glares ever so slightly. "I was worried about you. I heard about Dr. Lawrence and that you were the one who was with him when it happened. I also heard about your apartment."

I puff out an exacerbated breath. "How did you hear about all that?"

"I'm in your class group chat."

That takes me aback. How did I not know that? "You are? Since when?"

He smirks. "Since we broke up."

He says it like I should be flattered that he's encroaching on my chat or like it makes him a secret hero who is still obsessed with the heroine he did wrong. Only this isn't our romance book, and all that does is make him a douchebag of epic proportions and a stalker.

I glare. "You have no right being in that chat. You're not even in my program."

He shrugs unrepentantly. "I wanted to keep tabs on you. What? Don't give me that look. You can't be shocked. Just because we broke up doesn't mean I stopped caring about you. I wanted a break, not a breakup."

I snort out a sardonic laugh. Because truly, that's a good one.

"Your activity hours after our 'break' would suggest otherwise." I put air quotes around the word.

He winces, quickly looking away as he runs a hand through his hair and falls momentarily silent.

Patrick and I met at Dartmouth but didn't start dating until our junior year. After that we were inseparable. So inseparable that I didn't realize the force he was having over my life until we ended two months ago. I never went to parties without him. I never hung out with my friends without him. It got to the point where he'd comment on my clothes, my style, and how he liked my hair done—and I'd listen and follow his suggestions. I planned on going to Columbia for medical school—it's where Oliver went—but Patrick kept pressing for Harvard and when we both got in, I gave up on Columbia for him. We moved in with each other when we came to Boston last fall. Well, I moved into the apartment his parents got him.

Everything was great until about four months ago.

He's doing the health sciences and technology route for people who want to become physician-scientists. It's a joint program with MIT and with it, you take several classes at MIT. One of the girls in his class, Molly Lin, started getting close to him. Started texting him regularly. Some of the texts were bordering on flirty and then some were straight-up sexting.

We'd fight about it, and he'd assure me she was nothing more than a friend and that he only wanted me and not her and blah, blah, blah.

Then two months ago he told me he wanted us to take a break. That things were too serious between us and that he needed to focus on school more and less on me. A break but we could still date. Like, what the fuck is that?

We yelled. He left. And then he called me the next morning after not coming home to tell me he had slept with Molly the night before. The same night we barely called a break. I moved out that day. He claimed he was telling me so I wouldn't hear about it from someone else.

So cool. So casual. So unaffected. So brutally fucking honest.

He broke my heart by wanting a break and then he dug the knife in deeper by fucking her that same goddamn night. After that, I swore I wouldn't do that to myself again. I'd never lose my identity, and I'd never sacrifice the things I want for my life for a man.

"I already told you I'm not with Molly," he persists. "It was just that one night."

"Good for you. I don't care. Bye now."

I start to walk again, and he grabs me, pulling me to yet another halt.

"Let go. I have somewhere to be." I jerk my arm free of him.

He growls under his breath. "I just want to know that you're okay."

"I'm okay. Clearly. It's just stuff." Not really but screw him.

"Where are you staying? Because if you need a place to stay, you can always move back—"

"Oh my God," I sharply interject, my hand flying out toward him, making a stop signal right in his face. "Shut your mouth, Patrick. You have no freaking right to be here let alone to say that sort of bullshit to me."

He shifts his weight, growing agitated. "It doesn't have to be like this between us, Layla."

My hands go to my hips. "Actually, it does. This is what happens when you break up. It ends. The relationship is over. Now legit, fuck off."

He steps into me, not liking that at all. "That's not what I asked for—"

"I believe she said to fuck off."

Chills race up my spine at the sound of his smooth whiskey voice and it's like Friday night redux. Only this won't end with him eating me out in a random office or taking me back to his house for the night.

Patrick's head snaps in the direction of Callan's voice and reluctantly, mine does the same. Callan Barrows is sauntering our way. Tall. Broad. Confident. Sexy in a way that should be illegal. The sleeves of his pale blue button-down are now rolled up to his elbows revealing impressive forearms, and I might stare a second longer than socially appropriate.

"I don't believe this concerns you—"

"Ah, but it does," Callan cuts Patrick off once again as he reaches us, standing directly beside me, so close I can smell his intoxicating cologne. "Miss Fritz and I are overdue for a conversation." His blue eyes meet mine. "Isn't that right, Layla?"

Damn. The way he purrs my name is nothing short of diabolical in how my body reacts to it. "Yes. That's correct." I don't even bother looking at Patrick when I say it and that's what's bothering me. Not Patrick. It's the fact that I can't seem to remove my eyes from Callan.

I haven't stopped thinking about him all weekend.

Not Patrick when Patrick and what he did to me had been living rent-free in my head like a cockroach that won't die for the last two months.

Callan is saving me again after I ran out on him. He's saving me even though I'm now his student and he shouldn't be looking at me or even speaking to me this deliberately. The heat in his eyes is telling me he doesn't care about any of that. Though I know that's not the case.

He cares. He cares a lot.

I don't know him well, but I don't have to, to know he's that sort of guy. Honorable. It's written all over him as it was Friday night. He doesn't like what Patrick is trying to do with me, and damn him if it doesn't make me like him a tiny bit more than I should.

"I'm sorry, who are you?" Patrick is nonplussed.

"Dr. Callan Barrows. I'm the interim professor taking over Dr. Lawrence's class. Miss Fritz skipped out early on me and she has some explaining to do about that." Callan's gaze finally breaks away from mine and he takes Patrick in with a slow, disdainful sweep. "Who are you?"

"He's my ex," I answer for him. "And he was just about to fuck off. For good."

"No. Wait." Patrick angles in closer to me, panic striking his features as his eyes search mine. "Do you know him?"

I can't stop my wry smirk. "As he said, I skipped out early on him and owe him an explanation for it. Come on, Dr. Barrows." I grab his forearm, because *hell*, his forearms. "I'm running late now so we can talk while you walk me to the T."

"Layla! Wait!"

"Bye, Patrick. I assume I won't find you lurking around my class-room again."

We head for the exit and when we step out into the late morning sunshine Callan says, "That was the boy you mentioned who fell for you when you told him not to?"

That's how it started. Then the tables turned on me.

I shake my head incredulously. "You've got a real thing for coming to my rescue," I muse, walking across campus toward Brigham Circle. With any luck, I'll make the train and escape this entire morning.

"You've got a real thing for attracting clingy losers."

"Present company included in that?" I toss him a quick smug glance.

"I said clingy, so no."

"Ah. Right. Well, professor, what can I do for you?"

He grunts. "Have you told anyone about Friday?" he asks as we hot-foot it through the bright and humid Boston summer air.

"Just my best friend Stella and my sister Amelia. It wasn't as if I knew who you were or that you were my professor at the time. Besides, they won't tell anyone," I assure him.

"But will your sister tell Oliver? Fuck." He catches my waist and pulls me to a stop before walking us over to a shady tree. "You're Layla *Fritz*. I know your sister and brother-in-law. Hell, I work with basically your whole family at the hospital." His voice climbs.

"I know." I shift my weight. "I know exactly where they work." My gaze hits the hardtop. I'm being a bit of a bitch and it's not his fault this is our situation or that Patrick decided this was the day to show up. I temper my tone and mood and lift my chin. "Listen, I... um. There's something I need to tell you and I was going to, but you were surrounded by your horde of admirers, and I didn't want to be late. I'm headed to MGH now."

"What?" Callan grasps my arm only to just as quickly release it when he remembers where we are. "Why?"

I peek up at him through my lashes. "Oliver got me a position in the emergency room for the summer."

"A position?"

"Sort of like an early clerkship. I'll be working with Andrew Albright who is his friend. Watching mostly. Learning. Helping when I can." Andrew Albright or Drew as he prefers to be called is the chief of the emergency department, so therefore Callan's boss.

"Christ," Callan hisses, scrubbing his hands up and down his face before they land on his lean hips. "There is no escaping you. I'm going there now. I have a shift."

"I'm sorry. I didn't know who you were Friday."

His head bobs and he stares sightlessly out onto the med school grounds as he thinks. "I thought you looked familiar, but I couldn't place it, and in truth, I never would have put it together that you're Oliver's sister-in-law. I think I met you once very briefly and that was a few years ago at a charity event."

I shrug. "Maybe. I don't remember. I've been to a lot of those. Being Octavia Abbot-Fritz's granddaughter is like that."

His gaze snaps back to mine and he squints. "Granddaughter?"

"Amelia was my guardian. Our parents died when I was little. When she married Oliver years later, he adopted me. I was only fourteen at the time. Anyway, when he did that, I changed my last name to Fritz and his family became my family."

"So you're more than simply his sister-in-law. You're his kid. Great. I not only fucked my student but my colleague's kid. And now you're going to be working with me." He's breathing hard. "Christ, Layla, I feel like a real son of a bitch."

That raises my hackles. "I'm an adult, Callan. I make my own decisions and they have nothing to do with Oliver or any other member of the Fritz family. Besides, Amelia and Stella won't tell anyone. Least of all Oliver, who hates hearing about my love life. And we both know it won't happen again."

Callan bites out a sarcastic laugh. "You mean because you ran out on me or because of our current situation?" He shakes his head. "Never mind. Don't answer that. It doesn't matter."

"I told you that night I was a one-night-only girl. You met the main reason why inside. I had fun with you Friday night, but that's all I was looking for. A night of fun."

Only now that I'm here with him, I almost wish I hadn't run out. I wish I had stayed, and we'd had a bit more fun together as Layla and Callan before everything else got so damn complicated.

He exhales a heavy breath, and his face softens. "I know you did, but I won't lie and say I wasn't a little disappointed to wake up and find you gone." Another breath and he grits his teeth and rolls his eyes in a self-deprecating way. "Whatever. That's useless. Clearly, it was for the best since this is where we find ourselves now. It'll be fine. We'll be professional with each other. Nothing more. In a few months, summer will be over, and you'll be moving on to start your clerkship rotations and I'll hopefully be done teaching." His eyes bore into mine. "We can get through a few months."

He ends it there, but I hear his unspoken words ringing through my head all the same. *Without ripping each other's clothes off.* Or maybe those words are my own. I'm brutally and painfully still attracted to him. I still feel that thing between us. That kinetic energy we seem to put off when the other is nearby.

I want him.

And I can't have him.

But more importantly, I don't want to want him.

So I repeat his sentiment, "We'll be professional and nothing more."

He nods absently, rubbing at his jaw as he takes me in. "This is going to be hell. Come with me."

He doesn't give me a choice. Instead, he takes me by the arm and leads me in the opposite direction of the T.

"You need to stop saying that to me if we're going to be professional," I quip, trying to get myself free of his grip but to no avail. "Hey. Stop. I need to catch the T."

"I drove, so I'll give you a ride. It'll be faster than taking the E-train this time of day and then switching to the red line."

Even though I know he's right, I should argue it.

But I don't.

Because I like his grip on me and I like the way he sort of manhandles me and doesn't give a shit when I fight back. I like that he charged in and told Patrick to fuck off just as easily as he did the asshole in the bar the other night. I like the way I feel when he looks at me and how he's a lot forbidden.

I shouldn't like any of this.

But I do.

I won't fuck him again. I won't even flirt with him. I'll keep this juicy secret to myself, but it'll be one I hold onto and enjoy more than I should.

We don't talk much in the car. Likely because neither of us knows what to say. He asks what I want to specialize in, and I tell him either emergency medicine—hence this summer in the ED to feel it out—or trauma surgery. The conversation ends there as he parks in his spot in the garage and then we walk toward the ambulance bay and the patient area of the emergency department.

"I'm meeting Oliver and Drew in there," I inform him when he throws me a questioning look as I follow him.

Before we reach the ambulance bay doors, he stops me, taking me by the shoulders and moving us just over to the side. For a moment he simply stares into my eyes, deliberating something. Finally, he sighs, but he doesn't release me. One hand slides to the nape of my neck, his other curls into a fist, and he drags his knuckles up my cheek.

"I have no right to ask you for anything. You don't know me, and I don't know you. But can I ask a favor?"

I swallow past the lump in my throat and nod cautiously.

"It's a big favor."

"Okay." I laugh at his warning expression.

"Don't fuck anyone in my emergency department. And if you fuck anyone in the class, just make sure I don't hear about it."

I'm completely caught off-guard and snap in response. "I wasn't planning on it. Despite what you think, I don't sleep my way around Boston."

"I wasn't judging and that's not what I was trying to imply." His grip on the back of my neck tightens and his knuckles take another swipe. "I feel something I shouldn't when I look at you, and I don't need to make that stronger by becoming jealous of you with another guy right under my nose."

"Oh." And if I thought I was caught off-guard a moment ago, that has nothing on me now. I'm impersonating a goldfish. But worse, my heart starts to pitter-patter in my chest, sending a heady rush of girlish endorphins through my veins. It's warm and tingly and feels incredible.

"Is that okay?"

"Yes." I lick my lips, unsure of what's happening. "Can I ask the same?"

He makes a noise in the back of his throat. "You don't have to. I don't fuck people I work with, and I'd never fuck a student." He tilts his head, giving me a lopsided grin and treating me to his damn adorable dimples. "At least not knowingly."

"Then we're good," I say, forcing confidence in my voice and a smile to my lips.

"I guess we are." He releases me and takes a step back, his gaze still on mine even as he takes another, creating more distance between us. "It's weird. All my life I've followed the rules and done as I should. But looking at you... you make me want to break all the rules."

With that, he turns around and heads into the building, the mechanical doors swallowing him up. And all I can think is... me too.

CLEARANCE 12'

C allan

I'VE ALWAYS BEEN a master of compartmentalization. Being a doctor, especially in the emergency room, you have to be otherwise every patient will break you. So that's how I start my shift. Compartmentalizing my job and my responsibilities from Layla. Only that's proving to be impossible.

She's everywhere.

Oliver is beaming with pride as he parades her around like a trophy, introducing her to everyone he passes. He doesn't spend a lot of time down here as he's a family medicine doctor, but I do sometimes see him around and he works with my best friend Greyson Monroe's girlfriend, Fallon. It's a tighter circle than I like. One that could easily rain shit down on me if anyone found out.

"Cal," Oliver greets me, slapping me on the back. "Hey, man. Glad you're here today. Have you met my sister-in-law Layla yet? She's going to be shadowing a bit down here this summer."

"Hey. Yes, I have. She's actually my student for the summer as I'm filling in for Dr. Lawrence."

Oliver's green eyes go comically wide with surprise. "Right. Yeah. Sorry about your loss. It's been awful for Layla. I still can't believe she was there when it happened."

"Oh?" That's news to me. All I heard was that a student was with him when he had his massive heart attack, and they did CPR until EMS arrived and pronounced him dead. I didn't know it was Layla.

She blinks her pretty blue eyes up at me but doesn't comment further.

He peers down at Layla. "Well, it's great that you'll have your teacher both here and in the classroom. You'll learn a lot."

Layla rolls her eyes at him. "And you have plenty of eyes down here to watch me so I don't get into trouble." She climbs up on her toes and gives him a kiss on the cheek. "Go back to work. I'll see you in a few hours and you can grill me all about my day on the drive home."

Oliver laughs and ruffles her hair. "Fine. I get it. I'll go. Be good and be helpful."

Oliver walks off just as Drew Albright approaches. "You ready, Layla?"

She rolls up on the balls of her feet. "I am. Thank you again for having me here, Drew."

His eyes sparkle at her. "It'll be great. In fact, you should shadow Dr. Barrows for a bit. He's been working here since he was an intern. Then we can see if any of the nurses need some help."

All the color drains from my face but I have no solid reason to say no. Med students shadowing and working with residents and attendings is part of the gig.

"Uh. Okay," Layla mumbles. "Great."

Yeah, only not so much.

"You good with that, Cal?"

No. No, I'm not. "Sure."

"Awesome. I'll check back in with you in a bit. Thanks, man."

Drew walks off, his attention going to his phone, and I'm left here with Layla.

"Sorry."

I shrug. I have to get used to her at some point. Maybe this is the way to do that. Some immersion therapy and then I'll be cured. I can no longer think of her as the beautiful, sexy, and alluring woman from Friday night. The one who made my head spin and my body insatiable. From here on out, she can only be a faceless medical student to me.

"It's fine. Let's go. Just stay behind me, and don't speak or touch anything. You'll watch unless I direct you otherwise. Got it?"

Her expression grows serious. "Got it. I know the score down here and I'm not going to get in your way. I just want to learn all that I can."

I respect that about her. She's a Fritz, stepchild or not, and that name pulls a lot of weight in this city. Especially in the medical community since all the Fritz children are in the medical field. She used that to get this position, but she's not spoiled, and she's not enti-tled. She's in scrubs with her hair tied up, ready to do whatever is asked of her. I also reviewed some of her course discussions and lab scores earlier this morning, and she's at the top of her class.

I smirk at her. "Then come with me."

She laughs. "I thought we discussed you not saying that anymore."

"You did. I never agreed."

For the next few hours, Layla follows me around and does my bidding. We see patient after patient. She stays behind me. She keeps her mouth shut. She watches everything I do with interest and curiosity. When we leave the patient rooms, I drill her with questions and challenge her on differential diagnoses. She runs labs and by the end of the day, I allow her to stand in the corner of the room during a trauma that comes in.

Being around her gets easier but it also gets harder.

Easier because everything we're doing is work-related. There is no time for anything else. Harder because I still catch hints of her fragrance or a coy smile or the way her eyes light up when I praise her, or she gets diagnoses correct.

I've never been happier to see the end of my shift as I am right now.

"Thank you for today, Dr. Barrows," she says simply as I finish signing out the last of my patients to the oncoming doctor. "I learned a lot and I'm very grateful for your time."

"When are you back next?"

"Wednesday after class. I'm going to be here Mondays, Wednesdays, and Fridays. Tuesdays and Thursdays are lab and simulator days plus I need to study and get my work in."

"Then I'll see you Wednesday."

I spin to leave, wanting to flee this woman when her voice stops me. "Why did you pick emergency medicine as your specialty?"

I freeze, just like that. My hands go to my hips and my head falls forward as my eyes close. I don't get asked this question frequently anymore, and back when I was a student or an intern, I had a bullshit answer. I'd say it was because my father was an Army surgeon and I wanted to help those in crisis.

Originally, I had wanted to become a surgeon for that very reason. Then Suzie died.

Just dropped dead in the shower. She was with Zax, he did CPR, and then Greyson and I came in. I took over for him because I knew what I was doing because I was CPR certified—my father always made sure of that.

I also knew there was going to be no saving her that night.

Suzie. A girl larger than life. A girl whom I had known my entire life. And there I was, doing chest compressions on her dead body.

She had a stroke. A brain hemorrhage, but before that she'd been having headaches. I didn't know about those and neither did Zax who was her boyfriend. Only her twin brother Lenox knew, but there were other signs he missed. Other signs we all missed. Like she'd had some episodes of blurry vision. Some tingling in her fingers and even occasional weakness in her hand.

It was a lot of little things that were never caught, but after she died, I wanted to be the one to catch all the little things so something like that wouldn't happen again. I couldn't save Suzie and it broke me apart in a lot of ways, so that's why I did it. I've never told another living soul that's the real reason I went into emergency medicine. Not my father. Not my older brother. Not my friends—especially not them.

I turn back to her and debate how forthcoming I should be. Layla is part of a very wealthy, very famous, very private family. I suspect she's no stranger to keeping secrets and things close to the vest. Suzie's death was everywhere. Central Square was one of the world's largest bands at the time and her death was big news. I've never talked about it publicly, only with the guys. Trusting her with this is no small thing, but for reasons I can't figure out, I want her to be the one to know the truth.

"Because no one should lose their Suzie the way we lost ours. If I can save at least one person by catching something bad before it strikes, then that's all I need."

She swallows the distance between us by half and stares up into my eyes. "By my count, you saved the lives of at least three people today. Nice job, Doctor. I'll see you Wednesday in class."

My heart clenches like she's squeezing it in her fist, and I leave the hospital—and her—behind. It's going to be a long fucking summer.

"UNCLE CAL, can I come stay with you next week?" my niece Katy immediately asks the second as I hit answer on my car's screen as I drive over to Zax's place for dinner. All the guys are in town tonight and whenever that's the case—since it rarely ever is—we always get together.

"Hey, Katy, my favorite lady," I answer, smiling for the first time in what feels like all week at the sound of her high-pitched voice. "You can stay with me anytime, but what's going on next week?"

It's been one week since I met Layla. A week's worth of classes in the morning and then seeing Layla in the emergency room after. She was paired with me again today and it was a special form of hell. What is it about her that makes me want to look at her all the damn time? That makes me want to reach out and touch her?

I don't understand it. I've never been like this before with a woman. Instead of things getting easier, they seem to be getting harder.

"Ladybug, you weren't supposed to call him." I hear my brother admonish her in the background since Katy has me on speakerphone. "I asked you to get my phone, so *I* could call Uncle Cal."

"But he likes talking to me more," she defends.

I laugh as I pull up to a red light. "It's true. I do like talking to Katy more."

"That's because she has you wrapped around her finger."

"Also true. I won't even deny that."

My brother groans playfully and then his voice comes through louder. "Can I have the phone, please? Thank you. It's time for your bath. Mommy is upstairs waiting. She has the blue bath bomb you wanted. Say good night to Uncle Cal."

"Good night, Uncle Cal."

"Good night, sweetie. Talk to you soon. Love you."

"Love you."

A crackling sound fills my car and then my brother Declan is back just as the light turns green and I continue on. "Hey, Cal. Sorry."

I laugh. "Hey, Dec. It's fine. That was actually the best part of my day so far. So what's this about next week?"

My brother sighs into the phone. "One of Willow's friends decided to elope in the middle of the week and wants Willow to be her maid of honor, but the wedding is on Cape Cod and of course, children aren't allowed. Any chance you're not working next Wednesday or Thursday?"

I tap the steering wheel. "Wednesday I am, but as luck would have it, I'm not working Thursday."

"Any chance you want to watch Katy for a night or two?"

I take a left and head toward the Seaport district, inching along in Friday night Boston traffic. "Always. Her room is waiting for her."

"Awesome. You're a lifesaver. She'll be very excited."

"Me too actually." I tap the steering wheel. "I could use a little Katy distraction right about now."

"That sounds serious coming from you. What's her name?"

I roll my eyes though he can't see me do it. "Ha. You're very funny."

"But I'm right, aren't I? There's a woman."

I pull up to another red light, absently staring out the window at people on the sidewalk. My brother is a doctor too, but we've lived very different lives. I got to play rock star after high school, doing college entirely online. He went straight into the Army, doing college that way, and then became a reserve when he went into medical school. My brother and I are very close, but I know he never understood what I was doing with Central Square.

He's a lot like my father in that, though I'm not all that close with my parents and rarely see them since they live in Florida now. With that in mind, I absolutely cannot tell him about Layla. Not only is she my student, but she's also a subordinate at the hospital.

"It's nothing," I tell him. "Just a long week of teaching classes and working."

"You can tell—" I hear my sister-in-law call to him in the background, cutting off his words. "I'm coming," he calls back to her before he returns to the phone. "I gotta go help with the bath. Katy is asking for me. If you change your mind and want to talk about it, I'm here."

"Thanks. I'll see you next week when you drop her off."

"Sounds good and thanks again. Later."

He disconnects the call and I continue on, finally reaching Zax's penthouse.

His fiancée, Aurelia, opens the door with a smile. "Hey! You made it." She gives me a hug and then shuts the door behind me.

"I did. Am I the last to arrive?" I ask, searching around only to hear voices coming from the direction of the dining room.

"You are, but that only makes you right on time. Everyone is hanging out having a pre-dinner drink."

Aurelia is a former model-turned-designer under the name Lia Sage. She was Zax and Grey's former stepsister and reunited with Zax when she came to work at his family's fashion empire as a design intern. The two of them had a lot of drama, but ultimately fell in love. I'll admit, Zax was the last one of us I thought would ever fall in love again after the way he lost Suzie. Her death haunted him for eight years.

"Speaking of, I brought alcohol."

She laughs, taking the proffered bottle of tequila from my hand. "Is this for me or you?"

I meet her blue eyes. Blonde hair and blue eyes. Though she looks nothing like Layla, their basic features are similar and it's throwing me a bit. "Both," I answer honestly. "Do I look that rough?"

"You look like a man who has more on his mind than he wants to think about."

Never in my life have I heard a more brilliantly accurate description of myself.

"You hit the nail on the head."

"Then come on and let's get you a drink."

I follow her through the massive penthouse in the direction of the kitchen which is open to the dining room. Zax, Asher, Lenox, Greyson, and Fallon are all sitting at the table, laughing about something I missed as they sip on drinks and pick at appetizers. But seeing Fallon makes me think of Oliver because she works with him, and thinking of Oliver makes me think of Layla. Yeah, I might be a tad bit fucked.

Not to mention everyone here knows Oliver as well as the rest of the Fritzes. Boston celebrities are a small club, and we attend the charity balls the Fritz's family foundation hosts a few times a year. Hell, Oliver even does some modeling for Monroe Fashions, Zax's fashion company. I wouldn't exactly call us close since they're a bit older than us, but we're definitely friendly with them.

"Hey!" everyone exclaims when they catch me walking in. They stand and we all do the bro hug-shake thing and I give Fallon a hug.

Aurelia—bless her—returns with a glass of tequila on ice for me, and once again, that makes me think of fucking Layla.

Goddamn her!

The tequila wasn't even a conscious thought. I just saw the bottle and grabbed it, but it was the same one she and I drank.

"I fucked my med student." And yep, it came out just like that.

Everyone pauses, a lot of blinking eyes in my direction, and a heavy silence ensues because this isn't me. I'm not this guy. I'm calculating and cautious, but I wasn't that night. It was a rough night and I saw her, and I wanted her, and I took her.

Fallon is the first to come out of her fog. She's a doctor and I know has had med students of her own. She clears her throat, her violet eyes on me. "Did you know she was your student when you did that?"

"No."

I'm glad she asked, giving me the benefit of the doubt because she knows me. Fallon was Grey's and Zax's neighbor growing up. Grey was best friends with Fallon's brother, but they were close too, and he's been in love with Fallon since they were teenagers. They only recently reunited and got together. Out of all of us, Grey is the only one who continued with music. He's still a huge rock star, bigger than ever actually.

"I didn't," I continue. "I met her last Friday night at my sushi place. One thing led to another and I took her home. I didn't know who she was until Monday."

Zax leads me over to the table, practically shoving me into an empty chair, and everyone else retakes their seats.

"When you say you didn't know who she was, why does it sound like she's more than simply your student?" Asher questions. Asher Reyes is a championship-winning NFL quarterback. His entire family is football royalty, but he almost blew his shot by being on the road with Central Square. He and I had wanted to leave the band, me to become a doctor, and him to finish college at a big football school so he could hopefully get drafted. We've never talked about that since Suzie died and I wonder if he ever felt as guilty as I did about it. Anyway... I digress.

I lean back in my chair and swallow half of my drink before looking straight at Asher. "That's because she's Layla Fritz."

Once again suffocating silence fills the room.

"Here." Aurelia goes somewhere only to return a second later with the bottle. "Top yourself off. You need it."

Which I do, as I wait on them to fill the tense silence.

"Layla Fritz? As in Oliver Fritz's kid?"

"Is that what he calls her?" I ask Fallon.

She nods and then gives me an apologetic shrug. "Yes. Any time he talks about her with us, he calls her his kid. I know she's technically his sister-in-law, but..."

"Wait!" Zax holds up his hand. "I get why that's awkward, but if she doesn't tell anyone and you don't tell anyone outside this room and you don't do it again, why is this a thing?"

"Because she's working in the emergency department this summer with him," Fallon supplies for me, picking up a piece of cheese from one of the platters and popping it into her mouth.

"And he still wants her," Grey states, watching me carefully.

"It's all over your face," Lenox says and since he practically never speaks, any time he does it's always real. The silent hacker is sporting new ink on his forearm. No shocker there since he also owns a tattoo parlor near where he lives in the middle of nowhere Maine.

I could deny what they're saying, but why bother? "Nothing is going to happen again."

"Then what's the problem?" Asher finishes off his drink and then swipes the bottle of tequila from me, pouring himself a small glass. "I mean, other than the obvious. She's now your student and she works at the hospital and is a Fritz. That's all unfortunate, and yes, a bit sticky, but not insurmountable. Especially for you who never goes back on something once you've set your mind to it. You're the most focused motherfucker on the planet."

"True," Zax muses, tossing his arm around Aurelia and dragging her body in a bit closer to his. "You didn't know who she was at the time when you hooked up and it's in her best interest, as much as it's in yours, for her to keep her mouth shut. So explain why you look like Ash just broke Rocky's leg again."

"Christ!" Asher cries. "That again." His hand smacks the dark wood table before he points an accusing finger at Zax. "It was an accident, dude. What kind of dog chases after someone on a skateboard?"

I snicker, and so does everyone else, and I know that was Zax's intention. He wanted to lighten the mood and I appreciate it.

"The truth is..." I mumble, staring down at the clear liquid swirling around my glass. "The truth is there's something about her. I've hooked up with women and been around them after and it was never a thing. Never a second thought half the time. But last Friday with her is all I've been thinking about for a solid week. Every time I close my eyes, she's there and every time I open my eyes, she's also there because she's fucking everywhere. In my class. In my emergency department. In my head. It's a nightmare."

There. I said it. Only I don't feel any better about it. If anything, that truth reminds me I'm stuck in a situation for the next few months that I can't do anything about. It sucks.

"Then you'll just have to fight it, brother. And fight it hard if need be."

I raise my glass to Asher and then polish off the rest. "Easy as pie."

Only we all know it's a lie.

8

C allan

AFTER I DROPPED my truth bomb on my friends, we let the topic die. There wasn't much else to say about it, and instead, we ate dinner and then played poker. I lost to Aurelia, but that's no surprise as the woman is a card shark phenom. But for the first time since last Friday, I wasn't thinking about Layla. I was with my friends—women and men I consider my family—and everything was starting to feel a bit better.

Now Asher is riding home with me since he suggested watching a movie at my place, prattling on about training camp that starts back up in August and how he's been doing this new workout routine that's made him stronger than he's ever been. I'm close with all the guys, but Ash and I are the closest, even if we couldn't be any more different from each other and are two years apart.

"You should come with me to the gym this week."

"I have zero time for that, brother. I'm lucky I'm able to get an hour in at my house."

"It's weird," he muses, his voice going distant. "We used to live for the tour and live for the release of albums. Now I live for the season. It's a constant cycle."

I chuckle lightly. "I guess your life sort of is. You simply traded being a professional musician for a professional athlete."

"I'm better at this than I ever was at that. If Grey and Lenox hadn't been so damn talented and we weren't all best friends, we'd never have gone anywhere with our band."

It's true. I still occasionally bang on my electric drums—having traded in my regular drums for these when I moved into my town-house—but I'm mediocre at best. Ash is okay at guitar, but he didn't have to be anything better because Greyson is, as he said, pure talent. Both with his guitar and his voice.

"I think it all turned out the way it was supposed to."

Ash runs a hand through his reddish-brown hair, his voice somber as he says, "I know, but it feels wrong somehow to say that though."

I bob my head in agreement because it does. I've often wondered if I ever would have had it in me to leave the band if we continued to be as successful as we were.

"Damn. Those are some seriously long legs."

"Huh?" The sudden topic change and obvious interest in his voice make my head reflexively turn toward him and then outwardly search in the direction he's staring. And sure enough, those are some seriously long legs that are attached to a tall, blonde woman who isn't wearing much more than a cocktail napkin for a dress as she walks along the sidewalk as if she owns it.

Which she might considering she's Layla Freaking Fritz. "Goddammit."

"What?"

I growl and change lanes, sharply pulling my SUV into a random vacant spot.

"Dude, what are you doing?" Ash sits up straight, swiveling toward me in alarm.

Without answering him, I'm out of my car, practically getting hit by traffic as I go, slamming my car door shut with more force than I should. Ash is climbing out of the passenger side, racing over to me, his face twisting in confusion and concern.

"Cal. What the hell, man?!"

"That's Layla." The words grate past my clenched teeth. I point at the blonde up ahead who is walking alone. Alone at close to midnight looking like that.

"Oh." Asher snickers, his gaze casting back over to her and then he's patting my shoulder. "Now I see what the problem is. Yeah, she's something alright. I'd tell you not to do anything I would do, but I'm starting to wonder if maybe that's exactly what you need. Something, or in this case, someone to shake you up a bit."

"I'm not going to do anything with her," I grumble, but that doesn't stop me from heading in her direction. "She's my student. Remember?"

"Right. Sure. Whatever you say, man. Condoms save lives. Remember *that*, Doctor."

I flip him off.

"So, I'll just drive your car home then?" he calls after me. "Cool, man. Thanks. You can swing by and pick it up from my place tomorrow."

I throw my hand up over my shoulder acknowledging that, and then I take off into a jog to catch up to her because there are two college-aged guys near me staring at her like she's their next meal and saying things that will have me toss their lifeless bodies into the Charles River if they're not careful.

For a moment I take in the woman walking ahead, head held high, purse tucked against her side, heels clicking on the sidewalk, blonde hair bouncing. She's unstoppable and unmissable and for a lesser man, unapproachable. Just looking at her makes you think you could never have a shot with a woman like her, and that might in fact be true. She told her ex to fuck off plain as day without a backward glance in his direction and she remorselessly snuck out of my place after getting exactly what she wanted from me.

I don't think Layla needs my protection at all.

She's her own force of nature. A powerhouse living by her own carefully crafted rules. She's too smart, too beautiful, too irresistibly wild for us mere mortals to possess her.

It only makes me want to try harder to do just that.

But I won't.

I'll just make sure she gets somewhere safe so I can sleep tonight without worrying about her and that will be that.

"Are you trying to become a statistic?" I bark as I reach her, grabbing her arm and twisting her to face me. I'm angry and I have no right to be angry, but right now I don't care so much. She's been fucking up my world all week and now here she is like this.

Her giant doe-like ocean blue eyes blink wide at me, her fist balled up, clutching a black canister. Pepper spray. Good girl.

When she registers that it's me, a smirk curls up her glossy pink lips. "Did you know that pepper spray can reach an assailant from as far away as ten feet and will last anywhere between fifteen to forty-five minutes as it causes involuntary eye closure, difficulty breathing, and burning of the face and skin? Incidentally, I also carry a knife in my purse."

My hand dives into her hair, cupping the back of her head as I drag her body closer to mine. She lets me without even an ounce of resistance.

"Doesn't mean it's safe to be walking alone on the city streets at this hour of the night looking like every man's fantasy."

She's smiling at me now in a way that tells me she's beyond amused by my overprotective routine. "Slow your roll there, Dr. Hottie McSterious. My car is two blocks up." She points out to her side with her pepper spray hand.

I don't bother looking. I'm still too fired up. "Who were you out with tonight that let you walk out here alone?"

She squints at me, shirking off my touch. "No one, and since I am my own woman and keeper, I don't have to ask permission for anything I want to do. I was at Stella's restaurant. She had to work the bar tonight since two of her bartenders called out on her and I helped her for a while."

"Dressed like that?"

She shrugs indifferently. "More tits, more tips."

Jesus. I scrub my hands up my face, breathing harshly.

"Oh stop. You're being way too dramatic about this, and frankly, it's not your business. Stella made me promise I'd call her the second I got to my car or she'd—" Her phone rings in her purse and she gives me an I told you so quirk of her brow. She fishes her phone out and answers it. "I'm fine, Stella. I ran into a friend on the street." She listens for a minute and then puffs out a half-laugh. "No. An actual friend. Not a hot streetwalking frat boy I can make my bitch for the night. Do those even exist and not spread PID?"

I grin and then laugh, all the tension in my body evaporating along with it.

"Oh my God, Stella." Her arms flail. "I'm being serious with you." She cocks a hip and rolls her eyes. "Fine. Fluffy marshmallows. Happy now? Dr. Hottie McSterious is going to walk me to my car since he's unhappy I'm walking alone in my current state of sex-kitten perfection." She gives me a wink as she continues to listen to Stella on the other end. "I know you were too, but you have a business to run, and I didn't want *you* walking back to your restaurant alone after you walked me to my car." She lets out a heavy sigh as Stella continues on. "Stella, I'm legit fine. I swear. Here." She thrusts the phone out to me. "Say hi so she knows you're real and that I'm fine since she's not taking our safe words as gospel."

"Hi, Stella. It's Callan Barrows."

"Oh my God!" I hear Stella scream. "Layla! The fuck?!"

I laugh and so does Layla. She brings the phone back to her ear and listens as Stella yells at her. "No, I didn't plan to meet up with him. It was coincidental. I swear." More listening. "You can't say anything to anyone, not Meils or even Delphine because your lady lover has a mouth like an old woman in a beauty salon. I'm hanging up on you now, but I love you and I'll talk to you tomorrow."

"No! Layla, wait—"

Layla cuts her friend off by hitting the end button and then she shoves her phone back into her purse.

"Well, Dr. Barrows. This is certainly a surprise. Were you stalking me?"

"Definitely not. I was driving home."

She glances around. "If that's so, then where is your car?"

"My friend Asher took it since I left him stranded when I came after you."

A smile blooms sweet and pretty across her pink lips and her eyebrows bounce suggestively. "Asher Reyes is hot. Too bad he left. I've always had a thing for athletes."

"Brat."

She laughs and then takes my arm, giving me a solid tug. "Come on. You need a ride now."

We fly up the street and then she's unlocking her Tesla X for us.

She starts up the nearly silent car, music blasting through her speakers that she immediately lowers. We buckle up and then she's pulling us into late-night traffic.

The way she's positioned in her seat makes my cock throb in my jeans. Her legs are slightly spread, her foot pressing in on the gas, making the hem of her dress hike up so high that if I angle myself forward and dip my head, I'd have no trouble seeing what color the panties covering her pussy are.

"What were you going to do if I hadn't saved you?" she teases. "You're like... miles from your house and dressed like a sexy guy." I get a quick once over before her eyes turn back to the road. "Women would have been jumping your bones left and right, desperate to get a piece of you."

"I'm sure I could have managed."

She tosses me a dubious look. "Doubtful. You should start carrying pepper spray."

"Ha, ha. You're very funny, but your point has been made."

"I doubt that," she mocks. "Anyway, you should know I wasn't headed home."

"No?" I remark, shifting on the soft leather so I can be just a bit closer to her. Her car smells like her. Sweet and edible. It's also very her on the inside. High-energy music and a metal water bottle sitting in the cup holder that says, daily reminder to stay hydrated and not give a fuck what other people think. She has a Dartmouth sweatshirt on her back seat and an extra pair of ratty old sneakers on the floor.

"Nope. Wanna go on an adventure with me? It's a little dark and twisted."

"I don't see how I can allow you to go alone."

She plays with her smile, the tiny stud in her nose glinting against the huge screen in her car. "All right, hero. You've been warned. Now you're stuck with me."

She could be taking me to a cemetery or the morgue right now and I wouldn't care. Good thing too because twenty minutes later we're pulling through the neo-Gothic gate of a cemetery in Jamaica Plain.

"Something you want to explain?"

She weaves her way through the dark cemetery, clearly knowing where she's going. "What? Some of these graves are hundreds of years old and hold the remains of some of Boston's wealthiest people. Don't tell me you're not into grave robbing."

"Only in the winter when it's more of a challenge to dig."

Her uninhibited belly laugh fills the car. "You know you might be as weird and deadpan as I am." She stops the car, putting it in park. "There," she says, pointing to one large stone that boasts two epitaphs. "My parents. Today is my mom's birthday and with school, the hospital, and helping out Stella, I didn't have a chance before now to come and visit her."

Oh. Guilt interlaced with sadness hit me like the stench of week-old trash. "I'm sorry for your loss."

She waves me away. "Thank you. That's sweet, but I was six when they died, so I'm not about to break down or anything if you're worried. Visiting them makes me happy instead of sad. I tell them things and they hear me and it's all good." She twists so she's angled toward me, her eyes all over me, and I love it when she does this.

Gives me her undivided attention. I'm only too happy to return the favor. "You're not the sort of guy who is freaked out by dead people, are you?"

I point to my chest. "You're talking to a guy who did an extra pathology rotation."

Her nose scrunches up, her face only illuminated by the dash and the large computer screen. "Ew. Why?"

"I don't know. The science of it is fascinating."

"You're a total geek," she accuses, but there's no hiding her smile or mine. Or the way we can't stop staring at each other.

"You say that, but you haven't seen my Marvel collection yet."

She giggles, reaching out and ruffling my hair. "God, you're cute. Let's do this. Midnight's burning. Come meet my parents." She cackles as she climbs out of her car, nearly flashing me her ass as she does and catches me staring. "I saw that."

"You're the one wearing that. I'll look because I don't think I can help it, but I promise not to touch."

"Maybe I should have you take off your shirt," she tosses out as I get out of the car and walk around to her. "You know, even things up a bit."

"I feel like that's a bit disrespectful given where we find ourselves."

She taps her bottom lip with one hand, grabbing my hand with her other as if it's the most natural thing in the world. As with every time we make skin-to-skin contact, I feel the warmth she radiates vibrate through me.

"Perhaps," she agrees. "Here. This is them."

She releases my hand and takes a seat on a stone bench right in front of the grave. She gives a little wiggle and a small shudder as the cold stone touches the bare skin of her legs.

Without offering, I unbutton my shirt and drop it over her shoulders. It isn't very thick, but it's better than nothing.

"Boo. You're wearing a tank top undershirt. Though I do appreciate the arm candy, I was hoping you had changed your mind."

She slips her arms through the sleeves and *fuck*. Her wearing my shirt is something else.

I ignore the arm candy comment even if my still semihard dick doesn't. "Definitely not. And thank you for not calling it a wifebeater."

She shakes her head. "Never." Her face tilts down toward her parents' grave. "Hi, Mom and Dad. This is Callan. He's my professor." She laughs, her head flying back and everything.

"Ha. So very funny." I pinch her side and she squeals, bouncing in place and smacking at my hand.

"Sorry. I didn't mean to laugh. Actually, I did so I'm not really sorry." She turns back to the grave. "Anyway, happy birthday, Mom. I haven't had a chance to come here in a few months. I miss you guys and I have so much to tell you." She launches into an account of what happened with her ex and Dr. Lawrence dying on her and her apartment flooding and how she's moved back in with Amelia and Oliver and her nieces.

All the while, I sit here and listen, watching her, unable to drag my gaze away for even a moment. Hell, I hardly want to blink.

I'm infatuated with her. Fascinated by her every thought. Enraptured by her every move.

I'm wholly, completely, irrevocably cast under her spell.

And as I sit here beside her, teasing her, touching her, laughing with her, telling her stories from when I was on tour with the guys as Central Square, talking with her until the wee hours of the morning on a bench in a graveyard, I'm not doing anything to stop it or change it.

I'm allowing myself to be dragged in. Tugged along. My smart, responsible side is telling me to cut it out and get my shit back together, but it's not driving this bus.

The parts of me she already owns are.

Still, despite all that, I won't cross any more lines with her.

Layla Fritz became off-limits to me the moment she walked into my classroom. And that's how she'll stay until we go our separate ways.

EMERGENCY

9

L ayla

THE EMERGENCY DEPARTMENT can be like Candy Land to healthcare workers. Some days, you hit it right and you sail through your shift, reaching the end in flying rainbow colors. Other days, you keep pulling up those damn gingerbread or candy cane cards and are sent back to the beginning.

Today is the latter for me.

I'm not supposed to be working now. Hell, I don't even get paid, but whatever. I'm here to learn and I'm grateful for the experience. But on a random summer evening when every asshole with a beer in their hand thinks that they're freaking invincible is not the best day to be a volunteer.

Today is Wednesday, not even a Friday or Saturday, but you'd never know it with how this place is lighting up with patients.

I was supposed to be off an hour ago, but the ED is swamped and there aren't enough hands. I've been running labs and comforting kids and helping people to the bathroom. Then Drew comes at me and says with a no-bullshit expression, "I need your help."

Instantly I swallow hard. "Sure. What's up?"

"I have a family coming in. A tractor-trailer on I-95 slammed into their car, spinning them around and smashing them straight into the guardrail. It's bad. The parents were critical and intubated on the scene, but the kid appeared unharmed. I need you to be on the kid after pediatrics check her out."

My insides turn to slush, and I gulp down the sudden rush of tears. Once upon a time, I was that child. My parents were killed in a car accident, and I was unharmed in the back seat, and I... how do I look at this kid? I will do what I need to do for her, but *fuck*.

I send up a silent prayer, asking for her parents to make it and then stand in the exact place Drew tells me to. His wife, Margo, who is the nurse manager here gives me a reassuring wink, but then she's all go and no stop.

The parents are wheeled in with a paramedic straddling the husband, giving him compressions. They're not even working on the wife anymore. They simply wheel her into the trauma room, the monitor reading asystole—no heartbeat—with blood coming up her ET tube.

"There!" Drew points to the neighboring trauma room and I run like my ass is on fire straight in there. A girl, maybe five or six, sits on the gurney. She has dark-blue eyes and chestnut hair and a fractured look on her face.

She's quiet, but the second her eyes meet mine—freaked and distrustful—they immediately start to water. "Where's my mommy and daddy?"

I don't know what to say. I can't answer her because it's not my place to, but she doesn't need me to answer. She already knows the way I knew when I was her.

I die along with her mother because I can't... I just can't. This little girl...

"Hi," I say, swallowing down every emotion I've ever felt along with copious amounts of air. Doesn't matter. My voice trembles like a leaf in a hurricane. "I'm Layla. What's your name?"

She stares at me and then starts screaming. Like *screaming!* "Mommy! I want my mommy! Daddy! I want my daddy!" She's thrashing and kicking and fighting and attempting to fly off the gurney to get to the trauma room.

Oh hell.

I don't know what to do. I'm too new at this and I haven't been trained. I grab her in my arms and hug her as tightly as I can, compressing her body with my own. She fights me and she's strong and incredibly good at it, and all I can do is hold on. I just hold on and hug her, and I don't let her go. I tell her I know she's scared. I tell her that I'm here and that she's not alone, and after more struggling and screaming and kicking and hitting, she shatters.

Just completely breaks apart in my arms, and finally, her small body gives up and she lets me hold her as she sobs. I start sobbing too because I have to sob.

We cry and cry and cry for so long that there aren't any tears left, just gasps and body-racking hiccups and painful shudders.

I peek up to find Drew's grim face in the window of the trauma room. He shakes his head and I fall apart some more. I just lose it right here, holding this little girl while I question everything. Like how maybe I shouldn't be doing this, and maybe I was wrong when I thought I was impervious and over losing my parents and that nothing affects me.

It's not supposed to, but it feels like I'm holding myself that night all those years ago and I can't stop it. I want Amelia here. I want to hug her and thank her for being my person. For dropping her life for mine. For doing absolutely everything she could for me when she was also losing our parents right alongside me.

My eyes close and time seeps away from me as I hold her. Eventually, she grows limp in my arms having worn herself out, but I don't let her go. Even as I sense that we're no longer alone.

"Has anyone called him?"

"Not yet."

"We need to. He's listed as the emergency contact for the girl and her parents."

"Is she okay?"

"I don't know. She's been like this for at least twenty minutes."

I open my eyes, cloudy and crusty with tears, to discover Drew and Margot talking in hushed voices in the corner while the little girl is asleep in my arms.

"What is it?" I ask, clearing my throat of the gravel and tears.

Margot steps forward and gently pries the little girl from my arms, setting her down on a clean gurney and tucking her in with a blanket and a stuffed animal I've seen in the gift shop.

"The parents didn't make it."

"I know," I say in response, staring straight at Drew, trying to force myself to breathe through the grief.

"Their last name was Barrows."

I blink at him about ten thousand times.

"You're telling me—"

"That was Callan's brother and sister-in-law, and this is his niece." Margot cups my chin and tilts my face up. "Are you okay?"

I stare at her. Then at Drew. Then over to the little girl. "Does he know yet?"

"No," Drew answers.

"I'll call him," I tell both of them, rising off the gurney. I wipe my face, suddenly feeling foolish for losing it that way. I shake my head, staring around the room. "I'm sorry. I know this was unprofessional of me and it will never happen again." I release a breath, taking in the little girl's sleeping form. Callan's niece. Jesus. "I was her once and this was my first experience with that here." I clear my throat and straighten my spine. "I'll call him."

"No, you won't. I will," Drew says sternly but with tenderness to his features. "I was the attending on the case and I'm his boss. It's my job. Not yours." And with that, he marches out of the room, his cell phone already in his hand.

My hands run over my face and back through my hair. I'm a mess so I undo the elastic from my bun and quickly redo it into something tidier. "What does this mean?"

Margot sits on the gurney beside me and both of us watch the little girl sleep. "It means a whole lot of sadness." Her hand lands on my shoulder and her brown eyes meet mine. "And we've all been there. Certain patients hit you harder than others. Something like this? It's impossible for you not to feel it. Especially if you've lived it personally. Breaking is part of the job, Layla. But so is picking yourself back up and helping the next patient because they need you just as much."

I nod, filled with gratitude. "Thank you."

"Don't thank me. Not being able to save them all is the worst part. It's nights like these that used to drive me to a lot of alcohol and bad decisions. I'm sorry this was your night." She gives me a wan smile. "Can you stay with her until Callan arrives?"

"I won't leave her," I assure her.

"Call if you need anything."

Margot leaves me alone in the room with a sleeping orphaned little girl, her uncle presumably on his way. Her uncle. My heart lurches in my chest when I think about what he's about to go through. Callan and I sat on the stone bench by my parents' grave until about five in the morning. Then I drove him home and that was that.

This morning he was in class and then here in the hospital, and it was as if I wasn't here at all. All week we've treated each other as indifferent acquaintances with no past. And I thought that was... well, I *forced* myself to think that's good. I was paired with another doctor today, but I saw Callan. I saw him sneaking glances and watching me when he didn't think I was paying attention. Truth is, I was only paying attention because I was doing the same with him.

That's all this thing between us is. Stolen moments, sneaking glances, and watching from a distance. And I'm good with that.

Great with it even.

That doesn't take away the strange, anguished gratitude I feel for being the one who was able to hold this little girl tonight. For being the one who gets to stay and be part of this. It's not something anyone should go into without someone on the other side who has lived it for themselves, and I have.

And just as that thought hits my brain, a harried Callan comes flying into the trauma room, his eyes manic, swirling every which way before snagging and on me for a heavy beat, taking in my red face and puffy eyes, and then bouncing down to his sleeping niece.

I don't even know her name, I realize.

He sucks in a broken breath, his entire body trembling, and tears start to roll down my cheeks once more.

"Is she..." He can't even finish the thought. "Drew only said..."

"She's asleep," I whisper, my voice thick and crackly. "She wore herself out."

"But she's okay?" His eyes implore mine. "Physically I mean."

I nod. "Yes."

His hands go to his hips and his chin tilts up as he stares at the ceiling. He's breathing so hard, his chest rising and falling out of sync as he tries and fails to contain himself. Anguished tears hit his cheeks and those only make mine come harder.

"She was supposed to stay with me for the next couple of nights. My brother"—he coughs and clears his throat—"and his wife were going to a wedding on Cape Cod." His hands run up his face, wiping away the tears, but they don't stop and neither do mine. "I was going out of my mind. They were supposed to be at my house to drop her off more than two hours ago and he wasn't picking up his phone. Now they're gone and she's..."

He shakes his head, spins in a circle, and slams his foot into the door of the trauma room, making it snap open and then sharply swing shut. I start, but the little girl doesn't even stir. Climbing off the gurney, I amble over to him on unsteady legs. I have no words. There's nothing to say. So instead, I wrap my arms around his waist and press my head into his chest.

Right over his thundering heart.

"Fuck. Layla."

He starts shaking uncontrollably and despite being wooden and solid, he cracks as if some inner part of him he never allows the world to see is made of glass. His arms encircle my back and then he's hugging me fiercely, his face in my neck, unable to catch his breath. Tears soak into the shoulder of my scrub top as he cries into me, his hands balling the fabric on my back.

"Are you okay?" he rasps, his voice hoarse, wrenched in grief.

God. This man. He's so fucking strong in so many ways, but I think this makes him the strongest person I know. Who thinks of others when their life is falling apart around them?

"That should be my question for you," I counter.

"I'm not okay."

"I'm not either."

He nods because he already knows and because he knows and because we're both not okay, he squeezes me tighter. For a moment, that's all this is. All we can do. We take comfort where we can—in each other.

But then that moment ends because it has to, and he releases me and steps away.

"I need to get her home. I don't want her to wake up here. She won't understand. She's six." He sucks in a breath. Then another. Wipes at his face. "She knows this hospital as the place I work. Not the place where..." His eyes cinch tight, and he takes more deep, steadying breaths. "I have to get her home. I have to call my parents. I have to call Willow's parents. I have to call my friends."

I reach into his pocket and slip his phone out. He watches me do it, bewildered as I unlock it with his face and then program my phone number into it with the initial L as my name.

"You don't have to use it," I tell him. "But it's there if you need it. For anything. Anytime."

I hand him back his phone and he stuffs it in his pocket, and then he's all business. Picking up the sleeping little girl in his arms, he cradles her securely against his chest. His lips and nose plant in her hair and he breathes her in, unstoppable tears on his face, and then he walks out without another word.

Mechanically, I count to twenty to make sure he's gone and then I go gather my things and leave the hospital. I climb into my car and drive to my sister and Oliver's house. It's not even that late. Just a little after eight, which feels bizarre that it's still early and life is going on all around me as it should. The lights are on and there's so much sound coming from inside as I park my car in the garage.

Music.

My nieces are listening to Taylor Swift, no doubt having a dance party, and on any other night, I'd go inside and join them. But tonight isn't any other night.

Shutting off the car so I don't asphyxiate, I text Amelia, asking her to come out to the garage. A minute later the back door opens, and her inquisitive head pops out. She searches around and when she spots me sitting in my car, she frowns and then heads my way, opening up the passenger side door and climbing in.

Her hand immediately cups my face, her thumb dragging along my puffy eyes, her features lined in worry. "What is it?"

For what feels like the tenth time today, I break down. Unbuckling my seat belt, I reach across the console and hug my sister fiercely. "Thank you," I mumble to her.

"What?" She emits a mirthless laugh. "That is not what I thought you were going to say. Why are you crying and thanking me?"

"Because when Mom and Dad died, you dropped everything in your life, left school, left your boyfriend, and came home to take care of me. And I'm not sure I ever properly thanked you for it, but fuck Amelia, I'm thanking you now because you are the bravest, strongest, most caring person I know, and I love you. I love you and I'm so eternally grateful for you."

"Oh, Layla. Jesus, don't do this." Amelia starts crying and then we're both crying and hugging each other. Her hand runs down my hair, soothing me as she's always done, ever the big sister. "I wouldn't change it. Not for a second. Being there for you was the best thing I ever did." She pulls back and cups my face, her gray eyes piercing into mine. "What brought this on?"

I tell her about Callan. About his brother and sister-in-law and his niece. About how he's my professor and I work with him.

"I knew it was him," she says softly, almost sheepishly. "I mean, how many Callans are there in Boston? I didn't say anything about it because I didn't remember he worked in the emergency department of MGH, and I hadn't realized he was going to be your professor. I've only met him a handful of times along with his former bandmates, and those were all at Abbot Foundation events. Are you okay?"

I shake my head and then shrug, wiping my face that feels miserable and raw as hell. "I'm not sure I ever really cried about this on a deeper level, so to that point, I'm okay and I might have needed it more than I realized. But my heart hurts for him and for that little girl, Meils. I know what they're going through."

"So do I. It's the worst, and there are no words and there is no comfort. My heart breaks for all of them and I'll tell Oliver when we go inside." She holds her hand up when I start to protest. "Not about you and Callan. Obviously. That needs to stay quiet, but he'll want to know about what happened to him tonight."

I fall back against my seat, my eyes closing. "I just wish there was something I could do to help."

"I know, but I'm not sure there's anything to do for him right now."

I nod absently, my mind spinning.

"Do you have questions? Things you want answers to or things you want to discuss or even just to talk about any of it?"

"No," I say. "I don't remember the night they died, but I remember how it felt, and I... I don't *need* to talk about it. You know?" I squint at her, hoping she understands and because she's Amelia, she does.

"You were courageous tonight. I know you don't see that in yourself, but some would take their own trauma and use that as an excuse to run and it would be warranted given how obviously triggering it is." She stares into my eyes. "But you used your own experiences to help, and that takes a certain kind of heart and a certain kind of bravery. That said, I think for tonight, you've done all you can. Go inside and take a shower. Take some time for yourself. There are leftovers on the stove I can reheat for you and then we'll dance off all the rest of this."

I hug her again. Soundly. So fucking grateful for her.

I smile and climb out of the car, ready to do just that. Amelia and I go inside, and I quickly go upstairs so the girls don't see my face. But when I get in my room, my phone pings with a text.

C: Thank you for making sure she wasn't alone tonight.

My heart skips a beat and I sit on the edge of my bed, reading and rereading his words. I don't know what to say in return. But he texted and I doubt that was easy for him. Nothing right now is easy for him. And the urge to comfort him is overwhelming. The urge to drive to his house and crawl into his bed and—

I shake myself away from that.

I heart his text without directly responding to it because words don't feel appropriate and after tonight, I need a bit of space from it all. I plug my phone in on my nightstand and power it down. I go shower. And then I dance my ass off with my nieces until I'm so sweaty and exhausted I can't think about anything other than bed and sleep.

Certainly not the man who seems to occupy more and more of my thoughts.

10

C allan

THE ONLY GOOD thing right now is that I have people. People who are surrounding me. People who are here with me, helping me, taking care of things I can't focus on. Amelia and Fallon arranged the funeral. Everything from the flowers to the food to putting an obituary in the newspaper. Everything.

My parents flew in and as we stood over Declan and Willow's graves, behind me—and beside me—were my friends, their hands and bodies touching me in a silent show of solidarity and love. Never have I been more grateful for them in my life than I am now.

My parents left a few days after. My mother couldn't take it, and I don't blame her for that. They took Katy to the zoo and the Children's Museum and then got back on a plane to Florida.

Willow's parents are a different story. They didn't fly in for the funeral. They have zero money, but even with my offering to fly them in, they declined. I also hadn't heard from them much during all of this until last night when they suddenly demanded that I immediately fly Katy out to visit them.

I refused.

Maybe I'm wrong in that, but Katy doesn't know Willow's parents very well. Any time Willow mentioned her parents it was never in a favorable way, and I know she didn't have the happiest childhood with them growing up. So while I understand that they lost their daughter and I feel for them, I also wasn't about to drop everything for them.

Hell, they wouldn't even fly in for their only child's funeral and now suddenly they want Katy—a six-year-old little girl who just lost her parents—to fly out to Michigan to be with people she hardly knows? No. Not gonna happen.

They fought with me, telling me I'm not her guardian, which is true. I'm not.

At least not yet.

I want to keep Katy with me as mine. I know it will change everything in my world, but I love her with all that I am, and I can't imagine another way for this to go for her.

It wasn't even a tough call for me to make.

I think it's what my brother and Willow would want, but who knows for sure?

They didn't have a will. They each had a life insurance policy that goes to Katy—or her guardian when she gets one to help care for her —but that's it.

So here it is, Monday, everything is over, and Katy is back at camp because she asked to go. She hasn't been talking much. When she woke up that night at my house, she asked about her parents, and I had to tell her that they were gone. Other than some screaming night terrors that she can't tell me about or explain, she's been lost in her head.

I have two appointments this week. One is today after class with my lawyer, the other is later this week with a prominent child psychologist who came very highly recommended to me by Fallon, who is a pediatrician.

Until then, I have to get through this stupid fucking class that is the absolute last thing on the planet I want to deal with. Life goes on. I have responsibilities I can't shirk. The distraction will be good for me is the bullshit I keep feeding myself.

But the truth is... I want to see *her*.

I haven't seen Layla since that night in the trauma room, and I haven't texted her again since. Drew forced me to take extra time off, so I don't return to work until Thursday. I don't even need to talk to her. I just want to see her face and that should scare me and raise all sorts of alarms and questions, but I don't care right now.

I can be selfish just this once and it won't matter because nothing will come of it.

I get to class early to set everything up and go through what I missed on Friday when the door to the classroom opens. My head snaps up and I immediately lock on the prettiest blue eyes I've ever seen. Layla sets her stuff down on the table in front of the chair she usually occupies in the back and then with determined strides, marches in my direction.

"What are you doing here? Class doesn't start for at least another thirty minutes."

"I know," she says, stopping right in front of my desk. "I came in early thinking you'd be here. I wanted to see how you're doing."

I wish she hadn't, because she's wearing a tight black tank top that shows off the fact that she's once again not wearing a bra and tiny shorts that reveal her long, long legs. Her hair is up in a high ponytail that I can't help but want to wrap around my fist. She smells like fucking cherries and almonds, and since I know exactly what her pussy tastes like......fuck, I'm already wound too tight.

"I'm fine," I clip out because I need her to go before I do something I can't undo.

Her eyes cling to my face, studying me, and then she glances around the empty classroom. In a flash she's around my desk, standing before me and forcing my head to crane back so I can take her in.

"What are you doing? You can't do this." Though somehow, my

hands are already on her hips. Probably to push her away, but I don't. Instead, they start to climb, sinking under the hem of her tank top so I can feel her soft skin. Just for a moment.

"I can either drop to my knees out here or you can take me into that closet, and I can do it in there."

I choke on my own saliva, startled by her bold offer. She licks her lips, showing off that goddamn tongue ring, and fuck do I want her to drop to her knees. I've wanted that since I first saw her and that piece of metal spearing her tongue.

"You should go back to your seat, or better yet, go get a coffee before class."

"How close to the edge are you?" she asks instead, and I hate that I'm so visible to her.

I stand and I shouldn't because it kicks the fantasy she's offering me up a notch, but I can't look serious and forbidding when I'm sitting. "Leave, Layla. This can't happen."

"Here or in the storage closet?" she demands, her gaze unwavering. My cock is visibly hard, and I know she's aware of it even though she hasn't glanced down. Her hips rock toward me ever so slightly in a move I'm not even sure she was conscious of. "You have five seconds before I decide for you."

"You're not going to give me a blow job here at school or anywhere else. No."

"Yes. Five. Four."

"Layla, stop. Just go. Fuck, just go."

"Three. Two. On—"

Before she can finish her countdown, I grab her arm and haul her toward the closet. I open the door and then toss her inside, slamming the door behind us. "Cut it out! I know you think you're helping me or whatever, but I don't need you complicating my life any more than it's already complicated."

She steps into me, her chest pressing to mine, her tits to my shirt, and her hip bone against my aching cock.

"I'm not going to complicate your life," she promises so sincerely my chest quakes. "This will only be right here, and it will only be right now, and it will stay between us. We'll keep it simple. It'll just be a release because you look like you're ready to snap. I think you need to unleash yourself on someone and I'm telling you, *begging* for you to unleash on me."

I just about lose my mind with that. My hand snatches her ponytail, wrapping it around my fist as I had imagined. My forehead falls to hers and I lick the seam of her lips. "There is nothing simple about you. Nothing simple about any of this. If we get caught—"

"You better push me down onto my knees and come down my throat before that happens."

I groan, my eyes clenching tight. Fuck. She's right. I need this. I need her. But how...

"Fuck my mouth, Callan. I can take it. Hell, I want it. It's making me so wet just thinking about it. So do it."

My hand goes up her shirt and I savagely palm her tit, pinching her nipple to punish her for doing this to me. "Do you ever wear a bra?"

"Not if I can help it. I hate them and lucky for me I have cute, perky tits that are small enough I can get away with it."

"I love your fucking tits."

"You're about to love my mouth more." She drops to her knees right in front of me and stares up at me, waiting for instruction. She is a siren men would willingly jump to their deaths for. A temptress that is impossible to resist. Never have I wanted—*craved*—a woman the way I do her.

"Take me out."

She licks her lips again and then eagerly goes for my belt, undoing the buckle with a heavy metal jingle and then my button and zipper are next.

"I don't know how well I can control myself right now," I warn. "I might... I might be rough with you. You're sure you want that?"

"Should I stick my fingers in my pussy to show you how much?"

My hand lands on an open shelf, rattling something glass on there. "Yes. Then wipe it on my cock before you swallow it."

She moans and shoves her other hand down into her shorts at the same time she takes me out of my boxer briefs and pumps me a few times. Frizzles of light spark behind my eyes at the feel of her hand on me.

This is wrong. So fucking wrong. Any second someone could come into the classroom and find us in here.

That's not a small thing either. The repercussions of this could be massive and I can't afford massive right now, but I don't have any power left in me to stop her either. If I could, I'd take her home and shove my cock so hard and so deep inside her she'd feel me for weeks after. I'd take every ounce of emotion I can barely breathe past out on her body.

But that's not going to happen.

This is going to be it and if this is it with her, then I can't turn that down.

I can't see what she's doing inside her shorts and it's driving me mad, but then she pulls her hand out and shows me her two fingers absolutely coated in her wetness. I dive down, sucking them into my mouth, licking every drip of her arousal clean because I want the taste of her sweet cunt on my lips as I teach her class today.

"Are you going to make yourself come?" I ask as I stand back up and push her head toward my aching dick at the same time.

"Would you like me to?"

I think about that for a half beat. "No. Not here," I decide. "I want you to stay wet and wanting all day and then when you get home tonight, I want you to take your time and make yourself come as you think about what a dirty girl you were for your professor today."

"Fuck, Callan. Jesus. You keep talking to me like that and I'll come without even having to touch myself."

She takes me in her mouth, pumping me into it, testing out my length and girth to see what she can take. The barbell swirls around the head of my cock and holy motherfuck does that feel insanely good. I've never had a woman with a tongue ring go down on me and it might be the best thing ever.

"That's it. Now deeper. Fuck, Layla. Fuck that's good."

I push her head down a little, using the tight fist I have in her hair to do so. I don't even know who I am right now. This isn't me. I'm not rough and while I like control in all things including in the bedroom, I'm not typically overly domineering.

But I'm strung so tight, a rubber band ready to snap, and she's giving me what my body and mind evidently need. To be a brutal fucking animal. To take and not care. To shut my mind off from reality for just a few minutes.

She starts to suck me in earnest, flattening her tongue as the barbell drags along the sensitive underside of my dick. The muscles of her throat roll and constrict when I hit the back of her throat and she swallows reflexively, gagging ever so slightly.

It's heaven—all of it—and I tell her that as I start to fuck her mouth, pumping in and out.

I watch her, enraptured as she holds the base of my cock with one hand and fists my pants with her other. Her eyes water and she's struggling to breathe through her nose, but she keeps going. Keeps taking. Wanting more of me even as I try to pull out to give her a break to catch her breath.

I grip the shelf, already so close as she continues to lick and suck and take me as deep as she can. Her head bobs up and down. It's noisy. Messy. And hot as sin. I've never done anything like this before and that's only adding to the pleasure of it.

"Christ, Layla. Ah. God, that's so good. I'm so close."

The hand that's been gripping my pants slides inside and cups my balls, giving them a firm squeeze and gentle pull and that's enough to have me shooting without warning down her throat. I groan, low and deep in my throat, watching her pretty face as she swallows every single drop I'm giving her only to lick me clean after.

She pulls off me, sitting back on her haunches to catch her breath and I tuck myself back in, quickly redoing my zipper, button, and belt. I help her to stand, peek out the door to find the class still empty, and then press her against the wall and cover her mouth with mine.

Like I said, if this is the last time... I have to kiss her.

I can taste myself on her and instead of it being weird or gross, it's hot. Knowing what we just did, what she just did for me... I'm crazy about her. I am. I think I have been from the second she came over to my table and asked me to be her fake date.

But that's useless right now, so I shove it away and settle for shoving my tongue down her throat instead. I kiss her with my hands on her face, gentle now after I was anything but with her.

"Thank you," I whisper against her lips. "Thank you."

She smiles and then pushes me back, adjusting herself and I help her along so I have an excuse to touch her for another second. One last second.

"Is the coast clear?" she asks, and I look once again out the glass pane of the storage closet window.

"Yes. Go."

She does and I wait a beat and then follow her out. The moment she reaches her chair, the door opens and the girl I've seen her talking with in class, I think her name is Murphy, comes in and takes the seat beside her.

That's how close we were to getting caught.

Thirty seconds at most.

That was a risk I can't take again.

I watch Layla laugh and chat with her friend, both young, eager med students, and here I am, a quasi-professor and an attending and hopefully soon to be a single dad of sorts. She's twenty-three and at the beginning of the race and I'm thirty-one and have already hit the finish line.

Our worlds are light-years apart.

And there's nothing that can change that.

11

Callan

FOR AS RELAXED and more like myself Layla's incendiary yet incredible blow job had made me feel, standing here in my attorney's office right now I am anything but. I'm pacing a tight circle while I wait for him to enter. I know how to be an uncle. I know how to have fun with Katy.

Being her guardian is going to be an adjustment for us both.

At thirty-one I didn't expect to become a father to a six-year-old. I didn't expect first grade and homework and class projects or whatever will come with that. At least we have the rest of the summer to figure this all out. We'll both be learning—her how to live without her parents and me how to become one.

Yet I don't want this to go any other way. I want Katy with me. Not just temporarily, but always. She's mine. My girl.

The door opens and in walks Tom Daugherty, a highly revered family attorney.

"Callan." He greets me with a firm handshake. "It's nice to meet you. Have a seat."

I do, trying to calm myself down.

"It's my understanding that you'd like to become a permanent guardian for your niece?"

"Yes. I would." It's at this moment I realize I'm angry. Angry with my brother and Willow for not creating a will and appreciating the notion that we're all mortal and have no direct control over when it's our time and when it isn't. Angry that my parents just got back on a plane, leaving me to take care of everything without their help or support. Angry that Katy has to grow up without them.

Because what if I'm not enough?

I have a feeling at some point every parent asks themselves that question, but in my case, it's an extremely valid one. What if I'm not enough for her? What if she needs more? More than I can give her, and I don't mean financially because I have plenty of money. Not only am I an emergency room attending, but the only thing I ever spent my Central Square earnings on is my condo and medical school.

And we earned a lot of fucking money as Central Square.

Four years at the top of the charts and touring around the world almost nonstop—we earned more money than we could have ever imagined.

"All right. It's a pretty straightforward procedure since the child is already in your home. We will have to go to court quickly and petition to have you named as fiduciary guardian as well as legal guardian."

"Quickly?" I parrot.

"Yes, Mrs. Barrow's parents are making waves."

My face scrunches up. "I'm sorry, I don't understand what you mean by making waves."

His lips form a thin line as he explains. "Willow's parents are petitioning for fiduciary guardianship of Katy."

"Why?" is my first question because I'm shocked. "They hardly know her."

"They had a pro bono attorney from legal aid file the petition this morning."

"That's because they don't have a pot to piss in. And I'm not even saying that cruelly. Willow used to tell me and Dec stories about how poor they were when she was growing up to the point where she was worried that her parents were going to give her up because they couldn't afford her. Her father hasn't worked in decades, and I don't think her mother has either. Why on earth would they want to take on the financials for an elementary-age child?"

The truth is, neither has been able to hold down a job. They'd work someplace for a few months and then either quit for one reason or another or get themselves fired. They did much better on welfare, and Willow moved out the first second she could. They were never close.

"They didn't even come in for Willow's funeral."

Tom leans back in his chair, resting his hands on his stomach. "Do you want their story or what is more likely the truth?"

"Both," I tell him, gripping the arms of my chair.

"Their story is that they miss their daughter so much that they want whatever piece of her they can have. That they were too distraught to fly in for her funeral and watch their only child be buried. That they love Katy and want the opportunity to take care of her and give her the best life possible."

I sigh, my stomach twisting in painful knots. "And the real reason?"

"One point eight million dollars from life insurance that's in Katy's name, plus whatever revenue there is from the sale of your brother's house. Because Katy is a minor, that money will go to a court-appointed custodian to oversee the funds in Katy's name, which will be whoever becomes her fiduciary guardian."

I haven't even started to think about selling the house. Aurelia and Fallon offered to go there and pack up Katy's room and toys and belongings from it. I couldn't do it and I didn't want to put Katy through that either. I planned to have everything else packed up and either donated or sold off.

I just hadn't gotten there yet.

"Meaning if they become fiduciary guardians of Katy, they get at least one point eight million to spend at their discretion as long as 'it's in the name of taking care of Katy?'" I put air quotes around the last part.

"That's exactly what I'm telling you."

I fall forward, my elbows digging into my thighs, my hands covering my face. No wonder they suddenly wanted me to fly her out so they could see her. We were informed there was life insurance for Katy Friday afternoon. I just didn't put it together.

"What about legal guardianship of Katy? They're not seeking that?"

He sits up, talking directly to me. "At this time, no. I also don't believe a judge would grant that without a pressing reason. It takes a lot to move a child who just lost her parents out of the home she's currently living in especially if the person she's living with is petitioning for custody. You're single and work long hours, so that's not a mark in your favor, but right now, I don't think it'll be an issue. Willow's parents want the money. Not the little girl."

That last part doesn't shock me, and it's also a relief.

I grit my teeth. "Can we stop them from having any stake in Katy's life?"

"We can certainly try, but that doesn't mean we'll be successful."

"Whatever you need to do, make it happen. I don't want them in control of anything that has to do with Katy."

"I'll get the paperwork filed this morning and I'll be in touch."

We shake hands and I leave feeling worse than when I arrived. The crushing weight that's been moored on my chest like an anchor since Declan and Willow died isn't getting any lighter. I start to walk the streets instead of climbing back into my car and driving home.

I never have free time during the day. Not ever. It's a weird feeling.

I don't want to go home alone to my thoughts. Part of me is almost tempted to go to the hospital and put in a few hours. Then I remember Layla is there and the desire to see her again gnaws at me to the point where I immediately shove that idea away.

I need to figure out a way to be around her again—something I was sort of just starting to do—but now it feels like I'm beginning from square one with that. I want my voice in her ear, my words in her head as she touches her sweet body the way I told her I wanted her to, and then I want it to be my name on her lips when she orgasms.

Shaking all that off—because I will not call her, and I will not text her, and I will not go to the hospital to see her—I find myself in front of Katy's camp just as my phone rings in my pocket. Asher.

"Hey," I answer.

"How'd it go with the lawyer?"

I wipe a hand along my jaw as I stare at her the building for her camp. "Ash, some bad shit is going down."

I can practically hear the smile in his voice as he says, "Some bad shit as in you need an alibi, or some bad shit as in it's too late for an alibi and you need bail money?"

I grin, squeezing the back of my neck to release the tension that's built up there. "Maybe the first one if I can't pull all this off. Willow's parents are seeking fiduciary guardianship of Katy."

"I know a guy who could make them disappear."

"I don't even want to know if you're kidding or not."

"Then I won't tell you. I'm going to assume you do not feel that is in Katy's best interest."

"No. I don't. And I don't think I'm being selfish or emotionally irrational on that either."

"Right. Okay." He pauses. "But as long as you get Katy, the rest can be handled with court and money."

"True," I concede and start to meander up the sidewalk again. Maybe I'm making too big of a deal out of the money side. I have plenty for Katy and I can hold them up in court if I choose. "My attorney doesn't think they'll petition for legal guardianship, but you never know. He said it doesn't look good that I'm single and work long hours, but he also doesn't think they'll pull Katy from my care."

"If you're about to propose to me, I accept. As long as I can still sleep with women on the side."

I snicker. "You're not exactly my type, but you think Lenox would be in for that?"

He laughs and so do I. "Maybe. It's always the silent ones who surprise you the most. Or you could just get together with your hot med student again."

I freeze midstep in the middle of the sidewalk. "Uh."

"Uh what, Cal?" he asks, his voice leading.

"Something might have happened this morning." I hedge, kicking at a pebble on the sidewalk and watching it skip into a bed of patchy grass.

He barks out a laugh. "Alright, now we're talking. Tell me about it. Give me all the sexy details."

I roll my eyes and lean against the wrought iron fence in front of Katy's camp. "What are we, in high school? I'm not going to give you details."

"Boo. Boring. Just tell me where you fucked her. Was it at school since I know you're not at the hospital today?"

"I didn't fuck her." Technically.

"Then what?"

"Shut up, asshole. Whatever happened won't happen again. It was... a stress reliever."

He snorts sarcastically. "Uh-huh. You know you already told us it wouldn't happen again and then bam, looks like it did."

"It's different. And it really won't this time. It can't."

"Fine. Whatever," he remarks dubiously. "But I don't see any harm in you and her having an occasional *stress reliever* with each other as long as you both know what it is and where it can't go."

"Other than it being ethically wrong, I can't do that with her."

He pauses, and when he realizes I'm inferring she could never just be an occasional stress reliever, he says, "If that's how it is, then put her out of your head. You have enough to focus on right now."

I tap the metal bar. "Yep, I do. In fact, I'm going to go take Katy out for ice cream. I'll catch you later, man."

"Give my girl a hug for me."

We disconnect the call and then I head toward the front door of the camp. I tell the admin person behind the desk that I'm here to pick up Katy early, and then my little Ladybug is there with her green backpack on her shoulders and her hair wet from the pool as she gives me a wary look.

"Hey, Katy my lady." I crouch down and lift her up into my arms, hugging her to my chest. She hugs me back and then I set her down, taking her small hand in mine.

"How come you're picking me up early?" she asks.

"I finished with my meeting and thought it might be fun to get some ice cream together."

Her blue eyes, the same color as mine and Declan's light up. "Really? Mommy never gave me treats during the day."

"Oh," slips out and once again I wonder if I'm doing everything wrong.

"Well, it's a special day then."

She bounces on her toes with excitement. "Can I get chocolate in a cup with rainbow sprinkles and a cone on top?"

"Absolutely. Let's go."

We walk out into the bright sunshine and noisy streets of the city. It's hot and humid as it always is this time of year in Boston. Katy fills me in on her morning at camp. Everything from the arts and craft project they did to swinging on the tire swing with her friend Holly to swimming. At least she has this camp that I know she loves.

Finally, we reach the ice cream store and when we sit down and she's digging in, getting ice cream all over her mouth as she does, I say, "I'm working on becoming your guardian. Do you know what that means?"

Her eyes flash up to mine and she shakes her head.

"It means you'll continue to live with me, and I'll be the one to take care of you. Does that sound okay?"

She gives me a nod this time as she starts swirling her spoon through the melting chocolate in her cup. I feel like a heel for sucking all the fun out of this. Maybe now wasn't the time to broach the subject.

I take a bite of my ice cream, trying to soften my approach, even as uncertainty churns within me. "I know I'm not your mommy and daddy, but I love you very much and I want us to stay together."

"You do?"

I reach over and run my fingers along her forehead and then down the slope of her nose. "With all my heart, kiddo. With all my heart. It's you and me now and I can't do this without you."

She considers that. "Can I keep my toys at your house?"

"Of course. It's not my home anymore, it's our home." I hope. "In fact, I was thinking we could make one of the extra rooms on the first floor into a playroom. Anything you want."

This seems to please her as she cracks a small smile and then shovels in another bite of her ice cream.

She doesn't say much after that, just continues to eat her ice cream, and I force myself to do the same. It'll all be okay, I tell myself. It has to be.

12

L ayla

MY EYES close and I blow out a heavy breath as I tilt my face up to the sun that's shining high over the hospital. I pop my AirPods in my ears and start blasting Saint Blonde, bopping my head to and fro to the upbeat track.

Today is dragging, and I'm starting to feel the exhaustion of it all. Between classes, simulator lab, coursework, hospital work, and commuting from Oliver and Amelia's house, I'm feeling it.

I need to work on finding a new place to live closer to the city. I hate driving in the city and fighting traffic only to then have to try to figure out where to park. It's expensive and not always so convenient, but Oliver and Amelia don't live on the train line, so I must drive to the T-stop, park, and then take the train into the city.

For anyone who knows the Boston T system, it's a mess. The trains are hardly ever on time and they're epically slow—especially the ones that run on the street, which are the ones I have no choice but to take on days I'm at school.

All this means I'm forced to get up super early, and then I don't get home until super late. It's starting to wear on me.

With a heavy breath, I raise my turkey sandwich to my mouth and bite into it, chewing, and trying not to think about all that much as I enjoy a peaceful minute while on break. That is, until someone grabs my shoulder. A scream wrenches out of me and I jump, banging my elbow into the brick wall. *Ouch.*

My eyes snap open and I blink to find Callan, who isn't even scheduled here today, peering down at me. "You scared the absolute crap out of me!"

He says something I can't hear.

"What?"

"You're shouting!" He points to his ear, indicating I'm still blasting music through my AirPods.

Oh. I slide my phone out of my pocket and hit stop on the music and then pull the buds from my ears, tucking them back into the case.

"Sorry," he says a bit sheepishly. "I said your name a few times and you didn't respond. I didn't mean to startle you."

"Well, you did, ya booger butt. My elbow and my heart might never be the same." I rub at my smarting elbow. Who grabs someone's shoulder when they have earbuds in and their eyes are closed? I mean, for real.

A giggle down by his side has me dropping my chin to find Katy standing there beside him with her hand tucked in his.

"Hi," I squeak. Katy immediately recognizes me. There is no doubt in my mind. I'm sure I'm the last person she ever wants to see again, but she doesn't scream or yell at the sight of me. "Sorry, I said booger butt." Thankfully not something worse.

"I think it's something this little troublemaker would have said, right?" Callan asserts.

Katy nods. "Jamie McAlister in my group at camp is a booger butt."

Callan nods. "I wholeheartedly agree with that." He glances back up at me. "Can you do me a favor since you're already out here?"

I squint up at him since his face is blocking the sun. "Sure. What's up?"

"I forgot my watch here yesterday and I need to charge it tonight. Katy does not want to go inside. Is there any way you can keep an eye on her for a few minutes while I go and grab it?"

"I've got her. Go. I mean it," I urge when he hesitates. "I'll stay with her." I twist my head down so I'm nearly eye level with Katy. "Can I stay out here with you while your uncle goes in and gets his watch?"

She shifts her weight from one foot to the other and chews on the corner of her thumbnail. Finally, she nods her head.

"I'll be right back, Ladybug. You stay here with my friend, Layla."

"I will," Katy promises, and then Callan gives me a meaningful look and runs inside the building.

I hold out my hand to her. "Do you want to go sit on the bench? It's hot out here in the sun." She doesn't answer, but she places her small, warm hand in mine and allows me to lead her over to the bench.

"He's mad at me," she says in a low voice as we sit down, taking in not a whole lot other than the steaming asphalt the ambulances use to bring in traumas.

"Why would he be mad at you?"

"Jamie McAlister was teasing me on the playground today. He called me an orphan."

That little shit. He's lucky I wasn't there or I would have kicked his ass, six years old or not. "He sounds like a real booger butt."

Her face turns up to mine and she smiles, the sunlight reflecting off her blue eyes that are so much like Callan's it nearly steals my breath. "I told him he was a dick and kicked him in the shins."

I spit out a laugh and then start choking as I try to stifle it. "Where did you learn that word?"

"Uncle Cal's friend, Asher. He swears a lot."

I don't know the guy, but I'm guessing Asher is going to have to learn to watch his mouth around this one. "What did this boy do when you did that?"

She puffs out a breath and drops her cheeks to her small fists, her elbows digging into her thighs. "He cried like a baby and told the teacher on me. They called Uncle Cal and he had to come and pick me up. The teacher made me say I was sorry, but I'm not sorry."

Damn. I seriously love this girl. She is *so* me. "Do you think there was a better way to tell him you didn't like what he said?"

She hikes up her shoulders. "He's never nice to me. He chases me around and throws dirt at me. I don't want to be nice to him if he's not nice to me."

Wow. Kids set it straight in ways adults do not. "I get that. What did Uncle Cal say?"

"He told me it's always good to stand up for myself, but violence is never the answer and that next time I shouldn't use a bad word. He said Jamie is only looking for my attention and to ignore him."

I think about that. "Uncle Cal has a point. Boys tend to bother us the most when they want our attention. But you know what? I understand you being upset and reacting the way you did even if there are better ways to do it next time. I'm an orphan too," I tell her. "I lost my parents when I was your age, and it hurts a lot. When someone reminds you of that, it makes the hurt worse. Still, this guy isn't worth your attention and certainly not worth getting in trouble for."

She sits up straight and peers at me through her lashes. "How do you make the hurt better?"

Good fucking question. "When I figure that answer out, I'll let you know. Having people you love around or people who make you laugh helps. I read a lot of books, particularly when I'm feeling sad, and they make me feel better."

"How?" She presses.

"It takes my mind to another place, sometimes another world depending on what I'm reading. I talk about my parents too, but you might not be ready for that yet."

She shakes her head and gives a little sniffle, wiping her nose with the back of her arm the way kids do. "Do you think he'll take away my tablet?"

I hold in my smirk at the horror on her face. "I don't know." I scrunch up my nose. "Do you think he should?"

"Maybe," she answers honestly. "But I won't tell him that."

"Probably smart. Can I braid your hair?" I don't know why the urge comes over me. Maybe because her long brown hair is a bit of a tangled mess. Or maybe because Amelia used to do this to me when I was little and having a bad day and something about it always made me feel better.

Excitement flitters over her face. "Okay." She turns her back to me and I yank the elastic from my hair since it's the only one I have.

I shake out my head and then start combing through her hair with my fingers, making sure I don't snag on any knots. Then I separate the strands into three sections and start plaiting it until it's a long, thick rope down her back. I tie it off with the elastic and then pull out my phone and take a picture of it.

"Here. Look." I twist her little body back to me and show her the pic.

She smiles and nods approvingly. "Can we take a selfie?"

I'd ask how she knows what a selfie is at her age, but that's ridiculous. I think toddlers likely know what they are. "Sure!" We press our heads together and I snap the picture. "Oh, that's so cute. Here, I'll send that to your Uncle Cal so you have it."

Just as I hit send on the picture the doors of the ambulance bay open and he comes out. He hears the ping on his phone, pulls it out of his pocket, checks the image, and then throws me a questioning glance.

"What's this?"

"I braided her hair," I tell him.

"Cool." He smiles. "I love it, Ladybug. Maybe I should watch a YouTube video and learn how to do that for you."

My heart does a little somersault in my chest at him wanting to learn how to do that for her, but I push it away.

"YouTube saves lives." I stand. "Speaking of, I should get back though I don't know why. It's Q-U-I-E-T in there."

"Shhh," Callan hisses at me. "Never say that word here."

I roll my eyes. "That's why I spelled it. Duh."

"Thanks for watching her." He gives me a lingering look and then tucks some of my wayward hair behind my ear. "Better." He shifts his attention to Katy. "Are you ready for the park? I likely shouldn't reward you with that, but it's too nice of a day to stay inside."

"Can Layla come too!"

Both Callan and I freeze. "Erm." My lips pull sideways, and I give him *an I don't know what to say* look.

"Please, please, please, please," the kid tacks on, jumping up and down and yanking on my arm now.

Yeesh. How do I say no? Especially when I sort of want to say yes. I mean, how many times in our non-parenting adult lives do we get to go to the park on a summer day? Like never, right?

"Uh, I'm sure Layla has to—"

"But I want her to come. Please, Uncle Cal." She presses her palms together and holds up them to him, her face pleading.

"I'm okay with it if you are," I murmur so only he can hear.

"Are you sure? I feel like that's also a reward and while I'm insanely proud of her for what she did this morning, I don't think any parenting handbooks would applaud my being so. You're a reward. I think we all know that."

I laugh because it's a good line and I like it. "Up to you. I'm good either way."

He sighs. "Fine. She can come. But Ladybug—"

"I know, I know. Next time I'll ignore him." She groans and then huffs.

I try to hold in my snicker, but it escapes all the same. "You're a spitfire, kid. I like you."

"Now you know my dilemma." Callan takes her hand. "Come on. Let's go to the park."

Quickly I run inside, let Drew know I'm bouncing for the day with Callan and Katy, and grab my stuff. Once I'm back outside, we cross the street in front of the hospital and walk our way up Charles Street and then bang a left to head to the Common. The Frog Pond is filled with murky water that kids are splashing in, both in their clothes and bathing suits, and the playground is *the* social place to be if you're a parent or even a nanny.

Callan and I manage to find a place to sit, and Katy goes running off like her ass is on fire, her hands waving wildly in the air as she runs.

"It's one of the few places she forgets and acts like a kid for a while. Same with camp. Usually. That little fucker is lucky I didn't hear him, or he'd find himself down a set of nuts."

"Alpha Uncle Callan. She's a lucky girl."

He throws me a sideways smirk and then both of us go back to watching the playground.

"Everyone in here is staring at you," I observe. "I can't tell if it's because you're a hot dude or if it's because you're a famous hot dude."

He coughs out a laugh. "That's hot *doctor* to you and they're not all staring at me."

I snort. "You're a horrendous liar. Everyone is one hundred percent staring at you. I bet if you got up and walked around, you'd have at least five women hit on you, married or not."

"Is that a bet?"

I gleam at him. "Absolutely."

"Layla!" Katy yells out from the top of the playscape. "Come play with me."

"That's my cue."

"Wait." He stops me. "What do I get when you lose?"

"I won't lose, so how about whatever you want." I give him a cheeky wink and then stand.

"I'm holding you to that."

I wave in acknowledgment over my shoulder and then climb up to play with Katy. She and I chase each other and go down the slides all the while I keep a surreptitious eye on Callan, who does, in fact, get hit on by woman after woman. Only after he rejects the third woman—can't say I'm upset about that—it stops.

He catches me watching him from above and steps beneath me, like Romeo beneath Juliet on the balcony, and throws his arms out wide to me. "How do you like that? I was right."

I laugh, shaking my head at him. "Did you cheat?"

"I simply told them I'm a one-woman man and am already spoken for and to pass it on. Technically, it's not a lie, so it's not cheating."

My heart pinches in my chest. Even though I know he's not talking about me. He's clearly talking about Katy, but still, it's a powerful statement. Especially after what I went through with Patrick.

"Fine," I relent, making a show of rolling my eyes in feigned derision. "You win."

He fist pumps. "I'm holding you to that," he repeats. "Whatever I want? That's a powerful weapon."

Especially when there isn't a whole lot this man could ask me for that I'd say no to. And he's about to test that.

13

C allan

JUST WHEN I think things are starting to get easier, when I finally feel like Katy and I are getting into a groove, everything falls apart. Katy pulled one hell of a stunt yesterday at camp. She eloped, which is a fancy term for ran away. My six-year-old niece ran away from camp. They called to inform me of this and then they called the police.

I raced over there, and I just so happened—miracle of miracles—to pass the hospital when I saw her little body walking down the goddam sidewalk in the middle of Boston headed that way.

A six-year-old. Walking alone. On a busy sidewalk. In Boston.

I nearly got in an accident pulling over as quickly as I did and after freaking out on her, I brought her back to the camp, so I could rip them a new asshole.

How does a little girl escape a camp that has a gate in front of the building as well as security cameras? She's impossibly smart and crafty and I love her for it, but it's also giving me premature gray hairs.

When I asked her what she was doing escaping like that, she clammed up on me. At first, she said she was on her way to see me there, but I could see the lie in her eyes. The police spoke with her too, and then Katy finally broke down and admitted to them that she was leaving camp so she could go and visit Layla.

The fuck? Of all the people in my life she had to bond with and fall for, it's Layla.

The camp had to file an incident report—a second one since Katy kicked that kid earlier this week—and since the police were involved and Katy is a minor child in the middle of legal guardianship proceedings, they had to notify social services.

Yep. Social. Fucking. Services.

Tom and I spent two hours yesterday morning ensuring that social services wouldn't pull her from my house before our prescheduled hearing on Monday.

Now Katy and I are at Zax's place where I'm supposed to be playing poker while Katy and Fallon watch a princess movie in the other room. Fallon—bless her—is not into poker and told me she'd much rather watch *The Little Mermaid* than watch us play cards. But instead of playing cards, Tom called me this evening to serve me with the second blow in this fiasco.

"Willow's parents are now petitioning for custody of Katy."

My eyes cinch tight, and I fly out of my chair, storming over to the window and banging my fist against the glass. "What? Why would they do that?"

I hear concerned murmuring behind me and feel my friends' eyes boring into my back.

"Callan?" That's Aurelia.

"Hold on, Tom. I'm putting you on speakerphone so my friends can listen in."

"Good," he says. "Their input might be helpful."

I press the speakerphone button and then walk back over to the card table and drop my phone on the felt so all of us can hear.

"Sit, Callan," Zax practically orders me. "Calm yourself down so we can talk about this. What's going on?"

With my jaw clenched tighter than a nun's asshole, I retake the chair I just vacated and fill my friends in on what Tom just told me. They're as stunned and raw with this as I am.

Tom's serious voice through the speaker calls all of our attention back to him. "Willow's parents somehow found out about Katy's elopement from camp and the subsequent social services intervention." He releases a breath. "They are claiming between the incident yesterday and the incident earlier in the week with the little boy that you are unfit to be her guardian."

"That's bullshit," Asher barks out, and I drop my hand to his shoulder, settling him down.

"Sorry, Tom, but it's true," I state. "Willow's parents want the money. They didn't even try for Katy until this. They're pissed because they didn't do well the first time we went to court over the life insurance." The court didn't officially rule that day, but their lawyer didn't present much of a case in their favor to be Katy's fiduciary guardian.

"Perhaps," he concedes. "Regardless, this means that in addition to going to court on Monday to continue to argue for fiduciary guardianship of Katy, now we have to face the judge about Katy's safety in your home, and right now, it's not looking good."

A lead weight of fear drops in my stomach. "I could lose her."

I meet each of my friends' uneasy gazes across the table one by one. Thank God Katy is in the other room and can't hear this. She doesn't want to leave me. She just needs more than I can fully give her but that doesn't mean she needs Willow's fucking lowlife parents.

Tom takes a breath. The sort of breath that typically precedes bad news. "It's going to be a fight, Callan. If the court agrees with them, then Willow's parents will have the life insurance money to raise Katy with, and they're in decent physical health per the documents. You're a single man who works long hours and that's a solid strike against you. It has been since day one."

"So just like that, they could pull her from his care and a city she's lived in her entire life and move her to Michigan?" Grey asks, his hands plastered to the back of his head, his elbows butterflied out.

"If they win custody of her, yes."

Fuck. Just fuck. My hands rake through my hair. I can't let that happen. I can't let their greed hurt Katy. And it would hurt her. I have no doubt that Willow's parents' motives are less than altruistic or based on love.

"In the weeks since Declan and Willow's death, they haven't called to speak to Katy. Not once," I boom, gripping the edge of the table. "Other than that initial request for her to come to visit them, we haven't heard a peep about it. One point eight million dollars is a lot of money, and they could use that money however they want since there's no will to stipulate otherwise."

"Yes," Tom agrees. "This is all true. And we will argue about their blatant lack of interest in Katy herself, but their argument is that they want what's best for Katy and they're saying you're not it."

I shoot out of my chair again, needing to move because I think best when I'm on my feet and in motion.

I know Katy. I love Katy. She has a room in my house that she helped me decorate two years ago. I know her school and her teachers because I've picked her up there at least a dozen times. I know her favorite foods and favorite color and favorite shows and favorite things she likes to do on the playground.

And yes, this week hasn't been ideal, but she's safe with me. She is.

I can't let her move away with them. I can't.

How do I stop it?

Tom's right. I work long hours. That I can adjust. I have plenty of money from my Central Square days and I can tailor my schedule to fit her school schedule even if that means I have to switch jobs.

But yes, I'm single.

I know the courts will be hard-pressed to give me Katy as a single man, especially when we've had some safety issues with her in my care, and there are two adults who are saying they want her.

"What about the psychologist's notes?" I throw out.

"Those will help, Callan, but Katy doesn't speak a lot during those sessions. She did mention that she likes living with you and doesn't want to leave, so that's a bonus we can use. But it still might not be enough given the present situation."

"What if Callan wasn't single?" The words blurt from Asher's lips and everything in the room grows quiet. I spin on my heels and face him, my thoughts swirling chaotically as our eyes collide. I don't even know what he's saying. It makes no sense.

"What do you mean?" Aurelia questions.

"What if Callan wasn't single?" he repeats as if it's an obvious question. "What if he were engaged or married even? Would that change things for him?" Asher continues to speak while looking at me. My eyebrows pinch together, and I shake my head.

"What are you doing?" I mouth at him, but Asher holds up a hand stopping me, indicating I should wait for Tom to reply.

Tom clears his throat. "With Callan's money and the fact that Katy knows him and feels comfortable living with him, yes. I think that would make a big difference in demonstrating a more stable home life."

"Hmm. Okay. Callan will call you back, Tom." Asher disconnects the call and I fly for my phone only to have him snatch it off the table and hold it away from me, his eyes saying I dare you to try and get it.

He'll win. I'm not small, but this is Asher Reyes we're talking about and I'm no match.

"What the fuck are you doing, Asher?" Zax is on his feet now and so is Lenox, who hasn't made so much as a peep this entire time.

Asher stands too and walks backward toward the window, holding my phone in his hand. "What are you going to do about Katy, Callan? Tell me your battle plan."

I shrug a helpless shoulder and meet my friend's uneasy gaze. "Throw myself on the mercy of the court. I don't know." My hands fly up.

"I could take care of Willow's parents. See if there's anything there," Lenox offers, retaking his seat and placing large arms on the table. His question isn't threatening, though if you didn't know Lenox and simply encountered the silent beast on the street, you'd likely piss your pants. In addition to being a brilliant pianist and a tattoo artist, Lenox is a white-hat hacker. One of the best in the world from my understanding. He's done things like this before for us.

"What would that entail?" I ask cautiously.

"Depends on how deep you want to go. We're talking court and minors so there isn't a lot I can provide that won't show up as sketchy or gained by unfavorable means. I can grab financials and basics for now if you want."

"Tom's people are already doing that," I say with a rough sigh and give up going after Asher and my phone and retake my seat.

He gives me a nod. "The offer stands if you change your mind."

"Thanks, man. I might if things go south for me on Monday."

Asher is rubbing at his mouth with a look in his eyes as he too comes over and sits back down beside me. "You've been ignoring my question."

"What question?" I shoot at him when he doesn't follow that up. "You mean the ridiculous one about me not being single?"

"It's probably crazy and I know that's not your jam."

"What is?" Grey asks, just as much at a loss as I am.

"Asher," Aurelia warns. "No. I can see what you're thinking because I've read that romance book too, and no."

"What the hell are you talking about?" Zax pushes, his dark eyes narrowed in caution.

"This isn't me wanting to get him laid," Asher protests, pointing at Aurelia and then at me. "This is smart, and it could solve a bunch of shit for him *and* for Katy."

"What could?" I snap, brushing the longish strands of the front of my hair back from my face as I start to lose my patience. "Just fucking tell me."

"Dude, how are you not seeing this? Tom just put it out there for you. If you weren't single, you'd get to keep your girl."

I make a noise in the back of my throat. "Ash, I'm not asking you to marry me, man. I mean, yes, it would look better if I weren't single, but you're not the answer."

He rolls his eyes dismissively at me. "No shit. My reputation with the ladies precedes me."

Zax coughs out, "Bullshit," and we all snicker.

Asher throws a balled-up napkin at him. "Twat, that was one time in the bathroom after I had a few too many shots and a muscle relaxant. I had just won the Super Bowl." He grunts and then gets a wistful look in his eye. "God, if I ever get another chance with that woman, I will rock her fucking world till she can't walk straight for a month." Asher waves all that away and comes back to the room. "Forget that. I'm not talking about her or that night or even me. I'm talking about you, Cal"—he points yet another finger at me—"and your lovely forbidden medical student."

Aurelia hisses under her breath. "You just said it, Ash. Forbidden. This isn't the answer he needs."

"No, you're not getting it." Ash is back on his feet, working this all through for us as he calls the plays. "Katy loves Layla, right? She's the reason Katy eloped or whatever they call it from camp, isn't she? Katy feels Layla gets her because she does. So, what if you ask Layla to marry you?"

I laugh. It's a hard fucking laugh too, because that's no joke, the most insane, ridiculous thing I've ever heard in my life, and I'm an emergency room physician. We hear it all. Trust me on that.

"Don't laugh, brother. A fake engagement or marriage might just be your ticket to keeping your little girl and Layla Fritz is the perfect woman for the job. Though I do have to say, given the restrictions on things and the fact that the court already knows you're unmarried, a fake engagement is far cleaner than a marriage."

For a long moment, no one has anything to say to that including me.

Finally, Zax clears his throat and remarks, "As much as I hate to agree with jock shorts over there, I think he could be onto something. I don't know if a fake engagement is your only way, but you had mentioned that her place flooded and she's temporarily living with her sister and Oliver, right?"

"Yeah, so?" I push, already tense at where I know this conversation is headed.

"So, ask her to move in with you. You live a hell of a lot closer to the medical school and the hospital than Oliver does."

"It's a thought," Grey agrees, sipping his scotch. "You have a big place. If she moved in there and you were together as a couple, an engaged couple even, well, Tom said being in a position like that will make you appear like you have a stable household. She can hang out with Katy while wearing your fake rock and the courts will be all over it because it will ensure Katy's comfort and well-being. No one will take her from you then. How could they?"

I fall back in my chair, staring incredulously at my friends. "You can't be serious. You want me to offer a *fake engagement* to *Layla Fritz*? She's a goddamn Fritz. You can't just do that with those people. Besides, things like that don't work. It's a lie. A huge one. One that will be discovered the second we try it."

I toss back the rest of my drink and slam my glass down on the table, at the end of my patience with everything.

"Not necessarily," Aurelia hedges and I throw her a look. "What?" she exclaims, waving her hands around. "I'm sorta seeing this now. It actually makes brilliant sense if you can pull it off."

If I can pull it off. Meaning deceiving the courts and living with Layla for who knows how long until I gain permanent custody.

"I can't have Layla live with me." Because that's some stuff right there. It's not a smart play. This would have to be all business and when I look at Layla, business is the last thing on my mind.

I'd be forced to keep my hands to myself.

Fine. I can do that. We've been doing that anyway, but having her in my house... It's madness. It makes no sense. But it's like what Ash and Tom said...

"No," I declare. "No way. It can't be done, and I can't do it." Layla will cut off my balls for even suggesting this.

"Not even for Katy?" Grey throws out.

I growl, low and pissed, and scrub my hands up and down my face. "Layla won't agree. She won't. Why would she?"

Only in my head, somewhere I start to think this through. See the possibility of it. *Would* Layla say yes? Would she consider this arrangement? Not for me, of course, but for Katy. A girl whom I know she relates to on a deeper level.

My hands drop and I stare at my friends. "First of all, she's my medical student."

"Not a problem if you're not fucking her," Asher states. "When I was at Alabama, I was messing around with a graduate student who was renting a room off-campus in her professor's house. There was nothing scandalous about that. Besides, the school doesn't have to know anything you don't want them to and you're not officially an employee there. You're an interim professor and your work there ends at the end of August."

"What about the hospital?" I counter.

"Same deal only in reverse," Zax states. "Layla isn't an employee of the hospital and you're not technically her boss. But again, I'd keep the engagement locked up tight and not spread that word around either."

"Okay, so lie to pretty much all the people in my life, but have it not be just one lie, but two?" I shake my head. "It doesn't matter. This can't happen. Layla and I..." I trail off.

"Have heat," Aurelia voices for me.

"Yes," I admit, shifting in my chair and planting my elbows on the table. "We have heat. A lot of heat. I have enough trouble keeping my hands to myself when we're around each other. I have no idea how I could do that if she were living in my home. I'm her superior, boss or not. I have to keep my hands to myself because it's fucking unethical if I don't."

"Then you do it for Katy," Lenox says, and I hate it when he speaks as much as I love it because the man doesn't speak unless it's words meant to be heard and right now, he just flayed my argument.

Because what they're saying makes so much sense. It does. It would make Katy happy—I know it would—and honestly, it would be good for her to have Layla around, both as another female in the house, but also as someone who gets her. The courts would approve as well because it would show them how focused I am on taking care of Katy.

"She'll never agree," I say again, but it's weak. I mean, that's likely true because why on earth would she agree? But still, my argument has run out. My mind is working and it's wanting to do this despite the lunacy of it.

I keep racing back to one universal truth: Katy.

"Make her agree," Asher asserts, going all QB on me again. "The court doesn't like that you're single. So don't be single. And don't be single with the woman who your kid is in love with."

The way he says it... it's so simple. So easy. When it's anything but.

"It's a lie and that's not a small thing. If the courts found out, I'd lose Katy for good and possibly risk criminal charges if they felt like it."

"If you're engaged to Layla, then it's not a lie," Zax counters. "It's real. Well, fake real, but that's just semantics, right? A word. If you ask her to be your fiancée and she agrees, you're engaged. Engaged isn't married and engaged doesn't have to necessitate love or sex. It's a title. A designation. Think of this as business, not pleasure, and your business right now is securing Katy and her future by any means necessary."

I puff out a breath and stand, walking over and looking at the the Boston skyline just beyond Zax's floor-to-ceiling windows. "You're all serious about this? You think I should ask Layla Fritz—Layla Fucking Fritz—to be my fake fiancée?"

They're silent and I turn around, catching all of them exchanging glances.

Aurelia looks over to me with a smile that somehow soothes my ravaged nerves. "Talk to her about it and see what she has to say. No harm in that. If she says no..."

"We'll figure out a plan B," Ash promises, finishing where Aurelia left off. My heart swells in my chest at the way he uses the word we. As in my best friends are in this with me all the way.

"You think I can do this?"

"I think this is something worth fighting and bending all the rules for," Zax says. "Whatever you need from us, you know you have it."

"Yes," Ash agrees. "Plus, Layla Fritz is hot and kind of feisty, so there are worse women to get fake engaged to."

And that right there is part of the problem with this plan.

An hour later I'm driving Katy home, giving her a bath, and then tucking her into bed. By the time I'm in bed, I'm restless, sleep eluding me as I stare up at the ceiling. I haven't stopped thinking about Layla. About her moving in here, wearing my ring on her finger—even if it's fake—and what that would look like.

What that would *feel* like.

I don't think she'll say yes.

After all, there isn't much incentive in it for her. But the part that continues to stick with me is her playing the role of my fiancée. The court documents only stated that I am unmarried. They have no clue if I have a steady girlfriend or a string of one-nighters rolling through here.

So, I could potentially get away with saying that I am stepping things up with my girlfriend by moving her into my home and asking her to marry me, and oh, she just so happens to be the person Katy considers to be her person.

It's risky.

If the courts were to find out we were lying about that, there would be trouble.

But how would they find out? *How could they not*, my snarky side asks.

I groan, rolling over and stuffing my face into my pillow.

Do it for Katy.

Isn't that what they said? I could do this for Katy. I could play this game and keep my hands to myself. Right? I am an adult. One with amazing self-control. That always seems to fly out the window where Layla is concerned, but I'll try harder. If I have Layla with me, by my side, living here, the courts will give me Katy.

I know they will.

Now I just have to get Layla to agree.

14

L ayla

CALLAN WAS ACTING weird toward me this morning in class. Typically, he just ignores me or treats me with the same casual indifference he does every other student. Today he made eye contact. And held that eye contact. But it wasn't just any old eye contact, and it wasn't heated eye contact either.

It was contemplative.

To the point where I gave him a *what's up* look that he quickly dismissed with a headshake. So, I let it go. I have a ton on my mind right now including going to look at apartments tomorrow. Oliver and Amelia spent hours with me yesterday afternoon and evening scouring the internet and we came up with a handful I can afford that Oliver will agree are suitable enough—and in a decent neighborhood.

"Layla, are you done?" Lisa, one of the nurses asks as she passes me.

"I am," I practically hoot in response, washing my hands in the sink. "Friday night. Finally."

"If you're interested, a few of us are hitting up The Hill tonight."

I consider that for a moment, and then think about how I'd have to drive back out to Amelia's, shower, change, and then drive back in. "Can I give you a maybe? I'd love to, I'm just not sure if I can make it work."

"Sure! No problem. If you come, you come. If not, we'll see you next week."

"Sounds good and thanks for the invite. See you."

She walks off and I finish washing up. Then, with a twist of my back and an overhead stretch of my arms, I exit the hospital, only to find Callan standing against the wall with his arms folded, his ankles crossed, and his eyes directly on me.

"Hey," I say. "What's up? Everything okay?" Then something else hits me. "Are you here for me?" At that thought, my heart picks up an extra beat and butterflies erupt in my belly.

"I am." He pushes away from the wall. "Are you busy?"

Am I? I should say yes. That I am busy. That I can't go anywhere with him because I like spending time with him.

"Um."

He smirks, sauntering like a lion—slowly, methodically, yet determined to capture his prey—in my direction. "Let me rephrase it in a way I know you'll have a different answer. Are you hungry?"

I snort. "Is that a legit question? Always. But wait." I hold up a hand. "Are we talking about food or other activities?"

His eyes dance about my face, but there is something very dark and oh-so-very serious about him that's making my heart race. "Food," he says simply.

"I'll be honest, you're doing that Dr. Hottie McSterious thing again. It's kind of freaking me out a bit." And turning me on, but that's my own issue.

"Do you want some sushi at my place?"

"Didn't you once proposition me that exact same way?"

"Yes, only I'm about to make you a very different sort of proposition."

Wow. Okay. It's going to be like that. "I want gyoza too."

He reaches up into my hair and gently removes the elastic from my ponytail and then starts massaging my scalp. Holy hell in a handbasket, I try not to moan at how good that feels.

"Pork and pan-fried?" he practically whispers it.

I smirk, grabbing onto his upper arms before I pass out right here. "Is there any other kind?"

"Not for me." He sigh. "Please say yes," he mumbles, his hands slipping from my hair and falling to his sides.

"To the sushi or something else?"

"Yes."

Oh, God. I already know this isn't going to be good, but when he stares at me like this, like I'm the air he needs to breathe and the only thing capable of making his heart beat, he could ask me to pole dance naked around a streetlight in the middle of Boston Common and I'd consider it.

"If you feed me, I will come."

He groans, shaking his head. "Such a fucking temptress," he mutters under his breath. "Come with me." He pulls back, gives me a naughty wink, and then leads me away from the hospital toward his car. He orders the sushi on our way and within half an hour, I'm sitting on a stool in his kitchen watching him remove everything from the brown paper bag with the same focus he exudes during a trauma.

"Can you just tell me because the suspense is raising my blood pressure and heart rate to scary levels."

His hands freeze on the container of sushi and then he spits out in a rush of jumbled words, "I need you to move in with me and be my fake fiancée so I can win guardianship of Katy."

I blink. And I stare. And I try to make sense of what I think he just said, but I know that's impossible because—

I laugh. Kind of hard and it's weird and out of place and not actually based in humor. I'm laughing because I think Callan Barrows just asked me to move in with him and be his fake fiancée and that's a similar proposal Oliver made to my sister once upon a time.

So this just feels... I don't know. Comical? Ironic?

It's not though, and I appreciate that, so I force myself to shut up and ask, "Did I hear that correctly? You want me to *move in* with you and be your *fake fiancée?*"

He licks his lips, gripping the edge of the counter and pressing his weight into his hands as he leans in my direction, his gaze unwavering. "Yes."

I blow out a breath. Then another because I think I'm actually hyperventilating a bit. I pick up the now empty brown paper bag, wrap my hand around the top of it and start breathing into it. The room goes fuzzy, and then suddenly I'm on the floor blinking up at him.

"Did I just pass out?" Now that would be fucked up.

"No," he says, hovering over me, two fingers on my wrist, his eyes on his watch as he checks my pulse. "I moved you to the floor because your eyes were starting to roll, and I didn't want you to fall and hit your head. Your pulse is racing."

"Gee, I wonder why," I deadpan. "I'm fine." I'm actually not fine, but I don't want to be on the floor anymore. I move to get up and he helps me until I'm reseated on the stool. "Well, that happened and was definitely awkward, but not as awkward as what you just said to me. Explain why you need this."

He tells me all about what happened with Katy at camp this week and how he has to go to court on Monday and not only convince a judge he should be responsible for her finances, but also that she needs to stay with him and not be forced to move states and live with people she hardly knows. Now that social services got involved when she ditched camp to come and look for me, he's afraid he might lose her because the biggest strike against him is his lack of home life stability for her.

"And you think this is something I can fix?"

He sighs and then boosts himself up until he's sitting on his counter. He pops the plastic top on one of the to-go containers, picks up a piece of gyoza, and pops it in his mouth. I do the same because I'm not sure what else to do right now and eating always helps.

Plus, who am I kidding? I'm a total whore for gyoza.

He swallows, wipes his mouth with his napkin, and then says, "I don't know if you can *fix* it. I do, however, believe you can help. Especially with Katy. You reach her in ways I can't. You seem to speak each other's language and it's not one I'll ever be able to speak. So, from simply a Katy angle, I'm hoping you'll consider, at the very least, spending more time with her."

"And the other side of this?"

"The other side is I know having a live-in fiancée that Katy is in love with will show a more stable home life, both for me and for her." He has the grace to wince, and then stares silently at me, watching me like I'm a cornered animal as he waits for me to react in some way.

Only I'm not sure how to react just yet, so I go about digging into one of the sushi containers. I grab a piece of spicy tuna roll with my hands because I'm too lazy to use the chopsticks, and then swirl it through the soy sauce and wasabi before shoving the entire piece in my mouth.

"Why me?" I garble around my mouthful. I hate the thought that I'm having with that, but it's there. I'm a Fritz.

"You're the obvious choice. Katy skipped out on camp just to see you," he says simply. "I could entertain someone else if I was desperate enough and felt I *needed* a fiancée or wife to make it so they don't take her. I don't know if that's the case. I just know Katy needs you, and with that opportunity, I need you as well." He grins, making his dimple pop as he glances down at the counter for a moment only to look back up at me through his lashes. "Both you and your current situation make you the perfect woman for this."

"How do you mean my current situation?"

He rips the paper on a set of chopsticks, splits the wood, and then hands me the sticks so I can use those instead of my fingers.

"You're living with your sister and brother-in-law, which I know you're not entirely thrilled about. You're young, beautiful, single, and we have a chemistry that will appear authentic to anyone who might challenge us."

"You're asking me to lie in a court of law that I'm engaged to you?"

"I'll be the one who lies, and if you're wearing my ring and living with me and agreeing to be engaged to me—even if temporarily—then it's not exactly a lie, is it? We'll be engaged. People enter into arrangements like these for various reasons all the time."

He has a point in that.

Hell, I asked him to be my fake date the night we met. Granted, there wasn't a child on the line, and it certainly wasn't in a court of law, but he's not asking me to do anything other than help a little girl who is struggling and help him keep said little girl with him in his home.

"And the fact that I'm Layla *Fritz*?" I cock an eyebrow.

"It doesn't hurt, but it isn't the reason. Not even close. If you were simply Layla Atkins, it would still be you."

Good answer. Damn him.

He sighs, shifting on the counter so he can see me better. "Listen, I know this isn't a small thing—it's a huge fucking thing. I'm asking you to move into my home and pretend like you're in love with me and to also be in Katy's life until all this goes through. Even possibly for a bit after since I believe Katy needs you to get her through this. It's a lot and I'm not making light of that. I don't even know what to offer you in return, but whatever you want that will get you to say yes, name it." His eyes beseech mine. "I wouldn't ask if I weren't desperate."

He's right when he says that it's not a small thing. I remember all that Amelia and Oliver—and even I—went through when they did something similar, and we weren't even living with Oliver.

"Tell me why you need this?" I want him to say it. I don't even know why. I think I already know where his heart is, but... I want to hear it straight from him. If I'm considering this...

"I love Katy," he says simply. "She's my niece and I believe my sister-in-law's parents don't. Or at least not enough. I lost my brother, and we were close. But the moment I held my newborn niece in my hands, she was part of me. Part of my blood. She's struggling right now, and I'd give anything to fix that for her. Anything to make it easier for her. I can't let her move away from me, Layla. Both of us have already lost enough. She and I... we need each other."

I swallow and look away. Thinking. Thinking hard.

I'd have to move in with him.

I don't even know what I would tell people. My family would immediately know it's bullshit and I don't want to lie to them. He's my professor. Not to mention if word gets out, there are people who could call the validity of this into question. People like Patrick or Murphy or hell, anyone in my group class and chat for that matter.

I suppose I could say we were keeping it a secret for obvious reasons, but damn, it'll be bad for me. Really freaking bad. It's a stain on my reputation, both at school and in the hospital.

There are a lot of ways this could all go wrong and there is a little girl's life at stake with this.

Plus, there's the other piece to consider. The piece of myself that already likes Callan Barrows more than I should. What would moving in and living with him do to that? I don't have time for this. I don't have time to get myself entangled with his life and his drama all the while risking my reputation and my heart.

No thanks on any of that.

But...

I rise out of my seat. "When do you need an answer by?"

He pales. "By Monday morning if you can. I have court that afternoon."

"Okay. You'll have my answer by seven Monday morning."

I turn and head for his door, but I hear him hop off the counter and then he's running after me. "Layla! Wait." He rushes in front of me, stopping me, only to stand here in silence as he gazes at me. "I..." He releases a heavy, tormented breath. "Can I drive you somewhere?"

"No. I need to walk for a bit, I think."

He shifts his weight, looking miserable. He doesn't touch me and I'm grateful for that along with the distance he's put between us. "I'm sorry."

"I know." With that, I push past him and thankfully he lets me go this time. I walk out of his brownstone and then down the street, looking both ways. Well, this is certainly not how I saw my day going.

"Are you talking to me?" a man passing by asks, giving me an appalled look. Yeesh, this outer musing thing is a real bitch.

"No. Definitely not."

Inwardly shaking my head, I walk and walk, unable to organize my thoughts. I keep picturing Katy—the way she was screaming for her parents, the way she passed out in my arms—and Callan's face when he walked into that trauma room. The way she let me braid her hair and played with me on the playground.

Then I remember other things with Callan.

I walk through every detail of the night we met and then the day we saw each other in class. The night we hung out in the cemetery. All the time we've spent together since and all the times we did our best to ignore each other and do our work when ignoring each other seemed impossible.

Our chemistry is undeniable, and I'm obviously very drawn to him, and that's the main reason I'd say no. Which feels fucked up, but I still should say no. Right?

I'm torn... which is why I need help. Stat.

15

L ayla

SOMEHOW, I find myself standing in front of Stella's new restaurant in the South End, which means I've walked a hell of a long way. They aren't open yet—they actually have their soft opening this coming Thursday—but I have a key and I decide to use it because it's hot as a mofo out here and I'm very visibly sweating and there's a bar full of alcohol, and air conditioning inside.

Unlocking the door, I scoot in, quickly relock it, and then shut off the alarm before it goes off and the cops come. The restaurant is dark and cool, and I sigh and then shudder because it's also a little creepy being in here all alone.

"Stella? Delphine?" I call out. "Anyone here?"

Nope. Just me.

I head for the bar, running my hand along the smooth, polished wood, and then slip under it at the waiter opening on the far side. I take in the wall of liquor and refrigerators filled with wine and

mixers, all ready to help make this restaurant yet another success for
Stella and Delphine.

"Poison, poison, bubble, and doom, I likely should not drink you."

But I will.

First things first.

I slip out my phone and shoot out a text to my core Fritz ladies.
When Patrick broke my heart, I sent a massive text and then had a
fun pity party with all the Fritz women, but this is too delicate a situation to call in the extended crew.

Me: Emergency girl meeting at Bon Bagay.

Bon Bagay in Creole means good stuff, but since it also has the
word gay in it, it was my top pick and they ended up going with it.

**Me: This is a top secret event so please do not share this with
your other halves. And no, it's not a scary emergency and I'm physically fine.**

My phone immediately starts blowing up in my hand like bottle
rockets on the Fourth of July.

**Stella: Why are you in my restaurant? I just got the alarm
notice. I'm on my way.**

Amelia: Me too. I'll be there in fifteen if I hit the traffic right.

Gotta love my ladies. They don't even ask questions. They just
show up.

**Octavia: I'm already in the neighborhood, so please unlock the
door as I'll be there in five minutes.**

Oh. Score! I race out of the bar and over to the front door,
unlocking it for her and then I return to the bar, flip on some music
through the sound system, and start shaking up martinis because I
know I could use one and I need something to occupy my hands
before the others get here.

I pour a line of four martinis that I'll likely end up drinking most
of, and then I slip off my shoes and climb up on the bar because I've
never done this before. I've danced on tables in bars before—shhh,
don't tell Octavia that—but never on the actual bar and this feels like
the right time to let my wild girl out of hibernation.

I pick up one drink and start swaying my hips to the hypnotic beat of the light house music Stella likes to play and just as I'm taking my first sip, Octavia waltzes in, ever the perfect and polished queen of Boston. She spots me dancing on the bar with a martini in my hand and then comes and takes one of the barstools a few spots down from me.

"How many of those have you already had?"

I hold up my drink. "This is my first. I swear. I just got here, but I'm in crisis mode and I needed a sip or two before I could tell you all what I have to tell you."

She grins up at me. "If I weren't in my sixties and afraid of falling and breaking a hip, I'd climb up on there and do that with you. It looks fun and I've always been curious."

I cackle out a laugh at that thought. Not of her breaking a hip, of course, but of Octavia Abbot-Fritz dancing on a bar. That's insane. She's the epitome of regal and perfectly refined manners and honestly in the top three of the best women on the planet.

"It's a bit wild and freeing," I admit, doing a small dip and then smacking my ass like I'm in *Coyote Ugly*. "I won't lie and say it's not."

"I was never wild nor free when I was your age, so keep dancing for both of us, but as you do, please inform me on a scale of one to ten just how worried I should be."

I peer down at her, scrunching my nose. "I honestly don't know how to answer that. A six, maybe." I shrug and then take a long sip because this might be the best martini I've ever made. It's freaking delicious and hitting me in all the right places.

She purses her lips to the side, a classic displeased Octavia gesture but lets it go as we wait for the others to arrive. I keep dancing because why not, and as I do another booty swivel, Octavia asks, "You're not going to start stripping, are you? Because that's a very un-Fritz-like thing to do."

"In front of you or in general?" I snicker and then pull it back in when I see she's serious. "No stripping," I solemnly promise, holding my free hand over my heart just as the door to the restaurant opens.

Stella races in and talk about being displeased. She's ready to murder me and then throw my lifeless body in the dumpster out back. "Girl, I'm going to have to sanitize my bar now. You're barefoot and wearing the scrubs you no doubt wore to work in the *hospital* today."

I glance down at my light green scrubs and bare feet. Yeah. That's pretty gross now that I think about it.

I look back at my friend contritely. "Sorry. I'll do it. I promise. I'm getting down now."

"Much appreciated." She takes the seat beside her grandmother and then scrunches her face up in disgust. "Why do you always insist on drinking lemon drops?" Her mouth puckers reflexively.

"Because I know you won't drink them and that way I can drink yours," I reply honestly, sitting on the bar and swinging my legs to and fro.

"This is that bad, huh?" Stella checks with Octavia.

Octavia holds her hand up. "She wouldn't tell me anything, but considering how I found her, I'm going to assume the answer is yes."

Stella squints at me. "If you tell me you're back with Patrick, I'm going to shave your head and eyebrows in your sleep and then glue the hair to your face so it looks like a mustache and a biker beard."

I choke on my sip of lemon drop, some of it going down the wrong pipe, and I hack out half a lung until it's cleared. When I can breathe normally again, I glare. "Are you kidding me with that? You had to say that while I was drinking? Are you trying to kill me?"

"If you're back with Patrick, I am."

I roll my eyes at my friend. "I'm not back with Patrick. Loser can spread his cooties to someone else's cookie because he isn't getting access to mine again."

"Ladies," Octavia cuts in smoothly. "While this is a scintillating conversation and I too am glad to hear you're not back together with Patrick, can we stop talking about men spreading cooties to your cookie?"

I snort out a laugh and so does Stella because Octavia just repeated that.

"Absolutely, Grandma. That was all Layla being gross. Not me."

I smack Stella's shoulder. "Suck-up."

She gives me a cheeky grin. "Will you finally tell us why we're here?"

"Let's just wait for Meils to—"

"I'm here." Amelia comes rushing in and locks the door behind her. "I couldn't find a fucking—er, freaking parking spot. Sorry, Octavia."

Octavia is not a fan of cursing—or using obscure euphemisms for that matter—but quickly waves her away.

"What's up?" Amelia speed walks to us. "Spill it because I have like an hour, tops before I have to go and pick up the girls from a playdate. Oliver is working late tonight."

I gulp down the rest of my martini because these puppies flow like Niagara down my throat. "Callan Barrows asked me to move in with him and be his fake fiancée."

I get a lot of owl eyes pinned on me.

"You're joking, right?" Amelia questions, awkwardly and uncomfortably smiling like I'm pulling a prank. "I mean, you're punking us or whatever?"

"Um. No," I reply, lifting Stella's drink since we all know she won't touch it. "And you really need to get over your Ashton Kutcher obsession because that show ended like twenty years ago."

My sister is not amused. Her face is turning as red as her hair. "Layla, you cannot be telling me that he actually asked you to be his fake fiancée when you know about how Oliver and I got together."

"Except he did. You all know that he lost his brother and has been taking care of his niece. Well, he's filed for custody, which is amazing of him, and all was going well, but Katy—that's the little girl—is struggling. She and I hung out a bit this week and bonded a little, and then the other day she ran away from camp so that she could come to the hospital and find me even though I wasn't actually there yesterday, but she didn't know that. Anyway, his sister-in-law's parents, who are already after the life insurance money that goes to the little girl, are now petitioning for custody because they weren't going far with winning the money. They're saying he's unsafe, which is total BS in my opinion. He's planning to fight this obviously, but it doesn't look good that he's single and so he asked me to be his fake fiancée both so I can spend time with Katy and help her out and also help him win guardianship by making his homelife appear more stable."

I blow out a breath since that was longwinded as hell and then sit back a bit on the bar, waiting on them.

"Wow. That's..."

I nod at Stella. "Some stuff, yes."

"Wait." Stella throws her hand up in the air, tilts her head, and then goes around the bar and grabs a bottle of Jameson 18 because that's how she rolls. She pours herself a shot but doesn't drink it. Instead, she holds it out in the air and asks, "Is this like already a done deal?"

Octavia taps her nose. "That was my question as well. Stella, dear, while you're back there would you mind fixing me a Manhattan?"

"Not at all, Grandma."

"Crap, why do I have to drive and be responsible for children tonight?" Amelia bemoans.

"I can send one of the staff to pick up the girls and take them back to the compound," Octavia offers. "They can swim and play and have dinner there."

Amelia looks like she's about to weep in gratitude. "You're my favorite mother-in-law. Have I mentioned that before? Yes, please have him do that and I'll be eternally grateful."

Octavia taps something into her phone. "Done. Now that that's settled, please continue, Layla, so we can help you sort this out. Are you telling us this as in it's a done deal or are you still contemplating it?"

Stella sets a Manhattan in front of Octavia and an apple martini in front of my sister and then attacks her shot with gusto.

"To answer your questions," I start. "No, it's not a done deal. This was him asking me if I would consider doing this for both him and Katy. Anyway, Callan asked me before I came here, and yes, before you ask, he knows what he's asking of me. He knows the implications of it. I think he's stuck and doesn't know what else to do because he truly wants to help his niece through this while gaining guardianship of her."

Amelia stands and walks away for a moment and all three of us watch her as she does. With her back to us she puts her hands on her hips and Octavia, Stella, and I all exchange puzzled looks.

"Meils?" I question.

"I might not be the person you should speak to about this."

"Really?" I scrunch my nose in bewilderment. "I figured you were the perfect person."

She spins back around, her gray eyes glassy. "Layla, after Mom and Dad died, I would have done anything including lying, stealing, and cheating if someone told me I had to in order to be your guardian and help you. You may not remember, but you cried every day for six months after Mom and Dad died. I was broken too, and didn't know how to help. I can't imagine the fear and helplessness Callan is feeling right now at the prospect of not only losing his niece after he just lost his brother and sister-in-law but of her struggling so much and not being able to help."

"Oh," Stella mumbles.

"What she said," I utter as I impersonate a goldfish.

Amelia frowns. "I want to be impartial and help you figure this out, but I'm unfairly biased."

"So, you think I should do it?"

Amelia throws her hand up in the air. "That's what I'm saying. I shouldn't be the one to give you advice either way. This is a big thing, Layla. A huge thing. It requires a lot of lying and hiding things. He's your professor and you work with him at the hospital, and that, too, has far-reaching implications for you. Not to mention, you've vowed to put yourself, your life, and your work ahead of everything else, which I applaud because I'm not sure how much you did that when you were with Patrick. But for me, I'm afraid to sway your opinion on this when I already have very strong feelings about it."

I spin around on the bar, bringing my knees up and planting my feet on the top, so I can lie down. I already have to sanitize the thing. What difference does it make now?

I close my eyes. "I think that's why I wanted to say yes," I acknowl-edge and then just start spewing everything that's in my head. "Like, I was sitting in his house, looking at this man, and thinking, okay, sure, yeah. I mean, that was after I freaked out and hyperventilated to the point where I nearly passed out."

I blow out a breath and pinch my eyes tighter.

"I was Katy once. I was that little girl, but I had you, Amelia, and I was okay because of that. I want this little girl to be okay and she has Callan, and he wants to be her hero because he's a good man. Like, a *really* good man. Like Superman style, he'd be the first one you'd call if you were ever stranded because you know he'd always show up to help, good man. He wants to help her through it, but Katy sees herself when she looks at me just as I see myself when I look at her. We get each other and that's no small thing."

"But?" Octavia asks.

"But I tried to talk myself out of that because what he's asking me to do is crazy and wild and a little dangerous and it's as you said. I am trying to focus on myself and my life and my work and I wasn't always so great at that with Patrick. The last thing I want is for another man to come in and mess with that. Plus, there is the risk that comes with the fact that he is my boss and my professor."

"You're afraid of getting your heart broken again."

I point in Stella's general direction. "It's a consideration. I won't even lie about that. It's a real fear. He's hot, sweet, deadpan funny, and sorry, Octavia but the best sex I've ever had. We have a thing between us and there is no denying it. But it's more than that. It's everything."

"How long would you need to live with him and keep up this ruse?" Octavia questions gently, ignoring *the best sex I've ever had* comment, which is very gracious of her.

I sit up and polish off my second martini. I wish I had eaten more of the sushi, but drama waits for no woman. "I'm not sure. My guess is a few months."

"What would you ask for in return?" Stella challenges.

I set the glass down. "That's another thing, I don't know. There's nothing I need in this world that I don't already have, and I don't like the quid pro quo of it. It's not like what you and Oliver did when you got fake engaged. That was a very different situation. This is about the little girl and if I do this, I'm doing it for her and not for me."

"What's your gut telling you to do?"

I give Stella a good, long, hard look as I think. "It's telling me to do it. It's telling me that I'm in a unique position where I can help her, and I can help him. Like fate brought me into his life at the right moment so I could do this for them."

"And your heart?"

I turn back to Amelia. "It's telling me to be cautious and guard it like it's the Hope Diamond. I could get attached to him, and I could get attached to her, and neither is in my best interest right now. He and I are worlds apart."

"True," Octavia agrees. "You have a lot of other things you're focusing on, and Callan is in a different position in life than you are. Especially if he comes with a child."

"Right." I nod in agreement.

"How would you feel if you said no for those reasons?" she presses.

I glance down at my hands in my lap and speak a truth that makes chills race up my spine. "I'd never forgive myself."

In my heart, I know that's the truth. I think I was always going to say yes. I just needed to work it out with people I trust.

"Then you've made the right decision," Octavia declares, sitting up and placing her hand gently over mine. "Now you have to come up with a plan that will give you some power in this situation and safeguard the parts of yourself you need to protect."

16

L ayla

Armed with my brilliantly crafted plan that I've aptly named Operation Heart Block, I find myself knocking on Callan's door a little drunk and a lot determined at close to nine at night. Stella made me food—love her—and yes, I might have had another drink, but I needed the liquid courage otherwise I wasn't sure I would be able to pull this off.

The door swings open and a rumpled Callan is there wearing a fitted white T-shirt that shows off his chest, abs, and arms, and low-slung gray sweatpants. My panties are instantly wet at the sight of him. Because *dammmn* he's fine.

That's why this plan is so essential, I remind myself.

"Hey," he says, his eyes wide in a way that speaks to the fact that he clearly wasn't expecting me.

"I'm in but we can't have sex," I blurt out, but it comes out almost as a shout, loud and resonating, and someone walking down the street glances in our direction.

"Uh." Callan scratches the back of his head as he glances over his shoulder in the direction of the stairs and then turns back to me with a playful smile that isn't helping my wet vagina situation. "Katy is asleep and that's been a bit of a challenge for her, so if you feel you're capable of declaring your moratorium on my penis quietly, you can come in."

Riiiight. Katy. The whole reason I'm here. *Doink.* I mentally smack my forehead.

"I can try. Do you have a basement or something?"

He chuckles. "I do, but I don't go down there without backup. This place was built in the eighteen-hundreds and though it's been renovated several times over the centuries, I can tell you, the basement hasn't been."

I shudder and make a mental note never to venture into his basement. "I'll be quiet. But do you think you can change?" I ask as I step inside, and he closes and locks the door behind me.

He spins around, his eyes cast down to his body as he does. "I'm dressed. What's wrong with what I'm wearing?"

"You may be dressed, but you're wearing *that*." I swirl my finger around, indicating his chest, and then down to the noticeable bulge in his sweats. Why do gray sweatpants always show the bulge? "My next rule is you can't wear bulge-revealing clothing when we do this."

His dark blue eyes pop up to mine, his eyebrows at his hairline. "Bulge-revealing clothing?" He's visibly laughing at me now. "How much alcohol have you had tonight?"

I do a spin around his foyer. It's pretty. I'm not sure I ever noticed before, but it is. Black-and-white marble floors and pretty white moldings and a cool modern-ish chandelier. "Ohhhh, a lot. More than usual for me actually, but Stella made me eat a big bowl of creamy delicious pasta to absorb it since I didn't get to eat all the yummy, yummy sushi."

I narrow my eyes at his bulge.

"Do you think maybe we should have sex one last night? You know, to get it out of our system?"

"It's definitely a thought, but maybe one we should readdress when you're sober. Can I get you a water?" He grasps my arm and walks me into his house a bit more. The stairs where I stripped for him the first night we met are right in front of me. I already know with absolute certainty, I won't be doing laundry here. I'll have to do that at Amelia's or I'll orgasm every time I walk into his laundry room.

"Water would be the right call there, Doctor. Hydration is key. I'm going to hide in your office until you return," I whisper.

"Do you know where my office is?" he counters.

Do I? My face scrunches up but then softens as I gaze into his oh-so-blue eyes. "I think so?"

His hand covers my mouth and then he spins me around and points with his other hand. "It's that way. Go, please, because you're still loud." He releases me and gives me a small push, urging me on.

Crap, I swore I was whispering.

"Well, you weren't."

Argh! I forgot to ask my family tonight about this. How can I properly adult if I can't keep my thoughts and opinions a secret?

Callan points in the direction of his office again and I find my way, closing the door behind me. I glance around. He has a desk with two monitors, a closed laptop sitting on top of it with a mouse perfectly placed in the center of the mouse pad beside it.

There's a massive built-in bookshelf loaded with books, everything from medical textbooks to what I think might be classic first editions—fuck, I'm getting wetter by the second here—to contemporary thrillers. The couch is leather and gray and large and that's where I go because if I start scrolling through his library, I'll jump his bones for sure and that's *not* what I'm here for.

The room is fastidiously neat and tidy like every space he has in his home is, and I wonder how he's managing a little girl disrupting that. A few seconds later he returns with a glass of ice water for me, and I take a large sip before setting it down on a coaster on the distressed wood coffee table.

I offer him a contrite smile. "Hi. Sorry. I didn't mean to come in here like a hot mess and throw off your night, but I wanted to tell you as soon as I figured it out and I didn't want to wait."

He takes a seat on the couch beside me, leveling me with a seriousness I've come to expect from him. "I'm glad you're here, but before we start talking, I want to make sure that everything we say is what sober Layla would say. I can't have you agreeing or not agreeing to something tonight and then when you sober up tomorrow, you change your mind. Moreover, I don't want to tell Katy something and then have to go back on it."

I meet his gaze head-on. "I'm not going to change my mind."

He swallows hard and then nods slowly. Nervously. "Okay. The floor is yours."

"I'm saying yes, Callan. I think I already said that, but it might have gotten overshadowed by the no-sex stuff I blurted out after."

He exhales a breath I think he was holding and his eyes glass over as his expression warms with gratitude. "Jesus, Layla. Fuck." He shakes his head incredulously, laughs lightly, and fidgets all around as if he doesn't know what to do with himself now. "Thank you. Holy shit, thank you. I want to kiss the hell out of you, but I know that's the wrong reaction to have. Especially now. I also know thank you is ridiculous and simple to say, but I'm having difficulty adequately expressing my level of gratitude."

"I couldn't not say yes."

"May I ask why?"

I give him a dubious look, quirking an eyebrow at him. "Come on, Callan, I think you know. I was almost exactly like Katy once. I had Amelia who gave up her entire life for me. She dropped out of college and gave up her medical school dreams. Her boyfriend was a prick and broke up with her over text about it. She moved back home to Boston and accrued an insurmountable amount of debt so she could get her BSN and then worked for a misogynistic douchebag for years and years because he paid well. We had no money and she struggled endlessly, and she did all of that for me."

Annnd I'm totally crying again.

He reaches over and wipes at my tears. "She's an amazing woman."

"The very best in the world, but Katy deserves an Amelia and I think you're her Amelia."

"That's what I'd like to be."

I knew it. My gut is never wrong. His response does all the wrong things to my insides and this... this is the problem.

"But I don't know if I'm enough right now," he continues. "Amelia was also going through the loss of her parents. Yes, I lost my brother and sister-in-law, but as you know, it's not the same as losing a parent, and while I'm trying the very best I can, you reach her in ways I'm unable."

"I'm attracted to you though." Insanely. Painfully.

He coughs, giving me that playful smile again complete with dimples. "Um. Yeah, I know."

"No. That's my problem. I'm attracted to you, and well, I don't want to be."

That takes him aback for a moment. "Ah. Okay." He wipes at his jaw. "I think I'm starting to understand all this now. That said, I'm not sure what to do about it or how to change it."

Here goes nothing. I sit up straight and clear my throat. "That brings up the words I blurted out to you when I first arrived. I think we'd very easily and very quickly fall into bed with each other and while I know it'll be fun, I don't want to confuse fun for feelings. Plus, there's the whole other side of this coin where we actually shouldn't because of our jobs."

He leans back against the leather, kicking his ankle up onto his opposite knee and giving me a steadying look. "Alright. So that means no sex."

"It does. If I move in here and we live this fake life with each other, I can't have sex with you. It complicates and confuses things."

"I had already reached that conclusion and I agree. No sex. What's next?"

Well, that's a relief. "So, that's a no on the getting it out of our systems thing?"

His hand comes up and touches my face, dragging down my neck and across my shoulder, pushing the top of my scrub shirt aside. "I'm not touching you when you're drunk like this. But if at some point you decide you want one more time with me, you have it. Anytime. Anywhere."

"Woo." I start fanning my face. "Let's table that for now, but then again, I'm not taking it off the table if you know what I mean."

His thumb grazes the dip between my collarbone and shoulder. "I do."

"Great, now stop touching me because you're clouding my thinking and I need you to know there will be no falling in love. If that starts to happen or if we begin to have stronger feelings beyond attraction for the other, it has to end, and I know that's putting a lot of—"

"No falling in love," he repeats, holding his hand up to stop me, suddenly all stern and businesslike.

I sigh. "Callan, love hasn't been my bestie in the past and I don't have time for it or romance or feelings. I did that and it backfired on me, and when that happened, I realized just how much of myself I had sacrificed for him. I need to put myself and my goals first. I have three years left in med school and a minimum of three years after that for my residency."

His expression softens. "You don't have to explain. I understand it fully. I was where you are once before and I know I am not only older and already an attending, but hopefully, I'll have Katy permanently as mine. You're young and just starting out with your life and career."

"Good. Thank you for understanding that." I blow out a breath. This is easier than I thought it was going to be. "One year."

"One year?"

"Max."

"I'm Callan."

I burst out laughing, falling into him a bit only to right myself quickly. "Same goes for him too, cheeky bastard."

"I don't think that will be an issue, but absolutely. I imagine you'll be out of here long before that, though you're welcome to stay for as long as you need. And if after you need help with an apartment or a recommendation or anything else, you'll always have it from me."

"I appreciate that. Do you have any parameters you want to voice?"

"We share a bed."

Doink. "Uhhh."

"If you're agreeing to become my fake fiancée, then it might be necessary. My attorney explained that the upshot of this will very likely be family services making unannounced visits. It has to come across like we're in love. I can't have any visible signs of you sleeping in another bed even if we're not having sex."

He has a point and truly, I had already considered that. "What else?"

"You wear the engagement ring I get you whenever you're not in school or at work."

Vomit.

"What do I tell people at school?"

"Nothing. With any hope, this will all be taken care of quickly and we don't have to tell anyone who doesn't need to know anything. The school especially because I don't want any issues with your classes or rumors. It might come down to a meeting in court. It might come to more. I'm honestly not sure."

"When should I move in?"

"Whenever you'd like, but I'd appreciate sooner rather than later if that's possible."

"Considering I have zero furniture left and very few clothes, we're talking little more than one or two suitcases. Oh, and you should know Amelia is telling Oliver about all of this."

"Great," he mutters with feigned enthusiasm. "So, should I expect him at my door with a shotgun now or in an hour or so?"

I squeeze his shoulder. "Trust me on this. That won't happen. It's a good thing Amelia is telling him because Amelia is now your biggest fan ever. She was you and I was Katy once."

He shifts and takes my hand. "Layla..."

"Don't. I'm doing this for her." Then I hesitate. "What if Katy doesn't want me living with you guys or she outs us?"

He practically rolls his eyes at me. "She'll want you living with us. That I'm more worried about than almost anything with this. And she won't out us. She's smart and sweet and wants to stay with me."

I pick up the water glass and hold it in my hands before taking a sip. "And the courts won't consider that?"

He gives me a helpless shrug. "They've already spoken with her, and she told them that off the bat. Then social services got involved and now everything's up in the air."

I give him a fierce smile. "Then it's a good thing I'm a badass bitch here to save the day."

17

C allan

"Do you want me to call an Uber to take you home?" I ask Layla because if she doesn't leave now, I'm going to jump her and kiss her until the only oxygen she's able to breathe is the oxygen I give her. She's saying yes. Holy shit, she's saying yes.

This is happening.

I'm going to have to lie in a court of law. I'm going to have to pretend to be engaged to Layla Fritz, which means I'm going to have to pretend to be in love with her without actually falling in love with her.

"Sure," she says, her eyes hazy from whatever alcohol she slugged down before coming here tonight.

I stand and reach for her hand. She takes it and lets me help her up, only I immediately drop it when I hear a scream from upstairs. Layla gasps, her hand clapping over her mouth, but I'm already flying up the stairs.

"What is that? Is Katy okay?" Layla asks, racing behind me.

"She's been having night terrors since the accident," I explain, reaching the top step and going for her bedroom. "Give me five minutes and I'll call you an Uber. Please don't leave until I get back. I'd like to make sure you get off okay."

Without waiting on her response, I open the door to Katy's room. She's thrashing about, screaming and crying. "Daddy!"

My heart rips to shreds and I climb on her bed, running my hand through her damp hair. "Shhh, honey. It's okay. Shhh."

"Daddy! I want my daddy!"

I want your daddy too. I miss him. So much.

"Come here, Ladybug." I wrap her up in my arms and lay us both down. "It's okay, Katy. You're safe. I've got you and you're safe."

I don't know if she's awake or asleep or somewhere in between, but I hold her tight and continue to speak soothing, comforting words in her ear as I stroke her hair. She's a ball of sweat, but if I change her pajamas, she'll be up for hours. I learned that lesson the first week she was here.

Eventually, Katy settles down, her body going limp in my arms, and I carefully extricate myself out from beneath her and climb off the bed. "Better dreams now." I kiss the top of her head and creep out of her room, making a mental note to mark this down in the sleep journal her psychologist recommended I keep for her to chart her night terrors.

Shutting the door behind me, I slink along the hallway and then back downstairs. "Layla?" I call out, going from room to room only to find one after the other empty. Dammit. I asked her to wait. I don't like the idea of her being drunk in a car with a strange driver.

I slip out my phone and text her.

Me: I wish you had waited for me before you left. Please text me when you get home, so I know you're safe. Tomorrow if you're ready, we can move your stuff in, and I can make you dinner and we can talk some more.

I hit send and then slide it back into my pocket. With a heavy breath straining my lungs, I jog up the steps, flipping off light switches as I go. I need to give her space, I remind myself. This has to be about Katy, not her and me.

It's easier said than done.

I long for the woman I brought home that first night. The woman who wanted me back with equal vigor. The one with no complications. The one I could fuck wild and make mine for a few hours without repercussions. She mentioned a *get it out of our system* fuck and I want that more than I can even begin to handle, but I also know there is no getting her out of my system.

I won't just want a one-and-done. I'll want more and more and more.

Control, I remind myself. *Control*.

I hit the top step and head toward my bedroom only to freeze midstep when I reach the precipice of my room. I sag against the doorframe, taking in the sight before me. Layla is on my bed wearing my old Harvard Medical School hoodie and a pair of my track shorts completely passed out on my bed. She's on her side, her sweet face slack and peaceful, her blonde hair scattered across my pillow.

She looks so good wearing my clothes it nearly knocks me sideways.

Without thinking twice, I reach behind my head and tug off my shirt and then shuck myself out of my pants. I shut the door to my room, go brush my teeth, and then climb into bed, adjusting Layla so that she joins me beneath the covers. For a few minutes, I stare at her unconscious form. Words like lovely and beautiful and even stunning have been invented to describe women like her.

She surpasses them all, even in her sleep.

"Just don't ruin us," I plead to her, knowing it might already be too late. I might be ruined on her.

I push her hair back from her face and then roll over, intentionally giving her my back so I don't have to look at her all night, and then will myself to fall asleep.

~

WARMTH ENGULFS me from head to toe and I groan at the sensation.

"Layla."

Her name sprouts like a geyser from my lips as she tugs my cock. My hand drags along smooth, soft skin, up, up until my thumb reaches the gentle undercurve of her sweet tits. Tits I want to devour with my tongue and teeth and lips.

"Layla."

Again her name drips from me and my groan builds higher, harder when yet another tug on my dick rips the sound past my lungs.

"Callan."

"You feel so good."

"Callan, wake up."

Do I have to, I wonder, already somewhat aware this is a dream because real-life Layla already made me painfully aware that my dick is a no-go for her.

"Callan!"

My eyes slash open to find Layla's face right before mine, the side of her head on her pillow exactly where I left it.

"You're moaning," she accuses.

I blink. Then I think. Then I *feel*.

"Your hand is on my dick."

Now it's her turn to blink and then she glances between us. I follow suit because her hand is wrapped around my painfully hard shaft encased in only thin boxer briefs. I also take note of the fact that one of her legs is hiked over my hip and my hand is under her sweat-shirt, cupping her bare breast.

I should pull away. I don't.

Instead, I ask, "Are your nipples hard for me or is this part of their morning routine?"

"I can't answer that."

"I figured." It doesn't stop me from squeezing her tit. "Can I make you come or am I reaching for the stars with that?"

A blink. A swipe of her tongue ring. A gnaw of her bottom lip. "I said no sex, right? I mean, I was drunk last night, but I said that?"

It's a question to which I remorsefully reply, "Yes, you said that."

"So you should probably stop rubbing my boob."

I grin like a high schooler. "And you should probably stop rubbing my dick unless you want me to come in my briefs."

Her breath hitches and suddenly she's staring back down at the space between us. "You'll do that if I keep this up?"

"Don't seem so enthralled. You're jerking me off through stupidly thin cotton. I'll come and I'll come hard if you keep doing that."

"I'm not jerking you."

"No," I amend because I guess she's technically not now. "You're just gripping me like my dick is your favorite toy."

"He might be though."

That's it. That's all she gives me. But her hand is still on me and I'm close. Like no joke close. It's Layla after all so I'm close any time she enters the room, let alone touches me.

Her eyes flash up to mine. "I'm going to stop."

"Sure. Smart plan."

"Then I should go home. I didn't mean to fall asleep here."

"I have no complaints. Incidentally, I like you in my sweatshirt."

"It smells like you."

I groan. There is no helping it. I want her body painted with my scent. "You can keep it. Wear it all fucking day."

She smirks at me. "Would you like that?"

Fuck. "Am I supposed to answer that honestly?" I shake that off. "Now that you're sober, are you still doing this with me?"

Her mouth twists. "I am. I didn't agree because I was drunk. I drank because I wanted to agree."

Hmmm. Not sure what to make of that. "Can we move you in later today?"

"Sure."

"Will you let go of my dick now?"

"Oh!"

Her eyes flash, slingshotting back down, and yeah, her hand is still on me. And though I'm not playing with her nipple or doing much other than holding her, my hand is still on her breast.

"You first," she demands.

I smirk. I could wake up like this every day for the rest of my life and be so fucking happy. "Is that what you want? You want me to stop touching you?"

"I believe I also mentioned a one and done?"

"You did," I tell her. "But Layla—"

"We've done that before, right?" she cuts me off. "A couple of times now. One more time won't hurt anything and then it's out of our systems."

I want to ask her if she genuinely believes the bullshit she's spewing, but I'm so fucking hard, and she's still holding my dick, and I'll hate myself for the rest of my life if this is truly a one and then officially done and I talk her out of it.

Still, I can't have her regretting this either. "You're sure? One hundred percent, you won't freak out after and run or get weird?"

"I won't. I need one last taste before I go the way of the nuns."

Before I even know how I got here, I have her body pinned beneath mine and my lips slamming down on hers. Fingers twine through my hair, holding on tight as our mouths open in sync and my tongue slides inside. I didn't get this the first time around. She left before I woke up, but this... this is everything I wanted that morning.

Our lips move with urgency, hot and hungry while our hands roam everywhere. Impatiently, I rip my sweatshirt over her head, my hand once again toying with her tits. My other hand slides beneath the track shorts she's wearing before continuing down between her thighs. I run a finger along the crotch of her thong, finding it damp.

"You want this?" I ask again, breathing hard against her mouth.

Her eyes hold mine and she whimpers, "Yes."

I slide the satin to the side and then thrust two fingers straight into her, meeting no resistance, because she's already so wet for me. Her lips part on a moan, her eyes hazy and heavy-lidded as I curl my fingers and find the spot that'll make her fly.

Her hands latch around the waistband of her shorts, pulling them down to give me better access as I continue to push my fingers in and out of her slippery pussy.

"You're dripping on me, baby girl. Do you know what that does to me?"

She moans, her neck arching. "Tell me," she pants.

Instead of telling her, I show her by thrusting my dick up between her spread thighs, the motion pushing my fingers deeper inside her. She cries out and I bite into her lip in warning. It may be early, only a little after six, but the last thing I want right now is for Katy to wake up and come in here.

"More?" I bark gruffly against her lips as I nip on the bottom one again. "You want me to shove my fingers in deeper until you come on them?"

"Yes. Give them to me. I want to come so badly."

Pulling back, I take in the naked woman beneath me. The rise and fall of her chest that's flushed rose right in the center. Her perfect tits perked up and desperate for my mouth. The flat slope of her abdomen curving into her hips and smooth mound. The wet thrust of my fingers between her spread thighs. Yeah, no fucking way will once be enough, but for now, it's all I've got.

My mouth attacks one nipple as my fingers pump faster. My thumb starts to rub her clit to the same rhythm as my tongue flicks her nipple. The walls of her pussy convulse, clamping down around my fingers as her body squirms, both seeking more and moving away. Her hands rip at my hair, her voice hoarse as she quietly begs me to make her come.

My other hand comes up, twisting her other nipple and she detonates, loud enough that I have to abandon her nipple and swallow her sounds down my throat. She keeps going and going, so wet, and when she's done, I lick her off my fingers, grab a condom from my nightstand, sheath myself up, hook one of her legs up over my shoulder, and then slide home.

She squeals at the intrusion, her back arching as she tries to fit me past her tight, swollen walls. Immediately I set a pace that isn't necessarily fast—I want to make this last forever—but is hard and deep with the kind of fucks she'll undoubtedly feel all day and hopefully into tomorrow.

I don't want to punish her—hell, if anything I want to worship her —but I do want her to remember what being fucked by me feels like. Even if we can't have this again. Even if she's right, and this is wrong, and we shouldn't.

I still need her to remember because I'll never forget.

I keep going like this, moving us, adjusting her, telling her things that I know make her even hotter and wetter. I lose myself inside her, savoring every pass of her slick pussy over my ragingly hard cock. Staring down at her, her eyes closed, I take in the lines of her face. She's young and beautiful, and bitterly I hate that I might not be the right man for her because I'm not sure I'll ever find a woman more right for me than her.

That thought spirals like a corkscrew through me, suffusing me with urgency. I start to pound into her, harder and deeper than before, but faster this time. Her tits bounce as I take her and make it so that all she can do is press her hands into the headboard to stop her head from slamming repeatedly against it. I fuck her till we're both sweaty and breathless and then watch as she comes—so fucking pretty I can hardly stand it—the tight grip of her cunt pushing me over the edge with her into dizzying bliss.

And because this was a one and done, a get-it-out-of-your-system fuck, we don't linger. I pull out of her and throw back on my boxer briefs and dispose of the condom and by the time I return to my bedroom, she's already up and standing by the door, wearing my hoodie and shorts again, her scrubs from yesterday balled up in her arms.

"I'm going to grab an Uber home since I have nothing here. Yet," she tacks on, all matter-of-fact. All business.

I swallow a hundred different things and say, "If you wait, I'll drive you."

She shakes her head, her tongue ring rolling along her bottom lip, and I've noticed she does this either when she's nervous or uncertain about something. I think I fit both of those for her right now.

"No," she says, "I need space. And Amelia to make me coffee."

"Okay," I agree because I get that. "I'll order an Uber for you."

"That's sweet of you, thanks." She's smiling at me. It touches her eyes, but weirdness is already settling in, so I give her a questioning look as I order her Uber. "We're good, Callan. I promise."

I'm going to get my heart broken.

I can already feel it.

"I'm keeping your sweatshirt and I'll be back tonight with my stuff."

I walk over to the doorway she's lingering in and stretch my arms up and over my head, grasping the frame. "I can help," I offer and suppress my own devilish grin when she takes me in.

Her fingers run across my abs and then down the indents on either side where they slip into my briefs. She moans. "Those are hot." She pulls her hand away with a mournful sigh. "I'm going to go wait for my Uber, Callan, because I definitely need some space to get my head back on straight. No more sex. I mean it."

"Got it. Message received."

Her blue eyes glimmer at me. "Do you know what's super annoying about all this?"

"You mean other than the fact that I have to lie in order to keep my niece and pray no one who shouldn't finds out?"

She pats my shoulder. "Yes, other than that, though that's certainly no joke. You're sexy and the sex with you was amazing. But I think if we start screwing each other, we'll be in trouble and that's not the sort of trouble I want to take on."

I release the doorframe and fold my arms over my chest. "I get it, Layla. I do. But I think *you're* sexy and it's going to be seriously painful and difficult not to try and get in your pants every second of every day. Especially when I wake up and you're gripping my dick. But we'll be good. Adults, even. We'll find a common ground and hopefully, this doesn't last longer than it has to."

"Sounds like a plan, hot man. I'll see you tonight."

"Can I come down and wait with you?" I want to make sure she gets in the car safely.

"No. But I promise to wait inside until it arrives, and you can watch the car like a stalker on your phone."

I can live with that. "Deal."

I toss her a wave, watch as she walks down the stairs, and then hit the shower to, unfortunately, wash her off me. Fifteen minutes later, I go into Katy's room and wake her. It hits me that I have no idea what to tell her about Layla. I don't want to lie, but she's six, and six-year-olds aren't known for being the best secret keepers.

"Morning, Ladybug." I kiss the top of her brown head. "How'd you sleep?"

"Good." She yawns noisily. Half the time, she remembers her dreams and half the time she doesn't. "Am I going to camp today?"

"No, honey. It's Saturday."

She rolls over, picking at the sleep in her eyes. "Can we go back to the park then? Or maybe find me a new mermaid book?"

"Sure." I hesitate. "Katy, I need to tell you something."

She yawns again, slowly sitting up and adjusting her pajama shirt. "What is it?"

"You know Layla?"

She starts playing with her comforter. "I won't run away again," she promises. "I'm sorry."

"Oh, bug, I'm not talking about that. I was going to ask if you'd want to spend more time with her?"

Her head snaps up and her eyes light up for the first time since her parents died. "Can I?"

"I was thinking she could move in with us for a while. Hang out with us."

"Really? She can do that?"

"She can." I smile, tapping the tip of her nose.

"Why is she moving here?"

"For you, honey. For us. She's... special to me. She's my... well, I guess she's my fiancée now." Guilt hits me, but I push through it. When this ends, Katy may very well hate me, but I'll cross that bridge when it comes. "If someone asks you who she is, that's what you'll tell them. Okay?"

I watch her face as she thinks about what I said and then she simply shrugs. "Okay. I'm hungry. Can I have waffles for breakfast?"

Inwardly, I laugh. Kids are so easy. If only adults were like that. "Sure, kiddo. Whatever you want."

I kiss her forehead and then set out her clothes and leave her room. A wave of anxiety hits me when I think about what I'm doing, the risk I'm taking. All I can do is pray this lie is what saves us instead of ruins us.

18

C allan

LAYLA DIDN'T END up moving in Saturday night. I think after our sexcapade, she needed more time, and I didn't argue about it since I needed it too. Despite what Layla said, Oliver did, in fact, show up on my doorstep. It was two days later than I thought it would be. Shockingly, it wasn't with a shotgun, and it wasn't to beat the shit out of me. He gave me a hug and a handshake and told me not to fuck Layla up or he would return with the shotgun and his brothers.

He brought Layla's suitcases in and left.

Then she and I spent an hour or so unpacking and moving her into my place.

Into my *bed*.

She had maybe a suitcase and a half and I have a big house with a lot of closet space and her stuff fit in my room with zero problems. I gave Katy a bath and gave Layla her space and all was fine. The problems started at ten when we both got into bed. Friday night she was passed out. That wasn't the case this time.

First, I could smell her. Like, smell her skin and smell her hair.

Second, I could feel the warmth of her body under my sheets.

When you go from a party of one in a king-sized bed to a party of two, the difference is staggeringly not imaginary.

Third, when I woke up at five thirty to work out after a less than restful night's sleep and found Layla sleeping in bed with Katy because Katy no doubt woke up with a nightmare I somehow missed and Layla went in and took care of it, I knew I was screwed.

But I also knew that wasn't a new feeling for me when it came to Layla.

Part of me questioned if I was in trouble from the first moment I met her.

So now I'm running on my treadmill like zombies are chasing me while I try not to listen to the room above my exercise room. The room that happens to be Katy's. I don't have earbuds in my ears this morning. There is no music pumping through me. It's silence and that zip noise treadmills make when you run on them and that's it.

It's barely day one, and I have no clue how I'll keep any of the promises I made to Layla about this arrangement, but I have to, and I will if I'm going to make this work.

I have no other option for Katy.

My phone rings and I insert one earbud so I can still hear out of the other ear. "Hey," I answer.

Zax's growly voice comes through my ear. "Hey. I got your message just now. I'm sorry I didn't call you back last night. My phone was on silent for some fucking reason I can't figure out."

"No. You're fine. It wasn't urgent. But..." And fuck, how do I ask this? Ash suggested it when we spoke yesterday, but again, how do I ask this? "I... Zax, I have something big to ask you."

"Ash also texted me about it because he didn't want you to have to deal with it while you're dealing with everything else."

Christ. "I don't know if I'm relieved he did that or pissed."

He chuckles. "Relieved because yes, I still have it and it's yours to use as you need."

I wipe the sweat on my face with my towel as grief and elation slam into me. "Zax. I can't. I mean, how can I?"

"Because you need a ring ASAP and I happen to have one," he says matter of fact.

"It's Suzie's though."

He breathes into the phone, and I lower my treadmill speed to a slow walk. "If Suzie were still alive, she would be fighting this with you the hardest."

"She's the reason I'm in the emergency room. I never want to miss what we missed again." There. I said it.

He laughs like I'm a fool. "You think I didn't know that all these years? Shut up, Cal. I know you, brother. We all know you as you know all of us. You are the best of us and I'm not saying that lightly, but you are. We're more than family and stronger than blood, so I'm offering you the ring I was never able to give Suzie because it would make her fucking smile like the devil she was if she knew what you were using it for."

It would. I can practically see that smile now as I close my eyes and offer him my most heartfelt, "Thank you."

"My one ask is that Katy is the flower girl for me and Aurelia if I can ever get her to pin down a wedding date."

"Done."

"I'll drop it by this morning before I head into the office."

"I owe you. Don't say I don't."

"You don't. You'd do this for me. See you in a bit."

I swallow my breath. "See you in a bit."

Stopping the treadmill, I snatch my towel and wipe my forehead and neck down as I head into my kitchen for some water. I haven't called Tom yet. I wanted to give Layla some time or maybe some sleep to reconsider.

The problems with this will be my own.

She doesn't want to fall in love. I'm already halfway there with her. She said no sex. She makes my cock hard every time she walks in the room. Somehow, someway, I'm going to have to power through this like a warrior. I'm just not sure if I'll come out stronger or weaker on the other side when she's gone.

Creeping up the stairs, I softly pad to Katy's room and listen at the door. Voices. They're awake, but it's what they're talking about that keeps me from opening the door and entering.

"Were you sad?" Katy asks, her voice scratchy with sleep.

"Yes. I was. Very sad," Layla replies to whatever they're talking about.

"I am too."

"It's okay to be sad, you know, and it's okay if you want to talk about it, or if you're not ready to. It's okay to cry and shout or simply keep to yourself and your thoughts."

"I want my mommy and daddy back, but they're gone."

My throat closes up on me as my chest squeezes impossibly tight. My hands meet the doorframe, and my head bows forward. My eyes close as I listen to them.

"I know you do. I'll be honest with you, that won't change. You'll always want your mommy and daddy back."

"Do you still?"

"Yes. I do. But I have my sister who took care of me the way your Uncle Callan is taking care of you, and I have my family and friends who help me feel better when I'm sad. I also go to where they're buried and talk to them sometimes."

"I don't want to do that." Katy sounds horrified.

Layla giggles lightly. "I don't blame you. I didn't do that for the first time until I was in high school. Crying helps me though."

"Like you did when you held me in the hospital?"

I suck in a shuddering breath, rubbing my fist over my aching heart. I knew Layla was there and I knew she had been crying. I didn't know she held my girl and cried with her.

"Like that," Layla says. "But you're lucky. You have so many people who love you, Katy. And their love is magic and will help you through this."

I pace down the hall, needing to get away from the room. Away from what Layla is saying. I don't know when or how it happened, but she blew into my life like the storm that initially brought us together and tore every piece of foundation I'm comprised of apart. If she doesn't want me to fall in love with her then she needs to stop making it so effortless to do so. She's going to steal Katy's heart as well, and how will I explain any of this to her when Layla walks away from us for good?

Getting my shit back together, I head toward Katy's room, tapping lightly on the wood and then opening the door. They're in bed together, cuddled up and still talking.

"Hey," I say, entering the room. "Morning, Ladybug. How'd you sleep?"

Katy sits up, all brown hair, blue eyes, and a freckled nose. She stretches her arms over her head, yawning as she does. "Good," she says after she's done with all that and then twists her head to glance down at Layla, who is still lying on her side beneath the covers, and then back to me. "Uncle Cal, are you going to marry Layla?"

Oomph. "Uh." Fuck. What do I say? "Well..."

Layla sits up and gives me a look that tells me she's at just as much of a loss on this as I am. "Uncle Cal and I are two people who care a lot about each other. But right now, your uncle is very focused on you and that's how it should be."

"Right." Brilliant answer.

Katy shrugs. "Okay." Her expression twists. "Oh, I have to pee!" She scrambles out of bed and then hops like a bunny toward her bathroom. "Can I go back to camp today?" she calls out just as she reaches the bathroom door.

"That's why I came in to wake you. We have to get going if you want to make it."

Layla jumps out of bed, running her fingers through her hair and wiping under her eyes. "Yes, and I have to get going to make class on time. I'll see you later, Katy. I had fun snuggling with you."

"Bye, Layla."

Katy shuts the door to her bathroom, and I pull out a T-shirt and shorts for her to put on and set them on the bed before quickly making it.

"Brush your hair and teeth, bug. Your clothes are on your bed," I yell through the door. "I'm going to take a quick shower and I'll be downstairs to make you breakfast in a bit."

"Okaaaay!"

I turn to Layla who is lingering by the door. "Morning, fiancée. How'd you sleep?"

Layla rolls her pretty eyes at me, following me back out into the hall. "Like crap, but I suppose I should start getting used to no sleep now."

"One of the many joys of becoming a doctor. Did you need to get in the shower?"

She gives me a look, her gaze dropping to my chest, and then immediately returning to my face. "We're going to have to figure all this out, aren't we?"

"You mean not showering together when we both need one?"

"Yes." She licks her lips, flashing me that damn barbell I'm just a little obsessed with. Her gaze dips down once again to my chest and I hold in my smirk.

"Problem?"

"You... uh." She waves a finger around at me. "You don't wear a shirt when you work out."

It's a statement and not a question, but I answer her anyway because it's too good to resist. "No. Is that a problem for you?"

She clears her throat and looks away. "Nope. Your house and all."

"You can look. Looking isn't touching. You think I'm hot. No shame in that."

She emits a self-deprecating laugh. "Shut up. I'm just not used to this. I lived with Patrick for like six months and it was different."

I brush some of her long bangs back from her face, tucking them behind her ear. "I have four full bathrooms in this house and a huge hot water tank. Shower wherever, whenever you like. If you want me to start wearing a shirt when I work out, I will. I want you to be comfortable here, Layla. I know this is awkward, and yes, we'll have an adjustment period, but please, don't walk on eggshells, and don't skulk around me. Make it your home as best you can. The only thing I asked for is that your stuff stays in my room and that's where you sleep because I don't want it to be obvious the other bedroom is being used."

"I know and as you said, I'll adjust. I sort of want to pierce your nipples but that's my own thing and I'll get over it."

I laugh. "As much as I love the idea of you thinking about my nipples, I'm not sure I'm a pierced nipples sort of guy. If that's what you're into then Lenox is more your man, but if you touch my friend, I'll be forced to kill him, and I love him like a brother."

"Noted. No screwing your friends." She takes a step backward, and then another, but her eyes are still all over me. "That goes tenfold for you, fiancé. It appears as if we're both the jealous types. I'm going to shower. In your guest shower."

"I'm going to shower. In my shower."

She smirks. "Don't think about me when you're in there."

I smile like a bastard. "Same goes for you."

"Pfft." She rolls her eyes. "As if."

She spins around and heads toward the bathroom and I do the same, already running a few minutes late now. But that doesn't stop me from stripping down and automatically picturing Layla naked, wet, and soapy in the shower with me. My cock has been hard since the moment she looked at my chest like she wanted to lick it.

And with the mental image of her in my head—the one where I sat her on my washing machine and licked her clit while the machine vibrated into her cunt—I start to jerk myself in earnest.

Her tits. Small and perky as she likes to boast about. The taste of her sweet nipples and delicious skin. The smell of her. Fuck. I groan. The goddamn smell of her. That's enough to get me off right there, but remembering her face when my tongue flicked her clit, how she gripped my hair and rocked into me, her glazed expression and hungry eyes...

That does it for me and I continue to jerk until I'm spraying my shower walls with cum.

I'm embarrassed by how fast and how hard that happened, but there's no one to be embarrassed in front of because it's just me in here as the object of my obsession and fascination is down the hall.

I shampoo and wash up quickly, then wrap a towel around myself and head into my bedroom. Katy is going to be hungry, wanting her Mickey-and-Minnie-shaped waffles. I need to feed her, make her lunch, get her dropped off at camp, call my attorney, oh, and wait, I forgot—

I freeze, my hands in my drawer on a pair of boxer briefs, my mouth pooling with saliva. I feel like I'm stuck in one of those reels Ash always shows me.

When your fake fiancée is wet from the shower wearing nothing but a towel standing in your bedroom, and you can't touch her.

That's me. Right this very second. Layla is naked beneath her towel, soaking wet because she walked into that bathroom with nothing clean to put on and I've never been so grateful for that mental blunder in my life.

Long legs. Creamy skin. Wet, slicked-back blonde hair. Bright blue eyes. Adorable sparkling nose ring. Tiny white towel. Small swell of cleavage. I'm in fantasy overload and I can't move or speak.

All I can do is stare.

In my head, she asks, *are you naked under your towel?* And I reply with something somewhat clever like, *if you care to find out, I can drop it right now.* Only my life isn't nearly that cool despite my former rock star glory. Which is why she appears a bit shell-shocked and a little disoriented and mumbles out something along the lines of she'll get what she needs to change in the other bathroom.

She goes for the closet and misses and walks into the wall and I'm furious the towel didn't drop when she did that, but I can't even ask if she's okay. Because all I can say is, "Or you can get dressed in here."

"What?"

I don't know. That just came out. But... "You can change in here. You know, since this will be your bedroom for a while."

She tilts her head, squinting at me. "Where will you get dressed?"

Solid question. "The bathroom?" It comes out as a question.

"Oh. Um. You're sure?"

"No. I mean, yes. I'm sure."

She smirks. I grin. We stare. My stare starts to drift because of all her aforementioned sexiness. Her gaze starts to drift and catches on my hardening cock because coming with my hand isn't nearly as enticing as what she has to offer.

"You should go in there then."

"Uh-huh. Wait. Where?"

Her eyes are laughing at me now along with her lips that are quirked up. "In the bathroom. You should grab your clothes so you can get dressed in there."

"I should. But I'm having a hell of a time forcing my legs to move or my eyes to leave what they're very happy staring at."

"Maybe we should add no flirting or staring? You said looking is fine, but I can tell you, looking is so not fine with all the ways my mind is going."

She could be right on with that. Because I'm a half-second from ripping the towel from her body.

Before I can answer the doorbell rings. "Shit. That's Zax with your ring."

"My ring?!" Her voice shoots up in alarm along with her eyebrows.

"Yes. It was Suzie's. Or... was meant to be hers." I scrub my hands up my face, blow out a fucked breath, and grab the first pair of boxer briefs, T-shirt, and shorts my hands land on. Then I'm running out the bedroom door, throwing on my clothes and tossing my towel in the direction of the laundry room before heading down the stairs, practically tripping and falling down them as I do.

I disarm the alarm and fling the door open only to step outside and crowd Zax on my front steps. He's confused, but he quickly gets over it when I tell him, "I think I'm already in a lot of trouble."

He laughs, his brown eyes flickering in the early morning light before his expression sobers. "Might be, by the look of you. Is that a possible outcome for you?

I give him my worst truth. "No."

"All right. We can work with that. What's your end goal?" he asks, righting his features and turning this into business, something he does exceptionally well as the CEO of Monroe Fashions.

"Katy."

His hands meet my shoulders. "How do you get Katy?"

"By convincing the courts I'm the best guardian for her."

"And what will help sway them in your direction?"

I sigh in defeat. "Layla."

He gives me a *now you're starting to get it* look and squeezes my shoulders. "So what can you not do?"

"Fuck her or fall in love with her."

He gives me a pitying frown. One I fully deserve. "Love is a special thing, Cal. It rules not only our hearts but our minds. It slams into us when we're least prepared for it. It moves in and doesn't care if it's invited or not. It removes our choices and our rational thinking, and either makes us whole or leaves us in ruin. But no matter what, love comes with one universal truth—you cannot fight her. You can only hope to survive her."

Numbly, I reply, "It's just a lot all at once. I'll adjust. I always do. I'm not in love with her." *Yet.*

"Best advice?"

"Shoot."

"Remember that right now, this is bigger than just you. Focus on what you have to and push aside what threatens you."

I swallow thickly at that and force myself back under control. "I will."

If only it were as easy as it sounds.

EMERGENCY

19

CLEARANCE 12'

L ayla

I END up pacing Callan's bedroom, staring around, taking it all in, trying to figure this out. It's a lot. I went from being me, Layla Fritz, med student, to... fake engaged to Callan Barrows, who looks way too lickable only wearing a towel and helping with a traumatized little girl.

I don't regret it. I don't.

I'm just freaking out a little.

It's a normal reaction to this level of rapid change, so I'm not fighting it. I'm embracing it, hoping it passes quickly because there is a little girl waiting for me downstairs, a classroom after that, and a fucking ring. It's the ring that pushed me over the edge.

I don't know how to wear the ring.

I remember Amelia's. It's the same one she's still wearing on her hand now. It belonged to Oliver's great-grandma, and it meant something to him. This ring means something too and it feels wrong to slide it on.

I'm doing my best to remember the higher purpose for why I'm here. But between a hot and sexy Callan with abs for days, wet and wearing nothing but a towel, staring at me like he wanted to devour me while being adorable and flirty, my baser instinct is screaming for me to run and run fast.

I won't.

I'm a pull-her-shit-together-and-rise-to-the-challenge sort of bitch so I know I can master this one. It's just an adjustment. This situation is nothing a double espresso, electrolyte-infused water, bacon, egg, and cheese on a bagel, and a little perspective can't cure.

There's a tap on the bedroom door and I jolt, which then makes me laugh because that sound wouldn't have startled a mouse, and here I am jumping like someone just poked my ass with a branding rod.

"Come in," I call out, laughing even harder because this is his room and not mine, and I've officially lost it. The door opens and in walks a cautious Callan, his face now stoic and reserved without a drop of the heat and smolder he was showcasing before.

I blow out a relieved breath. Thank God, right? If he had even an ounce of sex in his eyes, I would have climbed him like a mountain and claimed his land for my own.

"Hey. Sorry. I..." He shakes his head and stares down at the box in his hand. "It feels weird to give you this, doesn't it?"

My legs collapse on me and somehow I'm sitting on the edge of the bed. He joins me, holding it between us as we both stare down at it.

"Zax bought it for Suzie only she died the day he was planning to give it to her." He releases a heavy breath. "Layla..." His eyes rise to mine. "I think you're amazing. You are all passion and fire and unbridled wildness. But within all that is a heart of pure gold. You are fierce and loyal and smart and funny and quirky. I thought all these things about you before you showed up on my doorstep Friday night, but they're multiplied by a billion now." His elbow hits his thigh, and he props the side of his face up with his hand, twisting to meet my eyes. "I know giving you this ring sucks. I know it does. I know I'm asking a lot from you, and so far, you haven't asked for anything in return. You're a selfless angel and it's not lost on me." He stares down at the box. "I don't think I would have bought you a diamond," he muses, almost as a side note, and I smile, weirdly curious and a lot flustered after all he just said about me. A man has never been so effusive with me before and it's doing things to me, so I focus on the easy question.

"What would you have gotten me?"

A smile blooms across his lips and his gaze cuts to mine. "My first thought is a sapphire because of your eyes, but that also feels a bit generic. You're not generic so I doubt I would have found what I was looking for in any regular jewelry store. It would have had to have been special and unique like you."

My heart is fluttering like a jackrabbit and I'm growing breathless with it.

He opens the box to reveal a huge princess-cut diamond bracketed by two smaller heart-shaped ones. It's absolutely stunning and not meant for me and it gets me choked up that the man who bought this ring with so much love in his heart was never able to give it to the woman it was intended for.

It's a ring that deserves to be on a beloved's finger.

"Suzie was a lot like you in many ways," he murmurs absently, staring at the ring. "I think that's why if I have to give you anyone's ring, I guess I'm glad it's hers even if this thing between us is not real. Suzie was fire and earth and air and water. She was life and rode it hard and to the fullest each day. That's what I think of when I see this ring. So wear it when you need a little bit extra, and it will get you there."

He takes the ring out of the box and slides it on my finger and fucking hell, it's a perfect goddamn fit. His thumb plays with the stone on my finger, sliding it back and forth and I hear his breath catch.

"It's beautiful," I whisper.

He swallows audibly and nods. "It is." He closes the box and sets it on the bed between us, clears his throat, and then stands. "We're running a bit late, so we should get going. I'll drop Katy off at camp quickly and then take you to school."

"Okay." It's seriously all I can manage, and I'm grateful he doesn't have any more words that are like a love potion flowing through my veins.

"I made you an egg sandwich and an espresso. I figured you could use both. They're downstairs whenever you're ready."

And yup. Thanks for that. Because there goes my heart.

He shuts the door behind him, and I scramble for my phone, pulling up Stella's name and shooting her a quick text.

Me: I said I'd pull out if I started to develop feelings. I think I should pull out, but I can't pull out and I don't know what to do. It's the first morning I'm here, Stella! He was all hot and flirty and only wearing a towel after the shower and then he gave me a fucking diamond and said all these incredible things about me. How am I not supposed to fall for him when he does shit like that?

By the love of Moses even though it's very early for my friend who works very late hours, she replies instantly.

Stella: Remind me why you can't fall for him because he sounds perfect.

Me: Not helping! You're supposed to help! I'm freaking out.

I start pacing, staring at my ring. No, not my ring. Suzie's ring. This is a prop.

Stella: Okay, keep your tits on. Mamma always said there'd be days like this. You knew the first day would be the hardest. You also went into this already crushing on the guy, which isn't help-ing. But you're Layla Fritz. If anyone can do this, it's you. Poor bastard should have asked me. I would have done it and he'd have no risk of me falling for him.

Me: It's moments like these that I wish I was a lesbian too. You and I could have fallen in love and moved to an island and had babies while we opened restaurants and cured local people of disease. Instead, I'm here wearing a diamond bigger than my face

and pacing a bedroom that isn't mine after I slept next to my fake fiancé.

Stella: In another life, it's you and me, boo. Until then, focus on yourself, and what you have to do to protect your heart while helping them. If protecting yourself is still what you want.

Me: It is.

Stella: Then get your shit on lockdown. You let it out of the cage, but now you have to shove that bitch back in there and remind her of all the reasons you designed your plan and set up rules.

She's right. Deep breath. I can do this. It's just a crush like she said, and I won't let it become anything more. Nothing about us is right. A professor/student relationship is not cool and I don't have time for that. I'm here to help and that's what I'll do and in the interim, I'll protect my heart from his infiltration at all costs.

I give myself a shake and crack my neck and then my knuckles because I've got this, even if my heart isn't totally sold on that.

Me: He's the sperm and I'm the condom protecting my heart. He shall not pass.

Stella: Um. Are you allegorizing Gandalf the Grey to a condom? Because straight up no on that. Besides, this all sounds very weirdly sexual and reproductive so... can't you just say something simple like you've got this?

Me: I've got this.

Sorta.

Stella: Better. Thank you. Just stick to your goals. Once he wins the kid, you can walk. Help him do that and this ends quickly.

Me: <3

Help him win the kid and I can walk. Something inside of me pinches. Something I shove away because it's not helpful and then I head downstairs, listening as I hear Katy giggle at whatever Callan is doing.

"No! You have them on the wrong feet."

"Are you sure?" Callan questions and when I round the corner, I discover him wearing his shoes on the wrong feet.

"Yes!" Katy giggles louder. "Uncle Cal, you have to fix them, or you'll trip."

"You think so?" He takes a step and then dramatically goes tumbling forward straight into me, forcing me to catch him. Katy breaks into a full-on belly laugh. His hands plant on my shoulders as he rights himself. "Anything for a cheap laugh," he whispers to me, giving me a wink. "All right, Ladybug. Go get your stuff while I fix my shoes."

Katy flies off the stool and then runs to the back hall to grab her backpack.

Callan drops to his knees, fixing his shoes one by one, not looking at me as he speaks. "Your sandwich and coffee are on the counter. I'm sorry we don't have time for you to eat them here."

My coffee is in a to-go thermos and my sandwich is wrapped in foil to keep it warm. Thoughtful bastard. "You don't have to do that for me, you know. I could have grabbed something on campus."

He glances up, gazing at me through thick brown lashes and then he smirks. That smirk. That killer fucking smirk with enrapturing dimples never fails to slice my insides to pieces.

"I didn't mind." His chin juts toward my hand. "You should probably take that off before class."

"Oh." I glance down at the sparkly diamond on my hand. "Good call."

I race back upstairs and slip it into the box and then immediately return, grab my sandwich, coffee, and my schoolbag, and then head for the door, following behind Callan and Katy who are already there.

Callan drives us while Katy belts out Taylor Swift lyrics at the top of her lungs. I join in with her, twisting around so we can duet. This is what I do with my nieces, and I love how Callan plays whatever she wants to hear. He pulls up in front of her camp and I say bye to Katy, watching as he walks her in.

A few minutes later he's back and then we're driving to school, which I shouldn't have let him do. "Next time I'll take the T."

He taps his fingers along the steering wheel. "Should I let you out on Huntington then?"

"Probably," I agree.

"Feels like we're living a double life, right?" he muses, and I bite into my lip, turning to stare at his profile.

"A little, but it's not forever."

He doesn't respond to that and a moment later, he's pulling over at the edge of campus so I can hop out of the car.

"See you later," he whispers, his eyes on mine.

Christ. The way he's looking at me.

"Later," I murmur, feeling my chest heat. I lick my lips and then leave him behind, making my way across campus while eating my breakfast sandwich and drinking my coffee, and forcing myself *not* to think about my present life choices. Trying not to imagine this as my real daily routine with him where I get out of his car but only after we say goodbye with a searing kiss.

I hike the steps to the front of the building, but before I can open the heavy doors, I'm intercepted by a tall, blond, not-so-welcome figure.

"Move, Patrick. I don't have time for you."

"You've been quiet in the group chat," he says, standing over me. I shift to get around him, but he's quick and blocks me.

"Move! I need to get into class."

"You have ten minutes, Layla. All I'm asking for is five of them."

I growl, in no mood to deal with his shit after everything that's happened the past few days. I peer up at him, squinting against the early morning sun. "Why are you here?"

"You've been quiet in the chat," he repeats like that's an actual answer to why he's on campus when he doesn't need to be.

"You're in the chat. That's why. I don't need you in my business, Patrick. You lost that right months ago. Go stalk someone else."

He grabs my arm and drags me along the front of the building and pushes me against one of the massive stone pillars. Then he gets right up in my face, his hands on either side of my head. "I need to tell you something."

My insides hiccup even as I feign indifference. "What is it?"

"Molly wants to be with me."

I roll my eyes. "No shit. You came all the way over here to tell me that?"

He makes an annoyed noise in the back of his throat, but his eyes hold mine, steadfast yet cautious. "No. I came all the way over here to tell you I'm going to be with her."

The wind leaves my lungs.

He pauses and then says, "That is unless you're willing to come back to me."

Instantly I shake my head, shoving at his chest. "*Eeen,*" I make a buzzer sound. "Sorry. You lost that round." I shove at him again, but the fucker just won't budge. "It's too late for that. Move."

"No, Layla, it's not. We were together for years. I got... I don't know. Overwhelmed. It was supposed to be a break, not a breakup."

I laugh caustically. "No, that's not what you wanted, and we both know it. You wanted to fuck Molly and you did that. Only you don't get to call a break, fuck someone else, and then expect me to be there waiting when you decide you're ready for round two with me. So go be with Molly. I'm done with you."

"You mean now that you're fucking your professor."

My heart stops, my partially digested egg sandwich and coffee churning in my gut. "What?"

"I saw the way he was looking at you that morning. He told me to fuck off. What professor does that? You're obviously fucking him."

I blow out a silent, relieved breath. Because if anyone could throw a wrench into this fake engagement, it's Patrick. By some miracle, he didn't see me get out of Callan's car, but damn, how close of a call is that?

I give him a bored, unimpressed look even though my insides are rioting. Folding my arms over my chest, I try and create some space between us. "Ah. Now I get it. You don't want me. You just don't want me fucking anyone else." Such a rotten bastard. I roll my eyes as if his accusation has no merit. "I'm not fucking my professor, dipshit. I'm not that stupid." *Anymore.* "Dr. Barrows works with Oliver, and he was being protective of me for him. Something you wouldn't know about. But if I decided to fuck every man and woman in this building, that would be my call to make, and you'd have no say in it." I redirect him away from Callan. "Why are you here? You could have told me about Molly over a text or better yet, not at all."

"I wanted to see you. I wanted to see your reaction when I told you. I wanted to see your face when I challenged you on your professor." He blows out an uneven breath, his posture crumpling in as his voice softens. "I wanted to see if you still want me the way I want you."

"You thought that rubbing it in my face that you're going to be with Molly would make me get emotional and beg for you to take me back?" I laugh. It's bitter. "Do you even know me?" The question hits the air, and I realize he doesn't. Maybe he never did. "Did you honestly think that would ever be an option after what you did? Hell, after what you're doing now?" I'm incredulous. And sick. I stab my finger into his chest as hard as I can as I breathe fire at him. "I'm over you. It didn't even take very long to happen. Now fuck the fuck off."

I was with him for two and a half years and though I initially fought off falling for him, once we both got into the same med school, I was game on, all-in. When he ended it, I thought my heart was going to die in my chest and then he dug the knife in deeper. And here he is, trying to hurt me yet again. I wasted so much time with him and he wasn't even half as good to me as Callan has been, and Callan isn't even my boyfriend.

Which would rattle me further if I allowed those thoughts to penetrate, but since I am the condom, they don't. This is the exact reason I have to be that fucking condom.

Patrick presses in on me, smirking arrogantly, but it isn't hitting his eyes. "You're not over me. You're just angry about Molly."

I return his arrogant smirk with one of my own. "Honestly, no. You fucked up a great thing when you let me go. That's on you. Girls like me don't have to give second chances. Especially not to douchebag assholes who get off on playing mind games. Bye, Patrick."

I duck under his arm and head for the door, making sure my back is to him as I enter the building. Making sure he gets the message once and for all.

I'm done with him.

Only the moment the heavy door shuts behind me, I scramble over to the side, hiding in an alcove. I cover my pounding heart with my hand, trying to slow both it and my breathing down. I hope this was the final act and now he'll be done with me. I hope he and Molly go off into the sunset and make each other miserable as hell.

For a moment, I debate texting Callan, but what would I say to him? Patrick didn't see us in Callan's car, and I pushed Patrick off the notion that I'm fucking Callan. Which isn't a lie because I'm not. Callan and I just have to be more careful with this fake relationship.

And I have to be more careful with myself.

That was my pledge in all this. It's as simple and as real as that. Seeing Patrick was the perfect reminder.

I don't want to get hurt again, and if I don't put myself out there emotionally, I won't.

From here on out, this is how it's going to be. My relationship with Callan is fake. That means I won't misread words or touches or any bullshit. I won't straddle any lines—or his dick. No more rides to school. No more breath-stealing looks. No more sexy-after-shower naked flirting.

No more flirting in general.

Or sweet words about how wonderful he thinks I am. Would it be weird if I ask him to be a dick to me instead? Or would him being a dick make me want him more because then it would be a challenge?

Argh. What is wrong with me?

This isn't who I am. I do not go all cuckoo for Cocoa Puffs over a guy. Attraction and lust aren't love. He's grateful I'm there, but we both have an end goal in this game and it's not each other.

School. This is what's important to me. This is my priority. Just as Katy is his priority.

Determination lighting a fire within me, I start to march off toward class when my phone buzzes in my bag.

C: Did you make it in okay? You're usually one of the first people here.

Me: I'm here. I just got sidetracked. Court this afternoon at 4?

C: Yes. Does that still work for you?

As his now live-in fiancée, I am going with him to show how awesome we are as a couple and how perfect and stable Katy's home life is.

Me: It does.

C: You're amazing. Thank you! See you in a few.

Me: See you in a few.

Here's hoping this arrangement ends quickly and no one gets hurt.

20

C allan

FOR THE LAST TEN MINUTES, the judge has been sitting here reading through the petitions that both Willow's parents and I submitted as well as the documentation from social services, the police, and the camp. Layla is sitting stoically beside me, twisting her ring around and around. Tom told me to sit still and appear confident, but I'm having a hell of a time doing that.

Behind me, sitting patiently and quietly, are my friends. I didn't ask them to come. They just showed up, and I must move or make a noise or something because I feel a hand hit my shoulder.

Asher.

I'd know his monster grip anywhere.

He leans forward and whispers, "I think Willow's parents' attorney just farted."

I bite into my lip to hide my smile and Layla coughs a small laugh under her breath. Asher is such a kid in so many ways and I love him for it especially right now.

"Good thing no one is sitting beside him then," Grey quips, and I clear my throat, rubbing at my lips.

Layla casually leans back in her chair and angles her head in my direction. "He totally checked out my ass too. Do you want me to nail him and see if I can make this all go away?"

I smirk in her direction, relieved she's looking at me. It's the first time all day. "Would you, baby? That's so sweet of you to offer."

Asher makes an amused noise he's trying desperately to cover and so do Zax, Grey, and even Lenox.

"Hey, helping is what I'm here for."

I lean into her, my mouth by her ear so no one else can hear us. "Your blow jobs are very effective."

Her breath catches, but before she can say anything else, the door to the courtroom opens, startling all of us and casting our reflexive gazes over our shoulders in its direction.

"I'll be a son of a bitch," Layla murmurs with an obvious smile in her voice, but I can't drag myself away from what I'm seeing.

"Octavia?!" the judge practically gasps in surprise. "What are you doing here?"

Octavia Abbot-Fritz, flanked by Stella and Amelia, comes to a halt in the center of the aisle, surprise lighting her elegant features. "Oh. Fredrick. How lovely to see you. I didn't know you were presiding over this case." Octavia's manicured hand goes to her chest, her flawless designer pink suit that matches her nails is everything you'd expect it to be. I swear, the sun just beamed in through the windows as if any clouds outside parted in her presence. It's as if Queen Elizabeth—before she died—just walked into the room.

Even Willow's attorney is in shell-shocked awe.

"Y-yes," the judge stutters only to clear his throat and right himself. "Lovely to see you too, as always. I have a tee time with Dr. Fritz tomorrow morning."

She winks at him. "I know he's looking forward to that. He rarely gets extra time these days to go out and play. I'll have to call Leah and make plans for lunch. Maybe the four of us can dine together after you play?"

"I'm sure she'd love that."

Zax pinches my shoulder in an *is this really happening* way.

Octavia glances in our direction and gives me what I can only describe as an indulgent smile before turning back to the judge. "I apologize for interrupting. I meant to arrive earlier to support my granddaughter and Dr. Barrows, but traffic at this time of day can be so difficult to get through. I'll just take my seat and let you get on with what you were doing."

"Your granddaughter?" the judge blurts out incredulously.

"Yes." Octavia beams a smile that could melt the polar ice caps. "Layla Fritz is my granddaughter and Callan Barrows is her wonderful man."

I think I just died. Can a person die of gratitude? Behind me, my friends are shifting around, murmuring things I can't hear to each other. All except for Fallon, who says "Brilliant."

Octavia didn't even mention engagement, which, as Fallon just said, is brilliant on her part. She didn't have to lie that way. She called me Layla's man and that's more than enough.

Layla takes my hand and I squeeze the hell out of hers, my head bouncing in her direction as I search her eyes. "Did you know?" I mouth at her, and she shakes her head as she chews on her bottom lip, smiling like the devil.

The Honorable Fredrick Clutchfield blinks at Octavia, and then blinks at me, and then Layla before returning his bewildered gaze back to Octavia, Stella, and Amelia. Wheels start visibly clicking into place, and he grabs a piece of paper he had previously discarded and then reads it again. He must not have caught Layla's last name when he quickly glanced over the pages since we only added it to the documents this morning when we modified it to say that my living arrangement had changed.

Octavia Abbot-Fritz might have just won this for me.

"Holy fuck." That's Asher and I totally and completely agree with him on that.

Octavia, Stella, and Amelia all come over to us, and Stella stares me down only to say, "I haven't decided if I like you yet or not."

I give Stella a hug even though I've only met her a couple of times in the past at Abbot Foundation events. "I get that. But I'm the guy who wins everyone over in the end."

"You're banking pretty hard on that one, aren't you?"

I shrug. "Only if I have to."

Stella gives me a wry grin and then takes a seat, giving way for Amelia to come at me. She gives me a squeeze and whispers, "You'll get your girl now for sure." I squeeze her back, thanking her in so many ways. I think she's a large part of why Layla said yes.

"Hello, dear. Smile. It always helps." Octavia pats my cheek and then kisses it, wiping away her lipstick smear. I catch her hand before she gets away, words failing me as I look at the woman before me. A woman who—much like Stella—I've only met a few times at one of her Abbot Foundation balls. Her green eyes hold mine, and then it's as if some realization hits her and they light up from within, and then she states, "My instincts are never wrong."

I shake my head at a loss as to her meaning, but then she goes for Layla and the two have a moment.

"Your Honor?" Willow's parents' attorney cuts into the lovefest. "I realize Dr. Barrows has a long list of wealthy celebrity friends, but I don't feel as though that should be a consideration in this case. My clients are poor and just trying to do what's right by their grand-daughter."

The judge holds his hand up, silencing the attorney.

"I have a few questions for both sides before I make my verdict." He sits up straighter, rubbing at his bald head. "Mr. Salucci, if your clients are named either fiduciary and/or legal guardians of Katy Barrows, what do they intend to do with the proceeds from the sale of Mr. and Mrs. Barrows' house as well as the life insurance policy, all in the name of Katy Barrows?"

Mr. Salucci places his hands on the wooden table before him. "They intend to use that money to help raise Miss Barrows, giving her everything a child would need to grow and thrive into adulthood."

The judge nods his head and then turns expectantly to me. "And you, Dr. Barrows. What do you intend to do with that money?"

Tom puts his hand on my arm, stopping me before I speak. "My client's plan is to take that money and put it into a trust for Miss Barrows so her future will always be secure. Dr. Barrows does not need nor has any intention of using that money for himself or to help raise Miss Barrows."

The judge turns back to the other attorney. "Mr. Salucci, in reviewing the documents provided by your clients, it appears they reside in a one-bedroom mobile home, and neither is currently employed. Is this correct?"

Mr. Salucci shifts though you can tell he did not want that question. "Yes, Your Honor. At present, that is correct, though my clients intend to move into a larger home in a better school district upon receiving the proceeds from the sale of Mr. and Mrs. Barrow's home. This would be solely to accommodate Miss Barrows if she were to live with them or come for regular visits."

"I see." The judge reads something over on one of the documents and then peers at me and the group of billionaires and celebrities surrounding me. "And, Dr. Barrows, will you have any need to move residences?"

"No, Your Honor," Tom answers for me. "Dr. Barrows lives in a great neighborhood in Beacon Hill and already has a private room fully decorated for Miss Barrows in place. He also lives within ten minutes of the private school she attended last year, so she won't have to change schools."

"I see. And Dr. Barrows, are you able to explain what happened with Miss Barrows last Thursday?"

Tom proceeds to explain everything that is already reported in the court documents but adds that Katy was searching for Miss Fritz as the two of them have become quite close, and Katy was upset about how she had been teased by that same little shit about being an orphan. Again. Tom continues with how Layla has been able to provide immense comfort and empathy for Katy with this.

The judge examines Layla for a very long moment and then turns back to Tom. "Dr. Barrows is engaged to Miss Fritz? This was not mentioned in the prior document. Only that Dr. Barrows was unmarried. Am I understanding this correctly?" The judge presses. "There are two adults now living within this household and Miss Barrows feels a kinship with Miss Fritz?"

I tense, and so does Layla, and the room grows uncomfortably silent, though I know much of that is in my head.

Tom doesn't so much as shift or blink. "Yes, Your Honor. In the previous documents, it was not necessary to present Miss Fritz as there were no challenges to Dr. Barrows' legal guardianship of Miss Barrows. At present, Miss Fritz is living in the same household as Dr. Barrows, and Miss Barrows and Miss Fritz are extremely close."

Not a lie. Go Tom.

The judge bobs his head about twenty times, possibly a bit displeased that Layla wasn't originally mentioned, but he doesn't comment on it further. He continues reading over document after document.

Finally, he clears his throat. "Well, after reviewing both arguments and taking in what this court considers to be the best interest of the minor child, I will rule in favor of Dr. Barrows being Katy Barrows' fiduciary guardian. As for the elopement from the camp, that is concerning. However, given the updated information on Dr. Barrows' living situation and that Miss Barrows clearly has the support system of both Dr. Barrows and Miss Fritz in addition to family and friends, it is the ruling of this court and the state of Massachusetts to maintain sole guardianship of Katy Barrows to Dr. Callan Barrows."

My chest rises until he continues and drops the bomb I was hoping he wouldn't.

"However, this ruling will be subject to four visits over a ninety-day period by a court-appointed liaison. We will reconvene after that time period and based on the results of those visits and the findings of that liaison, the court will then make a final determination on the legal guardianship of Miss Barrows. Adjourned."

He bangs his gavel, we all rise, and he files out.

I plant my hands on the table. On the one hand, he ruled in my favor to take care of Katy's money and I've officially gotten rid of Willow's parents with that. On the other, it's now ninety days until he'll rule Katy as permanently mine, and that's only if everything goes smoothly with the court liaisons.

I turn to Layla. "Three months. Do you think you can do that with me?" Suddenly I'm wary. That's ninety days of lying in school and ninety days of lying at work all the while pretending to be a couple outside of both.

It's a lot to juggle.

A lot that can go wrong.

"I can do three months. If Octavia can put on a show like that, so can I."

It's a sucker punch. One I clearly needed.

"Right. That's great. Thank you."

"Sure. Like I said, it's what I'm here for." She pats my shoulder like I'm her fucking buddy and then turns to talk to her sister and Stella almost dismissively. Something feels... off.

My expression clouds over, unsure how to speak or interact with her now. What was so easy and natural this morning is now onerous and forced. Did something happen that I missed? I thought we were in a good place. I thought we had figured it out, but now I'm not so sure. It's as if I've hit a barrier she's erected between us.

Hard and fast, I unexpectedly slammed right into it.

Regardless, I have no choice but to play her game and concede to her every desire. Too bad her desire isn't the *spread your legs wide and let me make you come* kind. It's the *back the fuck off and no one will get hurt* kind.

"You okay?" I ask when we start to shuffle out, trying to gauge her.

"I'm fine." She forces a smile that doesn't touch her eyes and then she moves past me, joining Stella and her sister as they reach the exit of the courtroom.

I pause for a beat, staring after her.

"Never believe a woman when she says she's fine," Lenox advises.

"He's right. We're never fine when we say we are." Aurelia gives me a wan smile.

I continue on, working through the crowded courthouse lobby and then heading outside. "I'm not sure what to do there," I admit. "We were good as far as I knew. I dropped her off at school this morning. Maybe she's having second thoughts or maybe I'm reading more into something I shouldn't. If it weren't for the ninety days, I'd cut her free. Should I talk to her and figure things out or back off?" I blow out a desperate breath. "I'm being a high-school chick and I don't even mean that in a sexist way though I know it sounds like it. That's how I feel. I'm overanalyzing everything."

"It is sexist, but it's also true," Fallon says. "It's unfortunately part of our DNA. Can I make a suggestion?" She comes in beside me.

"Please."

"Decide what you truly want from her before you do that."

I tilt my head curiously. "Meaning?"

Fallon touches my arm. "What is your end goal with her, Callan? She's young. She's a med student. You're now a single dad. You're in very different places. Is this just some fun you're after or are you interested in something bigger with her? If you are, that's amazing and I'm all for it because I think you're both great—possibly perfect—together. But if you're unsure..." She shrugs as she leaves that hanging. "She was here today. Her family was here today. She moved into your home and is doing everything you asked of her for no personal gain. She's trying to set boundaries for herself. So, the question is, why are you so determined to tear them down?"

I stare at Fallon, words stuck in the back of my throat.

She's right. I have no right to talk to Layla about anything. She's free to set boundaries. She's free to do as she needs to for herself. Yes, I want Layla. In a perfect world, I'd love to try dating her. But we're not in a perfect world. Nowhere close to it.

Other than the sex, which I agreed would just be that one time, she told me she didn't want to fall in love, and she told me didn't want a real relationship. In fact, she told me exactly how she needed this to go for her even though she was agreeing to help me.

Which sucks. I was riding something with her I shouldn't have been. Behaving in a way I shouldn't have been given the requirements she made in order for this to work for her. Obviously, I was already in over my head.

But I was alone in that.

That's not what she wants from me. Not at all.

I knew it. I agreed to it. I just didn't adjust to it as I should have. Layla isn't the one doing anything wrong. I am.

"I'll back off," I say. Even if the idea of it hurts like hell.

21

C allan

"*THE LITTLE MERMAID*," Katy demands, standing on the edge of the kitchen wearing her mermaid pajamas and holding the mermaid doll Asher bought her earlier this week. She bumped up another level in her swim lessons last Friday because she is determined to become a mermaid when she grows up. Everything in this house is mermaids.

I even had her bedroom walls repainted to look like the ocean—I figured it's also soothing.

But when I was having her room painted, something occurred to me. An idea for Layla I hope I can pull off even though she's been avoiding me like the ghost of one-night stands past. Regardless of that, she's here for three months with me and I want her to feel comfortable in my home, which I don't think she does yet.

"*Tangled*," I counter, putting the tray of cookies into the oven. They're the slice-and-bake ones because I tried—and failed miserably—to make them from scratch Monday after court and they came out like hockey pucks. They were Aurelia's recipe and when I sent her the photo of their charred remains, she suggested trying these because they're foolproof.

Katy places her hand on her hip, her expression pure determination. "*The Little Mermaid.*"

"I love the music, Ladybug, but I don't love the message." Fallon pointed out that in *The Little Mermaid*, Ariel changes who she is and gives up everything for a guy. Maybe it's worth taking a stand and maybe it's not. I honestly don't know. I'm too new at this and half the time feel like I'm doing a shit job. But I think I'd be a bad guardian if I didn't at least mention it.

Katy narrows her blue eyes at me. "What if I promise to stay me forever? Can we watch it then? Boys are gross anyway. Joey Long picked his nose and ate his boogers today. Holly and I nearly threw up our ice pops."

I match her position. "As long as you promise to continue to think boys are gross until you're thirty, I'll agree."

"Deal."

I extend my hand and we shake on it, but instead of releasing her, I drag her into me and start tickling her sides and belly. She peals out a squeal of laughter, writhing in my arms to try and get away from me. I wrestle her to the floor, blowing raspberries on her belly and tickling her everywhere I can. She rolls back and forth, her laugh a full-on belly laugh now that has me in stitches right along with her.

I go in for another raspberry when the doorbell rings, startling us both. "Stay here, kiddo." Hopping up, I jog over to the door. "Who is it?" I call through the wood.

"Mrs. Joanna Bible from social services."

Oh shit.

I unlock the door and fling it open to find a woman who, well, is terrifying. She's tall and broad like a linebacker, wearing a green floral dress and matching green shoes that both might be from the early nineteen thirties. Her hair is pinned up in a tight, austere bun, and her simple glasses are hanging from the tip of her nose.

But that's not why she's terrifying.

It's the no bullshit, I'm here to challenge everything about you and prove that you're an unfit parent look on her face that has me shuddering and breaking out into a cold sweat.

I plaster on a smile. "Hi. I'm Callan Barrows." I extend my hand which she breaks when she shakes it. Good thing I'm not a surgeon. "Please come in. Katy and I were just about to put on a movie."

A crisp nod, and then she's stepping over the threshold, visibly scrutinizing everything she sees and then she starts making notes on a tablet she pulls out of her worn messenger bag. "How long have you resided in this home?"

My heart starts to pound in my chest and through my ears as I think. I swear, being an intern wasn't this stressful. "About five years now, I believe."

Her lips purse to the side in dismay as if that's the wrong answer. Fuck. Maybe it is. I can't remember now.

I scoot past her, heading for Katy. "Katy, this is Mrs. Bible. She's here to meet with us and will ask us some questions."

Katy gives her the stink-eye. Probably because she's six and the woman smells like cabbage soup and appears to hate everything she sees—including us.

"Hello, Katy. Is that your real name?"

Katy looks at me and then back to the woman in confusion. "Yes."

Mrs. Bible stares skeptically at her. "It's not short for anything?"

Katy shakes her head, and this is not how I thought any of this would go with these check-ins. I thought they meet us, take a look around, check off some things on a form, and go. Katy pulls on the bottom of her pajama shirt, shifting her weight. She doesn't know what to make of this woman and neither do I.

Mrs. Bible turns back to me. "You're a doctor?"

Gulp. "Yes. A physician in the emergency department."

"So that means you're exposed to any patient carrying any disease that walks in through the hospital doors. Is that correct?"

Motherfuck, is she kidding me? "We take universal precautions with all patients to prevent the spreading and transmission of diseases."

"And your shift hours?"

I do my best not to squirm or twitch, but I'm sweating bullets. "It varies, but I've already cut back my hours to accommodate Katy's schedule."

She stares at me for a solid minute before she makes some sort of noise in the back of her throat and then types more into her tablet. Then her eyes are back on me.

"It is my understanding that you're engaged?"

"Yes." The lie burns like acid on my tongue.

"Where is your fiancée?"

Good question. I have no clue. All I know is that she's not here because she never came home after her shift this afternoon at the hospital. In fact, the only times I've seen her since Monday in court have been in class or the emergency department, both places where she completely ignores me. She sneaks in late at night and leaves early in the morning, and she barely speaks to me when I'm able to catch her for two seconds. She's been ignoring my texts or responding with one-word answers.

It's brutal. It's eating me alive actually.

I fucking miss her. I miss her smiles, her teasing, her laughter, the way she looks at me, and a thousand other things. I've spent this week thinking about what Fallon said to me outside the courthouse and I know what I want.

I want her.

But she doesn't want me back—hell, at this point I think she hates my guts and resents me ever entering her life—and that's glaringly obvious.

The only thing that hasn't changed is her relationship with Katy.

Layla picked her up from camp on both Tuesday and Thursday afternoon and the two of them hung out. Layla took Katy to the bookstore at the Prudential Mall and Katy came home with about a dozen books. Layla had told her how reading, getting lost in fictitious worlds, helped her not be so sad and focus on something other than what she was missing.

Katy is flying through books—at the age of six—and I can't say

I'm upset about that at all. I love that Layla still prioritizes Katy. I'm just trying not to feel the afterburn her absence has left on me.

"She's out with friends," I say, hoping my tone is light and casual.

"Out with friends?"

Oh, boy. Mrs. Bible does not approve of that.

"I can call her," I offer hastily, and she gives me a firm nod. Awesome. Now I just have to pray Layla picks up. I pull up her contact info and hit call. It rings and rings and then finally she picks up.

"Callan?" Her sweet voice tinkles in my ear, though wherever she is it's loud and there are a lot of people. "Everything okay?"

"Hey, baby. Yeah, everything's fine. I'm sorry to bother you when you're out with your friends, but Mrs. Bible from social services is here paying us our first visit. Is there any way you can come home early?"

"Oh, hell. Callan, I'm so sorry I'm not there. I'm on my way now. It'll take me no more than fifteen minutes tops."

"Perfect. See you soon, baby. Love you." I disconnect the call and slide my phone back into my pocket. "She's on her way. Would you like something—" *Beep. Beep. Beep. Fire in the kitchen. Beep. Beep. Beep.* "Fuc-dge. The cookies!"

I fly into the kitchen where black smoke is billowing out of the top oven like a chimney. Fuck! I nearly said fuck in front of a woman named Mrs. Bible and now the smoke alarm is blaring, and it won't shut up about a fire in the kitchen, and the cookies are burned beyond recognition, and just *fuck*!

Grabbing an oven mitt, I open the oven, waving away a gust of acrid-smelling smoke, and remove the smoking tray of black bricks. I set it down in the sink and then open the window right above it, waving the smoke in its direction. So much for foolproof.

"I'm sorry!" I call out, frantic and frazzled. Abandoning the window, I go over to the smoke alarm, waving the mitt under it to try and clear the smoke. But because I have everything hardwired, my phone rings in my pocket. "Hello?" I answer.

"This is Alarm Monitoring. We received an alert of a fire in your kitchen. Do you need us to send the fire department and police?"

"No, no. It's just some cookies that I burned." Again. "Everything is fine."

"Okay. Have a wonderful night, Dr. Barrows."

I deflate. "You too." Shoving my phone back in my pocket, I continue to work on the smoke detector until the thing finally shuts up—I swear it takes hours—and then I race back into the family room. Katy is sitting on the sofa, her ears covered and tears in her eyes. Mrs. Bible is still standing in the middle of the goddamn room, staring at me as if I'm the worst guardian in history.

Then again, she's not exactly comforting my kid either.

"Katy, my lady." I scoop her up in my arms and drop us both onto the sofa, tucking her on my lap. "I'm sorry." She didn't cry Monday, but Monday I caught the burnt cookies just before the alarm went off.

"It was loud."

I run my hand down her hair and hug her against my chest. "I know, honey."

"I didn't like the beeping noise."

I nod, rocking her into me as she sniffles. I can only imagine how traumatizing that was for her. The night of the accident was no doubt very loud between the sirens and being in the hospital, where everything beeps and everyone shouts.

"I've got you." I kiss the top of her head, holding her closer. "No more baking cookies."

"Next time we'll just buy them."

I laugh, sitting back and wiping her face. "Fully cooked."

Her head bobs up and down.

"How about some popcorn instead after Mrs. Bible is finished here?"

"Okay."

I hear the front door open and then two seconds later, Layla comes sprinting in. She's wearing black leather pants and a black crop top that dips low in front showing off her cleavage—no bra as always—a good amount of smoky makeup and her hair is down in soft, silky waves. She looks hot and sexy as hell. Like she was out on a date.

My insides plummet into my feet, replaced by a swell of anger rising up from within.

"Hey!" Layla exclaims, treating me to a smile I haven't seen on her all week. "What on earth happened in here?" She takes a couple whiffs of the air, and then her nose scrunches up.

"We burned the cookies," Katy answers.

Layla giggles. "Again? I think we're cookie-baking cursed." She gives me an indulgent wink and then walks over to Mrs. Bible. "Hi. I'm Layla Fritz." She reaches out her hand and grimaces when Ms. Bible shakes it. "It's so nice to meet you. I apologize for not being here when you arrived. It's been a long week of medical school and working at the hospital and I was just down at my cousin Stella's new restaurant. Have you been there? The food is amazing."

The woman blinks about ten thousand times at Layla. "I know your family."

Layla lights up like Times Square. "Oh really? How wonderful." Layla touches Mrs. Bible's arm. "Though I have to say, I'm sadly not surprised considering how many of them work in the medical field." Layla's hand covers her chest. "So heartbreaking." She shakes her head. "You do such important work and we're so grateful you're here checking in and making sure Katy is in the best hands possible."

Layla walks over to me, leaning in and kissing me gently on the lips before she takes the seat beside me and runs her hands down Katy's back.

"What happened, babe? Why the tears?" Layla whispers against Katy.

"The smoke alarm."

"Oh." She flashes me a grim look and then returns to Katy. "I bet that was scary. Glad it's all done." She kisses her forehead and stares at Katy with so much light and love in her eyes that it twists me up more.

My mind is spinning. Thrashing. My heart along with it.

"Well, I think this is enough for my first visit," Mrs. Bible says, cutting into everything. She stares down at her tablet for a moment as if she's reading through her notes, an indiscernible noise in the back of her throat. "Just a few questions before I go. How long have you and Miss Fritz been a couple?"

This is the question I had been hoping to avoid. Because if they investigate this any deeper, they'll discover she was living with Patrick only a few months ago. There are only so many lies we can juggle before they backfire on us.

"It's been... what? A few months or so," Layla says and then laughs. "It's so hard to keep track of when we actually got together versus how long we've wanted to be together. I've known Callan for years. He works with my brother-in-law, Oliver, and I've seen him at charity events hosted by the Abbot Foundation. We've been in each other's lives for a very long time, and I've always secretly been in love with him. But once he told me the feeling was mutual, that was it. We've been full steam ahead since."

"So you've only been together as a couple a few months?"

Shit. Not good.

"Technically, yes," I say slowly, trying to keep my features even. "But when you know, you know." I smile. She doesn't.

Her mouth pinches into a frown. "You both also work at Mass General Hospital?"

More shit. "Layla is only helping out for the summer. She's not an employee of the hospital."

A heavy silence fills the air as this woman studies us. Hard. Like, trying to read every word and nuance in our text. She does something on her tablet and then slides it back into her bag. "I'll be back another time."

"Great," I lie and then hop off the couch and lead her to the door. "Thank you for popping in tonight. Sorry about the alarm. Clearly baking isn't my thing." Ha ha ha. She doesn't laugh with me.

"Good night, Dr. Barrows."

"Good night, Mrs. Bible."

The door shuts behind her, and I lock it, and then my forehead hits the heavy wood and my eyes close. Breathing hard, I rub my fist against my rioting heart.

What do I do, what do I do, what do I do?

I should have never started with this lie. It's only going to be my downfall. My father would be appalled if I told him how I was trying to keep Katy. Then again, my parents aren't here. They're in Florida, practically fucking indifferent as they leave this entirely on my shoulders. I'm the one who has to manage this. I'm the one who is risking everything. I'm the one who could lose Katy.

Me.

And the one woman I *need*, the one woman I freaking *want*, wishes she was anywhere other than here with me.

I hear her footsteps and the words splash past my lips before I can control them. "Were you out on a date?"

"No," Layla says cautiously as if I'm a feral predator. Accurate since that's how I'm feeling right about now. "I was bartending at Stella's new restaurant."

"Why?"

"Because it's the only money I can earn, and I like bartending."

"Right. More tits, more tips," I bite sardonically.

"Callan, I'm sorry I wasn't here tonight. I know you're upset."

If I were a dick, I'd play this off. I'd blow past her as I said something dickish that I'm not even dickish enough to conjure up in my head. Nice guys always finish last, and most times, I don't care about that. I know who I am, and I've always been good with that.

But this woman challenges me in a way no one has before, and I was part of a rock band with four teenage boys for four years. Trust me, you see some stuff when you're on the road.

"If you don't want to wear the ring I know you find so detestable, at least carry it on you so you can slide it on your fucking finger when we have to put on pretenses."

I blow out a breath, needing to rein myself in. Needing to give her the out she might need. I right myself and then stare straight into her eyes. I wish she wasn't as pretty as she is. I wish she didn't look so remorseful.

"If you've changed your mind about being here and being part of this, then you should get your stuff and go. I won't hold it against you. Hell, I wouldn't even blame you. But this in between is killing me, Layla. The ghosting is fucking killing me. It's another burden I can't bear the weight of. I realize we might not have been friends, but I thought we understood each other and had enough respect to be honest. You told me that morning that you wouldn't get weird on me and you wouldn't run, but that's exactly what you're doing. So please, make the decision and live with it."

I plow past her, heading straight for Katy, ready to watch *The Little Mermaid* with my girl. Everything might be falling apart, but at least I have her. For now.

22

L ayla

GUILT SLAMS into my chest like a two-by-four as one wretched feeling after the other slashes at me with the subtlety of a razor. I. Am. A. Bitch. I could have—*and should have*—handled everything so differently. I thought that keeping my distance would keep me safe. I thought being detached and indifferent would protect my heart.

And by doing so, I hurt Callan instead.

And possibly Katy, though she didn't seem upset by me.

I agreed to this. I agreed to all of it. To moving in here and sharing a bed and playing the role I haven't played all that well. Mrs. Bible is no joke, and I could see the fear in Callan's eyes just now. This is bigger than me. Bigger than some feelings I'd rather not tempt out of hibernation.

This is about a little girl, and she is why I'm here.

I can be who they need me to be without giving away my heart. I have that bitch on lockdown anyway.

Peeling myself away from the entryway where Callan left me to lick my wounds like a diseased dog, I sheepishly make my way back into the living room. Only it's empty. I hear Callan and Katy in the kitchen. She's laughing at his latest cookie blunder.

When I came home Monday night around midnight or so, I could smell the charred remains of burned dough and found evidence of the atrocity in the trash.

"Movie theater butter," Katy demands.

"Kettle corn," Callan counters, and I inwardly throw up at that suggestion. What self-respecting person eats kettle corn when going to watch a movie? It should be illegal.

"Illegal?" Callan parrots, and yep, I did it again. Per Stella and Amelia, it's not something new that I do. Usually only when I'm upset or flustered, which lately is often, but not my usual baseline.

They're just so used to it by now that they hardly comment.

I enter the kitchen. "Do you have any Dermabond?" I ask, leaning against the white cabinets and beautiful brushed marble counters across from them.

"Dermabond?" he questions, his eyebrows hitting his hairline in worry as he does a quick scan of my body, likely searching for blood or multiple lacerations.

"Yeah. You know, to glue my mouth shut. It's been getting me in a lot of trouble lately."

His entire countenance darkens, and he quickly goes back to Katy, readily ignoring me. It takes me a moment to grasp the inference behind my words and I smack a hand to my forehead, registering the problem.

"Wait! That's not..." I sigh. And sag. "That's not how I meant it. I didn't mean it like I shouldn't have agreed—"

He shakes his head at me, cutting me off, visibly angry. His hands grip the edge of the counter, and he glances down at the stone between them. Finally, he blows out a breath and slowly raises his face until his eyes lock with mine.

For a long, pulsingly tense moment, his gaze holds mine, causing my heart rate to spike and my body to heat. "Solve the argument for us?" he asks, those deep blue eyes glimmering at me, and my knees practically give out.

"Movie theater butter. All the way."

Katy bounces in her stool, pointing at Callan and laughing. "I told you!"

He groans in defeat. "Fine. You both win. Butter it is." His eyes meet mine again. "Layla, do you want to watch *The Little Mermaid* with us, or do you have to get back to the bar since I pulled you from your shift?"

The disdainful taunt in his tone is unmistakable, but it's no less than what I deserve.

"I'd love to watch with you. I'll just scoot upstairs and throw on my pj's." There. I've officially impaled myself on my sword. Sorta.

I turn to go when Callan calls out my name, stopping me. I spin back around, and he sighs, not following my name up with anything. It's heavy, and a bit resigned, and also a little lost—and a lot scared.

Tonight rattled him and I've only added to his mounting stress.

"Thanks for coming tonight."

"Sure thing. I'll meet you in the TV room." I smile softly and then flee the kitchen, needing a moment to catch my breath and realign my heart to its normal rhythm.

The TV room is actually most of the third floor of Callan's house. It's a theater room complete with a super comfy sectional that has pullout bays that turn into recliners. The room is loaded with speakers, a bar that has an ice maker, a refrigerator, and shades that cover the floor-to-ceiling windows with a simple touch of a button.

It's essentially a bachelor pad.

A nice one though and I throw no shade at it. Oliver had a setup like this when I first met him. He was living in a Ritz-Carlton residence and had a concierge who legit used to bring me real movie theater popcorn and candy from the theater around the corner. For a fourteen-year-old kid who hadn't been spoiled a day in her life, it was a dream come true.

I remember wishing every night for Amelia to marry Oliver.

He adored her and she deserved to be treated like a queen. I remember wishing for all her worries—worries I know I was a huge part of—to disappear into the void of money and love. And they did. She had the fairy tale. Callan's stress and worries aren't lost on me. I just got too absorbed in myself to remember them.

Now it's time I play the role of his fairy godmother and grant him his wishes.

I change into a hoodie and a pair of heavenly soft joggers and then weave my way upstairs.

Callan jogs up the steps, Katy on his hip and the bowl of buttered popcorn in his other hand. My ovaries simultaneously explode and laugh mockingly at me. This is why I haven't been here. Every time I see him, my pussy goes from intentionally dormant to unintentionally active in a nanosecond.

It's biological.

A gorgeous, muscular man who knows all the best ways to fuck you and is also an amazing father figure to his orphaned niece is potent. It's female porn. Especially when his forearms are on full display and his biceps are making his soft cotton shirt their bitch. Plus, he's angry with me, and while that shouldn't be an aphrodisiac, it is.

What can I say?

The human psyche doesn't always make a ton of sense or act in our best interest.

He sets Katy down and she scurries over to her favorite spot, grabbing the *Frozen* blanket he keeps up here for her, and burrowing beneath it.

Callan picks his seat and I pick mine, and he puts on the movie and it's all so... tense. Especially because motherfucking Eric from *The Little Mermaid* looks like Callan. I never noticed it before, but yeah, he totally does, and now I have a new Disney movie crush, so thanks for that.

Katy is between us, the massive bowl of popcorn on her lap that all of us are digging into.

"Do you have a boyfriend?" he asks, leaning over Katy to whisper in my ear. He extends his arm along the upper edge of the sofa until his hand hovers on the leather near the shoulder farthest from him.

"What?" My head whips in his direction. I hadn't so much as cast him a second glance because hello, I have him in cartoon form on the screen, which somehow feels safer than the live-action version. But now the man himself is demanding my full focus. "N-no. You know I don't."

"A lover then?"

He's too cool. Too casual. And I'm too flustered.

"No."

He smirks and his finger snatches up a lock of my hair, twirling it around. "Good. So I don't have to worry about you breaking our agreement when you're out?"

Damn, jealous him is turning me on. Doesn't he understand straddling him is off the table? "No. I told you I wouldn't do that. This may be fake, but I stick to my word."

He releases my hair and his hand swoops around us and taps the ring I placed on my finger. I don't even know why I did it. Mrs. Bible is gone.

"If I could, I'd glue this diamond to your hand."

His hand swoops back around us, latching onto the back of the hoodie I stole from him. We've been playing a game with it. I leave it on the bed and when I come home, it magically smells like him again. Clearly, he puts it on, wears it for a bit to imprint his scent on it, and then takes it off again and leaves it for me. I knew he had recently worn it and I couldn't resist. I thought he'd find it cheeky. Now I'm reconsidering that line of thinking.

His eyes meet mine in the darkness of the room. Fierce. Intoxicating.

"Do you know why I want to glue that diamond to your hand and why I make sure that sweatshirt smells like me?"

I shake my head and gulp at the same time.

"Not because I dare to imagine that you're mine to possess, and not because I don't trust your word. But because I like that you smell like me. I like that you want to be surrounded by the way I smell. I like that if that rock is on your hand, it means you're off-limits. It's the only thing making me sane right now because I know exactly what every man who saw you tonight was thinking, and it pisses me off almost as much as you ghosting me all week has. I know I shouldn't tell you that. I know we're keeping it fake and casual—but I'm having a hellacious time feeling casual right now, Layla."

It ends there and he forces me to watch a cartoon version of himself. All the smiles. All the dimples. All the longer-on-top dark hair brushed back from his forehead. All the moments where he gets his act together and risks it all for Ariel.

The movie ends and then both of us glance down to find Katy asleep, the empty bowl listing in her lap. Callan takes it and places it on the coffee table and then lifts her into his arms. I quickly stand, following them and grabbing her discarded mermaid, and tucking it against her chest.

Callan carries her downstairs and right into her bedroom. "We didn't brush her teeth," he muses.

"I won't tell Mrs. Bible about it if you won't."

"She was a lot, right?" He smirks at me. "It wasn't just me?"

"No. She was a lot. But I think that's in her job description."

His head jockeys conciliatorily.

"Night, Ladybug." He kisses Katy's forehead and then the tip of her nose as he tucks her in, making sure the blanket is high up on her shoulders, and I force myself to look away. Trying not to grow emotionally attached to them is the equivalent of standing before the firing squad and hoping not to get hit.

He turns on her night-light and then he's leading me out of her bedroom, right into his with a firm grasp on my hand. He walks me toward the bed until the backs of my knees hit the mattress and bend, forcing me to sit.

He kneels before me, putting us at eye level. "I'm not sure what I have the right to ask and what I don't. This situation I've put us in is precarious. It's a lie. A lie I've sucked you into. I know that. You haven't asked for anything from me, and I'm asking for everything from you. But fuck, Layla, I don't know how to talk to you anymore."

His hands run through his hair. He's out of sorts, but so honest in how he speaks, it unsettles me.

"I know."

He shakes his head as if I'm not getting it. "I felt like we were in a good place and then you flipped a switch the moment you moved in here. If I did something or said something wrong, I need you to tell me. Because Mrs. Bible is coming three more times. And tonight didn't go well." His lips flatten into a thin line and he levels me with a look I can't ignore. "I'm scared this will all come crashing down on me and I'll lose Katy."

Staring into his oh-so-blue eyes, I reach up and run my fingers through his hair, feeling the soft, thick strands. I'm touching him and I shouldn't be, but I've missed him. I have. He's right. We used to be able to talk about anything it felt like, and then I ruined it all.

"You won't lose Katy. I got..." I lick my lips searching for the right word. I don't want Callan to know I'm fighting feeling something with him and how that's affecting me. "Spooked," I finish. "You put that ring on my finger and I moved in here and it all happened so fast. Then that same morning, Patrick showed back up at school equipped with his favorite mind games and it was too much. It just sent me over the edge."

His expression darkens and his hands move to my thighs, holding them firmly, almost possessively. "What sort of mind games?"

I shake my head, waving that off. I shouldn't have mentioned that. I don't want to talk—or think about Patrick. I just want to move on, but that was the tipping point for me with Callan and all this.

"It's nothing. I dealt with it, and I'm hoping he's gone from my life for good this time. You're my professor and a quasi-boss at work, but I care about you, and I care about Katy, and I had to figure out how to balance all that. I thought creating space here would be the answer, but it wasn't and I'm sorry. I didn't go about it the right way."

"Why didn't you say anything to me?" He squeezes my thighs, imploring me.

"Because you already have enough on your plate without me adding to it and the problem was my own to deal with."

"Yes, but it's easier if I know what's going on in your pretty head because then maybe I can help. I want to help you, Layla. You're doing so much for me, and I don't want you suffering from this in any way. We have three months left on this gig. Can you do this with me in an honest and open way?"

My nails scrape up his scalp and his eyes close for a moment, his lips parting. It shouldn't be this easy or this comfortable to touch each other, but it is. Even the talking is easy. He's so... rational. And smart. And passionate. And sexy. And fun. And caring. And just... good.

He's all the things, checks every box, and every time I see him, I'm reminded of that.

I'm reminded that he's the sort of man I want for my future. I'm just not ready for him yet. If this were five years from now, I'd fall into his bed—and into his heart—and I wouldn't hesitate or think twice about it.

But for now...

"Yes," I tell him. "I can do this with you." This time I mean it.

23

C allan

"ONE, TWO, THREE, GO!" Layla squeals and both she and Katy scramble to flip and set the turret-shaped mold before half the sand it's filled with pours out. Layla shifts it ever so slightly so that it's beside the main part of the castle, and then she pats the top of it. She looks at Katy. "Ready?"

Katy nods firmly. "Ready. Can I do it?"

Layla scoots back a little, giving Katy more room to work. "Go for it, babe. Slide it off slowly and let's see how we did."

Katy crouches up onto her knees, her entire body caked in sand. Using both hands, she slowly pulls the mold straight up, and there is the other turret of the castle, perfect except for one small missing chunk of sand.

Katy beams a smile. "We should have brought my princess figurines. That way they could live in the castle."

"Oh, that's a good call. Next time for sure. Right?" Layla checks with me as I pretend to read my book instead of watching them play and dig and create in the sand.

"Next time for sure," I agree, squinting against the sun.

After last night's fiasco, Layla and I seem to have worked things out. We talked and then fell asleep side by side in bed, and then this morning Katy woke up and asked if we could go to the beach so she could practice becoming a mermaid. I told her yes, and shockingly Layla agreed to join us.

It's hot out here. The July sun is high in the cloudless, pale blue sky, but neither Layla nor Katy seems bothered by the heat. Or the crowds considering the beach is packed. This is my favorite beach. It's about forty-five minutes north of Boston, but it's the one my parents used to take Declan and me to when we were kids.

We weren't like some of my friends whose parents had houses on Cape Cod or Martha's Vineyard. We'd pack into the car with umbrellas, blankets, towels, and coolers of food and drinks and would spend all day in the sand and waves. Katy loves to do the exact same thing. Even if I force her to wear more sunscreen than is likely necessary along with an SPF 50 bathing suit and a sun hat.

Layla sits back on her haunches and appraises their handiwork. The woman has been on her knees, bent over, with her ass in the air, cleavage on full display as she and Katy built this massive sandcastle. I've had a raging boner in my freaking swim trunks that hide nothing all damn morning. It's why I haven't gotten up to help much.

That and I love watching the two of them together.

Katy is missing Willow something fierce. Her therapist told me everything Katy is experiencing is normal, and that there is no rushing this, and there is no cure. She's missing a piece that nothing and no one else can fill. This will be a lifelong heartache for her.

Layla knows this better than anyone. It's what makes her so perfect for this.

It's also what connects the two of them together.

They seem to have an unspoken language already and I know Katy confides in her and tells her things that she doesn't tell me or her therapist.

"I feel like it's missing something," Layla finally declares, scrutinizing the sandcastle like it's an objet d'art.

"A moat?" Katy asks, mocking Layla's pose and expression.

"Yes! Katy, that is totally what this needs to be the best sandcastle ever. A moat is brilliant." Layla reaches out her hand to her and Katy high-fives it. "How about you dig the moat and I'll go fill the bucket with water to bring back?"

"Okay. But after that, I want to go swimming. I'll never be good at being a mermaid if I don't practice my swims and dives."

"Makes total sense. You dig and I'll be back in a jiffy."

Layla bounces up to her feet and heads for the water with a lime-green bucket in her hand.

"Having fun?" I ask now that it's just the two of us.

Katy is too busy furiously digging the perfect moat to acknowledge me as she answers. "Can I paint Layla a picture to go with her new surprise?"

"Absolutely. We'll have it framed and put on the wall."

She nods like that's an acceptable answer.

"So... are you having fun?" I press.

"Do you think Mommy and Daddy are watching us today since there are no clouds in the sky?"

Wow. What an astute question. "I think they are. I think they wanted you to have the perfect beach day to practice becoming a mermaid. Ladybug, just because they're not here with you every day doesn't mean they're not watching you and loving you. You'll always be their girl, honey. Always."

"Uncle Cal, I want to be a mermaid, but I think I also might want to be a bird so I can fly high up into the sky and find them in heaven."

Motherfucker.

"Ladybug, let's stick to the water for now. We can work on flying when you get older. A bird can't fly that high, but I promise you, they're looking down on you from heaven and are so proud of you."

Two minutes later, Layla comes running back with the water, and I swear she's doing that just to torture me. It's like *Baywatch,* only she's a million times hotter—and less fake—than Pamela Anderson ever was.

"Got the water." She bends and pours the water into the moat, and we all watch as it fills the canal. "Perfect. This is the best sand-castle I've ever built."

"I built one with Mommy once. It was twice this size. Then Daddy tripped and stomped his foot in it."

"Really? That's hilarious." Layla laughs loudly instead of being apprehensive the way I am every time Katy talks about her parents. "What a funny and special memory that is. One you'll think about every time you build a new sandcastle."

"Yeah. I guess I will," Katy acknowledges with a slight smile.

I need to learn how to do this better. I can be the fun uncle every day of the week, but being the parent is fucking hard. I never know what to say or if I'm doing the right thing.

Parenting needs to come with a manual, or at least a reference guide.

We expect our parents to be perfect, but we forget that they're human just as we are. Still, that doesn't help me in court and that doesn't help me when I don't get it right.

"You know, I didn't go to the beach a lot with my parents," Layla continues. "My mom had red hair and very fair skin like my sister. So whenever they'd go in the sun, even with sunscreen, they'd turn into lobsters." Layla makes pinchers with both of her hands and pretends to snap them at Katy.

Katy giggles, jumping away from them with a squeal, and I relax. "Like Sebastian."

"Like Sebastian!" Layla points at Katy. "Only Sebastian is a crab, not a lobster."

Katy stands and does a little body wiggle, shaking off some of the excess sand sticking to her. "Why did the crab cross the ocean?"

"Why?" Layla asks, smiling in rapt attention.

"Because he's a crab!"

Lamest joke ever, but I start laughing my ass off, and so does Layla, because the way Katy delivers it is pure gold.

"Water!" Katy runs toward the ocean and I follow after her. Layla joins us and right before Katy hits the wet sand, I grab her hand and walk with her.

"Murder, that's cold," I hiss between my teeth, grimacing as the frigid waters of the Atlantic come racing up the sand and splashing over my feet and up my shins.

Katy belts out a high-pitched scream, the bottom half of her bathing suit bearing the brunt of the wave. "Deeper," she urges.

"Ladybug, there is only so deep in I'm willing to go."

"You mean because you're afraid your balls will turn into frozen cocktail olives?" Layla whispers teasingly so only I can hear.

I throw her a side-eye, doing a quick covert glance at her in her bikini as I do. "One hundred percent accurate."

I get a crooked smile in return. "You know I saw that."

"What?" I ask innocently.

"Uh-huh. Women always know when a man is checking us out."

I shrug unrepentantly, giving her the same once over again, only this time not so covertly since I've already been busted. She has to be high if she thinks I haven't been checking her out all damn day.

"I like the color of your bikini is all. Red looks good on you."

And sexy as fuck. Triangles cover her pussy and tits, all held to her body by string. Her blonde hair is up in a ponytail that's pulled through the back of her Red Sox cap and white reflective sunglasses cover her eyes. She's my teenage dream. Everything from the sports hat to the body to the girl is my fantasy come to life.

I was smart enough to leave my sunglasses and Boston Rebels hat on my beach chair, having been to the ocean several times with Katy in the past. The girl gets everything wet. I have no idea how she does it, but no matter what, it happens without fail.

"Uncle Cal, just a little more," Katy protests, calling me away from the siren beside me. "You don't have to hold my hand. I'm not a baby."

"Fine. But you are to be no more than two feet away from me at all times," I warn.

Katy rolls her eyes at me. "Like, duh." She releases my hand and wades into the ocean a little deeper, clearly undisturbed by the cold water.

I blink about ten thousand times and then twist toward Layla. "When did that start?"

Layla giggles at my expression. "I think I was about her age when I learned the magnificent art of eye-rolling. She likely learned it at camp."

"Fantastic," I deadpan, watching Katy cup water in her hands and then launch it into the air sending sparkles of water every which way.

But now I have a serious problem.

"When did you get your nipples pierced?" I ask, stealing another glance at the outlines of barbells through her bikini top.

The diamond stud in her nose ring sparkles against the sunlight as she smiles. "The day after I moved in. You mentioned that morning how you're not a pierced nipple sort of guy, and I thought to myself, you know, I'm a pierced nipple sort of girl. So I went and did it."

"I realize I'm not allowed to care or be jealous, but is it bad if I admit that I'm annoyed that someone touched your breasts and nipples?" Someone who wasn't me.

"Actually, I drove up to your friend Lenox's place and had them done."

"What?!" I bellow, causing a few people walking by to stare strangely at me. My head fully snaps in her direction, my body wired up until I catch the amusement on her face. "You're fucking with me?"

She adjusts the brim of her hat, lowering it a bit to cover more of her face. "Of course, I'm fucking with you. He would have told you by now, wouldn't he have? Did you think he'd do that?"

I hesitate as I return to watching Katy play in the ocean. I mean, on the one hand, I think he would have told me, but on the other, maybe not because he knows I would have been jealous as fuck even if I know he'd never cross that line with her. He mostly inks people, but he does know how to pierce, and I know they do it in his shop.

"He would have done a good job for you, so now I'm not sure what to say."

She pats my arm in a placating way. "Well, I wouldn't have done that. Talk about awkwardness. The *woman*," she emphasizes, still visibly laughing at me, "who did it is very married—to a guy."

"Do they hurt?" *Are they sore? Tender? Sensitive? Tell me all about them or better yet show me.*

"Not so much anymore. The first few days they did."

"You know you're driving me crazy right now, right?"

She rocks forward onto the balls of her feet, staring straight out at the water. "Yep. But you already know what the sight of you shirtless does to me, so we're probably about even right now. All look and no touch make Callan and Layla horny-ass bitches. It be what it be, my friend. We are stuck in a sexless paradigm."

"At least we're self-aware," I quip.

"Uncle Cal!" Katy cries out even though she's practically within grabbing distance in front of me. "Watch me dive."

She spins and gives me her back as she reaches her hands over her head. Just as a rolling wave comes straight for her, she dives over it into the water. A couple of seconds later, she emerges, flipping her hair back the way Ariel did in the movie, a beaming smile on her face, and my heart clangs in my chest. It breaks me in two that Dec and Willow will never get to see any of this.

"That was amazing!" I exclaim, clapping my hands. "You know, when you get to be a bit older, we can teach you how to snorkel and swim with flippers."

"I only want to swim with fins," she informs me, but moves on as she stands and does it all over again with the next wave.

"Is it sexist if I say girls are trouble?"

Layla laughs. "I was, and I find it to be a compliment, so no. Actually, I'm not even sure I was trouble until I was sixteen. Then I was trouble, but good trouble."

"What does good trouble mean?" I ask, glancing in her direction, down to her tits, and then back out to sea.

I catch her smirking out of the corner of my eye. "I was a straight-A student and never wanted to upset or worry Amelia since she had already been through enough, but I liked coloring outside the lines whenever I could. I still do for that matter."

"Hence the metal. But no tattoos," I note.

She shakes her head. "Those are forever, or at least a lot of work to get rid of, and I like my skin as it is."

"Me too," springs past my lips without any filter, but before she can comment or tell me to quit it with all the boob staring and open innuendo, a warm, wet *splat* smashes onto my shoulder. "The fuc—"

"Uncle Cal! A seagull pooped on your shoulder." Katy's arms wrap around her tummy as she breaks out into a cackle of laughter.

Sure enough, there's a splatter of white goop on me. "Gross."

Layla giggles beside me. "It's good luck."

I turn to her, incredulous. "Why do people always say that? There is nothing lucky about a bird pooping on my shoulder. Now I have to go all the way in the water."

"You sure do." She's enjoying the hell out of this.

"You know, if I have to go in, so do you."

"What—" Only her words cut off, morphing into a scream as I loop my arms around her waist and lift her into the air. Without warning, I drop us both straight into the water. We go rolling in, hitting the sand beneath the icy water because we're not in all that deep.

Christ, that's cold.

Just as our heads spring up, both of us taking in air, a wave slams into our faces, knocking us back. We both go under, and I firm up my grip on Layla, pushing off the sand with my feet, forcing us up and back out of the water.

Layla comes up spitting water at me, right in the face. "That was so not cool!" she yells, disentangling herself from my grip so she can cup water in her hand and splash it at me.

I wipe it away and make sure my shoulder is also clear of the bird poop.

"You're no fun," I toss back at her, splashing her with a handful of my own water. "I thought you said you were trouble."

"You wanna see trouble?" She taunts as she moves her salt-coated sunglasses onto her soaked hat. She takes a step back from me and grabs hold of Katy's hand as if she means business now. Katy is still laughing her little brains out as if all of this is the most entertaining thing she's ever seen. "Come here, Katy. Let's get him!"

The two of them team up on me, both charging me with kicks and handfuls of water, dousing me further. My arms fly up protectively in a futile attempt to stop the onslaught of frigid water, and in doing so, I lose sight. A tactical error I should have known better than to make since Katy is now climbing up the front of me and Layla is climbing up my back, both pressing their cold flesh against mine.

I band one arm around Katy and then reach behind to grab Layla, pinching her ass.

"Jerk!" she barks in my ear, only there is no bite to it.

"We got you!" Katy exalts, doing an awesome impression of a spider monkey. With them both wrapped around me, I storm us out of the water, back up onto the warm sand, and over to our setup of towels, beach chairs, and umbrellas.

Katy slides off me, immediately grabbing her towel and wrapping it around herself, but I don't let Layla get off that easy. In a flash, I whip her around my body like we're doing a dance straight out of the fifties and when she's in front of me, I take her down for a second time, pinning her to one of the towels we have laid out.

"Ah! Your chest and swim trunks are so cold," she cries beneath me, laughing as she tries to push me away.

I press us in deeper and nuzzle my face in her neck, unable to stop it. Her hand presses into the middle of my back, her fingers splaying out, and at the same time, we both stop fighting and squirming and just lie like this—layered, connected.

"You ruined my hat," she accuses.

I grin against her skin. "I'll buy you a new one." I plant my hands into the towel and push myself up, gazing down at her. We're both smiling at each other, breathing a little hard from all the exertion. "Did I hurt your nipples?"

A laugh belts past her lips. "No. I think they're fine."

I glance down between us, noting her hard nipples and tempting barbells pressed against her wet suit before I look back up at her. "I could check them. Make sure there's no tearing or signs of infection. I am a doctor, you know."

She rolls her eyes at me. "You're pushing your luck awfully hard for someone who said bird poop wasn't lucky."

"But you said it was," I counter.

"Uncle Cal, I'm hungry," Katy declares, going over to one of the chairs, taking a seat, and digging into the cooler we have without even waiting on me to help her.

I groan, and Layla gives me a playful smirk, pushing me by the shoulders so I'll climb off her. I sit up, taking her hand and helping her do the same.

"Guess you were right. Bird poop is not lucky after all, Uncle Cal." She pats my shoulder as she stands to join Katy. "Sucks to be you, I guess."

She has no idea.

24

L ayla

"YOUR PATIENT IS EXSANGUINATING, and her vitals are tanking. What are you going to do?"

Fuck, I hate this woman. I've always hated this woman.

"Stop her bleeding." *Clearly.* I inwardly snap that last part. I press in on the profusely bleeding wound with a massive wad of gauze, but that's like sticking a piece of wadded-up chewing gum to fix a leak in the Hoover Dam. The wound overflows with red, sticky stuff that has no end in sight. My own pulse hammers in my chest as sweat coats my forehead, but I'm riding that high again. The one I can't seem to get enough of.

"What are your core focuses?" Dr. Swanson stares impassively at me with a self-righteousness I can't stand.

Not killing you with my imaginary scalpel.

"ABCs," I reply crisply. "Always." I know this.

"And those are?"

"Airway, breathing, circulation," I grit out. "She's bleeding and needs the OR. I can't fix a gunshot wound to the stomach, but my plan is to stabilize her so she's able to make it up to the OR alive."

"And how do you intend to do that?" she challenges with a smooth voice, though I can tell she thinks I'm about to crumble like a chip. Not gonna happen.

I take a steadying breath and force more of my weight into it to apply better pressure. "Secure her airway and stop or slow the bleeding while repleting what she's been losing with IV fluids and blood. She needs to be intubated and have a central line placed."

"Excellent. Philips and Brody, care to jump in and secure the patient's airway and start a central line just as Miss Fritz directed? Layla, you continue to staunch the bleeding, but feel free to direct your peers since you're the one running this trauma."

Philips and Brody come in, and between the three of us, we manage to stabilize the patient—well, our simulator patient— enough to get them up to the OR. Last time I worked this hard at building up a sweat, at least I got an orgasm out of it.

"Good work today, everyone. Dr. Barrows asked me to remind you all that you have case studies due tomorrow."

I groan as I twist my back to work out my stiff muscles. Between the simulator lab and working in the emergency room and the freaking stress that is my life, I'm a ball of tension and knotted sinews. The good news is I still have Stella's cooking and the homework I plan to do at her restaurant to look forward to.

After our heart-to-heart last week and then going to the beach on Saturday, things have been easier between Callan and me. I've come home at a reasonable hour, and I haven't been dodging him. Not too much at least. I still don't think spending extra time with him is a good thing for either of us because we have so much freaking sexual tension when we're together, and I do try to avoid that.

Especially when I'm in the house.

Callan, too, must recognize this because he doesn't push and he's great with giving me space. I've all up but taken over his office and he seems fine with that.

Other than some easy flirting and lingering heated looks that set my pulse on edge, we're managing. Wanting the hell out of each other while doing a pathetic job of hiding it—but managing. My issue stems from the more I think about him and the more I see him, the more I like him. So I actively don't think about him and I passively don't see him more than required, and that's that.

I can do the duck and weave for another two and a half months.

Stepping outside, I take a deep inhale through my nose. Freshly mowed grass and summer. I exhale a heavy, exhausted breath just as my phone buzzes in my hand.

Stella: What do you want for dinner or are you going to order from the menu?

Me: The menu is fine. You don't have to make me anything special.

Stella: Damn, I was hoping you changed your mind and were going home to the hot doctor who is waiting for you with adoring googly eyes.

Me: He's not waiting for me, nor does he have adoring googly eyes.

Stella: Any time you want to get off your crazy raft and stop floating down the river of denial, let me know.

Me: Quit meddling like your grandmother or I'll give you a one-star on Yelp.

Stella: Ha! Cute, but you'd never bite the hand that literally feeds you. See you soon, slutwagon.

Me: See you soon, whorebag.

I skip down the steps of the building, but before I can get very far, I feel someone grab my hand and then give it a tug. A scream starts to peel past my lungs when another hand covers my mouth.

"Shhhh," Callan breathes in my ear. "You want to get us caught? Come on."

His hand falls away from my mouth and then he's pulling me again, forcing me to race after him in the other direction from the T.

"What are we doing?"

"Going out for sushi."

"Huh?" I jerk on his hand, forcing him to stop. "Where's Katy?"

He gives me a dimpled smile that makes my belly swoop. "At a sleepover."

"What? With whom?"

He drags me over to the side of the building so we're not standing out in the open. He shrugs up a shoulder. "I don't know. Some girl from her camp."

"What do you mean some girl from her camp?" I squawk incredulously, my hand flying about. "How can you not know whose house your kid is sleeping at?"

He chuckles, stepping in closer to me, his hand still holding mine, his thumb grazing along the inside of my wrist. "Holly St. Nick, and yes, that's her real name. She's six. Her birthday is January fifth. Her mother's name is Noelle St. Nick. They live on the corner of Beacon and Arlington. The mother is an heiress from New York but works at a nonprofit for children's literacy. She has a clean record with not even a speeding ticket to her name. No boyfriend or daddy and Holly was the product of a sperm donation."

I shake my head. "How do you know all that?"

"I had Lenox run a background check." His smirk grows lopsided, the setting sun casting a pinkish-orange glow behind him. "But your confidence in me is overwhelming. Truly, I'm touched." He pokes the center of my chest with his free hand. "Did you actually believe that I'd let Katy go off with someone I don't know?"

I ignore that because, no, I didn't. "Lenox can run background checks?"

He steps in even closer to me. So close I can smell his cologne and see every beautiful fleck of blue in his eyes. So close I have to crane my neck to see him.

"I won't tell you all the things Lenox can do or you'd never sleep through the night again. Just know he's a scary force of computer nature, and I'm glad he's on my side." He rocks back on his heels and then forward until his chest brushes mine. He tugs on my hair, looping it around his finger. "So back to that sushi."

"Are you asking me out on a date?"

"Most definitely. But if you're more comfortable, we can simply call it me taking advantage of a child-free night. I hear single parents don't get a ton of those."

I squint, forcing my lips into a hard line so I don't smile. "Are you hitting on me?"

"That depends on your definition of hitting on you and whether or not you're against the notion."

I make a disagreeable sound even though my heart isn't totally sold on it. "Why the sudden change? We agreed to no nookie."

"Never in my life have I ever uttered the word *nookie*. I missed you today. I want to have dinner with you. Simple as that."

Swoon! Fucking motherfucking swoon! Sexy bastard. The truth is, I've missed him too. "Are you trying to break my rules?"

"Again, that depends on your definitions and willingness. The word *break* is a bit harsh, don't you think? I'm merely suggesting creating amendments. I am your fiancé." His gaze pins to mine, unblinking.

"Fake fiancé," I remind him.

"True, but practice makes perfect."

Ugh. He's so damn cute. "What kind of amendments are you proposing?"

"You're asking an awful lot of questions." He tugs on that lock of hair he's still playing with. "I thought you were supposed to be the wild, adventurous one in this relationship."

"Just answer me," I demand.

"Right now, I'm only asking to take you out for dinner," he says without missing a beat. "Sushi is your favorite and I know you can't say no to it."

Damn him. He's right. I can't say no to it. I'm also finding it more and more impossible to say no to *him*. I'm not sure I even want to.

"Sushi is also your favorite," I toss back at him.

"True. We have so much in common. I'm glad you pointed that out."

He pauses, humor dancing in his every feature, but beneath it, there's a vulnerability that tugs at me. It's as if I can feel his nerves, hear his heart racing. He's worried about being here, flirting with me, and asking me to dinner.

"So... do I get a date with my stunning fiancée?"

I hesitate.

"Don't say no, Layla. That's the easy response. Challenge me. Challenge yourself. See where it can lead you. I promise you won't bottom out. Not with me."

My heart gallops in my chest at the way he says that with such fucking sincerity. He twists me up and spins me around, and I can't help but love every second of the ride with him. It's when the ride ends and I'm dizzy and ready to hurl that worries me.

I scan his face, knowing I should say no. A date is a slippery slope. But that not-so-well-hidden vulnerability is a powerful weapon I'm helpless against. The man makes it so damn impossible not to like him.

"Is Katy really at a sleepover?"

"Yep. When the mom called to ask, Katy screamed, 'YES!' at the top of her lungs and started jumping up and down so high I thought she might burst through the ceiling. The mom knows about Katy's night terrors, and I've told both the mom and Katy to call me at any hour for anything. Incidentally, the mom also invited me for a sleep-over tonight, but since I'm a taken man, I declined."

"She what?!" I shriek, my spine snapping straight, my eyes narrowing, and my hands balling up into tiny fists. I want to kick her ass. "What kind of woman does that?"

He unrolls my fingers, relacing our hands together. His other hand drags along my cheek, his smile softening. "You have no idea how much I love that you're jealous."

"I'm not jealous," I snap, shoving him away because his touch makes me shudder and right now, I don't want to shudder. I want to be angry. "I'm just... indignant. And incredulous."

His shoulder hitches up. "It's okay to be jealous. I want to kill every man who looks at you. Especially Patrick." His jaw clenches and Patrick's name comes out as a slur.

"Well, I'm not jealous," I press emphatically, wanting to drive that home because I'm not. Even though the notion of him being jealous makes me inadvertently smile and squirm. I redirect him away from that train of thought. "Are you sure you can trust a woman like that to watch Katy for the night?"

He crowds me some more, that fierceness slipping back into flirtation. "I think Katy's going to be just fine. It'll be good for her even. So... sushi? You still haven't given me an answer." He cocks his head, making some of his slightly too-long-on-top hair flop onto his forehead.

This man is my fucking kryptonite.

I shake my head, clearing all that away. "I can't have sushi with you."

"Why not?" he persists.

Why not? I have reasons why not, but with him this close and smelling this good—and giving me that devil-may-care look—I'm having trouble remembering my reasons.

Oh! "I'm supposed to go to Stella's restaurant for dinner."

"Which you can do another night. Next?"

"I have a massive case study to complete because my professor is a dick and assigned it today and made it due tomorrow."

"He doesn't sound like a dick. He sounds like an amazing professor, and you should consider yourself fortunate that you're his student and able to benefit from his expert tutelage. But I heard this case study is hard, and lucky for you, I'm a doctor. You can bounce your thoughts off me while we eat. I can't do more than that for you because that would be cheating and wrong. To make up for that, I bet this amazing professor would allow you to borrow a particular sweatshirt he may have worn earlier today."

I grumble.

"Now that that's all settled, let's go."

He lands a smack on my lips and then twists our hands and takes off at a run again, weaving us this way and that. I can't help but laugh, even though I'm trying to fight it. He's all smiles and boyishness, and he came here for me because he wants to have dinner with me. I've been fighting him, and I need to keep that up, but he makes it impossible to do that.

Especially when he's like this.

So... irresistible.

An hour and a half later, we're sitting in his office after having eaten take-out sushi—my demand—while he reads a book on freaking parenting after loss, and I work on this case study that is no joke.

"When you created this, did you orgasm over the prospect of torturing your students?" I ask, frustration bleeding from my voice as I stare at my notes that don't add up to a whole lot. Something is missing.

"Orgasm? No. I only do that at night when my beautiful fiancée is asleep in our bed."

My head flies in his direction, my eyes wide. He doesn't so much as spare me a glance.

"This is a real case, Layla," he continues without missing a beat. "A real case I had as a resident. A real case that will be similar to the ones you'll face and have to solve as a doctor. I can give you easy, but that won't help you grow or learn as a provider. Second-years start their clerkships in less than two months. I'm giving you a leg up as I intend to have you all do these once a week."

I roll my eyes and grumble under my breath. "I don't want easy, and I love the challenge, but you gave us one night."

"That's all I had to figure it out as the resident on the case. One night. My attending wanted the patient discharged because he felt it was cut and dry and I didn't. Imagine the patient is before you and this is the only information you have because that's how it will be. One patient in front of you with only the information at your fingertips and you're expected to diagnose and either fix them or save them."

He's right. This is what I've been training for. What I've always wanted to do.

"Fine." I turn back to my laptop, reading through everything I have.

Suddenly, I hear him set his book down and slide in behind me. We had dinner together and I didn't make a thing about it. We talked and laughed, and it was a date. It was. I know it was. He made sure I felt that too, and I didn't stop it because I *liked* him wanting it to be one.

But now I've removed my hoodie—well, his hoodie—and I'm only wearing my Red Sox cropped T-shirt that was once Amelia's. She decided it was somehow unlucky, so now it's dead to her. The woman is more superstitious than any player ever could be.

I digress. Or maybe I'm simply distracted because the shirt is soft and old, and his strong, warm hands are under it. Going up and up and up as his thumbs and fingers rove circles into the flesh of my back.

My head lolls back and I moan. "How did you know my back was a hot mess?"

"I can tell you're tense." He continues to massage me under my shirt as he shifts in behind me, adjusting so his legs are straddling me from behind. "Talk it out with me, Layla."

Oh, say my name like that again. Pant it against my ear.

"You expect me to concentrate when you're doing that to me?"

"I can stop."

I give him a menacing side-eye. "Do and die. Keep going. I'll talk."

"Tell me about the case as if you're presenting the patient to me first."

"This feels like a trap."

"It's not," he assures me. "If anything, it's good practice."

"Six-year-old female presented to the emergency room accompanied by her mother, complaining of fevers of unknown origin times two weeks, abdominal pain especially in the right lower quadrant, and lethargy. The emergency room worked her up including a chest x-ray that was negative and an abdominal ultrasound. Ultrasound showed inflamed loops of bowel in the lower right quadrant that likely explained her pain in that region. Her appendix was inappreciable. Labs revealed an elevated white count indicating some form of infection. Urinalysis revealed the patient had a UTI. They discharged her home on oral Bactrim, only the patient rebounded inpatient within forty-eight hours. This is where I take over."

"Yes. That's where I met her."

His hands continue rubbing my neck and shoulders, massaging me, coaxing me along and into a slightly lulled state.

"I'm assuming since she rebounded and was readmitted and you're giving us this case study to work on, it's more than a simple UTI or kidney infection."

"You tell me."

I sigh, giving myself a moment to simply enjoy what he's doing. "I ordered a renal and bladder ultrasound that was negative, and her repeat urinalysis was also negative, but she's also on Bactrim, so that's to be expected." I sigh, sinking into his hands. "You're insanely good at that."

"I think you already know how talented my hands and fingers are, especially when it comes to your body."

"You're flirting again," I accuse, unable to hide the smile from my voice.

"Actually, I was being overtly sexual, but call it what you want."

My smile widens, but I quickly redirect us back to what I should be focused on. My work.

"I don't know what she has," I admit.

"That's the point. You're supposed to figure it out."

I roll my eyes in derision. "Thanks, Professor. I'm ruling out pyelonephritis (kidney infection) because the Bactrim seems to be working and now they have her on it through her IV just in case. She's still having abdominal pain and I ordered a repeat ultrasound since a CT scan isn't advisable in children so young if it can be avoided. Ultrasound was unchanged, and the loops of the bowel are still inflamed. It could be appendicitis, but I don't think so. She's been sick for over two weeks, and I believe it would have ruptured by this point or at least been visible on ultrasound if it was very inflamed."

"What else?" he commands, his voice low and rough, his warm breath brushing along my exposed neck, and I stifle my whimper.

"I also put in an order to repeat labs but added on a C-Reactive

Protein, a sed rate, and more comprehensive liver function tests. I was right in doing that because the results clicked through once I entered them."

"And?"

"And the kid's labs are a mess. Her white blood cell count hasn't gone down despite being on antibiotics for the UTI. I'm thinking the UTI is a red herring. I'm thinking that the abdominal pain and the inflammation in her bowel are the keys to all this. I just don't know in what way." I blow out a heavy breath, thinking this through. "She now has sores in her mouth, but none on her hands, feet, or buttocks. I don't think it's Coxsackievirus, but it still could be some form of an enterovirus?" It comes out as a question.

"It could be."

"Yes, it could be, and that would explain all the symptoms, but that doesn't feel right in my gut. The little girl has been sick for a very long time by this point and if it were just an enterovirus, she'd likely be improving. Not getting worse. She has weight loss. Poor coloring. Weird ultrasound. Mouth sores. Abdominal pain. Labs are all over the freaking place." At this point, I'm simply musing aloud, but I'm missing something. I know I am.

His hands slide down and outward, shifting around so he's holding my ribs. His diabolical thumbs continue their ministrations, rubbing into my back, but he's also skimming the undersides of my breasts with his pointer fingers as his hands move. He's closer now, too. His chest is practically right up against my back. His hard cock presses in the crevice above my ass and I lean back into it, unable to stop how my body reacts to him.

The way it craves his every point of contact, like a junkie seeking their next fix.

I know I should stop him, but I also know I won't. His hands feel too good, his touch too magical.

"Focus, Layla," he whispers in my ear just as his hands come up and cover my breasts. Fuck. I need to stop this. Because I do need to focus, and I said no sex—it was my fucking thing—for reasons I don't exactly recall at present, but at the time it felt vital.

His thumbs swirl circles over my hard nipples, teasing my piercings. He's the first person other than myself to touch those and holy
bejesus, they're sensitive as fuck to someone else's touch. I moan,
leaning all the way back into him, desperate for more.

"The patient," he prompts, and his hands stop moving, though
they don't leave my breasts.

I scan over my computer screen, reading everything through for
what feels like the thousandth time. Emergency room report, labs,
imaging, Mom's account of symptoms as well as the patient's account.
Everything is here. I'm not missing anyt—

"Family history," snaps out and I can feel him smile against my
neck as he places an open-mouthed kiss there.

I click on the family history button, and it immediately populates.
I scroll through it. "Both parents are healthy as well as both the
patient's siblings. Paternal grandfather has a history of type 1 diabetes
and hypertension." I shake my head. "No. It's not diabetes because
her glucose was within normal range each time it was tested. Paternal
grandmother has a history of Crohn's disease, depression, and anxiety. Maternal grandmother has a history of Graves' disease and high
cholesterol. Paternal grandfather has a history of Crohn's disease and
hypertension."

I bolt upright, forcing his hands to fall from my body.

"It's Crohn's disease. Oh my God." My head flips around to him.
"Right?"

He's smiling at me, rubbing his finger along his bottom lip, but he
remains silent. He can't tell me, and I'm glad he's not telling me
because I feel like I could fucking fly right now. That's how worked
up I am.

"It is," I declare adamantly. "Mouth sores, weight loss, abdominal
pain, inflamed loops of bowel, labs all over the fucking place. It's
new-onset Crohn's. She needs a GI consult, stool tests, more blood-
work, and a colonoscopy and endoscopy." I enter everything into my
case study and hit submit. Then I twist to him. "Did I get it right?"

"Are you asking me as a doctor or as your professor?"

"Both," I answer easily.

He inches forward and closes the lid of my laptop. Then his hands are removing the elastic from the messy bun on top of my head. My hair falls around me and he brushes it back over my shoulders.

"Yes," he says. "You got it right."

I fist-pump the air. "Fuck yeah!"

He laughs, taking me by the hips and moving me until I'm straddling his thighs. His head leans back against the couch and then he's gazing up at me, drawing circles on my lower belly.

"My attending didn't see it. He was positive it was simply the UTI and an enterovirus as you said. The patient's mother wasn't having it. She bitched me out for a solid ten minutes when I gave her that as the diagnosis. The nurse that evening told me to never underestimate a mother's intuition when it comes to her child. So, I followed that and my gut told me my attending was wrong. I dug deeper. Got a more thorough history. And yes, it was Crohn's. I called GI that night, and they agreed with my suspected diagnosis and confirmed it with colonoscopy and endoscopy."

"Wow. Nicely done, Doctor."

"Same to you, Miss Fritz." His hands cup my breasts once more. "And to reward you for getting it right, I'd like to make you come."

C allan

LAYLA'S NIPPLES pebble beneath my hands, and her hips rock on my thighs ever so slightly when I say that. She's let me touch her all night. She's let me invade her space. I have no doubt she's warm and wet and wanting. Now if she could only get out of her own way to let this happen.

I've tried to be good, and I've tried to give her the space she says she needs, but tonight when Katy was asked to go for a sleepover and I was alone for the first time in weeks, it was Layla who popped into my head. It was Layla who I wanted to be with.

It's Layla who I just plain want.

"You know I've only been letting you cop a feel in the hopes that you'd help me cheat on that case study."

I smirk, rolling her new piercings with my thumbs. I think she's about to come on my thighs just from that. I can't wait to get my mouth on them.

"Except you didn't cheat, and you're still letting me touch you."

She gives me a coquettish smirk. "Thanks for the reminder, Professor. You're right. I think we should stop, and I should hop off this ride before it becomes dangerous."

I move one hand to her hip and upper ass, grinding her forward up my thighs and along my hard length. Her gaze grows dusky. Especially when I ever so slightly twist the barbell in her nipple.

I lift her shirt and reach out with my tongue, licking around her piercing that I can tell is healed but still sensitive. Her breath catches, and she sinks her teeth down into her plump bottom lip. I flick the metal with my tongue and then lower her shirt again. She let me do all that. Not even an ounce of fight in her.

"We can do this for each other, Layla. You need my fingers and cock inside you, and I love the taste and feel of your pussy. I'm thinking this could be a very mutually beneficial arrangement."

She considers this. "We're not a real couple, and this isn't a smart play."

My body disagrees, but part of me knows she's right. We're not a real couple, and I'm risking a lot by trying to push us deeper into something. If she didn't care about me, she wouldn't be here. If she didn't want me, she wouldn't be sitting on my lap allowing me to play with her tits. She can tell herself anything she wants, but it all comes down to one thing.

She's been burned.

She trusted a man who used and abused that trust.

And as a woman who categorically doesn't like a man having that sort of power over her, she's protesting me on spec. Fine. I respect that about her. She doesn't suffer bullshit lightly, and she doesn't make mistakes twice.

Only I have no plans to be another mistake for her.

I'll have to show her just how good things can be if she's willing to open herself up to the possibility. It won't be easy with this wild one, and it won't be overnight. She's stubborn. A bull that doesn't want to be caught or tamed.

She doesn't see how we could fit, and maybe part of me agrees.

But sex? Sex she wants. And she wants it from me. That's how I'll catch her and make her stick. With honey. The kind she can't help but want to taste. It's not lost on me all that she's risking. How the entanglements of her life restrict her and why I'm a bad idea.

What if I don't care? What if all of that isn't a deterrent? What if she's the one? *The* girl?

Isn't it worth exploring to find out?

"You're here helping me out," I say softly, my voice a seductive purr. "The least I can do is return the favor."

"With orgasms?"

I pinch her nipple. "Will you accept another form of payment from me?"

She squirms. "No. And I already told you this form of repayment was off-limits."

"Then why are you letting me touch you? Why is your pussy grinding down on my dick even as you tell me no?"

Her lips mash together, displeased with my blunt observation.

"Does this feel good?"

She pants out a breath. "You know it does. It feels so good I can hardly stand it."

I pull gently on the barbell. "Then why fight it? I can make you feel so good, Layla."

A pretty rose climbs up her face, her pupils totally blown out. "Sex? Is that all you're offering me?"

"I don't know how to answer that. I feel like I'm Indiana Jones. One wrong step and I'm plummeting to my death." I sit up, taking her ass in my hand, and bringing her with me. "I'm also not some college douche who will only say what a woman wants to hear in order to get laid. So, if you want my particular brand of honesty, I'm happy to give it to you." I hold her face in my hand, and her eyes with mine. "I want you for more than just sex. I think you know that about me because I'm shit at hiding it from you. But I also appreciate the predicament that puts us in. If you'd rather live in the world of contentedly oblivious, we can play that game too, and I'll abide by it."

For now.

"Are you saying we could fuck each other constantly and it could be just fucking?"

No. Not even close. The notion that we could fuck each other casually is preposterous. She knows it, and I know it, but I can try. If it means I can have this piece of her, I can try for casual.

"I'll try." It's my best offer. "If that's all you want, we can cut this down to the basics."

I've known Layla for about six weeks. And in this time, shit has gone from fun and dirty to insanely complicated. I'm also the sole guardian of a little girl. A little girl I'm fighting to keep. So truthfully, I shouldn't be attempting to start a fake-relationship-with-benefits. Yet that's precisely what I'm doing. Because she's the one I want to keep.

In my bed. In my life. In Katy's life.

"You hold all the power," I admit. "But I think we both know that at this point, sex is on the fucking table. Whether it's our centerpiece or not is up to you. The decision is yours."

I shift beneath her and wait for her deliberation. But that doesn't stop my hand from playing with her nipple, and she's not stopping it either as she scrutinizes me with deliberate thoughts flickering through her eyes like an old movie reel.

"I don't want to fall in love again. At least not yet."

"What *do* you want?" I ask.

"You."

With both hands now on her hips, I glide her center harder against the bulge straining in my jeans, forcing her to feel every hard inch of me. "You've got me. I've never wanted a woman more than the way I want you."

"Then I'm saying yes."

"This continues until you tell me to stop."

Her hands slither up into her hair, lifting the golden strands and making the hem of her already short shirt rise higher. She grinds against me, and my eyes half close at the spike of pleasure.

"I will tell you to stop," she promises, but there is uncertainty there too, almost as if she's forcing that design into herself as well as into me. "When Katy is officially yours and our arrangement comes to an end, we will too. We'll have to." It's a warning mixed with regret, but she's decisive and fierce as she lands that blow.

Challenge accepted. "Until then…"

In a flash, I grab her ass and flip her over onto the couch. She lands with a soft bounce and a laugh, but then I'm on top of her, pressing her into the leather with my weight.

"God, Layla." I hover over her, staring down at the goddess beneath me. "Why do I want to fuck you again so badly? Why is it all I can think about? Even as my life is being turned completely upside down, all I want is you."

I don't allow her to answer as my lips consume hers. I wasn't lying. I crave her in a way I don't quite comprehend. It's deep in my blood. Restlessly rattling the marrow of my bones.

I wish you belonged to me.

It's a useless chant, one I've had for weeks now.

But fuck all to hell, if she wants me. I'm going to take and take and take until she's so spent and spun up on me, I'm all she knows.

My hands rip at her T-shirt, throwing it up and over her head. Her tits, so soft and sweet and playful, give a little excited jiggle. And her piercings? I never considered myself a guy who was into that, but I love her piercings. Once I get a good eyeful of them, I rip down her leggings, and when I get them off…

"You were naked under your clothes like this all day?" My hungry gaze shoots up to hers.

"Is it weird if I say I've not worn underwear since I moved in here?"

"Why?" I demand, staring down at her pussy.

Layla bites her lip, spreading her thighs a little wider for me. "Because every time I wake up next to you, I'm wet. And not wearing underwear turns me on because it feels like a naughty secret I keep for myself. It's been too long since I've felt you move inside me."

And then I'm on her, blood thrumming hot and brutal through my veins. There is nothing that can stop me. My mouth is all over hers, licking, biting, tasting, delving in as deep as I can go. I grind against her, punishing her for this. For all that we could have had, she's denied me, and I want her to feel that.

My jeans are still on, but she doesn't care about the rough fabric scraping her sensitive skin. She's taking it all. Welcoming it. Moaning into my mouth and begging for more.

"I can't wait," I hiss against her lips as her fingers rip open the button and zipper on my jeans.

"Then don't. Fuck me, and fuck me hard, and then fuck me slow and sweet after. I don't care. Just make me come until I'm flying so high I see stars. If we're doing this, we're fucking doing this."

I don't give her a chance to reconsider. Hell, I don't even give her a chance to move. I'm shoving down my jeans and boxer briefs and then my mouth is on her neck, licking and sucking at her skin as my hand grazes her bare, wet skin.

"Fucking soaked," I rasp into her. "You need to be fucked that badly?" I pull back and stare down at her glistening pussy. So fucking pretty, I need to taste it and fuck it and feel it all at once.

"Why don't you give it to me and find out."

Her hand grips the back of my hair, and she yanks me back to her mouth, kissing me soundly.

The angle isn't my favorite. I'm above her and she's below me, and we're on the sofa so it will require some acrobatics to make it good. I don't care though. I'm here with her. Kissing her. Touching her. Smelling her.

My finger flicks at the apex of her thighs and then rubs her clit. I pull back enough so that I can flip between watching her face and her pussy as I do. I told her I wanted to make her come. A thousand times over, that's exactly what I want to do.

"How many times?" I bark against her lips as I pick up the pace of my swirling finger. "How many times have you rubbed this clit and thought of me?"

"How many times have you jerked your hard cock and thought of me?" she counters.

"I've lost count," I admit. "At least twice a night for every one you've slept beside me."

"And while you're in the bathroom doing that, I'm fucking myself with my fingers, imagining it's your thick, hard cock."

Fuck. The dirtiest woman on the planet, and I had to go and fall for her.

Wait.

Fall for her? Is that what I've done? Already? It's too soon. Too fast. Too problematic. But...

It slams into me, wrings me dry with its truth, and suddenly there is no denying it. I knew I was halfway there before, but I had forced it all back. What a joke. There was no forcing her back. I was just a fool in denial.

I stiffen, staring down at her with new eyes. With the eyes of a man who has not only lost his head on the girl but now his heart. I liked her. I might have even been a little too crazy about her. But love?

She just told me she doesn't want to fall in love. How she's going to end it when Katy is mine. Christ. I assumed I'd get hurt when that happened, and I had already accepted that I'd fight to change that, but this...

It scares me. And thrills me. But it also makes this... *real.*

Real when it's not.

A hollow sort of ache starts to build in my chest. My falling in love with her doesn't change our problems, and it doesn't change all that will inevitably keep us apart. I'm essentially fucked.

It's a new experience for me. I'll give it that. I'm normally as in control of myself and my life as a man can be, but that hasn't been the case at all lately. Since she came into my life, it's been one thing after another.

She wiggles her hips, her pussy jutting up, and I realize it's because I've slowed my fingers.

Her eyes open, locking with mine. "What's wrong?"

What's wrong? Everything.

"I..." I swallow hard. "I..." I lick my lips. "I don't have a condom on me."

A smile blooms on her face, and my lungs empty. She sits up and removes my shirt, running her warm hands over my already heated body. My skin is so hot right now I'm shocked I'm not breaking out in blisters. She swaps places with me, hovering above me.

"Can I tell you a secret?" she asks coyly, pushing me back and then straddling my thighs once more.

"Tell me anything." My tongue swirls around her nipple.

"I'm on the pill. And I'm regularly tested."

"I'm not on the pill, but I am also tested regularly."

"Do you think we can fuck then, Doctor?" She grips my head and holds it against her breast. I push her up higher, giving my mouth better access to her tits and allowing for two fingers to slip inside her.

"You could fuck these first." I thrust up until I'm knuckle-deep in her.

She moans and starts doing just that. "What happened to all your urgency?"

I had a panic attack when I realized I'm in love with you.

"I decided I wanted to watch you come first." Definitely not a lie.

"Use your thumb as I'm using your fingers and I will."

My thumb starts to rub her clit as she continues to fuck my fingers. It's ridiculously hot and I pull back from her nipple so I can watch her ride my hand. I think watching her is my new favorite thing to do. Ever. The way her eyes turn smoky, half-drunk with her lust, and her skin flushes the sweetest pink. The way her lips part to accommodate her taking in more oxygen.

Her pussy is wet and tight and warm, and she makes this incredible noise as I crook my fingers inside her, hitting her front wall and that perfect spot.

"That's it, Layla. Show me how much you like this. Show me how pretty my girl is when she comes for me."

"I want you to do dirty things to me tonight."

I smile, cupping her breast in my other hand, lifting and squeezing it and rolling the piercing until she whimpers. "What kind of dirty things? You want my cock in your every hole? You want that kind of dirty?"

"Yes," she moans without skipping a beat as she continues to take my fingers in and out of her while staring down at me as she does. "Fuck my mouth. My pussy. My ass."

I groan. Jesus. She says that and I won't last through one of those holes.

"What else?" I rasp raggedly. "Tell me all the dirty thoughts in your beautiful head. I'll do them. I swear, I will."

"I want you to pull my hair and slap my ass as you fuck me from behind."

That's it.

My fingers slide out of her, and then I'm flipping her over and forcing her onto all fours on the couch. "Spread your ass cheeks for me," I tell her as I shove my jeans and boxer briefs off. "Show me exactly where you want to get fucked."

Her head swivels over her shoulder as she reaches behind and pulls one of her ass cheeks to the side, revealing her dripping entrance and the pink ring of muscles in the back. Bending down, I give her asshole a swirl of my tongue, dipping two fingers back into her pussy. She squirms and then whimpers as I start to fuck her pussy again while my tongue dips inside her from behind.

I keep going, getting her soaking wet in both holes, and then when she's just about to come, I thrust my thumb into her ass and my cock into her pussy.

"Holy fuck!" she cries, her pussy instantly convulsing around me. Blinding white spots cover my vision and for a second, I think I'm legit having a stroke. She's tighter than I remember and feels unlike anything I've experienced.

Probably because I've never fucked ungloved before.

But with her, I can't think of any other way to go. I need to feel her. All of her. And I need her to feel me in return the same way.

I pull almost all the way out, slippery and covered in her, only to push back into the hilt.

"It's not fake anymore, baby girl. My cock is inside you, and that makes you mine."

Then I start to fuck her.

Her hands claw at the sofa, searching for something to grab onto, only the leather doesn't accommodate that so well. It puts her at a disadvantage—and me at the perfect one—to control her movements and the pleasure she'll receive.

One hand grabs hold of her hair, twisting it around my fist only to yank it back, causing her back and neck to arch.

"Is this what you wanted?" I growl, increasing the pace of my thrusts. I give another tug. "Is this deep and hard and dirty enough for you?" My thumb pumps deeper into her ass, keeping pace as I slam over and over into her pussy.

"Yes!" Her voice is shredded. "Oh god! Yes! Don't stop."

I won't. I'm going to fuck her rough like this, punish her body, and push it to its limit, and then after, I'm going to bring her upstairs and fuck her nice and slow until she loses her mind over me the way I've lost mine over her.

With my other hand tight in her hair, holding her body firmly, I fuck her wild. Driving into her until she's screaming and begging and every muscle in my body is ready to snap.

"Fuck. Layla!"

"Yes!" she screams and then she's coming, so hard and so loud, her body seizing up and clamping down on me, and I lose it, coming harder than I ever have before as I spill everything I have into her.

All of me.

My cum, my sweat, my body, my blood, my love.

All of it is now hers. And it'll stay hers. Even when she walks away from me.

26

C allan

LAYLA FELL asleep after we showered, only instead of lying in bed beside her, holding her against me, I'm pacing the upstairs hallway in the middle of the night. Noel St. Nick sent me a text around nine-thirty, telling me that the girls were snuggled up in bed together, sleeping soundly. So this isn't about Katy.

No. It's about the woman in my bed.

The woman I foolishly agreed I'd fuck and keep it at that. Except I'm more than simply attached.

I'm in love.

Words I know better than to use with her, but why the fuck does she feel she has to walk away from me when this arrangement is over? Why is she so against being with me for real?

I get it. We have challenges. And yes, we should stay a secret at the school for obvious reasons. There are four more weeks left in the semester, but then I'm no longer her professor. That timing coincides with the end of her summer in the emergency department—so again, our restrictions aren't so restrictive at that point.

Is it because I have Katy? Is it because she's still in love with Patrick? Is it because he hurt her, and she doesn't want to get hurt again? Is it that she likes to fuck me but doesn't feel a tenth for me of what I feel for her? Is it the differences in our ages and positions in life? Does she honestly believe she can't have it all—a life with me and school and a career?

I don't know.

All those questions—those mounting questions that are relentlessly blaring through my ears like a fire alarm are what have me pacing. I don't know if I should say something to her because saying something to her will likely make her run, but on the other hand, I don't know how to continue feeling this way about her while acting like I don't.

I agreed to casual sex. I told her I'd try. What a fucking idiot I am.

I've never been in love before, and instead of exalting in it, I'm wrecked with the knowledge that I will lose this love, and I know I'll never be able to find one like this again. It's her. It's Layla.

And right now, that sucks.

Since this incredible woman entered my life and my brother and sister-in-law died, leaving behind their little girl, nervousness seems to be my baseline. I'm either terrified I'm going to scare Layla off by coming on too strong or terrified I'm going to lose Katy.

How can everything feel like it's coming together while simultaneously falling apart?

My hands run through my hair, and I blow out an aggravated breath, falling against the wall and leaning heavily into it. I need sleep. I'm half tempted to text Ash or Grey because both of them would make me laugh and tell me to regrow my balls or remove them from Layla's purse or something along those lines.

They'd be right to say that, and I'd listen and get my shit together.

Well, Ash would. Grey might not since he's all about love lately now that he's with Fallon.

The door to my bedroom creaks open, and Layla's curious head pops out into the dark. She doesn't immediately notice me as she squints in the direction of the stairs as if searching for a light downstairs that would explain my absence in bed.

"Hey," I say in a low voice, and she startles, clearly not expecting me to be lingering in the dark hallway in the middle of the night.

"Crap on a stick, you scared me." She puffs out a breath, covering her heart with her hand. "I was worried when I woke up and you weren't there. Is everything okay? Did something happen with Katy?"

"No."

I take a few steps in her direction, unsure of my course or intention.

"Then what—"

Without warning, I grasp her wrist and spin her around, pressing her up against the wall, and getting right up in her face. "I'm in love with you." It just blurts past my lips. Shit. I didn't mean to do that or say that, but it's too late to take it back now.

Do I even want to take it back?

I'm tired of it all being a lie. A lie that's chipping away at me piece by piece. A lie I don't know how to continue because I don't want to continue it. In public, we're nothing to each other but teacher and student. In private, we can't stay away or keep our hands to ourselves.

I want to hold her hand in public without fear. I want to lean in and kiss her lips simply because I can. I want to tell her I love her without fear that she'll bolt on me because loving me isn't what she wants.

It's too much. All of it. I'm in love with her, and she's not mine.

Layla's eyes widen, her eyebrows shooting to her hairline, and her lips part in an audible gasp.

"Callan—"

My name ends on a sharp sound and that's it. Her blue eyes hold mine, glimmering against the small sliver of moonlight that's leaking in from the far window, locked in indecision. I wait, my heart painfully thrashing against my rib cage. The words are there between us, only I feel no levity in setting them free.

"Say something," I clip out, finally reaching my breaking point.

"Tell me to fuck off. Slap my face for being a dick and telling you that even though I promised I'd keep this casual. Anything, Layla, just don't stand here in silence staring at me like I'm the Antichrist of your life. I know I shouldn't have blurted that out, but fuck, I didn't know how not to."

A tear glides down her face and she hastily reaches up, swiping the offender away. She stares out into the hallway behind me, her gaze flicking restlessly. "You're doing this here? Now?"

She's angry and I get that.

"I didn't exactly plan it."

"You don't know what you're saying."

I laugh. It's a little bitter because that's bullshit. "Layla, in the time that you've known me, when have I ever done or said anything I wasn't one hundred percent sure about?"

She swallows audibly and turns her head away, avoiding my eyes.

"For what it's worth, I don't expect you to say it back or come even remotely close to feeling the same way. But goddammit, Layla, I know you feel *something* too. No one has what we have and doesn't feel this." My hand slams into the wall beside her head when she doesn't respond, or look at me, or even fucking acknowledge my words. "Don't do this. Don't check out on me. Not again. Talk to me. That's what we do. Even if it's in anger or hate or whatever."

"You love me?" Another tear tracks down her cheek, only this time it's my hand that's there to wipe it away.

I turn her face in my hands, hovering above her, gazing directly at her, letting her see every piece of my heart that belongs to her. "So fucking much. I'm tired of trying to hide it, and I'm tired of trying to pretend, and I'm tired of not telling you how you've become my world. I didn't exactly realize to what extent my feelings went until last night, but once I did, there was no more fooling myself."

Her head falls back against the wall, and her eyes close as she releases a long, slow breath. My insides quicken, and I clench and unclench my fists, antsy and unable to stand still.

I release her and start to pace again, moving around in jerky circles in the small confines of the hall.

"Layla—"

All she does is shake her head, her eyes still closed, refusing to look at me.

"Dammit, don't do this," I repeat, rounding on her.

Her eyes spring open, blue fire and burning hot. "I need five minutes, Callan. Five minutes to think. You never give me time to think. You never give me space to fucking think!" she blasts, pushing at my chest and forcing me back a step.

She might have a point about that. I crowd her. I don't know how not to. Even when I think I'm giving her room to breathe around me, I'm not. I don't do indifference well.

The air conditioner clicks on, the vent directly above her, making her shiver. I peel off the T-shirt I threw on when I got up and drop it over her head since she's not wearing anything other than her under-wear. She slips her hands through the sleeves and huddles into it as she closes her eyes once more.

"I'm sorry," I tell her, moving like a shooting star across the hard-wood because I'm unable to stand still. "I know I shouldn't have blurted it out. It's not fair to you, and I know that. I also know this could mean you'll run out on me. But I can't help it. I love you and I need you and I can't go another day without you knowing that. You are the air I breathe and the ground beneath my feet holding me steady. Without you, I am lifeless and unbound. Without you, I am lost."

"I can't think with you saying this to me," she sobs, covering her face with her hands.

"Then stop thinking!" I boom. "What is there to even think about? I love you," I growl because she's so fucking stubborn it makes me want to shake some sense into her. Doesn't she see what's right in front of her? All that we can have if she just allows herself to try? "You don't have to love me back. But think about us, Layla. Us!"

"What does that even mean—us?"

That pisses me off something fierce. "Is it because of Katy?"

Maybe that's it. Maybe it's that I come with a kid.

Hurt flashes in her eyes. "Fuck you, Callan. It's not because of

Katy—I adore her. Yes, living with a six-year-old has been an adjustment. Yes, I have to watch my mouth and play house a bit, but I see myself in her eyes and it only makes me want to hold onto her tighter."

"Then what is it?!" I snap, desperation clawing at me because I knew better.

Part of me knew better.

The woman told me point blank she didn't want to fall in love again. She wasn't baiting me to challenge that. She meant it and I didn't care, but now look at us. I forced this on her. I was impatient and rash—two things I hardly ever am and only seem to be with her —and now here we are.

"Why won't you talk to me?" I soften my tone, only to flip the switch with my next breath. "Please, just give me something." I sigh as I crowd her again. "Is it because of Patrick? Because of what happened with him?"

"I'm not in love with Patrick." Her words clip out, her expression blazing. "But I'm still scared because of him. How does this not end in disaster? Tell me?"

I clutch her shoulders because it feels like she just gave me something. My face drops so we're inches apart, and finally, her watery and beautiful eyes lock with mine.

"I am not him, Layla." My voice shakes with sincerity. "I'm not. Do you know the difference between a man and a boy?" I question.

My body presses into hers, forcing her to feel me, to see me.

"What?" she whispers.

"Games. I don't play them. I'm not insecure or lacking in ego. I don't expect you to fall at my feet or pine after me. Nor do I want that. He played with you because it made him feel powerful to do so and fed a weakling of an ego. I wouldn't dare. Do you know what I find to be the sexiest thing about you?"

She swallows, her eyes searching mine in rapid, manic flicks.

"How irresistible you are to me. You're fierce and brave and smart and unpredictable. But I don't need to cage you and I don't need to tame you. I don't expect anything more from you than what you're willing to give me. I've been nothing short of honest with you. Do I want you? You know I do. Do I love you?" I blow out a harsh breath, holding her chin in my hand. "Fuck, Layla, I'm going to love you forever. But I am not him!"

"I'm scared," she says, her voice breaking as more tears overflow her eyelids.

"I know, baby. You're worried about what being with me means for your life. I have Katy and I pray that's not temporary. It's a lot. We're a lot. But it doesn't scare me because when I'm with you, I feel like we can do anything."

"Callan—" She shakes her head again, trying to stop me.

I press in against her, frenzied, needing her to hear me. "No, Layla. Please. Give yourself a moment to imagine the irresistibly wild notion that I could be right for you, and you could be right for me, and we could be it for each other."

"You broke the arrangement. You said you wouldn't fall in love."

"I never agreed I wouldn't fall in love with you. I just didn't argue when you told me you wouldn't."

I sigh, and then give her the only truth I have left.

"Being with me doesn't mean you have to lose yourself. It doesn't mean you have to give up on anything. Being with me is an adjunct. A bonus. It means you have someone else in your corner cheering you on and helping you to not only succeed but to win. Do you not see that? Do you not see how incredible I think you are? How one of the things I love most about you is your drive and determination and brilliance? This doesn't have to be all or nothing, Layla. You can have me, and you can have medical school, and residency, and a career after that."

She's breathing hard, her hand on her chest. "Tell me what happens now."

"That's up to you. I already told you I don't expect more than you're willing to give."

She contemplates this for a long moment. So long in fact, that I sort of die a thousand times over while she decides if she's going to kick me to the curb or not.

Finally, she whispers, "I like you. I'd be lying if I said I didn't and I'm not saying never to all of this. I'd be a fool to say that to you because you're everything, Callan." She pushes off the wall and then stands before me, in my shirt and little else, gazing at me in a way that quickens my pulse. "You are everything I want and deserve in a man, and so much more. I'd love to throw caution to the wind and ride this wave and see where it leads me because that's sort of how I roll. I think Patrick fucked me up a bit more than I realized. I'm saying yes to this, Callan, because I want it and I want you, but I'm also asking if we can take it slow?" Her hand finds my jaw, her fingers grazing up along my stubbled chin.

I belt out an incredulous laugh. "Slow? We can take it as slow as you'd like." I smirk as her fingers touch my lips. "I thought you were going to tell me to fuck off."

Her fingers glide up my face and into my hair. "Not a chance."

"You mean that? You'll be mine?"

She hitches up a shoulder. "I don't think there was ever a time I wasn't yours. Just don't break my heart or I'll punt kick your balls into the Charles River."

I snort out a laugh. "Never," I promise.

She smiles and climbs up onto her toes to kiss my lips. "Good. Now take me back to bed and don't make me regret this."

27

L ayla

"I DON'T THINK this is a good idea," I tell Callan as we glide through early morning traffic.

"You didn't answer my question, and there was no way I was going to let you walk and then take the T without knowing if you're wearing underwear today or not."

"Why does it matter?" I try to be indignant as a way to hide my Cheshire grin.

"Because you're wearing a skirt, Layla. A skirt!" His hands grip the wheel. "It's not even a long skirt, so if you're not wearing any fucking panties under it, I have to know."

"But why do you have to know?"

His head swivels in my direction, and he gives me a *do you really want me to answer that* look. I do, so instead of smiling like the smug devil I feel like, I smile sweetly at him. Callan loves me. It's wild. In a good way. I think.

All I know is when he told me that, my heart leaped out of my chest, and I'm taking that as a positive sign instead of a negative one and rolling with it.

After he fucked me six ways to paradise on the couch, he ate me out on the stairs and then fucked me against the wall of the hallway because he was too impatient to make it down the hall into his bedroom. Then a third time in the shower before my poor vagina had to raise the white flag.

That is, until he brought me back to bed after the *I love you* bomb and we did it again.

The man is a fucking insatiable dynamo in bed, only the bed isn't where we seem to do it most times.

He's officially ruined me.

Like reaching the summit of Everest on a clear day, no other view will ever quite live up to that, and no matter what, it'll forever be the view you compare all others to. So when we woke up late but horny and didn't have enough time for morning shenanigans because we snoozed past the alarm twice, I felt like being a little naughty.

Just to taunt him.

Just to make him think a bit.

Only it's backfired on me because he all but forced me into his car and now here we are.

"Show me," he demands, all flustered and adorable and hard. Yes, he's that too. I can see it through his slacks. This is going to be a long day and maybe starting this sort of game as we drive into school and have to play the roles of student and professor wasn't my smartest decision.

Too late.

I blink coquettishly. "Professor, I don't feel that's appropriate. In fact, I have to demand you let me out here so I can walk the rest of the way and not alert campus police that we're up to no good."

He blinks at me. "Huh?"

I roll my eyes. "It's hot role play, but that aside, I can't roll up to school and hop out of your Range Rover. We're living a double life right now, and while that's kind of hot and fun since now we're doing the naughty with each other, we still have to live the other side in public, if you know what I'm saying."

"Does anyone ever know what you're saying?"

I shrug. "Only those who know me best. Now for real, pull over here. We're getting too close to campus."

"Are you wearing underwear?" he demands, at the end of his patience.

He slows the car and I unbuckle, grabbing my bag and hauling the heavy thing up onto my lap before placing the strap over my head. "You'll just have to wait to find out, Professor." I give him a cheeky wink and then I'm flying out of his car as he swipes at me. I laugh, slamming the door shut and blowing him a kiss.

He smiles despite himself, rubbing at his jaw. It's a great look on him. He's all grumpy and flustered, but it's in a lighthearted way for once. It's cute and it sort of reminds me of the night we first met.

Callan isn't a grumpy dude.

He's just too serious for his own good sometimes, and I know he's tense about everything at the moment, so getting him to think about anything other than Mrs. Bible and Katy's guardianship is a good thing. And while I'm working on getting him not to think about all the serious stuff, I'm forcing myself to do the same.

I told him I wanted to take it slow, and he seemed okay with that. Which tells me he's on the same page as I am. There will be no confusion or misunderstandings between us, which I like.

I didn't lie when I told him I didn't want to fall in love again right now, and I didn't lie when I said I didn't want a boyfriend. But I listened to him, and he was right. It doesn't have to be all or nothing. I can have him, and I can have this. Even if it's tricky at the moment.

Let's face it, though, I'd be a fool to walk away from a man like Callan, even if our timing isn't ideal.

So for now, I'm a professional student and hospital scut puppy by day and a naughty bedfellow by night, and somewhere in between, I'm walking the tightrope of being his girlfriend, his fake fiancée, or someone he hardly knows.

As I walk along the stunning campus headed toward my classroom, I am officially back in student mode. I'm feeling good, and it's not all because of the sex or the morning teasing. I nailed my case study. In September, I'm going to start my second-year clerkships. Everything I've been building toward my entire life is upon me, and I'm ready for it.

"Dude!" Murphy comes flying at me just as I enter the building. "Where were you all night? I texted like a million times."

I swallow the oh shit, in the back of my throat and say, "Sorry. I had my phone on silent and missed them."

"Whatever." She waves me off. "That case study was a nightmare. What did you diagnose it as? I said histoplasmosis."

My face scrunches up. "What? Where did you get that one from? Isn't that regional? And come with a cough?"

Murphy looks like she swallowed a bug. "Does it? I Googled the symptoms, and that was one thing that came up."

My eyebrows hit my hairline. "You *Googled* it?"

"Well, yeah," she hems a bit sheepishly. "But I wasn't the only one, and I thought a fungal infection would be spot on given the symptoms."

My mouth pinches to the side. "Oh, that's actually a good call, and I didn't consider a potential fungal infection." Why didn't I consider a potential fungal infection? Probably because that's insanely rare in a young, otherwise healthy child, but still.

"What did you come up with then?" Murphy presses just as we reach our classroom.

I throw her a side-eye. "I said Crohn's disease."

Murphy blinks about ten thousand times at me as we walk into the classroom and take our seats, a little closer to the front of the room now.

"That's... specific. Crohn's disease?" She's confused, but also slightly aggravated. "No one else came up with that, and the group chat was going nuts with it last night. Where could you have picked that one up?" She stares me down and something about her stare makes me uneasy.

"I don't go in the group chat anymore since Patrick is still in there."

"Yeah, and you didn't text me back either. I got it. Where did you come up with that diagnosis?"

I set my bag down on the table and pull out my laptop, opening the screen. Her voice has an edge I don't quite get other than maybe she's just frustrated with this case study. "What did the group come up with?"

"Some said it was appendicitis, others enterovirus, food poisoning, parasite, or sarcoidosis. No one else said Crohn's." She winces at me. "The kid had like zero diarrhea or any blood in their stool."

I shrug. "Her family history was very strong for it, and she had other symptoms. Plus, Crohn's doesn't always present that way."

"We'll see what Dr. Hottie says."

"You mean Dr. Hottie McSterious," I correct since that's the name I gave him and therefore, it's the only one that should be used.

She laughs sharply. "Is that what you call him at work?"

No. Only in the bedroom.

I scrunch my nose. "Definitely not. I hardly see him at work."

Callan enters the room, and all the rustling immediately stops. Everyone is anxious about their case studies and from what Murphy said, they should be.

"Good morning," he says, his gaze skirting past me as he takes in the tiered classroom. "I know you're all anxious to get to your case studies, and I've had the chance to review your submissions. We'll go through all of it, and you can explain and defend your reasoning. Remember, medicine is both an art *and* a science, and the correct diagnosis isn't always so easily found. I will tell you this, only one of you in this class made the correct diagnosis. Several of you were on the right track but disregarded a crucial piece of information, and I think that's something we should talk about. This is also something I plan to do each week and will hand out rewards to those who get the correct diagnosis."

He starts to pace but stops when Daria raises her hand like she's in first grade. "What's the correct diagnosis?" she asks. "Who got it right?"

"Let me ask you this instead." He pauses right in front of her since she's in the first row. "What do you do when you first go in and meet a patient? What information are you there to gather and assess?"

Daria sits up and studiously thrusts out her tits. I mentally roll my eyes at her pathetic display to get his attention. Only I can do that with him. Because he's mine. Not hers.

"I introduce myself and get a history of present illness as well as a past medical history."

"Correct. What else?"

She falters, shifting in her seat. "Um. Well..."

"How about a family history?"

Her face flames up because that seems to be the thing we were all missing. Myself included, until I realized my blunder.

"The only person who clicked on the family history tab is also the only one who got the diagnosis correct," Callan continues, addressing the class once more. "Do you not believe family history plays an important role in your patient's overall health?"

"Well, yeah, but not as important as present symptoms," Murphy chimes in. "I've heard doctors say that family history can be misleading."

"Potentially," he replies. "But it can also be the key to your case. Genetics plays a role in all of us. In this situation, it did, and I had a feeling that was going to be what tripped everyone up. The diagnosis was Crohn's disease, and both the paternal grandmother and paternal grandfather had a history of it."

"But the patient had only a few symptoms that would correlate with that diagnosis," Daria protests.

"The patient had more than enough symptoms to correlate with the diagnosis. I think you'll find that most patients very rarely exhibit all symptoms in any disease process. Crohn's relies on a genetic component and an environmental trigger. If a thorough family history had been taken, that pathology would have made itself clearer given the symptoms the patient presented with, don't you think?"

The whole class grumbles, and I get a stink eye from Murphy. "You got it right," she hisses to me, and the note of accusation in her voice hits me strangely.

"It was right there in family history," I defend. "I just put the pieces together after that."

"Uh-huh. And no one helped you with that?"

I blow out a silent breath. "What are you suggesting?"

"Just seems as though you have a lot of doctors at your disposal. You live with Oliver, right?"

Um. Not anymore. "Oliver didn't help me with it. He was at the Red Sox game last night with Amelia and the girls." That's actually true. It's why I was wearing Meil's Red Sox shirt. She might not think it's good luck, but I still do.

"And what about one of your other Fritz uncles? Did you ask them for help?"

I narrow my eyes at the way she says that. "No one helped me." Which is true. Callan didn't help. He gave me no prompts or feedback until I submitted my work.

"And what about Dr. Hottie McSterious as you call him?"

Shit. That was a mental blunder. Not to mention the way she sneers his name is very different than the way she mentioned Oliver or the other Fritzes. Could she know about me and Callan? I don't see how, though even if Patrick had implied I was fucking Callan before. Still, I don't see how she could know anything.

There's no way. She's just grasping at straws.

"No," I snap, miffed she'd think so little of me. "I told you no one helped me. I clicked fucking family history and two of the patient's relatives had it. Look over the disease pathology, Murphy, and get a better history next time. And maybe don't consult Dr. Google."

Murphy turns back to the front of the room, as pissed with me as I am with her, and the lecture continues. Others attempt to defend their answers, and Callan patiently goes through each one, explaining his own experiences with the patient and his attending.

He's good at this.

I know it's not what he wants to do, but he's an excellent teacher. Even last night with me.

He's patient and listens and doesn't discourage, even when the answer isn't correct. As much as I wish he weren't my professor and wish the school would hire someone else to take over, I've learned a lot from him, both here and at the hospital. I'm going to miss that terribly when it's all over.

I shake that off and continue to listen as he instructs the class. We don't do our break-out groups today. Instead, everyone wants to continue to discuss and fight over the case study. I stay quiet, and he doesn't call me out as the one who got it correct.

Until the end of class.

"Miss Fritz," he says, his eyes on mine in a way that makes my pulse jump. "As the one who got the diagnosis correct, would you mind following me to Dr. Lawrence's office for a quick moment? I left the reward in there before class."

My nipples instantly harden. Thankfully I'm wearing his sweatshirt, though the way his molten gaze quickly bounces down to my chest, I'd bet he knows it anyway.

I don't respond. I simply rise out of my seat and gather my things as everyone else does to leave for the day.

"Enjoy your reward."

"Get over it, Murphy. It's not a competition. It's about learning." I can feel Murphy's eyes on me as well as a few others', but I ignore them, my head held high as I carry myself down the steps in his direction.

"This way." He opens the door for me, and I exit the classroom, antsy and edgy. We both have to get to the hospital and we're still on the medical school campus, so I know this won't be more than what he's saying—a reward for getting the answer right.

But hell, if he doesn't have my nerves on a short fuse.

He breezes us through the anteroom where the professor's assistants sit, only for us to find it curiously empty.

"They're at lunch," he supplies, answering my unspoken question. "In here, Miss Fritz."

Fuck. The way he's saying my name makes me think this will be more of a punishment than a reward. We enter his neat-as-a-freaking-pin office, which is also as barebones as it can be. He's only here temporarily, and his thought on that shows. There's nothing of him in here. It's just a desk, a bookshelf loaded with medical texts that I know aren't his since his are on his bookshelf at home, and a window that looks out into the courtyard.

He takes a seat in his chair and instructs me with a quirk of his finger to come around to his side of the desk. "Turn around," is all he says, and my breath hiccups.

"What?"

"Forearms on the desk, Miss Fritz. Your reward will be different from the other students in your class, but that's only because yours will come with a bit of a punishment."

I knew it!

"Punishment for what?"

He twists me around and places his hand on the center of my back, pushing me forward over his desk, and I'm soaked. Like totally freaking soaked. Because hello, I'm bent over my hot professor's desk in a skirt and—

"I knew it," he rasps as he flips the skirt up onto my lower back. "No fucking underwear."

His hand comes down with a crack right on my bare ass cheek, and I moan so loudly because I told him I wanted him to spank me last night and he never did, and I'm so turned on already and I want *alllll* of his dirty punishment right now.

He bends over the back of me, his chest pressing me down deeper into the desk. "Moan like that again and everyone in this building will know you like getting spanked by your professor."

Fuck, I love it when he talks to me like this. When he plays this game with me.

"Is that what you want?"

Yes! It's totally what I want. But only in the fantasy of my mind and not in reality, so I say, "No, Professor. I'm sorry. I won't do it again."

"Hmmm," he hums in my ear as his hand rubs the spot he just spanked. "What should I do, Miss Fritz? Should I punish you or pleasure you?"

"Both. Please, Dr. Barrows, both." I have zero shame in my begging. I'm in a constant state of arousal when I'm with him. Everything the man is—from being a freaking perfect father figure with Katy to a brilliant doctor and professor to everything he is with me—I can't get enough, and I know that's a slippery slope, but I refuse to question it because he makes me feel so good.

So alive. So wild and carefree.

So myself.

He sees me and knows me and wants to give me everything I want, and that's exactly what he's doing now. It's never been like this before for me. Patrick didn't get this side of me. Callan does.

The pressure of his body leaves my back, and then I hear him retake his seat, sitting directly behind me. I can only imagine the view he has right now. Both hands rub my ass, massaging the muscles, and then cool air is immediately followed by another *crack*. My eyes roll back in my head, and I bite my lip so hard to smother my moan I'm shocked I'm not drawing blood.

I grind forward, aching, desperate for friction.

He's not spanking me hard. There is no cruelty here. It's purely erotic and playful. Because that's Callan. The man doesn't have a cruel bone in his body.

He spanks me again and again, alternating cheeks, one after the other, some softer and some harder, keeping me on the edge without knowing what kind I'll get next. After the last one, his hand rests on my heated flesh, the skin smarting but not too raw. I can hear his breathing, labored and gruff, and I'd give anything to see what he looks like right now.

I start to turn my head over my shoulder, and when I do, I almost regret it. Our eyes collide, and in them, I lose everything inside me. Every piece of myself I had been holding onto is now gone. He owns all of it and I don't care. I want him to have it because I know he's going to do delicious and wicked things with it.

"Put your right knee up on the desk."

I don't lose eye contact with him as I do, exposing myself completely to him.

His hands run up my thighs, over my reddened skin, up along my hips. Everywhere he can touch me, he does. Reverently. Almost lost in the act.

"So pretty." He shakes his head. "God, Layla. You're so fucking pretty. All of you. Not just this." His hands continue to roam, and my chest quakes. He licks his lips, and then something in his eyes shifts as if he's coming back from wherever he was. "Do you still want to be my naughty student?"

I nod in earnest because whatever that was just gave me a little mental jolt.

"Then remember to stay quiet." His hands grip my ass, split open my cheeks, and then his mouth is on me like this—from behind. One leg up on his desk. My skirt up my back.

It's dirty.

To the point where I plant my face in my forearm to smother my sounds.

"Is this what you wanted?" he growls into my wet flesh, pushing two fingers inside me and making my back arch. "Is this why you didn't wear anything under your skirt? You wanted your professor to bend you over his desk and eat your pretty cunt out?"

Holy. Motherfucking. Hell.

"Yes," I whisper-cry, already so freaking close to the edge. Always so freaking close to the edge when I'm with him.

"I'm going to take this ass soon, Layla. We didn't do that last night, but soon."

I moan again, unable to stop myself. His tongue replaces his fingers, but those fingers don't go far. They work my clit, and that coupled with his tongue flicking inside me, and where we are, and what we're doing, and how we're doing it, I come and come and come. Wave upon wave of mind-bending pleasure twists through me and has me slashing around the top of his desk. It's so intense that the moment he slams his cock into me, it's strangely unexpected and shocks me with a new rush of pleasure to the point where I scream.

His hand slams over my mouth, and I blink open to find his eyes glaring down at me in a fierce warning. Sometimes it's so easy to get caught up in this, and I forget all that we're doing and all that we're risking, but he doesn't. He's too controlled for that, even when he's out of control.

I nod my head, letting him know I'll be quiet and then he starts fucking me. Fast. Hard. Nihilistically. His cock pierces me, taking, demanding my surrender, my pleasure. I give him both. He presses me harder into the desk and I can't do anything other than take his cock. His balls slap my clit, and I swear, stars dance behind my eyes.

He's so deep in me like this. So everywhere all at once. My nails scrape the wood of the desk, trying to latch onto something, but the desk is huge, and I can't reach the other side from this angle. He likes this. I can tell. He smacks my ass again as he pounds into me, the cut of pain mixed with pleasure nearly makes me come right there.

His chest falls to my back once more, and then he's breathing harshly by my ear, whispering a hundred things to me. All kinds of things I don't even know if he's aware that he's saying.

Things like "Mine," and "More," and "Yes," and "I'll never get enough," and "This is only the start," and "You feel so good," and "I can't let you go."

It pours from his mouth like a river. All of it. The dirty. The sweet. The I shouldn't say this, but I can't stop myself.

"Stay with me." He says that last, and then I'm coming. And I'm coming so fucking hard. Because *those* words send me flying. I don't even know what it is about them.

Three simple words. So different from those three forbidden words.

Three simple words that now hold my body on a tethered string, a lifeline I didn't know I was attached to. Stay. With. Me.

He repeats them. A harsh breath against my soul. Only he adds to them. "Stay with me, Layla. Always."

28

L ayla

"CATCH ME!" Keegan yells from the top of the waterslide.

"I'm waiting!" I call up to her, treading water at the bottom of the slide, though I've left plenty of room to spare so I don't get kicked in the face. You only need to learn that lesson once. Stella broke my nose in two places when I was seventeen, and I had to have it fixed.

Not my happiest day.

Keegan belts out a squeal, and then she's shooting down the slide, hitting some air at the end, and then plummets two feet from me into the pool. She emerges, and I make sure I'm right in front of her when she does. Keegan is a good swimmer, but the water scares her. Kenna had a near drowning when the girls were three. You'd think Kenna would be the one with the fear of water, but no. That girl is fearless.

As if proving my point...

"Here I come!" Kenna doesn't wait for us to move. Her battle cry is our only warning. I latch onto Keegan and move us to the side because Kenna—much like her cool Aunt Layla—loves to make a splash in everything she does. This is why when she hits the air at the bottom of the slide, she does a makeshift flip that ends in a cannonball.

The twins crack me up.

Keegan is all Amelia, and Kenna is all me—with a bit of Oliver in there too.

Kenna explodes up triumphantly, and Keegan is there to high-five her sister.

"Layla, it's five," Amelia says, walking along with Stella over to the pool, a towel for me in her hand.

"Awesome. Thanks!" I give the girls kisses. "I'll see you ladies soon."

"Why do you have to go?" Keegan pouts.

"Because Layla has a date." Stella's eyebrows bounce and I coyly flip her the bird making both her and Amelia laugh.

"It's not a date. It's just dinner."

"What's the difference? It's dinner with the man you're—"

I splash at Stella, shutting her up. "Silence, booger. We have young ears present." I hop out of the pool, and take the towel Amelia hands me. "Thanks."

"So tell me what you're doing again, because I don't know why it required you to be out of the house all day?" Amelia asks only to hold up her hand. "Not that we're complaining. We love seeing you."

I shrug, drying the end of my hair on a corner of the towel. "I don't know. He wouldn't tell me, and Katy was tight-lipped too."

"This sounds thoughtful and special, and thoughtful and special translates to a date. But are you dating him or just playing bedroom tag?" Stella questions for at least the fifth time since I told her last week that Callan and I are taking it slow. Incidentally, I also owe both her and Amelia fifty bucks each, because apparently, when I was in my drunken state at Stella's restaurant, I told them that I would not screw around with Callan and that if I did, I'd owe them each fifty bucks.

Oops.

"It's both," I tell them. "We're together, but right now with every-thing else that's going on, we're having fun. Stop doing the *what does this all mean* thing. It sets us women back centuries."

Amelia gives me a look as if she's questioning my basic sanity, which, frankly, is not a new look for her to give me. She folds her arms over her chest, throwing a quirked eyebrow on top of that look. "If you think you're not in as deep with him as he is with you, you're high. He's very much attached to you, and you're getting attached too." Amelia's hand shoots up when I start to argue. "I'm not upset about it. I'm actually thrilled because I like him a lot and I think he's perfect for you—"

"Will you stop with that already? Yes, he's perfect. I know he is. That's not the problem. Right guy, wrong time, okay? It's a lot all at once."

Stella lets out a sardonic laugh. "Well, whether it's the wrong time or not, you've found him anyway. I'm with Meils on this one. He's perfect for you, and I'll bet another fifty bucks that you and your hot doctor turn out exactly the way Amelia and Oliver did."

"Great," I grumble. "You're supposed to be on my side."

"I am, Layla. You just haven't figured out that it could all work if you're willing to give it a try."

"You mean if our situation wasn't all kinds of fucked up?" I toss at them, hoping that shuts them up, but I should have known better. I'm dealing with Amelia and Stella here.

Amelia levels me with her motherly glare, her gray eyes deep and intense, and suffering no fools. "You can be so absolutely right for someone and yet be stuck in a time that is so impossibly wrong you feel you have no path forward. But that doesn't mean you don't. All it means is you have to make adjustments if you want it to work."

"I know that," I reply adamantly, wrapping the towel snugly around my chest. "The truth is, I don't know what I want anymore. I don't. I like Callan a lot, and I care for him deeply, and I love Katy, but... I'm... I don't want to get hurt again. I don't want to sacrifice the things that are impor-tant to me. I don't know if I'm ready for what being with him entails. He's thirty-one and has a kid and I know he's at the point where he wants to settle down. I'm twenty-three and a second-year med student. I'm not ready for all that yet, and I don't think that makes me a villain either."

Amelia blows out a tired breath, shifting her weight and playing with her red ponytail. "Fine. I get that, and part of me agrees with it. I'm just keeping the promise you made me swear to keep. Deny it all you want, but you're getting attached to both of them."

I am. I know I am.

We have six weeks left on this. We're halfway through, and I'm crazy about them. Both of them.

We even got through another impromptu visit from Mrs. Bible Friday night, and that one went better than the first, though she's still clearly not impressed with us at all. No burnt cookies or fire alarms or sexy Layla coming home with her tits half hanging out. Mrs. Bible took a tour of the second floor, including Katy's and Callan's room, so it was a very good thing it was obvious Callan and I are both sleeping in there.

We played the role of a family, but for the first time, it didn't feel like a role. It didn't feel fake. And now Amelia and Stella are piling on top of that.

"What do you want me to say?" I snap, exasperated by everything. "I care about them, but that doesn't make me the right woman to be in their lives for the long term." I clear away any emotion that comes with it. "We have six more weeks left of me being his fake fiancée. After that, I'll figure my life out."

Stella snorts. "Uh, I fell in love with Delphine in like three weeks."

"That's you," I counter, a touch—or maybe a lot—defensively. "This is me, and I have a plan."

That's already going to hell. I love Katy, and I care a lot about Callan, but you don't casually get involved with a man like him. It's simply not possible, and I'm in no place to settle down and play house and stepmom for real.

But...

I mentally shake my head. No buts. I quickly shove away the weird, twisted part of my mind that balks at that.

"Well, have fun sticking to the plan while he's sticking his dick in you."

"Oh my god!" Amelia smacks Stella's arm. "Crude much?"

Stella raises her eyebrows expectantly at Amelia. "Tell me I'm wrong?"

Amelia gnaws on the corner of her lip and gives me a simultaneous hard look. "Yeah. Stella's right. You're fucked in a few ways, aren't you?"

"Annnnd, I'm gone." I throw them a wave and start to head into the Fritz compound. "But thanks for all that."

"It's what we're here for," Stella calls out to me. "Reality check and love."

"Next time, I'll take it from Octavia. She gives more love and less reality."

I brought a bag of stuff so I could shower here, but now I'm wishing I hadn't. Part of me wants to escape, wants to run and go home, only I don't exactly have a home. Callan's home isn't my home, even if it's starting to feel more like it every day.

Entering the Fritz compound through the back door, I take the stairs in the west wing up to the second floor and walk down the hall to the bedroom I used to have sleepovers in when Amelia and Oliver first got together. I quickly shower off the saltwater from the pool and sunscreen and change into white jeans and a pink crop top that's lined so my barbells aren't so noticeable in front of Katy. I go for a summer glow makeup look and blow out my hair into silky waves.

Forty minutes later, I'm unlocking the front door of the townhouse, sticking my head in, and calling out, "Hello?"

Katy and Callan told me I couldn't come home until six tonight. Whatever they're planning involves food, because I can smell something spicy and garlicky cooking.

"She's here!" Katy screams from somewhere upstairs. "Uncle Cal, she's here!"

"I heard." He laughs, and then I hear wild, light footsteps flying down the stairs, followed by Callan's slower, heavier ones.

I drop my bag on the floor and my keys in the small bowl on the entry table and then round the corner into the hallway. Katy hits me just as I reach the bottom of the stairs, but I don't get a chance to react to the blow of her body against mine. She's too busy grabbing my hand and changing directions, dragging me at a sprint back up the stairs.

Callan is coming down, and we nearly slam straight into him. He grabs hold of Katy's shoulders, slowing her. "Easy, Ladybug."

"What's going on?" I ask, taking him in. He's freshly showered. His thick, longish on top hair is wet and brushed back from his face, making his deep blue eyes somehow appear lighter. He's wearing a white T-shirt—he knows they drive me crazy—and low-slung dark jeans.

Without missing a beat, he leans in and kisses my lips. Softly. A little sweet, but with a smile he can't hide. "We have a surprise for you."

"Upstairs?" I can't stop the swell of butterflies that hit my chest.

His smile turns boyish, a little nervous, and he nods. "It's this way."

"Come on, come on, come on!" Katy is tugging on me like I'm made of string, and then she's yanking me back up toward the second floor. "We did it ourselves."

"Go on up, Ladybug. I want to talk to Layla for a minute."

Katy huffs and puffs, not happy with that at all, but she's too excited to contain herself and her little body—already bathed as well and wearing *The Little Mermaid* pajamas—zips straight up, immediately going for the third floor.

"Callan, what is all this?"

He takes my hand and slowly starts walking us up the stairs. His gaze partially holds mine, and I can practically feel his pulse racing through his hand. "After our first visit with Mrs. Bible didn't go so well, I realized something. You've lost so much. Your apartment has been destroyed, and most of your belongings along with it. You've been living in my house, but you have nothing of your own here except for your clothes."

He takes in a breath as we reach the second floor and pulls me to a stop at the bottom of the stairs that lead up to the third floor.

His eyes are full of apprehension. "Layla, this doesn't have to mean anything you don't want it to. You need to know that ahead of time. I wanted you to have something that was all you. Just for you. A place you could go where you'd feel comfortable and escape to if necessary. It's my way of saying thank you. It took longer than I thought it would to finish, but it's finally done."

My heart is racing in my chest, my skin hot and prickly with nervous anticipation. "Okay..." That's all I can manage.

We continue up to the third floor, but I don't see anything other than how it's always been. The couch, the huge television, the bar—it's all the same. Only Katy is jumping like a kangaroo in front of the bathroom door.

Callan turns me to him, his gaze intense. "The previous owners of this house had this floor as their master. When I moved in, I moved it back downstairs and turned this room into what it is. But they had a huge walk-in closet that I used mostly for extra storage. I turned that into your office slash reading room."

I blink at him. And then again. And then I turn to Katy, who has the biggest smile I've ever seen. Callan nods to her, and she opens the door beside the bathroom. The one I had never given any thought to.

He squeezes my hands, holding me in place. "Like I said, this isn't meant to imply anything you're not comfortable with. However long you choose to stay, whether it's for six more weeks or... longer, I want you to be happy here." He licks his lips. "I thought this might help with that."

I'm trembling like a leaf when he finally releases one of my hands and guides me toward the room. It's painted in the most stunning periwinkle, like a summer sunset. It's also bigger than I thought it would be for a former closet. It's double the size of my bedroom in my old apartment.

The hardwood floors from the media room continue through, but there's a light gray rug taking up the center of the space. On the right is a large picture window, and beneath it is a reading bay with a matching gray cushion and plush throw pillows. Taking up the majority of one wall is a built-in white bookcase, half filled with books. On the other wall is a large desk with two monitors and my closed laptop sitting on top. On the left is a set of overstuffed cream chairs with a small table between them.

The wall above the table is loaded with framed pieces of art my mother did. Ones I haven't seen in years. Not since I was a kid. There is also a picture of a mermaid in the ocean with blonde hair that is very obviously Katy's masterpiece.

"Callan. Where? How?"

I cut myself off there with a gasping hiccup of a sob. I cover my mouth to stifle it, but that's useless against the tears as they cloud my vision.

He leads me over to the bookshelf, turning to face me as I face the bookshelf, staring at one spine after the other. "You told me, and then you told Katy about the books that belonged to your mom that you lost in the flood in your apartment, but I didn't know which specific books you had. Amelia filled me in on some of those and said a few were first editions, but I couldn't replace them all because some I couldn't find. I know they're not the same. I know they're not your mothers. But I also know what they meant to you, so I did what I could."

I shake my head. I can't breathe. It's too much.

He releases my hand, and lifts a small painted wooden box, cradling it in his large hands. "Katy made this for you. Stella told us about your box. About the things you used to keep in it. And while we can't replace the memories you lost with it, Katy wanted to give you some new ones."

He flips open the box and inside is a seashell Katy and I picked up the day we went to the beach. There's a rock in there I immediately recognize as the one Callan had been playing with the night we went to the cemetery. There's also a fake jelly sushi, and I snort out a laugh when I see it.

My fingers run over the box, over the items in it, and then along the spines, my hand still over my mouth, my head still shaking, utterly incredulous, completely blown away. No one has ever done anything like this for me. The work that must have gone into this room.

"When—"

Fuck. I can't speak without my voice cracking. Stella and Amelia helped with this. They never hinted at a thing. Not even today.

"I had my contractor working on it for the last month. The bookshelves and window seat are custom, and that's what took some extra time. Plus, he had to work on it when you were out of the house. Today Katy and I spent the day putting the finishing touches on it."

That's when I break down. Absolutely start bawling my eyes out. My hands cover my face, and I cry in the most unladylike way.

"Does she hate it?" Katy asks, despair in her voice.

"I love it," I croak. "That's why I'm crying. I love it so much, Ladybug. So much." I fall to my knees and drag her into my chest, hugging her to me, kissing the top of her head, her forehead, her cheeks. "I love it as much as I love you."

I pinch my eyes shut because that slipped out, but it's true. I love this little girl.

"I love you too," she whispers against me, and what am I doing? *What am I doing?* I wait for the panic—for the need to run—but it never comes. Instead, this room does exactly as he intended. It makes me feel like I'm *home.*

Only it's not the room doing that, I realize. It's them.

I'm home with them.

I glance up through my watery eyes to find Callan staring down at us, a look on his face like I've never seen before. His eyes hold mine, and I see everything he's feeling. Love. Fear. Hope. Desire.

He clears his throat and then wipes at his face and says, "Ladybug, let's let Layla explore her new space. Why don't we go finish up dinner?"

Katy reluctantly peels herself away from me, standing before me with earnest blue eyes. "You really love it?"

"With all my heart," I promise her.

Callan takes her hand and before I can say anything to him, they're gone, and the door is closed. I stare around the room, at the books, at the cushions, at the colors—my favorite colors—at the art on the wall that he got from Amelia and had reframed and hung.

All of this he did for me, but he prefaced it by saying there are no strings attached to it. He did all this work knowing there was a possibility I'd walk away. Only how can I possibly ever walk away from them now? Do I even want to try?

29

L ayla

I'M NOT sure how long I lie like a starfish on the carpet, staring up at the pitched ceiling. At the bookshelves. At the reading nook against the window. At the desk ready for me to work at. At the chairs that I know he thought of and positioned for me to use with a friend or Amelia. I told Katy I loved her, and I meant it, but... fuck. I love him too.

I do.

I'm in love with Callan, and it's not something I could have avoided simply because it's not something that came on slowly. It didn't creep up on me, and it didn't slither its way into my heart the way it did with Patrick. Patrick only infiltrated my heart once I allowed him in.

That's not the case with Callan.

Callan hit my barriers like a wrecking ball, and my defenses didn't stand a chance at holding. But more than that, my attempts to thwart him were meager at best. I started this by telling him I didn't want to fall in love again, and I meant it, but I did nothing to prevent it.

Now what?

I hate that question and it has me scowling up at the ceiling and then wiping at the emotion that still clinging to my face in the form of dried, crusted tears. Callan loves me, and I love him. Could it actually be that simple? That perfect? That... right?

I love Katy and I love him.

So does it matter that the timing might not be ideal? That I'm so much younger than him in all the ways that feel like they matter most? Eight years isn't crazy, but given our lives, it feels like decades. Still... I'm not sure how much I care anymore.

Callan isn't Patrick.

As I think the words, they rattle the breath from my body, seeping deep, inward until they completely overwhelm and shake me to my core. Callan is nothing like Patrick.

I can't do anything about the past other than learn from it. But instead of giving up on love, I now know what it should be. What I want from it.

And what I will never settle for again.

I peel myself up off the floor and head into the bathroom that's up here. Grimacing when I catch the melted makeup on my face in the mirror, I splash some water on my face, washing it all away.

Washing everything away.

When I think I have my shit back together, I go downstairs to find Callan in the kitchen with Katy. She's standing on a chair beside him, both of them wearing aprons, as he helps her stir tomato sauce in a pot.

Could I do this with them? Could I be part of their lives permanently? What would that mean for school? For my residency after that? For myself?

Am I ready for all of this—*for them*—at only twenty-three? A smile spreads across my face as my heart and mind—for once—line up. Yes. I think I could be.

"Smells amazing in here."

Both Callan's and Katy's heads pop up.

"We made spaghetti and homemade sauce," Katy chirps with pride.

"Yum! I love spaghetti. It's my favorite!"

My smile grows as hers does, and then I shift to Callan. In his eyes, I can tell he's still nervous. He's worried I'm going to bolt or disappear on him again, and I hate that's where his mind is. Rounding the island, I wrap my arm around his waist and drop my head to his shoulder.

He relaxes against me, exhaling a breath, and dammit. I should say something, something reassuring, but I can't make the words come out. All I can do is kiss his neck and nuzzle my nose against him, and inhale his cologne and then whisper, "Thank you. It's the best thing anyone has ever given me."

His head pivots, and he glances down at me as I glance up at him. Our eyes hold for a long moment, and then he leans down and kisses me. Callan Barrows gives me the sweetest kiss of my life, and it's only made sweeter because I am totally butt-crazy in love with him.

The three of us eat dinner together, and then I clean up the entire kitchen while he takes Katy upstairs and gets her ready for bed. Tonight is Sunday, and tomorrow Katy has camp, and Callan and I have school and then work.

I finish up the kitchen, shut off all the lights downstairs, and then go upstairs. Katy is singing "Part of Your World" from *The Little Mermaid* as Callan braids her long hair into pigtails to give her mermaid waves when she wakes up.

He went from bachelor to single dad overnight and hasn't complained about any of it. Not once. No self-pity or second-guessing or despair over losing his bachelor status and freedom. He takes life as it hits him and adjusts accordingly, and that's that.

It's a strength so few possess.

"After you brush your teeth, can I read you a story?" I ask from the doorway of Katy's bathroom.

"Will you read *The Pigeon Needs a Bath*?"

"Definitely," I tell her. "It's my favorite."

Katy quickly goes through the motions of brushing her teeth while Callan prompts her along the way, and then she and I are snuggled up in her bed as I read to her, and we both giggle at the pigeon who refuses to take a bath even though he's past the point of being smelly and dirty.

She has me read it to her a second time, but before I reach the last page, she's out like a light. As gently as possible, I climb out of her bed, kissing her forehead as I go. "Good night, Ladybug. Sweet dreams." I pause. Gulp. "I love you."

Tiptoeing out of her room, I shut the door with a soft click, and then I gather my breath before heading straight into Callan's room. He's sitting up in bed, still dressed but barefoot, as he reads a freaking medical journal. I shut the door behind me and pull my shirt up and over my head, tossing it onto the chair in the corner.

"You never take a break, do you?"

The journal falls to his lap as he watches me get to work on the button and zipper of my white jeans. Those fall to the floor along with my underwear, leaving me naked.

"Not often," he admits, his voice gravelly as his gaze smolders. He sets the journal down on his nightstand and then shifts his position, uncrossing his legs as I climb on the bed, crawling straight for him.

I straddle his thighs and drag my fingers through his hair, tilting his head back until our eyes lock. "You're the most incredible man I know, and considering the men in my life, that's saying a lot. I don't know how to begin telling you what that room upstairs means to me."

His hands meet my hips, sliding me back and forth along his hard length. "I don't know how to begin telling you what you mean to me. You're mine."

"Yours," I say, and then pull back enough to look at him and ask him something that seems to knock the wind from his body. "Will you say it?"

He blinks. "Say what? That I love you?"

A soft, almost girlish smile curls up my lips. He hasn't said those words to me again since that night in the hallway. But right now, that's shockingly not what I'm after.

"No. What you said to me that day in your school office. What you say to me a lot when you're inside me."

It's as if he's working the farthest reaches of his mind, trying to discern what he's said and what precisely I'm asking for. "Help a guy out?"

I smash the crease between his eyebrows and then kiss a line up his throat. "Stay with me."

"Those were never intentional words. Those were a plea. A prayer. A hope based on nothing." He clears his throat, and I kiss right where his Adam's apple bobs. "Will you?" he asks softly. "Will you stay with me? Even when this arrangement ends. Even if it gets tough. Even if we fight. Even if we're so screwed up that we're both stumbling around in the dark, unsure how to make this all work." He grabs my head and forces my gaze to his. "Will you stay with me, Layla? Even then?"

My body climbs his, seeking more contact, needing to be closer. "Yes," I pant against him, my tongue licking the seam of his lips. "Yes, I'll stay with you. You and Katy both."

My heart pounds, but not in a scary way. In a way that's thrilling and death-defying. In a way that's telling me this is the way it's always meant to beat. For him.

I layer my lips with his, our eyes one, and I say, "I love you."

Bewilderedly he stares back at me. "You do?"

I giggle lightly. "How could I not? I trust you with myself, with my heart, with my life, with my future. I want this, Callan. I want us."

"Layla." That's the only warning I get before his mouth slams down on mine. This is more than friendship. More than lust. More than an agreement. No longer fake, this is real, and undeniable, and so powerful, I'm shaking with it.

He breaks the kiss, breathing hard. "Say it again."

I giggle. "You first. You haven't said it to me properly since the night in the hallway."

His hands cup my face. "I love you. Are you really doing this with me?"

I nod jerkily. "I love you."

A low growl builds in his chest, and his mouth takes back over, kissing me soundly. "I'm a lucky son of a bitch."

"I'm just a lucky bitch."

He smiles against my lips as his hand reaches up into my hair, and he drags my lips down to his. My breath shudders in and out as his tongue sweeps against mine. I rip at his shirt, desperate to feel his chest against mine, to have him touch me the way I know he will. And he doesn't disappoint. The moment his shirt is gone, his mouth is back on mine, and his hands are playing with my nipples, with my piercings.

My body is on fire, flames licking up my skin, burning me from the inside out in the most delicious of ways.

"More," I find myself begging.

"More what?" he asks against my lips, twisting my nipples until my head falls back and I moan, rubbing my clit against his jeans over his hard cock. "Do you know how beautiful you are to me? Do you know how sexy it is to watch you lose yourself on me? You make me depraved. You grind yourself all over me, and I smell my fucking pants the next day and jerk off to them, wishing I was face-deep in your pretty pussy."

"Oh god!" I can't control it now. I'm riding him, pushing myself higher, moving faster, harder. "Callan. Please."

"Look at me."

I immediately obey, and his eyes, they're wild. "I want to fuck your ass tonight. We've talked about it, we've teased, but we haven't done it yet. Can I fuck you there?"

I'm nodding before he's even finished. "Yes. Please, yes."

His mouth crashes against mine, and then he's kissing me hard. Swirls of his tongue against mine, and then we're moving and he's pinning me beneath him. He continues to kiss me as he removes his pants and boxer briefs. His mouth glides down my jaw to my neck where he sucks and nips at me. I feel his thumb on my clit, rubbing me in circles, his other hand on his cock, jerking it slowly.

It's mesmerizing. The way he touches me while he touches himself. Being with him has always been more than sex. Even that first night. It was trust and exploration, and hurricane force passion. I don't care if he's rough. If he leaves marks on me. Hell, I crave it. Part of me even needs it, especially now. Especially with where my feelings are.

I want to be branded by him because the truth is, I need to know how real this is. How deep and how far it goes. So much of us is still fake.

He continues to kiss my neck and then down to my breasts. "Are you dripping for me, baby girl?"

He knows I am. He's playing with my wetness as he asks.

With his hand on his cock, he rubs his head along my entrance and then pushes in. We both groan at the tight fit. At the hot feel of it. His hand cups my jaw, and with my eyes pinned to his, he starts pumping in and out of me, slowly, deeply. So slowly and deeply I can hardly catch my breath or organize my thoughts, because holy shit, does he feel good.

His grip on my jaw tightens and then he pulls out and whispers "Turn over," against my lips.

Nervous anticipation rolls through me like a tidal wave. I don't care how many times you've done this; you get nervous each time, and especially for the first time with a new partner.

I roll onto my stomach, and then climb up onto all fours. For a moment he's silent behind me, running his palms along my ass and up my back.

"Have you ever done this before?" he asks in a low tone.

I turn my head and look at him over the angle of my shoulder. "Yes."

"Was it with Patrick?"

My throat clogs as I answer. "Yes. Does that bother you?"

He's staring down at my ass, and then his eyes travel over the curves of my back up to my face.

He swallows, and his jaw clenches. "Yes. I hate that he's done this with you. I hate that I don't have any firsts with you. I hate knowing that he—that *anyone*—has even touched what I want to only ever be mine. It drives me insane with jealousy, and I hate that side of myself too. You bring out the caveman in me, cutting all my rationality out at the knees. You're sand shifting with the tides and always slipping through my fingers."

"But I'm not," I tell him. "I'm yours, Callan. Nothing with you is like anything I did with him. All of this is new. All of this is my first. You are nothing like him."

His grip on my hip tightens, pulling me back to him. His finger runs through my entrance, collecting my moisture, and then he's ringing my asshole with it before plunging inside me there. I hiss out a breath and rock against the air, my clit throbbing and my empty core clenching.

"Don't move," he breathes against my back and then he's gone, cold air replacing his warmth. I hold impossibly still. I listen, my eyes closing. A drawer opening and closing. The snap of a cap. The squirt of lube. I hold my breath as I feel his hand on my ass spreading me open and then his wet fingers are there, two of them, pushing back into my most forbidden place.

I squirm forward, but he's there, holding me, caressing my back with his other hand, whispering sweet and filthy words that he knows will get me to do anything he asks of me.

"Fuck," he rasps. "Look at you. You're going to kill me with how you look on all fours waiting for my cock in your ass."

"You have the dirtiest mouth." I don't know why I voice it now. It's been more than two months since the first time we met and came back here. But it shocks me every time. I'm not even sure why. It fits him, and yet it doesn't. All I know is that he loses his precious control when he's with me and his more primal side comes out to play.

I love it.

I love him.

"Baby, my mouth isn't the only thing that's about to get dirty." He splits my ass cheeks and removes his fingers. Cold lube pours directly onto my hole, and I suck in a sharp breath. "Too cold?"

"Ah. It's definitely close."

He swirls it all around me, lubing me up everywhere he can, and then his cock until he's slick. "Then let me warm you up."

In the next beat, I feel the head of his cock against me, working my ass. I've never done this with anyone his size, and I hold in a breath as I feel him start to push in.

I must tense because he pauses, his hand rubbing circles on my back. "Are you okay?"

I give him a shaky nod.

"Baby girl, you have to breathe and try to relax. If you need me to stop, I will. You just have to tell me. I love you, and I never want to hurt you. Ever."

I exhale the breath I was holding, and the head of his dick pushes in and in and in, then out. He does it again, going a little deeper each time. It burns, but in that way that borders on more pleasure than pain. On he goes until he's past that initial resistance, and once that's done, he pushes all the way in until he's as deep as he can go, his chest against my back.

My head falls forward, my breath short and choppy as he holds himself still.

"Are you still with me, baby girl?"

Baby girl. I love when he calls me that.

"I'm still with you." Because I'm not sure I can ever go anywhere else. Be with anyone else. He's my life. My future. And it doesn't terrify me anymore.

"Are you ready for more? Are you ready for me to move?"

His words slip past clenched teeth. His grip on my hip bruising. He's barely holding on, yet I know I'm his first priority.

I reach behind me to clasp my hand over his while my hips simultaneously cant back, seeking more of him, wanting to take him deeper.

His breath hitches, and he curses low and rough. "God. Layla."

That's his only warning for me before he slides out only to push all the way back in. His arm snakes around me, pulling me back up until I'm pressed to him, his chest to my back. His mouth roams along my neck, kissing, licking, tasting, and smelling my skin.

"More?" he questions in a gruff rasp.

"More. Give me more."

Turning my head to the side, his lips find mine, kissing me as deeply as he can from this angle while he starts to fuck me. My knees dig into the mattress of the bed and he's standing behind me, holding me, touching me, fucking me, kissing me.

It's dirty. It's erotic. It's bliss.

His hand slithers down the front of me, toying with my breasts and nipples, and then lower across my belly until he finds my clit. One deft finger rubs me in smooth circles, and sparks play in the periphery of my vision. All the while, he starts a steady pace. Even. In. Out. In. Out. Deeper and deeper each time he goes.

But fuck, it's not enough.

He's trying to be gentle, and he's trying not to hurt me, but I need more of him. I need everything he can give me. I like him unhinged. I like him rough. I like him desperate, and I must tell him so because he growls like a beast. A beast who grows wild and loses his mind. A beast who starts to fuck—and fuck hard.

"Is this what you want?" The hand not rubbing my clit comes up, wrapping around my neck, holding me tighter to him. "Me losing my mind over you?"

"Yes," I cry out. "Don't hold back. I want you, Callan. I want you, I want you, I want you."

"God, Layla. What you do to me."

I can feel his heart pounding against my back. His breath panting against my neck. His words rattling my soul.

Holding my neck, his other hand bands around my hip, and then I'm pinned against him as he pistons in and out of me. But it's not deep enough, and he feels that. He wants to hold me, and he wants to feel me, but we both want it deeper. With a growl of frustration, he releases me, and I tumble forward, my hands planting into the bed.

"Who do you belong to?" He grunts against my back, his teeth scraping along my spine. "Who owns this?" He spanks my ass and then cups my pussy, shoving two fingers deep inside me. My eyes roll back in my head, and I beg for more, whimpering at his force. At his possession.

He's not simply fucking me, he's infusing me with him.

His fingers pump in and out of my pussy at the same pace his cock pumps in and out of my ass. It's the most overwhelming, mind-bending, soul-flaying, body-consuming thing that's ever happened to me.

With every thrust of his fingers, the base of his thumb rubs my clit, coaxing every part of me to the edge. I don't expect it. My orgasm surges forth out of the abyss of pleasure I'm already encapsulated in. But it strikes like a missile, direct and deadly, leaving behind a shuddering, disjointed, uncontained woman.

I scream and then drop forward to smother it, my face in the blanket, my hands clawing and tearing. Callan follows me, a roar climbing past his lips and shredding through the air. His fingers slide back to my clit, rubbing me as his cock pulses in my ass.

And with it, somehow, I come again. It's almost too much, but I don't care because I want us to come together like this. I want him to feel what I'm feeling. I moan and writhe all the while he fills my ass, and I fucking love every second of it.

He collapses against my back, still inside me, rolling us to the side so he doesn't crush me. We're still as he holds me, panting, unable to catch our breaths. His face nuzzles against my sweat-coated neck.

"Layla."

It's all he says, but the veneration in his voice says all the words he can't.

I feel his hand against my ass, and then he's pulling himself out of me. I whimper, but before the sting can register, he's swooping me up into his arms and carrying me bride-style into the bathroom. He walks us straight into the shower and sets me gently down on the marble bench he has in here. I shiver against the cold of the stone, but then he's turning on the hot water and swooping back in, standing me up and drawing me to him, holding me close.

"Are you okay?"

Suddenly drowsy, I sag against him. "That was…"

His hands run over my hair, and he pulls my face back. Our foreheads meet, and our eyes lock. "You are…"

I smile, and so does he, and then he's kissing me.

He didn't fuck my ass and then roll over and fall asleep or go off to his dude-bros to gather high fives. He's caring for me. Holding me. Speaking soft words against my lips and washing my body with gentle strokes of his hands.

And when he's done with all that and we're back in his bed and I'm wrapped up in his arms and I start to drift into that perfect space between awake and asleep, he murmurs those words again, "Stay with me."

And I fall into the most beautiful, peaceful, contented sleep I've ever had. Praying that nothing tears us apart.

EMERGENCY

30

L ayla

I'M GOING to tell you a secret I never want Callan to find out about. I've met Greyson Monroe a few times, but I've never actually spoken more than a few words to him here or there. So he doesn't know that I grew up with a poster of him on my bedroom wall.

I've been a fan of his music since I was a teenager.

I didn't listen much to Central Square—another secret, though Callan knows and finds it hilarious—but Greyson Monroe as a solo artist? Yeah, I crushed, and I crushed hard. Even now, when he opens the door to the warehouse he and Fallon live in, I get a slight childhood, fangirl rush.

"Layla!" He greets me with a huge smile, the way his friends have whenever they see me. "Glad you could make it. Come on in."

"Thanks," I say, stepping over the threshold and surreptitiously glancing around.

I'm in Greyson Monroe's home. It's one thing to meet someone a few times, but it's something else entirely to be invited into their home. I sort of want to take covert pics, but that's creepy, so I won't. I did call Stella on my way over here to brag, though. She sent me a pic of her middle finger, and I mentally high-fived myself for that.

The entire first floor, which is freaking massive, is almost like warehouse space. There is a giant staircase in the middle of the floor, but I don't hear any noise. "Where is everyone?"

I spin around to face him, only to find him smirking at me. "Callan didn't tell you, did he?"

I blink at him and fold my arms as I slowly take in Greyson for the first time. He's wearing a Celtics T-shirt, gym shorts, and sneakers. "Tell me what?"

"That we're hanging out in the sports arena I have as part of my building."

The first thing that hits my head with that? The man has a sports arena as part of his building. Now, I grew up with billionaires. Like, mega billionaires. So that sort of thing shouldn't shock me. The Fritz compound has one, and it's professional to say the least. But I think I expected this more from Asher instead of Greyson.

Asher is the professional athlete after all.

The second thing that hits me is I'm pissed. Well, maybe not pissed. But annoyed? Yes, let's go with that because I'm wearing adorable sandals, a pretty lavender tank top, and white eyelet shorts. I came home after simulator lab, showered, and gussied myself up for this. Because he said we were having dinner at his friend's place, and I wanted to look nice since we're officially official.

This was after dealing with Murphy, who once again all but accused me of cheating on the latest case study we turned in on Friday because I was one of only a few who got it right and she got it very wrong. Our friendship has slipped to nonexistent, with the exception of glares and snarky comments from her.

"Oh."

He snickers. "It'll be fine. We're just hanging out and having some pizza and drinks while we shoot hoops and stuff."

"Oh," I repeat, folding my arms over my chest. "He's a dead man. Both on the court and off."

Grey laughs, kind of loud. "You gonna play barefoot, or should I see if Fallon has sneakers that will fit you?"

"Unless your woman wears a size nine and a half, I'm going barefoot."

"I couldn't tell you what size she wears, but I don't think her feet are as big as yours."

"Lucky woman. But lucky for me, I'm lights out on the court."

His head quirks. "Are you really?"

I smile at him. "Little known fact? I played D1 basketball at Dartmouth. I mean, I wasn't a starter until senior year, but I was a pretty decent point guard. Amelia told me I wasn't getting into an Ivy League school on grades alone and that I needed a sport to balance me out, and since I'm tall, she pushed me to basketball." I shrug.

Grey bursts out laughing. "This is our secret. It stays between us, and I'll be the sucker who has to take you out of pity. Got it?"

"All the way."

"Good. Because Ash is all, 'I'm the god of sports,'" he mocks. "And fuck him."

"Totally with you."

Grey gives me a fist-pound and then turns and starts leading me across the first floor to a large metal door in the center of the wall. He punches in a code and then opens it, and holy shit, this is incredible.

I think I just orgasmed.

"You know you said that out loud, right?"

I sigh. "It seems to be a growing problem. I'm on it." Sorta. "But for real, this is seriously cool. What do you do with all of this?" There is a full-size basketball court, a pool I can just barely see in a separate room, and an enormous, fully equipped gym across the way, also in a separate room. And that's just what I can see from here.

"I built it originally so the neighborhood kids could have a place to go after school. Some local youth groups run programs out of it."

I stare at him, flummoxed. "How did I not know this, and does the Abbot Foundation know?"

He shakes his head. "I fund it and I'd never take dollars from the Abbot Foundation since there are plenty of other charities out there who need their money. This is just my secret thing."

I slap his shoulder, beyond impressed by this man. "Not just a pretty face and a killer voice, huh?"

He laughs, throwing me a wink. "I try," he says to me before turning to the room. "Hey everyone!" he calls out. "Look who just crawled through my front door."

"Layla!" Katy comes racing over and launches herself into my arms. She's all fire and no smoke. I love it about her. Brave and so herself.

"Ladybug, you are fierce in this outfit." I set her down and take her in. "I see you're ready to play some ball, and yet someone forgot to extend that message to me." I raise my head and quirk a brow at the hot piece of man candy heading my way.

"I didn't think you'd come if you knew we were playing games tonight."

I inwardly laugh, and Grey throws me a smug smirk that only I can read.

"I would have muddled along. But in this?" I throw a wave down at myself indicating my cute outfit because, let's be real, I look damn good in it. "And here I thought you knew me," I quip.

Callan doesn't stop walking until he's in front of me. His arm swings around my waist, and he hauls me up against his chest. "I ordered you pizza with black olives, mushrooms, and bacon."

"Then you'll get laid tonight," I promise, and he grins.

"I know you. Just not everything yet." That's when he kisses me. Right in front of all his friends. And Katy. "We'll get there. But are you okay playing some basketball?"

"Does it come with alcohol?"

I hear a noise in the background. "Layla Fritz, come here." I swivel around to find Aurelia waving me over to a cart bar they have in the corner of the massive room. "Tell me your poison, and I'll mix it pretty."

"I like you."

She laughs. "I like you too. More importantly, I like that look on Callan's face. Especially now that you're drinking that particular poison with him." The pretty blonde waves her hand across the tray of various alcohols like she's a game show hostess. "What'll it be?"

"Bourbon. Double. Straight up. No chaser."

"If I was into chicks, I'd be into you," Aurelia tells me as she lifts the heavy bottle of Blanton's.

"If I was into chicks, I'd marry Stella, but you'd be my second choice."

She hands me a glass and then pours one for herself. "I'll take it. I've met Stella, and I can't blame you. Cheers."

"Cheers."

Our glasses clink and then we're both tossing back our drinks.

"I'm going to drop a hundred on you. You play, don't you?"

I choke out a laugh, shocked as I meet her eyes. "How on earth could you possibly know that?"

She shrugs. "I read people better than most, and I can tell you have something up your sleeve. You're too calm and coy, and I caught the look Grey gave you."

I give her a wink. "You're observant. I'll remember that. Triple that bet, and I'll go in for half with you."

"Ash!" Aurelia cries out. "I've got five hundred on Layla beating your butt."

Everyone gasps.

She pours me a second drink and I toss down the double and hand her the empty glass. I kick off my sandals and pad barefoot back toward the center of the court.

"Five hundred?" Asher questions, wearing a sleeveless Boston Rebels' shirt and black gym shorts.

"Five hundred," she confirms.

"What do you know that I don't?"

Zax shakes his head. "Uh-uh. You can't ask that. It's like Vegas. You either take the bet or you don't."

"You don't even play," Asher tosses back at him.

Zax gives him a careless shrug. "I don't make the rules, brother. You know how this works."

Asher grumbles under his breath as he dribbles the ball. "Fine. Five hundred." Then he points at me, smirking in a way that makes it seem like he just tipped the odds in his favor. "Grey, you've got Layla and Katy on your team."

"Fine," Grey grumbles but shoots Katy a wink.

"Works for me. Katy's my girl."

"Heck yeah!" Katy jumps up at me, and we high-five.

"All right, player." I turn back to Asher. "I'm ready to shoot some baskets."

"It's hoops," Asher smugly corrects me, dribbling the ball with a mocking grin.

I wiggle my fingers for him to pass me the ball. He does, and I start dribbling a bit, slowly and with not much purpose. "Oops. I had no idea that's what you call it." I bat my eyelashes at him and then I turn and hit a jump shot with nothing but net because those were my specialty.

Callan groans in defeat, tossing his head back. "She's totally playing us. She's about to wreck us on the court. Mark my words."

"No one plays me."

"Ash, you're going down, brother," Grey promises, high-fiving Katy who then cracks her knuckles like shit is about to get real.

I point my finger at Asher Reyes. "Bring it."

"Ohhhh!" Everyone else crows.

"Let's play some ball," Ash declares with a bit of defeat in his voice.

I crouch down to Katy, who is all beaming smiles and ask, "Do you know how to play?"

She shrugs. "My mom played basketball in college. I know how to dribble a little, but the net here is really high."

"True. We'll have to make up our own rules with that. Show me how you dribble." I hand her the ball, and she starts dribbling, bouncing the ball to an off-time tempo.

"Good. Now walk while you do it. Keep it going." She starts walking, her eyes on me, but she's dribbling as she moves. I give her some minor pointers, but then it's too late for anything else as Asher is calling the game. "Just keep doing what you're doing. You've got this, babe."

"Katy, girl, whenever you want to shoot, just wink at me and I'll lift you up so you can reach the basket," Grey tells her.

"Ladies and Grey get the ball first," Zax announces, since evidently he's reffing this game. "Go."

Grey gives me a firm nod that tells me I start, and I begin dribbling, reading the court and the opposing team. The sound of the ball smacking against the hardwood and sneakers squeaking fills the room. It's a bit weird playing barefoot, but I'm managing to move well so far, only to find Callan coming at me. Instinctively I lean forward, getting into a defensive position to protect the ball.

"He matched you up with me?" I throw out at him.

Callan's about two feet in front of me, arms out, body poised and ready, looking fucking hot in his tight sports shirt and gym shorts. He grins, cocking an eyebrow since he clearly just caught me checking him out.

"He thought I might distract you since you're so obsessed with me."

I cackle out a laugh. "Dude's got that reversed. I'm not wearing a bra. Or underwear." I blow him a kiss and then immediately skirt to my left right as he pounces for me. He misses, and I take aim and make my shot. Grey and Katy cheer along with Aurelia and Fallon, who are sitting on the sidelines sipping their drinks.

Callan hisses out a curse under his breath, coming in right behind me. "Are you really not wearing underwear with those tiny shorts on?" he growls against me. "If so, you can't bend forward again."

I laugh. "I'm wearing underwear. I just wanted to mess with you." I turn and give him a playful side-eye. "My game is all about psychological warfare." It totally was. I was *the* shit talker on the Dartmouth team.

He licks up my neck before blowing cool air on my skin and making me shudder. "Game on."

We continue playing, back and forth. Callan is all over me. Grabbing me and touching me and slapping my ass when he thinks he can get away with it. In return, I tell him all the fun things I intend to do with him later tonight.

Callan has the ball and he's going up the court with me on defense. He does a crossover dribble, switching his ball hand. He's able to dribble equally well with both, which is annoyingly impressive. Katy is down by the basket, guarding Lenox—which is freaking hilarious to see—and Grey is on Asher. It's just me and Callan, and he's loving it.

He fakes at me and then retreats, checking my reaction to his movements. I missed and I grit my teeth at him.

He continues to dribble, arrogantly now. "You can stay in that position all night, baby. I have an excellent view of your cleavage like this."

"If you think that's good, I should turn around and show you my ass."

He ignores that as he cuts one way and then spins to drive for the basket, using his shoulder and hip to bump into me and push me out of the way. I don't let him get any breathing room. I'm all over him, chest pressed against him, arms waving in the air, anything I can do to block his shot.

He bumps me back, getting just enough space to step back and make his shot from inside the paint when I whisper so only he can hear, "Because then you can see what you're fucking tonight."

He sputters out a cough, tripping over his feet and flying forward, only to catch himself before he goes down, but the ball slips out of his hand, flying nowhere near the basket. Unfortunately, Asher manages to snatch it out of the air, fight his way around Greyson, and then slam-dunk the ball.

He comes down howling and pounding his chest like a caveman. Great.

I turn back to Callan, who steadies himself, giving me a perturbed scowl.

"What?" I ask, feigning innocence.

His arm bands around me and he pulls me into him, his chest to my back. He thrusts into me, forcing me to feel every hard inch of him. "You're going to pay for making me hard in front of Katy and my friends in these fucking shorts that hide nothing."

"I look forward to it." I rub my ass against him.

"Gross! I'll never be able to unsee that," Asher yells, covering his eyes with his forearm as if he's been stricken.

"You're just jealous."

Asher grins at Callan. "Definitely. Your woman is hot. But save the naughty stuff for later. Katy's ball!"

Callan pinches my ass and kisses my neck, whispering, "Later," against my skin, and then we're back at it.

Asher bounces the ball at Katy, who grabs it and then starts doing a little dance as she dribbles in place. She is so much freaking fun. Everything she does, she does with enthusiasm and guts. She gives it straight to Asher and Callan, who tease and taunt her right back.

Lenox doesn't do much other than act as a massive wall of man and occasionally grunt. But he does smile and fist-pound Katy after Grey boosts her up and she nails a shot.

"Nice one," he tells her.

"Thanks, Uncle Lenox." She's all breathless smiles when Grey sets her down. She peers at the ink on Lenox's arms. "Will you tattoo a mermaid on my arm?"

"Noooo!" Callan comes racing over, shaking his head so fast I'm shocked he doesn't pull a muscle. "Absolutely not."

Lenox chuckles lightly, kneeling down so he's Katy's height. "I can show you how to draw a mermaid on your arm."

She thinks about this for a moment, and her pensive expression reminds me so much of Callan's. They look so alike sometimes that it's startling considering she's not his. "You've got a deal."

"Hey, are we playing ball or are we having art hour," Asher challenges.

"You only want to keep playing because you're losing," Grey declares, wiping the sweat from his forehead with the hem of his shirt.

"Not my fault you guys cheat," Asher throws back at him. "You boosted Katy so she could get a basket, and you've got a ringer on your team."

I throw my hands out at him. "Hey, you made the teams, and I don't remember you saying anything about the rules."

"Yeah, Uncle Asher," Katy taunts, her hands on her hips, all tiny attitude. "I'm only going into first grade but I'm already a better sport than you are. What's the matter? Can't handle getting your butt beaten by a girl and a six-year-old?"

"Oh, snap!" I choke on a laugh, as does everyone else.

Asher runs in and snatches her up in his arms. "Ladybug, where on earth did you learn such excellent trash-talking?"

"From you."

"Atta girl." Asher tugs playfully on her ponytail. "You want pizza?" Before she can answer, he runs her over to Fallon and Aurelia, who along with Zax, are setting up the pizza on a large table.

"Did you have fun?" Callan asks, drawing circles on the center of my back with his finger.

"I did. I beat your ass."

He laughs. "You did. That was awesome. I should have known you'd be a ringer. You're good at everything you do."

His phone pings with a text, and when he reads it, his entire disposition changes.

"What is it?"

He looks like he's seen a ghost.

Slowly his gaze rises to mine, and then he flips his phone so I can read it. And when I do, only one word comes to mind. "Fuck."

31

C allan

Tick, tick, tick. The gold clock on the medical school director Dr. Scabowitz's desk—everyone calls him Dr. Scab, and I know it bothers the shit out of him—is making me postal. I'm alone in his office, waiting on him to get here, and I'm a half-second from picking up the heavy timepiece and chucking it out the window. It feels particularly cruel to leave me sitting here when he texted last night that he has something so important to discuss with me that it requires me to come in early before class for it.

He knows about me and Layla.

He has to.

Why else would he want to meet with me before my class to discuss her?

That's what his text said.

Dr. Scabowitz: Good evening, Dr. Barrows. Are you available to

come to my office Wednesday morning before your lecture to chat about a situation surrounding Miss Fritz?

Me: Of course. Is it anything I should be concerned about? Is there a problem with Miss Fritz?

Dr. Scabowitz: We'll talk about it Wednesday, my boy. Wednesday.

My boy. I'm a doctor and a grown-ass man, but that was entirely beside the point.

I showed Layla the text, not knowing what else to do or say other than replying that I'd be there. When we got home and talked about it after we put Katy to bed, she started to lose it, and rightfully so.

"I don't know what it is," I start, taking her in my arms and pressing her back against my chest. "Not for sure anyway since he wouldn't say anything. My guess is he somehow knows about us. I can't think of anything else it could be."

She stiffens against me and then grows preternaturally still. "You told me I didn't have to choose between you and med school. You told me you were an adjunct, that I could have both, that I could have it all, but that's a lie. I can't have you and med school. Not right now."

Grief slams through me because she's not wrong. This might finally be out in the open between us, but there's so much that still has to remain hidden.

Inwardly, I flip off the irony of this. We went from having a fake engagement where we pretended it was real to a real relationship we now have to pretend isn't there. I love her, and she loves me, and I want the world to know it.

"I'll take care of it," I swear. "I'll make sure nothing touches you."

"You can't make that promise." She puffs out a breath and rolls over to face me. "You can't guarantee that, and I don't even want you to do that. I know you're trying to protect me, and I love you for it, but I agreed to everything we did. I was far from an innocent little coed who got swept off her feet by her older professor."

"No? Because I sort of like the way you phrased that."

She rolls her eyes at me in the dark. "It doesn't make sense. Why now?"

I run my fingers through her hair, relieved that she hasn't stormed out of bed or kicked me in the nuts. "What do you mean by why now?"

She pins me with a look. "We haven't touched each other on campus in weeks, Callan. We had sex in your office that one time and since then, it's been nothing. We don't talk on campus, and we don't interact on campus. We've been good. Careful. So why now?"

Her question gives me pause. I think through what he said, and she's right. It's not adding up. "I don't know. If he had known about us before, he would've said something. He would have had to."

"Exactly," she asserts. "So maybe he doesn't know about us. Maybe this is something else entirely. Maybe he's going to ask you to be my clerkship adviser since my first rotation is at MGH with you."

She did just receive her fall clerkship schedules this morning, and yes, she is in the emergency room at MGH for her rotation.

"Maybe," I whisper, gathering her back into my arms and holding her against me as I press my lips to her hairline. "All I know is that it involves you and it involves me."

Which is why I'm at my wit's end. Seconds turn into minutes. My knee is bouncing, and the incessant tick of the goddamn clock making me more and more agitated. Finally, the door swings open, and in he waltzes, heavy steps along with the cloying scent of cigar smoke clinging to him.

"Callan." He claps me on the back as he passes. "I appreciate you coming in. Sorry to keep you waiting."

I still my bouncing knee and sit up straight. "Not a problem, sir."

He takes his seat, the wheels of his office chair sliding back a foot as he drops his sausage fingers onto his round stomach. "I'm not going to beat around the bush. I have two reasons for bringing you in here this morning."

My pulse spikes.

"The first is the easy one," he continues. "I've received tremendous feedback from our board and students about your work in the classroom. I'd like to offer you a permanent position here at the medical school." He holds up his hand, stopping me before I can politely decline, but that's not what I was about to do. I'm too shocked by the offer to do much of anything other than stare bewilderedly at the man. Shifting in his chair, he scoots himself in and drops his forearms to his desk. "I know you told me you weren't interested, but the raving reviews I've gotten from your students rival those of Dr. Lawrence and far exceed those of other first-year professors."

If he's offering me a job, that means he doesn't know about me and Layla. He can't.

Relief cools the adrenaline that had been thrumming through my veins, and I take a deep, steadying breath. "Sir, while I'm beyond flattered and quite frankly a bit floored by that, I'm not sure I am the best fit for this role. My focus and passion have always resided in my work in the hospital doing direct patient care. I only agreed to fill in out of respect to Dr. Lawrence."

His head bobs, and he picks up his Monte Blanc pen, tapping it lightly against the base of his keyboard. "I assumed you'd say something along those lines to me. But please, do me a favor and consider it for a day or two before making your final decision."

"I can do that," I concede, and he gives me an absent grin, only for it to instantly slip from my lips.

"Now onto the second part of this. Murphy Wallace."

And just like that, everything speeds back up, but this time in shock "What about her, sir? I thought you mentioned Miss Fritz to me in your message last night."

He leans back in his chair once more, but his unwavering gaze tells me he's anything but relaxed. "First, I'd like to hear your impression of her."

I shake my head. "Which student?"

"Let's start with Layla Fritz and go from there."

Immediately I feel like this is a trap. Like there is no good answer and everything I say will be a setup.

"My impression of Layla Fritz as a student here at the school, in my emergency department, or in general?" I toss back at him.

"The first one and we'll work our way through the rest."

I refrain from wiping my hands on my thighs as I sit up a bit straighter and tell him the truth. "I'm a bit confused," I admit. "Who are we discussing here today?"

"Both students. You see, Murphy Wallace is failing. Her simulator scores are horrendous, and so are her case studies."

"I know about her case studies. I'm also relatively sure she's copying and pasting straight from Google in them."

He nods at me. "Murphy Wallace claims your case studies are unfairly difficult."

I scoff at that, my eyebrows raised in challenge. "Unfairly difficult? These are actual case studies from when I was an intern and resident, and this is Harvard Medical School. I seem to remember my professors doing something similar when I was here."

I get a crooked grin, almost as if I'm complimenting him, which I sort of am. Dr. Scabowitz was my second-year professor when I was a student here. "Yesterday, I confronted her about her scores, informing her that she's officially on probation and that if her scores don't improve, she's gone before second-year starts."

"I'm in agreement with that. But what does that have to do with Layla Fritz?"

He taps his pen twice and then drops it on the desk. "Murphy then came back to me with an accusation. She claims Layla Fritz cheats on her case studies. I know she's not only your student here but your student at the hospital, which is why I'd like your opinion of her."

Anger flares up inside me, but I do my best to quell it and answer him with an even tone. "Layla doesn't cheat."

"So you don't believe that accusation has any merit?"

"No," I tell him adamantly. "I don't. My opinion of Layla Fritz as a student is that she's extremely smart, dedicated, and hardworking. She sees details her peers miss. My impression of her work in the hospital is similar, but I'll add that she doesn't balk at being assigned scut work and has an innate compassion I've found lacking from other medical students, as well as many doctors, truth be told. And my general opinion of her is that I believe she'll make an excellent doctor."

"That's your honest assessment of her?"

Guilt and even some paranoia claw at me. I'm more than tempted to come clean.

But my honesty won't help her. In fact, it will only hurt her. If it were just about me, I'd tell him now. Putting the indiscretion of what we're doing aside, if I tell him Layla and I are in a relationship, he'll believe she's cheating because I make up the case studies. If I tell him I simply care about her and work with her, he'll investigate, and there is no way to prove she's not cheating. It's a no-win situation for her.

She's already taking a risk by being with me. I promised her I'd be an adjunct, not a hindrance, and I have to stick to that. She's worth more than my integrity.

What good can telling him bring other than assuaging my own guilt?

I run my hands through my hair and drop my elbows to my lap. "Layla isn't cheating."

"She could be asking her brother-in-law or one of her uncles for help. That counts as cheating."

"She's not."

He chuckles lightly, almost incredulously. "How could you possibly know that?"

I need to keep myself in check. "It's not who she is, sir. I've been working alongside her for a while now. She has too much pride and is too much of a natural competitor to do that. If you don't believe me, review Layla's performance throughout the year. It's consistent. I went through everyone's work when I first started. It sounds to me as though Murphy Wallace is saying whatever she has to to throw the heat off herself."

He rubs at his jaw as his demeanor shifts yet again. "So what would you say if I told you that in addition to accusing Miss Fritz of cheating, Miss Wallace also accused you of having an affair with her and that you're the one helping her cheat?"

And just like that, my world stops dead. He rocks back in his chair as he scrutinizes me with the diligent focus a detective would give a murder suspect. Silence. Heavy, deafening, consuming silence.

I can lie. I can try to cheat.

But it's not who I am.

Besides, if I lie and he digs and discovers the truth, it'll only be worse for Layla.

"If you believed that, you wouldn't have offered me a position."

"No. I wouldn't have, and that's because I didn't believe her. Not for a second. But I'm looking at you now Callan, and you look like a man who is not simply defending a student, but defending a woman he cares about."

I straighten my spine and meet his gaze head-on. "Layla is a woman I care about. Very much. She and I are together, but it's not as scandalous as it sounds."

"Shit," he hisses, opening his desk drawer and pulling out an unlit cigar. He pops the unlit thing into his mouth and starts chewing on the butt of it, and I refrain from cringing at him. What sort of doctor does that? "Callan, are you kidding me? What the fuck am I supposed to do with that?"

He rises from his chair, agitated in a way I've never seen him.

I just dumped a scandal in his lap with the name Fritz on it, and I have to fix it, and fix it now.

I sit up straighter, refusing to cower even as my heart pumps a steady dose of adrenaline through me. "Review her work throughout the entire year. Review the case studies she did with Dr. Lawrence. Review her work in the simulator lab. You'll see consistent work." I stand now too. "You asked me my impression of her, and that's what it is. I don't cheat, and neither does Layla. She and I have only recently started a personal relationship, but it's far from something sordid. I love her. Regardless of that, it doesn't enter the classroom."

"You want me to believe you're having a sexual affair with her and you're not helping her cheat or grading her differently than you are any other student? Come on, Callan. I wasn't born yesterday."

I try to hold in my ire because he has to ask that and if it were me in his position, I wouldn't believe me either. It looks bad. It looks really fucking bad because it is.

"I'd never do that, sir. Ever. And neither would Layla." I step forward, pressing against the edge of his desk. "You already said you didn't believe the accusation, and that's because you know me," I throw at him instead. "I was a student here and you were my professor. You were also my clerkship and rotation adviser for my second and third years. You know me to be a man of my word and a man of integrity."

He points the tip of the cigar at me accusingly. "Yet you've been hiding an affair with your student."

"Affair sounds dirty. I have no wife, and I'm not cheating on anyone by being with her, nor is our relationship based on favors of any kind. I met Layla the night I agreed to this position and at the time, I didn't know she was a student here. Once we discovered that, we both did our best to stay away from each other. Trust me, falling in love with one of my students was not something I anticipated or planned." I shrug helplessly. "I love her, but that doesn't make me a liar, and it certainly doesn't make her a cheater. If you don't believe me on that, take me out of the equation."

He gives me a bemused grin. "Meaning what?"

I retake my seat, and he does the same, blowing off some of the steam he was building.

"Meaning they have class this morning." I start to gather strength and determination. "You write them a new case study that I have no part of. You'll come into class with me this morning and administer it."

I get this long, drawn-out, contemplative, I'm a dirtbag stare. "What do you think that will show?"

"That Layla doesn't cheat, and that Murphy Wallace shouldn't become a physician."

He tilts his head and narrows his gaze. "And what about you, Callan?"

It's a valid question. "I'll go in with you, and you can hold my phone, so you know I'm not doing anything underhanded. I'm telling you"—I lean forward, scooting the edge of my chair and pinning him with a look he can't ignore—"Layla Fritz isn't cheating, and neither am I." I blow out a breath. "Honestly, sir. I don't care about me. I have no stake in this for the long-term, but Layla does. She is one of the best and brightest students I've seen walk through my emergency room doors in a very long time. I'm not saying we didn't do anything wrong, and I'm not making excuses for our actions with each other. I know I likely should have spoken up sooner, but nothing we have outside of school has impacted what she's done in this building. Test her, sir. Test her and you'll see for yourself."

He rubs at his jaw and then pops the cigar hanging precariously from his lips and chucks it onto the table. "I'll do it. I'll create a case study for them to do in class this morning. Honestly, the last thing I'd ever want to do is wrongfully accuse a Fritz. Her family donates millions to the school, and two of her uncles, as well as her grandfather, are alumni. And yes, I agree her work has been consistent over the year because I reviewed it last night after Miss Murphy's accusations. Her simulator scores are also exemplary, which you have no part of." A frown mars his face, and he scrubs a hand over his forehead. "Dammit, Callan. You put me in one hell of a position."

"I'm aware of that, sir, and again, I apologize for it. We love each other, and that couldn't be denied."

He nods his head, and then shakes it in dismay, and then nods again. "I'm agreeing to this because I do know you, and despite this infraction, I do trust you to be a man of your word and honor. However, I think it's best if you don't accept my offer."

I wipe away my smirk. "I wholeheartedly agree with that. What about Layla?"

A heavy, resigned sigh. "Layla stays pending the results of the case study this morning and a more thorough review of the case studies she's already done this summer."

Hope shoots through me like a geyser, but I'm far from feeling settled about any of this yet. "One hundred percent, sir. What about my remaining two weeks?"

"You'll finish them out, but I'll be the one to write and give the case studies from here on out."

"Thank you, sir." I stand and extend my hand. "I'm sorry if I let you down. Please, whatever your opinion of me, don't hold any of this against Miss Fritz. She's a brilliant woman and will make an incredible physician one day."

He shakes my hand, and then I leave, anxious to get out of there. I walk down the hall to the classroom, and when I enter, it's already filling up, and Layla is there, her expression questioning but grim and nervous. I give her a slip of a wan smile and leave it at that. I won't risk texting her, and I won't tip her off that anything is coming.

This needs to be honest if she's going to be exonerated.

Murphy Wallace is sitting three chairs down from Layla, looking smug. That is until Dr. Scabowitz enters the room twenty minutes later and explains to everyone his plans for their morning, and then her expression drops. I sit at the front of the classroom as everyone works diligently, Dr. Scabowitz beside me, watching with focused, critical eyes.

After class, he shakes my hand again and tells me he'll be in touch later today with his determination. I thank him, but by the time I leave, Layla is already gone, and I don't get a chance to talk to her. I figure I'll try at the hospital where we're both headed.

Only when I get there, there is a mass trauma, and for my entire shift, I don't see her. Not once. By the time I make it through the last patient, Layla has already left for the day.

I text her as I get in the car to pick up Katy, asking her to meet me at the sushi restaurant, and she counters by asking me to meet her at Stella's new restaurant. I agree, and just as Katy and I enter Stella's restaurant and immediately spot Layla chatting with a woman I don't recognize over by the bar, a text comes in.

Dr. Scabowitz: Layla passed with flying colors. Top of her class as it were and the only one to not only properly diagnose the abdominal aortic aneurysm, but also the fact that the patient had Marfan's Syndrome. I believe that neither of you cheated. Murphy Wallace failed and will be out before the start of second-year classes and clerkships.

A euphoric cocktail of joy and relief slithers through me while every tense muscle in my body starts to relax. Especially when the second Layla spots us, a smile lights up her face. She gives us a wave, says something to the woman she's with, and then comes bounding over to us. She lifts Katy high up in the air and gives her a hug before setting her back down on her feet and leaning in to give me a kiss.

It's normal. Natural. And everything I've wanted us to be for the last couple of months. So much so that I don't stop myself from taking her into my arms and deepening the kiss. Right here. Out in the open. I wish I had never decided to make her my fake fiancée. I wish she didn't have to wear the ring she has on her hand right now.

Our lies are out in the open, all except this one, and there isn't anything I can do about that until Katy is mine.

Someone from across the room whistles out a catcall. "Get a room!"

I pull back, laughing lightly. That had to be Stella. A point Layla proves by flipping her the bird behind her back in a way that Katy can't see.

"I take it your meeting with Dr. Scab went well," Layla exclaims, slightly breathless, and just like that, my insides sink.

"Sorta. I need to talk to you."

Worry creases her features, and she gives me a wan smile as she clutches my hand and leads us over to a small table already set up with menus. The three of us take our seats, and Katy hands me the kid's menu so I can go over it with her. She can read, but I know her mom used to do this with her so it's not something I argue about.

I read her each menu items
and she selects mac and cheese.

"Perfect choice," Layla praises. "It's so good here."

A waitress comes over and we order drinks and food, and then once it's just the three of us, I hand Katy my phone so she can play her Disney game on it, and I can talk to Layla without Katy giving us her undivided attention.

I reach over and take Layla's hand, playing with her long, delicate fingers and the ring that's sitting high on her hand. "Layla, how well do you know Murphy Wallace?"

The question takes her by surprise, and she shifts in her chair.

"I'm assuming not as well as I thought I did. I have a feeling you're about to confirm that for me."

"She accused you of cheating."

Her features harden, and she sucks in a sharp breath. With her hand gripping the edge of the table, she leans against it. "Are you fu"—she quickly glances at Katy—"f-ing kidding me?"

"Unfortunately, I'm not." I explain everything that happened today with Dr. Scabowitz when a shadow falls on our table.

"I thought that was you." My head flies around to discover Mrs. Bible standing beside me. "I was coming to see you after I had some dinner, but here you are."

I stumble out of my chair and extend my hand to her. "Mrs. Bible. How lovely to see you."

She breaks my hand with her grip. "I was taking Miss Fritz's advice and trying out Stella's restaurant. I don't typically enjoy Creole food, but I'll see how this goes."

Layla stands too, with a forced smile on her face that dies with her next heartbeat. She mutters something under her breath that sounds like a gritted curse, her gaze locked on something over my shoulder, and reflexively I turn to see what it is.

My insides plummet to my feet as Patrick and Murphy enter the restaurant and head our way.

32

L^{ayla}

I WON'T EVEN LIE and say I'm not ready to draw blood. Murphy accused me of cheating when she was the one copying and pasting from Doctor Fucking Google, and now she shows up at Stella's restaurant with my ex. Normally, I'd just verbally eviscerate her, flip him off, and then go home with Callan because the sex and love with him is a million times better than it ever was with Patrick, but I can't.

Because this had to happen right when Mrs. Bible—of all freaking people—decided to dine at Stella's. I can't even ask Murphy the burning question that's sticking to the tip of my tongue—how did she know about me and Callan?

I'm not sure what to do or how to play this. Beside me, Callan is a statue, staring at Murphy and Patrick and then back at Mrs. Bible as if he's watching two cars about to collide and he can't do anything to stop the destruction about to happen.

For a moment, I think Callan is about to pick Katy up and run.

Instead, he takes Mrs. Bible by the arm and starts to gently guide her away from the table. "Mrs. Bible, where are you sitting?" he asks. "I'd hate to have you miss your food being delivered."

"No, no," she tells him. "I was about to order when I saw you—"

"Wow," Murphy exclaims, cutting Mrs. Bible off midsentence. She's sporting a grin that makes the Cheshire cat look depressed. "What an incredible coincidence to find you here, bestie. With our professor. Hi, Dr. Barrows." She gives Callan a wiggly-fingered wave. "Or is it Dr. Hottie McSterious? Isn't that what you call him, Layla?"

"Professor?" Mrs. Bible questions, her gaze ping-ponging back and forth between Murphy and Callan. "I thought you were a doctor."

"I am," Callan says, ravaged defeat blaring like a siren across his face. His hands meet his hips, and his gaze dips to the table, then over to Katy, then back to Mrs. Bible. "I am also holding a temporary position at Harvard Medical School for the summer. Filling in for a doctor who passed away."

Mrs. Bible shakes her head. "So you're Miss Fritz's teacher? In addition to working with her at the hospital?"

"He sure is. Not the most ethical thing to do, is it? Then again, neither is cheating."

"Murphy," I snarl under my breath. "You don't know what you're talking about or what you're doing. Walk away. Now."

"You thought I didn't know?" she snarls right back at me. "You thought you could get away with it. But I saw you with him on campus one night after our simulator lab. I saw him take your hand, talk to you, kiss you, and then run off together. That was the night of the first case study. While we were all toiling at it ourselves and on the group chat, you were sleeping your way to answers. Naturally, you were the only one to get it right."

That was the night Callan and I started sleeping together. She saw us. It explains why she's been cold toward me since then. No wonder she accused me of cheating.

"I didn't cheat. That's not what happened, and that's not what's happening here."

Murphy laughs sardonically, folding her arms over her chest and popping her hip out. "Right. Sure. Real fucking believable." Her grin slips into a sneer as her voice turns acerbic. "You thought you were so much better than all of us. So much smarter. But you're a liar, and a cheater, and a slut. I told Dr. Scabowitz about you. You'll be expelled by the end of the week."

"This is why you wouldn't get back together with me?" Patrick jumps in before I can answer Murphy and tell her that she's the one who is out and not me. "Because you were screwing around with him?" He jabs an angry finger in Callan's direction before turning on Murphy. "Why the hell am I even here? You told me she wanted me back."

Mrs. Bible is rightfully confused. Murphy is positively gleeful. Patrick is pissed. Callan is a mess, and I'm right there with him.

"What is going on here?" Mrs. Bible asks, her voice rising.

I reach over and take Callan's hand, gripping it. "Mrs. Bible, that is the man I was with prior to being with Callan. It's been over between us for a long time now." I glare at Patrick. "And no, he's not the reason I didn't want to get back together with you. You are."

"How long, Layla?" Patrick demands, getting right up in my face. "How long have you been with him? You lied to me. You told me nothing was going on between the two of you."

Because, at the time, nothing was going on. Only I can't say that.

Callan pulls me closer to his side before he pivots like he's about to get in Patrick's face. "Back off, Patrick. This is the last time I'll tell you."

Patrick straightens his spine, pulling himself up to his full height, which is still a couple of inches shorter than Callan. He gives him an asshole-ish grin. "Or what? You'll beat my ass? I'd love to see you try. I deserve some answers."

"Can someone please explain to me what's happening?" Mrs. Bible is running out of patience. "What is all this about cheating and secret affairs? Dr. Barrows, have you been hiding your engagement to Miss Fritz from the medical school?"

"Engagement?!" Patrick roars. "She's not fucking engaged to him. She was living with me four months ago."

Oh, God. Oh no. My heart slams against my rib cage and my stomach roils, shooting bile up the back of my throat.

Stella comes racing over, breaking up the tension. Her hand lands on my arm, clutching me as her gaze flitters to each person standing around us like some sort of angry mob. I know we're causing a scene in her restaurant, and I feel terrible about that, but there's nothing I can do.

"Layla?" she questions, tilting her head to me.

It's too late to fix this now. I stare helplessly at my friend, rolling my tongue ring back and forth between my lips. I don't even know what to say. What to do.

"Stella, would you do me a favor and take Katy to the back and get her something to eat?" Callan asks calmly. Too calmly.

Stella's eyes are all over me, and I give her a nod.

Her features crease with consternation, but she says, "Of course. Katy, do you want to see how we make your dinner?"

Katy hesitates and Callan releases my hand, walking over to her and squatting down so he can meet her eyes. "Go on, Ladybug. It's okay." He gives her a smile that doesn't reach his eyes as he touches her cheek. "I'll see you in a bit." He kisses her forehead, his eyes pinching closed, and my heart breaks, watching the fear and agony on his face.

Everything is crashing down around us all at once.

Katy places her hand in Stella's, and the two of them walk off together. Stella throws me a meaningful look over her shoulder, and then they disappear to the back room.

"Dr. Barrows, are you engaged to Layla Fritz or not?" Mrs. Bible demands, making no bones about expecting an honest answer. We could lie. We could. But at this point, it'll only hurt us more if we do, and I know Callan knows that.

Callan's head is bowed, his hand gripping the arm of the chair Katy was just sitting in. Finally, he blows out a heavy breath and stands, addressing only Mrs. Bible. "When my brother and sister-in-law died, there was no will dictating who they wanted Katy to go to. I know you know this."

Mrs. Bible shifts her weight, her tone clipped. "Yes. I know this."

"I took guardianship of her because I love her, and I couldn't imagine her going anywhere else. She formed a bond with Layla and when she ran away from camp to find her, social services got involved. I wanted Layla for Katy." He shrugs. "Hell, I wanted her for myself too."

"I'm not sure I understand?"

Callan haplessly tosses his hands. "I love Katy. I've loved her since the moment she was born and I've been a constant part of her life since. I didn't hesitate to take her when Declan and Willow died. But when Willow's parents sought custody, it was suggested that I could lose her because I was a single man, and they were two willing parents." His mouth twists into a resentful scowl. "It felt ridiculous and wrong, but I knew it was true all the same. I couldn't let it happen. I couldn't lose Katy like that."

"How did Miss Fritz get involved?" Mrs. Bible queries.

Callan walks back to us and retakes my hand, his eyes adoring, even as his world falls apart. "Miss Fritz and I had recently met, and I will tell you, I was already more than halfway in love with her by that point. I asked Miss Fritz if she'd be my fiancée so I could gain custody of Katy. Miss Fritz, who has the most beautiful and selfless heart of anyone I know, agreed."

"What does her position in school have to do with this?"

He turns back to Mrs. Bible. "Nothing. It was an unfortunate coincidence. I met her prior to knowing I was going to be her temporary professor. She was there the night Willow and Declan died. She was the person in the emergency room caring for Katy. None of this was planned."

Murphy clears her throat, and Callan looks over to her.

"Layla never cheated, and I never helped her with her case studies. Not once. I have already spoken with Dr. Scabowitz, and he is aware that Layla and I are together. The case study you all took this morning proves that Layla didn't cheat. She never had to. You, on the other hand, are failing out and if anyone will be gone by the end of the week, it's you. Maybe you should learn to manage yourself and get all the facts before you try to ruin other people's lives."

Murphy looks like she swallowed a bug, her face pinching up, and she takes a step back. "I assumed Layla cheated. I saw you with her, and then she was the only one who got the case study right."

"Because no one else in the class clicked on something as simple as family history," Callan snaps. "But I will tell you, everyone else's work in the class has improved. Everyone's except for yours. You've never put in the effort ,and that kind of lazy, shotty work is dangerous and will put people's lives at risk."

Murphy stares down remorsefully at the floor and takes another step back. "I'm sorry. I didn't know."

"Now you do, and you've done your worst, so why don't you go," I hiss at her.

"I'm not going yet," Patrick states, standing his ground and pulling me back to him. "You love him? Like actually love him?"

"Yes," I tell him. "I love him. It's not simple and it's not easy, but it's real, and it's the kind of love that will never fade or die. I don't know why you're still holding on."

Patrick stares at me, running his hands through his hair and gripping the back of his head. "I always thought you'd find your way back to me. Couples do that. They take a break. Figure things out. Then get back together."

I shake my head at that. I don't want to get into this with him again. It's pointless. "You wanted to have your cake and eat it too, but that's not the type of person I am. It's Callan, Patrick, not you, and that won't change."

Without another word, he spins around and storms out.

Murphy looks sick, and I hope she is. I hope she realizes what she's just done. How wrong her accusations are. Either way, she doesn't deserve another second of my attention. I turn my back on her, giving Mrs. Bible my full focus. I don't know if Murphy stays or leaves.

All I know is it's now just the three of us.

"I didn't do it to hurt anyone," Callan starts, his voice fractured. "I did it because I love Katy, and I can't lose her. Please." His voice cracks and he clears his throat, staring beseechingly at her. "I can't lose her, and she can't lose me. She's already lost so much. Please don't take her from me."

Mrs. Bible's gaze bounces back and forth between the two of us before settling on Callan. "You lied to me. You lied to the courts."

Callan swallows audibly and nods gravely.

Mrs. Bible grows terse. "And you feel that's a measure of someone who will make a good guardian?"

His hand grips mine tighter, and I can feel his pulse hammering through his skin. I want to say something, I want to fix this, but I have no clue how to do that.

Callan doesn't cower. Not for a second. "I feel a good parent would do anything for their child and that includes lying if necessary. And I felt it was necessary. I couldn't have her go off and move to a new state and go to a new school and live with people she hardly knows. I couldn't. Lying is not something that sits well with me and it's not something I'm proud of, but if it meant I got Katy at the end, well, I'd do anything to have that happen."

Mrs. Bible takes that in, but it does nothing to soften her. Instead, she grows angrier. "You've given me no reason to trust you. If anything, you've just proven that Katy's grandparents are the better, safer option for Katy. I will not remove her from your home tonight because I feel that would be too traumatizing for her, but I will request an emergency hearing and I can tell you now, Dr. Barrows, when I file my report, I will not be siding in your favor."

Mrs. Bible leaves, and for a moment, we're too stunned to do anything other than stand here.

"What do I do?" he finally asks, his voice as shaky as I feel.

"I honestly don't know."

His eyes meet mine. "I'm going to lose her. It's so strange. I started this out of fear, but that fear has nothing on me now. I don't know what to tell Katy. Everything was starting to feel as though it was coming together, and now it's all being ripped apart. I was wrong,

Layla. I was wrong to do this in the first place. I should have never made you my fake fiancée."

My chest cracks open as I watch him grapple with this, tormented and ravaged in regret and uncertainty.

"When you asked me to be your fake fiancée, Amelia told me she would have done the same if it had been her. That she would have done anything to keep me with her. Hindsight gives us perspective and makes us question our actions, but it's useless after the fact. We can't go back in time. We can only go forward."

He wraps his arms around me, pressing me into his chest right here in the restaurant. "I can't lose her. It's you, and it's her. I went from just being me to having you both, and now I can't imagine my world without either of you. I've fucked up so much. So much for her and for you. If you're having second thoughts about being with me, I understand. I've compromised you in a hundred different ways."

I have no words of comfort, and I refuse to offer him hollow platitudes.

He's going to lose Katy, and I have no idea how to stop it.

33

C allan

I DIDN'T SLEEP. Not one wink. I put on a brave, happy face for Katy who is smart and intuitive and knew things had taken a turn the wrong way without me having to say anything. I told her everything. Feeling so awful I could hardly stand to sit still or be in my own skin when she looked me in the eyes and then broke down. After that, she was quiet and clingy, but so was I.

I had no reassurances for her, and I was done lying.

Tom called me at nine to inform me we have an emergency court hearing at three p.m. today and that Katy will be required to come.

He wasn't happy, nor was he hopeful about my chances of keeping Katy. He also told me the judge was fucking pissed. Asher came over at five this morning and dragged me from the house, forcing me to go to his gym to try and work off some of my nervous energy.

By the time I got home, Layla had to leave for the simulator lab, and while I knew she had to go because she can't miss it—especially after yesterday—I wish she were here with me.

My friends came over—with the exception of Lenox since he's in Maine—for moral support and to try and distract me. Fallon and Aurelia whipped up a spread of food that I hardly touched, and we ate while talking about nothing, and the day passed like that.

Now here we are, all of us entering the courthouse because according to Fallon, when your life doesn't go as expected, you need your people there to either hold you up or help you celebrate.

Layla isn't here yet, and that's not helping my edginess. I told her I'd understand if she left me, and I would. This was the last thing she said she wanted to have happen. Her work is her life, and I get that. That's how it should be for a young medical student and even a young doctor.

She didn't plan on me, and she didn't plan on Katy for the long term.

And while uncertainty with Layla slashes a new gash into my already torn apart heart, I'll have to figure it out later. For now, Katy is holding my hand and I have the strongest urge to run away with her. Something that must be written all over my face because Mrs. Bible is here, standing right outside the courtroom door.

"Katy needs to come with me. I have another court liaison who will sit with her during the proceedings."

Immediately I shake my head.

Zax's hand meets my shoulder. "It's just during the hearing, right?" he checks with her.

"For now," Mrs. Bible says without even a hint of emotion.

"No," Katy cries, clinging to my side. "I don't want to. I want to stay with you."

I glare—and I glare hard—at Mrs. Bible before I kneel down so I can look into Katy's eyes which are the same color as mine.

"You have to, honey. I'm so sorry." My voice catches, and I cup her face in my hand before I drag her into me, holding her, kissing the top of her head, smelling her sweet scent. "I will do everything in my power to keep you, Katy. But if the judge decides that's not what's best for you, I will talk with your grandparents and work something out. You won't lose me, Ladybug. I swear it, you won't."

"But being with you is what's best for me."

She clings to me, and I wrap my arms tighter around my girl, fighting my emotions that are already threatening to overtake me.

Mrs. Bible comes in and snatches Katy away, prying her from my arms, and my insides are being ripped away with her.

"No!" Katy screams, reaching for me. Tears well up in my eyes and my heart shatters as I stand.

"You're wrong on this," I tell Mrs. Bible, no longer caring. "You're wrong. I know you can see it." I shake my head at her. "I'll see you soon, Katy. It'll be okay. However this goes, I promise, I'll make it okay for you."

Mrs. Bible turns a corner with Katy, and even though Mrs. Bible is wrong for not seeing what's so blatantly in front of her, I have no one else to blame for this but myself. My actions have hurt Katy. My lies have hurt her, and I don't know how to reconcile that.

Slowly, I shuffle along, my heart in my feet, and drag my miserable ass into the courtroom.

Asher's hand is on one shoulder. Grey's is on the other. They're holding me up because I would absolutely fall apart if they weren't. I don't know what I did to deserve them in my life, but I thank my lucky stars each and every day that they are.

As we make our way inside the courtroom, the attorney for Katy's grandparents is standing, chatting with one of the court officers. When he sees me, he gives me a pompous look that I'd love nothing more than to knock off his face. Somehow that twists into awe and he immediately sprints over to us, which takes me by surprise.

Even more so when he rushes out, "Can I have your autograph? I realize this isn't the right place to ask, but after today, I'm worried I won't get another chance."

I look over my shoulder to where his gaze is locked and stumble upon Asher, who looks like he's ready to knock the guy out. "Nah, man." He waves him away. "No way. You're fucking with my guy here."

The lawyer blushes and shifts his weight, covering his mouth as he says, "Sorry, I didn't mean you. I was asking Lia Sage." He points to Aurelia. "I've followed your modeling career and am obsessed with your couture. I'm such a huge fan. Your gowns are everything."

I bark out a laugh, and it's the first one in I don't even know how long. Asher is affronted, which is part of what is making this so humorous. "For real?" he snaps. "You want her autograph over mine?" Incredulous Asher might be one of my favorite things ever.

The lawyer shrugs, still slightly embarrassed. "Football isn't really my thing. I run drag shows in the South End."

Zax, Greyson, and Fallon choke on their own laughter at that. I don't know if Asher's ego can handle that blow. "I like drag shows, bro. I support the hell out of that. I just don't like you."

The lawyer is undeterred as he encroaches upon Aurelia. "Be that as it may, would you sign something for me?"

Aurelia is taken aback but composes herself quickly. "Uh, well, first, I'm very flattered. And I too love drag shows, so if you ever need couture for your shows, you can message me. But you're here to take away my friend's niece, so I can't do that right now. In fact, I straight up want to kick your nuts so hard they pop up through your teeth and you choke on them."

"Yeah," Asher jumps back in. "What my girl Reils said. Go back to your table where your greedy ass clients *aren't* sitting. Because they straight-up suck at life. Think of how you'll feel if you end up giving a six-year-old little girl to a couple who only care about the money she comes with."

The lawyer scuttles off, and Asher turns to all of us. "Can you believe that guy? Fashion over football. That's insanity."

I snicker. "You set him straight, brother. Thanks for that." I slap Asher's shoulder, and then all amusement dies as I go over and greet Tom and my friends take their seats behind us. The court is called to order, and the judge is announced. We all rise, and then he's taking his seat, and yes, if the glare he's giving me is anything to go by, he's fucking pissed, and this time, there is no Octavia to bail me out.

There isn't even a Layla to hold my hand.

I sit heavily in my chair, which feels like a rock beneath me, as despair and panic slurry around in my stomach.

The judge shuffles some papers around and then he's addressing me as if I'm a Nazi at Nuremberg. "Dr. Barrows, it has come to my attention that you and Miss Fritz have willingly deceived this court."

I swallow down a noise, and do my best to appear calm, but I am anything but. I look to Tom and this time he gives me a nod, indicating that I should be the one to address the court.

"Yes, sir, though the blame is entirely on my shoulders and no one else's. Miss Fritz was simply trying to help me."

I won't let Layla take the fall for this. I am the one who asked her to do this. I am the one who put her in an impossible situation, playing on her heart and her past.

"Your Honor, if I may, I'd like to make a motion to—" Mr. Salucci jumps in, only to be silenced by the judge holding up a hand.

"It is not the time to make any motions as we're here to discuss the sudden change in Katy Barrow's custody situation." He turns back to me. "Dr. Barrows, in my years on the bench, I've had many people sit before me and lie. But never like this. Never with such a blatant lack of respect for the court and never going to such extremes as to make up a fake engagement. What do you have to say for yourself?"

Slowly I stand, my voice broken and desperate, as I already know I've lost.

"Your Honor, in the matter of a few hours, my life was turned upside down. My brother and sister-in-law died, leaving their little girl alone, and me the only one to take care of her. A little girl I held the day she was born. A little girl I was immediately in love with. So much so that I had one of the spare bedrooms in my home turned into her bedroom before she could even walk. I didn't think twice about keeping Katy with me when they died. It felt right and it felt natural.

"Mr. Salucci's clients haven't called to talk to Katy. Not once. Willow and Declan died nearly two months ago now, and they haven't checked in to see how Katy is doing with the loss of her parents. They don't care about what she's been doing in camp or that she wants to be a mermaid or that she still occasionally has night terrors. Simply put, they don't care about her. They're not there for her—I am. Katy doesn't matter to them. Her inheritance does. They want her money and care nothing of her."

I fall forward, planting my hands on the table, looking over at the judge through my lashes.

"Your Honor, I know you've been made to believe everything out of my mouth is a lie, but that's not how it is. I only care about Katy. Yes, I lied about the engagement. But even though the engagement was a ruse, the love was real, and Layla living with us, she's been a rock for Katy. I lied so that Katy could have the best possible chance at a happy future because *I know* I'm the only one who can give her that. When you read over whatever Mrs. Bible wrote in her report and you think about this, please consider that even though what I did was wrong, I did it all for Katy."

I wipe at my mouth, and take a deep breath only to exhale it slowly.

"I'm not perfect," I continue. "I'll never get everything right. But in my gut, *in my soul*, I know that Katy belongs with me. More importantly, she knows it too. If you don't believe me, talk to her. Get the facts from her. Don't discount me simply because it's the easy thing to do."

I sit down, and the judge leans back in his seat, still staring at me as if I just intentionally blew up a bus full of nuns. I can already tell he wasn't moved by my little speech. He views me as a liar. As a man who disrespected his court and his position, and I did. I did exactly that and I have no recourse.

An icy blade of fear stabs into me, flaying me open, and leaving me utterly powerless to stop myself from bleeding out right here. My head falls to my hands, even though I was trying for brave and strong. I know my friends are behind me, but my brother isn't here, and my parents are off doing their thing and aren't here, and fucking Layla isn't even here.

I'm angry with him for not creating a will, and I'm angry with myself for acting rashly in making Layla my fake fiancée, and I'm angry and frustrated at a legal system that would discount me as the best option for Katy after a minor safety issue simply because I'm unattached. It's provincial and sexist and biased. There are millions of single parents out there doing a damn good job. But because two greedy assholes made themselves look like sad victims, they're going to win, and I'm going to lose.

I was never a big believer on fair versus unfair.

I'm a doctor, and you see life shit on everyone equally. Rich, poor, ugly, beautiful—it doesn't matter within the walls of the emergency department.

But this... this is un-fucking-fair, and I want to scream that at the top of my lungs for all to hear. I'm not this Callan. I'm never this Callan. I'm methodical and a problem solver and a healer, but I have no control, and it's driving me to the edge of my sanity.

The judge clears his throat, and my hands fall to the table. Warily I meet his steady gaze.

"Dr. Barrows, I can see that you're visibly upset, as I feel you should be. While I hear what you're saying, and I can see there is genuine remorse for your actions, I don't see how this court can—"

The doors at the back of the courtroom fly open, and Layla comes rushing in along with... Lenox? Huh? What the hell is going on?

34

C allan

"YOUR HONOR, IF I MAY." Layla shoots to the front of the room, interrupting the judge. "I realize this is against every protocol you have, and I know I'm likely not your favorite person right now, but please, may I be heard? I have some evidence you need to see. I'd also like to express my own thoughts and opinions on Dr. Barrows as a father figure to Katy."

The judge presses his lips together, even more displeased than he was two seconds ago, and part of me wants to grab her hand and shove her into a seat. I don't though, because Layla is standing tall, beautiful, poised, and unflappable. The judge must see it too, because he pans a disgruntled hand in her direction as if reluctantly giving her the floor.

Lenox comes in and quietly sits beside Fallon, who is on the end. In unison, Grey, Ash, Zax, and I all twist our heads in his direction, questions clearly etched all over our faces. He ignores everyone except for me. I get a sly grin, but that's it. All silent muscles and tattoos, that's the only thing he gives me.

"Lenox?" I bark.

"Your girl is a fucking spitfire," he says, still with that grin. "I dig her."

Mr. Salucci is on his feet. "Your Honor—"

"Both attorneys, please approach." The judge holds up his hand as both he and Tom join Layla up at the podium in front of the judge. I can't hear what they're saying. All I know is Layla is handing them each several pieces of paper, and the attorney for Willow's parents is now arguing something and then Tom is jumping in, arguing equally as aggressively, if not more so.

"I'll allow it," the judge finally decrees. "This is relevant to the case." They continue to argue, but my eyes are on Layla, who skips over to me and lands in the empty chair beside me, immediately taking my hand. I grip her fingers, squeezing them between mine.

"If you didn't love me before, you're going to worship at my altar in a second."

"What is all this?" I question under my breath.

"So much juiciness." Her eyes sparkle like a reporter who just nailed the big story and is about to bring down an evil empire.

"What did you do?" I question, going out of my mind.

She leans in and whispers in my ear, "Two things. The grandfather was found passed out drunk on the side of the road three days ago. It wasn't a DUI. He was apparently walking home from whatever bar he was drinking in, and a cop picked him up. He became combative and belligerent, so the cop arrested him. He ended up sleeping it off in a jail cell overnight and then pled no contest to misdemeanor disorderly conduct and public intoxication in exchange for the report being expunged from his permanent record in thirty days if he completes twenty hours of community service. Evidently, he had to beg and plead for the thirty days because that's far from standard procedure, but the judge there agreed for some reason."

"We were supposed to appear in court for Katy's hearing in five weeks."

She bops my shoulder with her other hand. "Exactly. But since we're here early, Lenox was able to find it."

"How did you know to call Lenox?"

"You had mentioned the night you showed up at school that I would shudder if I knew all he was capable of with a computer, and the night we played basketball at Fallon and Grey's place, Fallon told me about how she and Greyson got together and casually mentioned how Lenox was able to do some stuff for them. I figured it couldn't hurt for him to dig a little."

"Wow. Okay." I'm utterly flummoxed. "You said two things though?"

She snorts out a laugh. "This is the best part. Mr. Ashlan, Katy's grandfather, opened his mouth and told the judge that he needed his record expunged because he's part of an ongoing custody battle for his granddaughter. By doing so, the court notified Mrs. Bible that the grandfather was arrested as she's the court-appointed social services liaison. She received the email two days ago to her work email and deleted it. Not to mention, she didn't follow up on this or make any sort of note about it in Katy's file. All of this is illegal."

"Why would she delete it?" I ask, unable to make sense of that. Before she can answer, both lawyers retake their seats and Tom leans into me.

"I assume Layla filled you in?" Tom asks, and I nod. "Good. It's messy. The legal evidence presented about the grandparents is legitimate, as is the deleted email from Mrs. Bible's work account since she works for the state. There is also no notation about any arrest in Katy's file. It's the other documents that the judge is deciding if he'll allow or not since those were obtained by unknown means."

I stop breathing. "What other documents?" I whisper to both him and Layla.

Layla leans back in and whispers in my ear. "Lenox discovered that Mrs. Bible has been in email communication with the Ashlans from her personal email. They promised Mrs. Bible ten percent of the life insurance policy and proceeds of your brother's home if she would determine you to be an unfit parent and they won custody of Katy."

"*Mrs. Bible did this?*" I cover my face with my hands, laughing incredulously into them. I never would have expected that. I assumed they were going to say she did this because she hates me—which I already knew and assumed. I never expected her to be accepting a *bribe* from Katy's grandparents. Nothing from the way she dressed to the way she conducted herself ever gave off the impression she'd ever do that.

She was by the book—no pun intended.

"Yes. There's other evidence—"

"Mrs. Bible," the judge's voice cuts Tom off sharply. "Would you care to explain why you deleted an email from Fallow County Court regarding the arrest of Mr. Ashlan and failed to make note of it in your case report for Katy Barrows?"

"Your Honor?" Mrs. Bible stands, visibly shaken, all the color draining from her face. "I'm not sure I understand your question. I came here today to testify about how Dr. Barrows is an unfit guardian for Katy Barrows."

The judge nails her with a look that could freeze over hell. "And you have no financial stake in that?"

She shifts her weight, pushing up the bridge of her glasses that immediately slide back down the perch of her nose. "I... um... Your Honor, I'm not sure I—"

"I have documents here that show you deleted a legal document sent to you along with a stream of emails between yourself and Katy Barrows' grandparents where they promised you money in exchange for you declaring Dr. Barrows to be an unfit guardian. Not to mention, I have another document here with your personal financial statements highlighting several large, random payments made to you that correlate with the dates of cases you worked on. Can you explain those?"

Mrs. Bible stares up at the judge and then, without a word, tries to book it for the exit. All of us gasp, shooting to the edges of our seats as we watch her run.

The judge bangs his gavel, his complexion ruddy as he shouts. "Bailiff, will you please stop Mrs. Bible from leaving and take her into custody?"

Mrs. Bible continues to race for the door, only to be blocked by a police officer and after a small skirmish, they manage to wrangle her out of the courtroom.

Holy shit. How is this happening?

"Holy hell. She tried to make a run for it." Asher is half-laughing, half-shocked. "This is like some insane TV shit going on."

"No joke," Grey agrees. "What the hell is going on?"

My head spins wildly, and Layla grips my forearm with the hand not holding mine and shakes me. "She was never going to side with you," she says in a low voice. "Which likely explains why she was such a megabitch and questioned everything you did and said when she came for her visits."

My forehead meets her shoulder. "I wasn't sure you'd come today, and then you show up and have done all this?"

She leans in and rubs her nose against mine. "Every Superman needs a Lois Lane to save them. Also, you can't beat the timing of Drunk Joe."

I grin, sitting up. "Drunk Joe?"

"That's not actually what they called him in the police report," Tom supplies.

I turn to him. "Is this enough for me to keep Katy?"

He doesn't crack a smile, but there is an unmistakable gleam in his eyes. "I think so, but we'll see. The judge is still unhappy about the lying, but I can't imagine he wants to make Katy a ward of the state when all you did is lie about having a fake fiancée. Then again, with how today has gone, I'm not sure anything would surprise me."

The courtroom is still buzzing with noise, and I can hear my friends behind me going nuts, grilling Lenox for answers.

The judge wipes at his forehead and bangs his gavel again, calling order back to the room. "Now that that's taken care of, Miss Fritz, do you still wish to address the court?" The man is clearly at the end of his patience, but despite that, Layla doesn't hesitate.

She stands, addressing him directly. "I do, Your Honor. Because my presenting you with those documents wasn't just to prove who the wrong people for Katy are, it was also to show you who the right person for her is. You see, I understand Katy's situation. When I was six years old, my parents were killed in a car accident. My sister Amelia, left college to move back to Boston to take care of me. I was lucky. She was my next of kin, and she wanted me. She was twenty at the time and it was a rough several years for us. But I never felt unsafe. I always felt loved and cared for. It wasn't easy and it wasn't perfect, but Amelia was what got me through. We were everything both of us needed, and that's what I've seen in the two months I've been living with Katy and Dr. Barrows."

She sucks in a deep breath and straightens her spine.

"They are it for each other. Callan's love for Katy isn't fleeting. It's not monetarily based. It's the sort of love that will sustain her through the hardest, darkest time of her life, and instead of constant tears and heartache, she'll have smiles and laughter in there too. He will take care of her. He would lie down in traffic for her. He would even go so far as to ask his student to be his fake fiancée because he would do anything not to lose her."

She turns and glances down at me, and then back over to the judge.

"I'm sorry we lied to you. Love and fear can drive us all to do wild things. Things we would never foresee ourselves doing in any other situation. Dr. Barrows is a good man. The best man I've ever known and considering who my family is, that is saying something tremendous. I love him, but Katy does too, and I know he will always put her first. Please, sir. We lied. But it was a lie of love. It was a lie of fear. But everything between us now is as real as it gets."

She sits back down, and I immediately take her into my arms and kiss her mouth right here. Right in this courtroom.

"Fuck Lois Lane, you're the Black Widow. Bold. Fierce. Savage.

And sexy as fucking hell." I hug her against me before dropping my forehead to hers. My hand caresses her cheek. "Thank you."

"You saved me with the school. The least I could do was return the favor."

I chuckle against her. "I love you."

"I love you."

I kiss her again, deeply, and then sit back in my chair. The judge rubs his forehead again and shifts in his chair. "Dr. Barrows, in light of all of the evidence presented today, I don't feel this court has much of a choice but to continue your temporary custody of Miss Barrows."

My heart leaps in my chest, only to snag on the word temporary.

He takes a breath. The sort of breath that usually feeds into things no one wants to hear. "I am going to be extending the probation period for another ninety days, and in addition to requiring another four observations by a *new* court liaison, I will also require parenting classes for you."

"Of course, Your Honor," Tom speaks for me now. "My client will do whatever is necessary."

"Good. Because if you show up here in ninety days or even before that with one more infraction, I will have no choice but to intervene and pull Miss Barrows from your home. For now, this court is adjourned."

He bangs his gavel, and I leap out of my seat, flying at Layla, hauling her body up and into mine, and slamming my lips down on hers. It happens so fast I'm not even aware I've done it until I feel the warm, sweet breath of her gasp against my lips.

I steal a quick taste and then murmur, "Thank you," against her mouth, against her lips as fierce, unshakable joy swirls through me like a tonic. "I love you. So fucking much. You never cease to amaze me."

She smiles against my lips. "All this time I was so afraid to fall in love again, but the truth is, I think I was always waiting for you."

I kiss her again, my hands in her hair, holding her to me. Never wanting to let her go.

Part of me is tempted to ask her to be my fiancée for real. I want to marry her and have babies with her, and watch Katy become a sister-aunt of sorts, but I'm getting ahead of myself, and I let the thoughts slowly fade away.

For now at least.

I give her one last kiss and then turn to find my friends. To find Lenox and grab the big man to bring him in for a hug.

"Thank you, brother. I owe you one. I owe you a million."

"It's what I do."

I laugh because it's true. It's what he does. And he's damn good at it. I have no idea where I'd be without him. Where any of us would be without each other.

"If there's ever anything I can do for you..."

He claps my shoulder, a smile on his face. "I know. Shut up already."

I snicker and decide to leave it at that, hugging my friends and thanking them for being with me on this wild ride.

It's not settled. I have ninety days, and yes, things could go wrong. With the way my life has been going lately, things could go very wrong.

But there are no more lies to strangle me or prevent me from keeping my girl. And no matter what, I know Katy isn't going to end up where she shouldn't be.

We leave the courtroom, and Katy is standing outside the door holding a strange woman's hand, but the moment she sees me coming for her, her face lights up and she tears herself away, running straight for me. I swoop her up into my arms and hug her fiercely against my chest.

I kiss her forehead. "Ready to go home?" I can't contain my smile.

She beams at me. "Ready."

I turn to Layla. "What about you?"

"Definitely ready."

Layla takes my hand, and we all head out of the courthouse.

No more lies. No more sneaking around. No more hiding what should never have had to be hidden. It's us. Forever.

EPILOGUE 1

L ayla
Ninety Days Later

IF YOU DIDN'T ALREADY KNOW this, life can change with every beat of your heart. Seconds aren't even necessary. A blink of an eye or an intake of breath might be all that's required. A rash decision. An impulsive move. And bam... your life will never be the same.

In the last ninety days, a lot has happened.

Murphy didn't wait until she was formally kicked out to leave school. She dropped out before simulator lab that very next day, and I can't say I was sad about it. Last I heard from the group chats, no one has spoken to her since, and I haven't bothered to look her up to see where she landed.

I also haven't heard from Patrick since he walked out of the restaurant, though I have no doubt I'll run into him since he too is doing clerkships and will be back on campus for classes starting in January.

Then there's Mrs. Bible.

She was arrested and started rolling over on all her charges, claiming parents and prospective guardians forced bribes on her that she couldn't turn down given her meager salary. I won't go into that. But I do know that several of the cases she closed have been reopened and reinvestigated.

The woman who took over for Mrs. Bible was a lot easier to work with and a hell of a lot less scary. She was also a huge fan of not only Central Square, but of Greyson Monroe and Asher Reyes, and it just so happened that both were over when she made her first pop-in visit. After that, it was easy street.

In the end, it didn't matter.

The last three months went smoothly for all of us, and as of two o'clock this afternoon, the judge ruled that Katy is permanently Callan's. Which is why we're celebrating and doing it in style. Octavia and Dr. Fritz senior invited everyone—all of my Fritz relatives and all of Callan's friends—over to swim in the indoor pool and play games and eat. She even rented a bounce house that she has set up inside because it's November in New England, which means it's too cold to be outside for any length of time.

I swear, the woman looks for any excuse to throw a party, and I'm certainly not complaining.

Katy has been running around with the Fritz kids all afternoon, and in the months that Callan and I have been together, she's grown especially close with Keegan and Kenna, who are only a year and a half older than her. It's been everything to see her blossom and hold her own with all these new people in her life.

It hasn't been all sunshine and roses though.

She misses her parents terribly, and though Callan and I do what we can to help with that, sometimes all you can do is be a shoulder to cry on, a pair of arms to hug, and an ear to listen. The night terrors have all but stopped and her psychologist recommended she keep a journal of feelings, which I think has been making a difference, especially on days she doesn't want to talk about it.

"What are you doing next week?" Stella asks as she sits on a lounger beside me in her tiny bikini, sipping champagne. Her newest restaurant is a massive success, just as much of one, if not more so, than Stella's. Plus, she asked Delphine to marry her, and Delphine said yes so, the girl has every reason to celebrate.

"Sitting on my ass, eating all the turkey and leftovers, and not studying," I answer, my eyes closed as I take a blind sip of my own champagne. Thanksgiving is next Thursday, and I can't tell you how much I'm looking forward to the break in school and clerkships. We do six-week rotations and right now I'm in the middle of psychiatry, which is fascinating, but not at all my jam.

"We should go somewhere maybe."

I blink open my eyes and roll my head in her direction. "Where?"

"I don't know. Feels like a lot of work to plan something."

"Totally." I snicker at how lazy we're both being today.

"Maybe over your Christmas break?" she questions, her gaze cast about the room, watching her cousins swim and play.

"That could be fun."

She laughs. "You don't even know what I was thinking. I could have said Iceland."

"Except I know you, and I know you do not like cold weather. You're thinking Aruba or St. Barts."

She finishes off her champagne and sets the empty flute down on the small table beside her. "It's freaky how well you know me."

"I'll miss vacations. Being a resident will suck like that. They get no time off."

"True. You should have become a chef. But for now, let's plan something over Christmas break otherwise we'll never do it and I won't see the sun again until May."

"If you're lucky. This is Boston." I sit up straight. "I'm down to go away. I wonder if Callan would be in for Aruba."

Stella bounces her eyebrows at me. "Well, my, my, my. We're in the planning and thinking about vacations with our guy phase now, huh? Last week you weren't even sure if you were going to continue living there."

Oh. That. I twist on the lounger to face her, giving the room my back. I chew on my lip. "He hasn't asked me to. That's why I'm unsure."

She scrunches her brow. "I thought you both agreed you'd continue living with them until the hearing was over, and then you'd reevaluate."

"Right. We did. The hearing was today."

She's still giving me that look. "Right. It was today, so slow your roll there, Suzie Homemaker. I'm sure he'll get to it."

I puff out a breath. "Stella, he hasn't asked me to stay. He hasn't even brought anything up to me. Do you know how un-Callan-like that is?"

She waves that off. "He wants you to stay. Obviously. The man is five-alarm fire obsessed with you. You could always bring it up."

"I did, last week," I argue. "He blew me off, and that's when I told you I wasn't sure if I was going to stay. Hello, it's like you don't know how my brain works."

"Dramatic, much?"

"Whatever. I haven't decided if I'm going to stay because he hasn't asked me to stay or given me any indication that it's even on his mind. I mean, I realize we're new at this and it's only been a few months of us actually being together, but the dude is a planner to the max."

"Maybe he just assumes you're staying." Her eyebrows bounce suggestively. "Or maybe he's going to propose to you for real."

"Ha. You're very funny."

"Why is that funny? Is it because you'd say no if I asked?"

My eyes snap to the size of dinner plates. Stella has the biggest shit-eating grin on her face, and right now, I want to kill my best friend.

"You'd never get away with it," Stella says. "You'd be the worst at trying to cover up a murder."

Ugh. Again, I'm speaking inner thoughts out loud. "The jury would acquit me. I can't believe you just did that to me." I reach out and smack her arm.

She shrugs unrepentantly, and I slowly roll over to face Callan, who is sitting on the chair directly behind me wearing swim trunks and a playful grin that's making his dimples pop. His wet hair is brushed back from his face, and he looks so hot and yummy right now.

I narrow my eyes. "How long were you listening?"

"Long enough. You never answered my question."

I blink about ninety thousand times. "What question?"

"If you'd say no if I asked."

I nearly fall off my chair as I attempt to sit up. I glance around us only to realize it's oddly quiet in here. The pool is empty, and at the far end of the room, I catch Amelia ushering the last Fritz grandchild into the room where the food is all set up, but before she closes the door behind her, she throws me a wink. A wink!

Stella walks past us, waving at me over her shoulder. "Traitor!" I yell after her and then turn back to Callan. "What are you doing? What is this?"

Something flickers in his eyes. "That's actually my question for you. What is this, Layla?"

"What do you mean?" I toss back at him.

"Is this something you want?" He takes my hand in his, playing with my fingers. Staring at me. Looking like he's about to decimate my planet. "Do you think you want to stay with us? Move in permanently?"

I lick my lips, my tongue ring swirling along my bottom lip.

"Do you, Layla?" he presses when I don't immediately answer. "What do you say? Can you imagine yourself in a whole new world with us?"

"What?" I bark out as a laugh.

"No!" Katy cries, coming out of nowhere as if she were hiding this whole time. She smacks her forehead like she can't believe he just said that. "That's the wrong movie!"

"Crap," he mutters. "What was I supposed to say?" he asks her, his face scrunching up as if he's trying to remember his line and can't. Despite the nervous butterflies crashing into each other in my stomach, I can't help but smile at how adorable they are together.

Exasperated, she does a starfish in the air as she jumps, flickers of water from her bathing suit and hair goes flying every which way. "'Part of your world', Uncle Cal! The song is 'Part of Your World' from *The Little Mermaid*!"

"Darn it," he mutters, shaking his head in dismay before turning back to me. "I was supposed to ask you to be part of our world, not join a whole new world. Crap." He scrubs his face. "I'm doing this all wrong."

I'm smiling like I've never smiled before. Could he be any cuter or more perfect of a guy?

"You two planned this?" I wave my finger back and forth between them, and then Katy drops down in the seat next to him. "You're asking me to move in with you like this? Here?" Of all freaking places, which means everyone is in on this. I mean, obviously, Stella was and clearly Amelia is no fool, but—

Suddenly, the overhead lights cut out, only to be replaced by strings of glowing fairy lights overhead, sparkling in pink, purple, and green. Music comes on too that I immediately recognize as "Part of Your World" from *The Little Mermaid*.

My head flies around, taking it all in, only to snap back to the man before me.

And now I see it all. The multicolored lights. The music. The guy suddenly dropping to his knees before me. Taking my hands. Staring up at me with eyes that pierce my soul.

I gasp and swallow, and then start breathing heavily.

"No passing out on me this time."

"Callan! What are you doing?"

He stares down at my hands in his, his thumbs brushing back and forth along my skin. He's shaking, I realize. I can feel his trembling that matches mine.

"I'm thanking you," he says, and I choke out a sound because that's not what I thought he was going to say. He glances up. "Layla, I'm thanking you because if it weren't for you, I might not have Katy. And I'm thanking you because if it weren't for you, I'm not sure Katy and I would be doing as well as we are. I didn't ask you to stay sooner because I didn't want you to think anything I asked of you was based on Katy's case. So I kept my mouth shut. But Katy is mine now. For good." He looks at her with a smile of pure love and affection before turning back to me. "We love you. We *want* you. *I* want you." He clears his throat. "Layla, I love you. I just... I *love* you. I want you to move in with us for good. I want you to stay with us forever. I want you to be my..." He hesitates and then laughs, shaking his head in a self-deprecating way. "I can't say it because I know you'll say no."

"Say what?" I manage, because at one point I would have said no. But right now...

"You really want to know?" He checks with a tilt of his head.

I nod in earnest, my heart thrashing in my chest. "I really want to know."

His entire disposition changes, and now he's closer, his body between my spread thighs, his face inches from mine. "Layla." His eyes lock on mine. "I want you to marry me. I love you. *I love you*," he repeats, this time with so much emphasis and so much love, air quivers in and out of my lungs. "I know I can't ask this. I know it's too soon. I know you didn't want any of this and I know I'm doing every-thing wrong. I mean, hell, I already got the song wrong. But the one thing I never got wrong was how I felt about you. It's been you, Layla. Since the first moment we met, it's been you." He shakes his head, his gaze dropping to our joined hands. "Baby girl," he looks up. "Stay with me?"

Stay with him? Those words—they never cease to shred my heart.

"Always," I promise.

I get the barest hint of a smile. "Then will you marry me?"

Marry him?!

"I thought you were going to ask me to move in."

He smirks. "I was. I am. I did. But then. I thought..." His voice dies off.

"You want to marry me?" I stare incredulously at him. Then over to Katy, who is now dancing about in the sparkling twilight of fairy lights. Then back down to him.

He smiles. That dimpled smile that hits every soft, squishy part of me he already owns. I'm so gone on him that it isn't even funny.

"I do," he says simply. "With no expectations. With nothing else on the line. With nothing left between us other than how I feel about you. What do you say?"

I slip one hand away from his and cup his jaw, running my fingers along his smooth skin since he shaved for court today. My heart thunders. But I feel no panic. No nerves. No uncertainty. "Okay."

He laughs at my banal word choice and tone. "Okay?"

I grin. And shrug like it's no big thing. "Okay. I guess I'll marry you."

He squints at me. "You guess?!"

I lean in and layer my lips with his. "Yes, Callan. I'll marry you. I'll marry you tomorrow if you want. I want you and I want Katy and I want us forever. I love you. But it's like I told you the night we met. I'm a lot. You sure you can manage it?"

He nips my bottom lip and then sucks my tongue into his mouth. "I'm positive I can manage it."

I lick the seam of his lips, smiling against his smile. "Then you got yourself a fiancée. A real one this time."

"Holy shit!"

"Uncle Cal!" Katy bellows as she twirls around and around.

Callan falls forward into me, wrapping his arms around me with a laugh so light and airy and happy it chokes me up. "Sorry, Ladybug." Another laugh, but then his lips take mine, kissing me with blinding passion. He kisses me, and he kisses me, and he kisses me.

And when he's done with that, he slips something onto my hand. Onto my finger. I pull back and stare down at the large, heavy rock. It's not a regular diamond. It's not the blue sapphire he had once mentioned either.

"What is this?"

I've never seen anything like it.

His finger glides along my knuckles, as we both stare in awe at my hand. "It's a pink diamond which naturally looks like the sunset because it's a pale pink. It's different. It's a bit wild and unexpected." His eyes hold mine. "Just like you."

The End.

WANT MORE of Layla and Callan's HEA? You can get TWO bonus scenes HERE. Turn the page for an EXCLUSIVE excerpt of Irresistibly Risky (Asher's book!)

END OF BOOK NOTE

Thank you lovely reader for taking the time to read Irresistibly Wild. If you're a fan of my Boston's Billionaire Bachelors series then I know you've been waiting for Layla's story for a long time. I hope I did it and her justice. I loved writing this couple. They were effortless. Their connection just flew off the page and the Layla was just so much fun!

I've fallen so hard for this crew of guys and I can't wait to continue their stories and this world. I will say that very few of my books make me cry while I'm writing them, but writing the scene with Layla and Callan in the hospital after Katy lost her parents broke me a bit. I also loved having Drew and Margot in this story. They're from The Edge of Reason if you haven't read it yet.

I want to thank Team J. Saman. Patricia, Danielle, Kelly, and Joy. I am SO grateful for all you do for me. You make it possible for me to get my words in when I need to and you're always there as a sounding board when I need to bounce ideas off you.

To my reader group, I love you all SO much. You are my happy place online and I feel so blessed that you're there to hang out with me and are always so excited for the books I bring you. Thank you!!

To my guy and my girls. You are eternally the lights of my life. I am nothing without you. Thank you for always encouraging me, always being my support system, and showing me the true definition of love.

Keep reading for your excerpt of Doctor Scandalous!!

Enjoy!

XO,

J. Saman